The
Crimson
Rooms

Also by Katharine McMahon

The Rose of Sebastopol
The Alchemist's Daughter
A Way Through the Woods
Footsteps
Confinement
After Mary

The
Crimson
Rooms

KATHARINE MCMAHON

Weidenfeld & Nicolson

LONDON

First published in Great Britain in 2009
by Weidenfeld & Nicolson
An imprint of the Orion Publishing Group Ltd
Orion House, 5 Upper St Martin's Lane
London WC2H 9EA

An Hachette UK Company

1 3 5 7 9 10 8 6 4 2

ISBN 978 0 297 85338 1 (cased)
ISBN 978 0 297 85534 7 (trade paperback)

Typeset by Input Data Services Ltd,
Bridgwater, Somerset

Printed and bound in Great Britain by
Clays Ltd, St Ive's plc

The Orion Publishing Group's policy is to use papers that
are natural, renewable and recyclable products and
made from wood grown in sustainable forests. The logging
and manufacturing processes are expected to conform to
the environmental regulations of the country of origin.

www.orionbooks.co.uk

The Kind Ghosts

She sleeps on soft, last breaths; but no ghost looms
Out of the stillness of her palace wall,
Her wall of boys on boys and dooms on dooms.

She dreams of golden gardens and sweet glooms,
Not marvelling why her roses never fall
Nor what red mouths were torn to make their blooms.

The shades keep down which well might roam her hall.
Quiet their blood lies in her crimson rooms
And she is not afraid of their footfall.

They move not from her tapestries, their pall,
Nor pace her terraces, their hecatombs,
Lest aught she be disturbed, or grieved at all.

30 July 1918, Wilfred Owen

This book is dedicated to Nuru

All the characters in the book are fictional with the exception of Evelyn's group of friends, including Carrie Morrison, who were among the first women lawyers; the barrister Sir Edward Marshall Hall (who receives a mention) and upon whose 'Holt' case the Wheeler murder is very loosely based, and Charles Bulpitt, an English 'home' child, who hanged himself in a Canadian barn in 1923.

With thanks to Stephen Irwin for an inspirational discussion on barristers in history, and Sue Sleeman who read the book in early draft. Also to the following for their advice on legal matters: Claire Beaver, Mary Groom, Mo Grundy, Pete and Kath Kinch, Gilly More, Sue Sandeman and Kate Thirlwall. Thanks too to Steve Cook at the Royal Literary Fund, Virginia Nicholson, Jack Milner, Helen Halpern, Mike Bateman and Charonne Boulton, who was as usual a wonderful sounding board. Also, thanks to my editor, Kirsty Dunseath, and, as always, to Mark Lucas.

I am very grateful to Amanda Ross and the Richard & Judy team for introducing my books to a much wider readership.

Chapter One

May 1924, London

I followed my brother across a plateau where a bitter wind howled and flashes filled the sky. A sudden glare revealed churned earth and a monstrous coil of metal. My brother marched ahead, immaculate in cap and pressed uniform. I tried to keep up but floundered thigh-deep in mud. Though I thrashed and scrabbled there was nothing to hold on to, neither root nor rock.

At last I wrenched a foot free but James was now yards ahead, far beyond my reach. I clutched at my other thigh with both hands and hauled until it was released and I could crawl forward. The front of my nightgown was a sheet of freezing sludge.

'Jamie.'

He trod lightly, springing from one dry patch to another. The sky flickered again and this time I saw a man fallen like a puppet on the wire, back arched, legs splayed. And in the next flash there was another boy, perhaps fifty yards ahead, waving. Tears made runnels down his filthy cheeks, his mouth gaped and the lower half of his body was a mash of blood and bone.

I faltered again. 'James,' I cried through lips clogged with mud, 'come back,' but he didn't hear me. His arms were extended towards the boy.

The sky roared. Above a shudder of gunfire came the ear-splitting whizz and crack of a shell. I yelled again, 'James,' but my voice was drowned by an explosion that swiped my brother off his feet, plucked him up and crucified him against a violent flare of light.

He thumped back to earth.

Silence.

He was face down, one arm torn away at the shoulder. When he raised his head I saw that the side of his face had been blown off and an eyeball dangled by a thread in the space where his right cheek should have been.

He looked at me with his good eye, a chip of ice.

'It's me, Jamie. Don't you know me?'

The eye went on staring.

'I'll be there in a minute, Jamie. One minute. Please wait ...'

But the mud held me fast. If only I could reach him, press his face to my breast. Then he would be covered and made warm, healed. Another shattering racket of shellfire. I fought the grip of the mud that was dragging me deeper, deeper, away from James, filling my mouth, nostrils, and eyes.

Another pause, this time prolonged. I was hot, breathless, shaking, my eyelashes wet. Moonlight shone through the thin bedroom curtains. My skirt and jacket hung ghostly on the wardrobe door, my heap of underclothes shimmered.

From two floors down came a knock on the front door.

I fumbled for my watch, carried it to the window, and found that it was two thirty-five. Though I yearned to be back inside the dream – this time I had so nearly reached my brother – my hands were already struggling with the sleeves of my dressing gown, my feet had pushed into their slippers.

The landing was quiet. Thank heavens nobody else had heard the knocking, no sign even of Prudence, jowls aquiver, hairnet remorselessly pinned to thinning hair. Stairs groaned under my bare feet, my hand, still trembling from the dream, skimmed the banister and my heel caught on the last stair rod. In the hall the trapped smells of the house fluttered like moths: dinners, rose water, endurance.

Knock, knock, knock-knock. 'Oh please be quiet,' I muttered. A seepage of yellow from the lamp outside oozed through the fanlight and fell across the hats on the hallstand – James's boater, father's trilby – and the silvery haze of the looking glass. As I grasped the latch, my jaw tightened to conceal whatever emotion, other than outrage (surely permissible in the circumstances), this sudden intrusion might provoke.

A child of about six stood on the doorstep, his face upturned; a neat, rectangular brow, shadowed eyes, lower lip drooping from fatigue. My body sagged so that I had to cling to the door frame for support. Dear God. James stepped out of my dream, whole, a child again. In a moment his clenched fist would unfurl to reveal the best, the shiniest, the weightiest marble.

My voice was a thread. 'No. No, it can't be.'

'Forgive us if we woke you,' came a voice from further down the steps and dimly I registered a transatlantic twang. 'Evelyn, is it? I would have known you anywhere. You are so like your brother and he described you so fondly, especially your hair.'

A woman's head appeared just behind the child's shoulder, her face bony, with neat features and a pointed chin. Despite her confident words she seemed as highstrung as a cat; the sinews in her neck were taut and her eyes were too wide open. Extending a small, gloved hand she said, 'I'm Meredith Duffy, and this is my boy Edmund. Perhaps we should not have woken you but the boat got in very late and though I thought of looking for an hotel in the end I decided to come right on here.'

I stared at the exhausted boy, who swayed slightly. 'James,' I murmured. 'Jamie.'

'Yes, he really is so like his father, it's uncanny. I'm hoping that you might have some photographs of James when he was a child so we can compare father and son at the same age.' She took another step towards me and I noted a trim ankle beneath a daring hemline. Behind her on the pavement was a collection of compact though shabby travelling bags. 'Oh, this isn't *all* we have,' she exclaimed. 'I have another trunk and assorted boxes, I'm afraid, but we couldn't manage them in the cab. The shipping company will send them on tomorrow morning.'

Mother and child were like a tide coming in up the steps, lapping against the threshold.

'I absolutely do not understand,' I said.

The woman gasped and put her hand to her mouth. 'Don't say you never got my letter. Oh, the post from Canada is so unreliable. No wonder you're surprised to see me. I must admit I was puzzled that nobody was there to meet us off the boat but now I understand completely.'

3

'But don't you see,' I said, still blocking the way, 'I have no idea who you are.'

She frowned. 'But you must. I'm Meredith and Edmund here is my son, your brother's child.'

The boy's eyes were fixed on my face, occasionally losing focus as his eyelids fluttered. Brown knees stuck out from beneath flannel shorts: my brother, at precisely the height when, if I knelt, his head was level with mine as he gripped me with monkey arms and legs. We used to call it a *cling*. But here, on the doorstep, in the small hours of Monday, 19 May 1924, with the dream of the real James still fresh, this other child seemed to exist out of time.

'I didn't know James had a son,' I said.

'Well, surely you must have done. Unless ... don't tell me your father kept it from you all this while?'

'My father died last year.' The boy's hair, I noted, sprouted up at the crown in a backward quiff, and his lips were moist and full.

'Ah, that explains a great deal. I'm sorry. I would so like Edmund to have known his grandpa. But listen, I must get this child to bed. We don't mind where we sleep,' Meredith was saying. 'After the ship we're just grateful not to be afloat, on *waves*. A sofa and a blanket would do.'

Surrendering, I leaned forward to take the child's hand – I knew that it would feel warm and a little sticky in mine – but he hung his head and held back so instead I picked up the luggage. Now I was terrified he might disappear, but mother and child came tripping into the house hand in hand, she with her little purse hanging from a chain over her shoulder while I struggled with a cluster of bags. 'We must be very quiet,' I whispered. 'I don't want anyone else to be woken.'

We crept upstairs, past James's hat and blazer on the hall stand, the urn of dried flowers on the half landing, the sleepers on the first floor and the gallery of Victorian Giffords above the dado, to my own landing, where the door to James's bedroom was kept tight shut but in the spare room next door a couple of empty beds were covered by candlewick bedspreads. I took armfuls of mothball-smelling blankets from a linen chest and starched sheets from the airing cupboard, although when we set to work I was put to shame: Meredith was an expert bed-maker who could create angular corners and shake a pillow dead centre in its case first time whereas I hadn't made a bed since Girton.

I showed them the bathroom but told them not to flush the lavatory at this hour. Meredith only gave me a preoccupied smile and it was clear that I was now expendable. She lifted the child's shirt over his head; I glimpsed pale, smooth skin, the little discs of nipple and navel, the fragile collarbone. My boy, my Jamie, how I would have kissed him between neck and shoulder.

They ought to be fed, I realised, and crept down to the kitchen to find something suitable. A hot drink was impossible as it would mean lighting the range, which was beyond me at the best of times. In the end I took up cold milk and biscuits, but by the time I'd climbed three flights of stairs there was no light under their door, so I went back to bed and lay picturing the boy tucked up under the white sheet, his palm beneath his cheek. In a little while he would turn onto his back and throw his arm across the pillow.

The house seemed to sag under the weight of these new arrivals whilst I, rigid as an effigy, relived the last half-hour: the dream of James, the child on the doorstep, James's child. As dawn thinned the darkness, I tried to work it out. James had written regularly, right up to a fortnight before his death, and never mentioned this woman Meredith. I thought he confided everything in me. Was it possible that he had time, in the midst of war, to conduct a love affair? And had my father really known? Why had nothing been said? And what did this woman, now installed with her son in the spare room, want from us?

At six o'clock, abandoning any attempt to sleep, I got up. Above me on the attic floor our maids Min and Rose (collectively known as 'the girls' despite both being nearly sixty) were astir. The light, reflected off the white tiles in the bathroom, was pitiless when I risked a glance in the mirror. The Canadian woman, Meredith, had been lying: I was nothing like my clear-eyed brother. My thirty-year-old face was all hollows and angles, my gaze haunted.

Fumbling with the small buttons of my blouse, I tried to decide how best to alert the household to our visitors' arrival. The process would be a tedious one and I was bound to be held responsible for the shock. The maids were straightforward: they must simply

5

be told that, for the time being, there were two extra mouths to feed – without additional housekeeping money. Grandmother (maternal), nearly deaf and partially blind, would be agog with interest but slow to comprehend the complexities of the situation. Prudence, father's elder sister, would have a hundred remarks and accusations. And mother would weep.

But she, after all, was father's widow and nominal head of the family. James was her son and Edmund her grandson. It was Monday morning and I was due to leave the house at eight. There was nothing for it but to break the news at once so I went down to the kitchen, had Rose make a pot of tea, and carried it up to mother's bedroom.

She had the infuriating habit, blamed by Prudence on poor circulation and lack of exercise, of being cold even in the height of summer. At any rate, I found her sound asleep under a winter quilt, the room a fug of sleeping female flesh and lavender. As I swept back the curtains she raised herself on one arm, grey-brown hair falling away onto the pillow, a hand shielding her eyes. In her youth, when a soft chin, melting eyes and tight lacing were all the rage, mother had been considered a great beauty. Now in her mid-fifties she was too thin and her lips drooped at either end as if weighted down by abandoned hope. 'What is happening? What's the time?'

'I've brought you some tea because I need you to wake up properly so I can talk to you. You'll need to be very strong, mother.' I perched on the edge of the bed, allowed her a sip of tea and then removed the cup and saucer because I was afraid her hand might jolt when she heard the news. 'We have a visitor whose name is Meredith. She has come with a small boy called Edmund whom she claims is James's son. From what I can gather, she and James had a love affair during the war. There now, that's all I know.'

I had seen her receive shocking tidings before, of course, and knew she did not manage it well. On this occasion she fell back on the pillow, arms taut on either side, shut her eyes and took gasping breaths while I studied the greasy film made by the milk on the surface of her tea and wondered if I might have been less brutal. Yet I was irritated by these dramatics, which were all too

6

predictable and ensured that the rest of us felt we had to protect her from bearing her responsibilities.

Mother covered her face with both hands and moaned, 'I can't believe it. I can't . . .'

I had always disliked her bedroom, which as a child I regarded as a distastefully private place to which I was summoned for little chats while mother put up her hair or fastened her corsets. At the very centre of the room, on a strip of Turkish rug, stood a round table covered by a lace-trimmed cloth upon which a writing box with brass fittings was placed, like a reliquary. This was the repository of James's school reports, his letters and the appalling telegram. On the mantel were twin oval photograph frames, one containing a picture of James aged thirteen when he started at Westminster, the other my father in his prime, dressed in top hat and tails, his belly round and his smile hearty between beard and moustache. Father, before James's death, had been powerful and noisy with a glint in his eye that spoke of a hunger to earn, own, conquer. The only photograph of me was relegated to a side table. Aged twelve years, I had been decked out in frothy gown and ringlets for a studio portrait in which my mutinous eyes and thrusting jaw were strikingly at odds with the soft curls and girlish throat.

'They woke me at about three,' I told the prostrate figure in the bed, 'so I put them in the spare room. I've asked Rose to grill extra toast when they get up. I'm about to leave for the office but I expect our visitors will sleep late and then they could go for a walk or something. That will keep them occupied until I get home.'

Mother's round eyes widened. 'Oh no. No, no, you can't leave me.'

'I must, I'm afraid.'

'But you can't ask me to deal with them on my own, Evelyn. I can't take in what you're saying. A boy? James's son? But how can we believe them? They might be impostors. What proof is there?'

'The child is unmistakably James's son, I would say. You've only to take one look at him to know that. Meredith says she was in correspondence with father but lately, of course, he didn't reply. Do you know anything about this?'

7

Mother's eyelid gave the merest flicker as she shrank down under the quilt. She had known of the boy's existence and had kept it from me; that much was clear. The knowledge diminished my sympathy still further.

'Well, I'm off to work now. Be prepared for the fact that Edmund is so like James it's as if James were a child again.' The image hovered between us, an echo of the miniature Jameses that hung from ribbons in the alcove by her bed: baby James in a bonnet on her knee, James the schoolboy in cap and over-tight tie, James in cricket whites. For a moment I thought I might reach her. I ached for her to recognise that I was suffering too, that I had been struck by the savage disjunction between one child and another.

Instead she wept. 'Ah no, don't leave me. Oh Evelyn, what shall I tell mother and Prudence? How could you be so cruel?'

'I can because I must. I am needed elsewhere.' I ran swiftly downstairs to the hall, where Min was passing through with a breakfast tray, bottom lip caught between her teeth as a sign that she was suppressing comment with difficulty. 'Please make sure that our visitors have everything they need, Min. I forgot to give them towels last night.'

Then I rammed on my hat, skewered it with a pin, buckled the belt of my jacket and seized briefcase and gloves. As I set off into a warm, breezy morning I thought, Thank God I have my work.

Chapter Two

Male Giffords had been lawyers for generations. Our house in Clivedon Hall Gardens, Maida Vale was adorned by portraits (bad oils or stiff daguerreotypes) of gentlemen with the same demanding eyes and fob watch as my father, each in his turn a luminary of the firm Gifford & Aldridge. Sometimes for a treat James and I, as children, were taken to visit father's office in Holborn, where James would be placed in father's chair, whence he would beam at a procession of admirers, his plump hands pummelling the arms and his cheeks bulging with toffee supplied by the elderly Mr Aldridge, who promised young Master Gifford that he'd be glad to teach him all he knew about property law the moment he was old enough.

Since nobody else was interested in my future, I plotted it myself. Hurdle number one was to get myself sent to a worthwhile school. Mother deplored the idea but father, more indulgent, said it would keep me amused, so each morning I went by omnibus to St Paul's in Hammersmith. On the way, from my perch on the top deck, I glimpsed other lives less ordered and opulent than my own. At twelve I was introduced to a bowdlerised version of *The Merchant of Venice* and fell in love with Portia, who contrived to be wayward, clever and successful – all qualities I wished to possess (I was resigned to being without beauty and thought I didn't care for wealth). Later we studied the French Revolution and found that the likes of Robespierre, with his compelling sea-green eyes (the same colour as my own), had also trained as a lawyer. The law seemed to be my destiny. I discovered that although the British Law Society stood firm against women lawyers ('If there's one calling in the world for which women are conspicuously unfitted . . .'), my legally qualified sisters were allowed to practise in the United States, in Canada, India, France and Denmark. Surely it was just a matter of time?

James was on my side. 'The main argument is: tradition dictates that women should not be lawyers and the law is governed by tradition. Just wait and see, Evie. Tradition is usually overturned in the end by historical imperative. One day you and I will be partners in a firm called Gifford & Gifford. And we won't deal in property, like father, we'll deal in crime and family law. We'll speak for those least able to stand up for themselves.'

But when I finished school in June of 1911 mother put her foot down and said my gadding-about days were over. She had me fitted with stays and rustling silk petticoats and hooked me into high-necked muslin day dresses and revealing evening frocks with tiers of lace in the skirt. I fumed and fretted at the wasted time spent piling up my hair, filing my nails, changing for tea and talking to stupid women in the drawing room, where I wasn't even permitted to read a newspaper. Whenever I dared, I pleaded a headache, stomach ache, fatigue, faintness, anything to escape to my room, where I had squirrelled away books and files borrowed from a clerk in father's firm. With my sharp elbows resting on the dressing table, I made careful notes in a series of red exercise books.

When war was declared, James was seventeen. Gripping him by the lapels I butted him playfully in the chest. 'Oh how terrible it must be, poor Jamie, to have a choice. Save the country or go to Wadham. Poor little James Gifford, which shall he do?'

'Father says I have no choice. He says fighting for one's country is the greatest glory a man can hope for. He says he wishes he were me.'

'But you might die. Has father thought of that?'

I had spoken flippantly – at that time the war was not yet real to me – and I was stricken by the dread in his aquamarine eyes. But he went to war and I signed on for work at the censorship office. And afterwards, when it was all over, I thought, Well at least I can work; at least that is left to me. When I pleaded to be sent to Girton, father was too deep in mourning to refuse.

In 1922 the Law Society at last opened its doors to women. But, as I soon realised, passing exams was only half the battle because who, given the choice, would employ a female? The handful of women who had qualified with me and found employment had usually done so through family connections. Though I applied to perhaps thirty firms in search of articles none would look at me. In the end I disguised my name and college on the application letter by writing *E. Gifford, graduate of Cambridge*, but the shock when I appeared in person wearing a four-year-old grey wool two-piece with drooping pockets and a skirt ending three inches above my ankles was always too much. Interviews rarely lasted more than ten minutes. Nobody wanted a woman, however she was clothed. 'We must give priority,' said the pinstriped legal gentlemen who deigned to give me an interview, 'to the poor fellows back from the trenches. And in any case, my dear young lady, the law is no place for a woman. What would your father . . .?'

As they well knew, my father would rather have employed a criminal halfwit than me, provided he was male. It was one thing to give your headstrong daughter an education, quite another to let her into your office. So I filled my time in those tense and dreary months of unemployment (during which I had to put up with a nightly chorus of lamentation from mother and Aunt Prudence that I should even dream of becoming a lawyer) by reading the *Law Society Journal* and applying for clerkships. Most mornings were spent observing in courts across London. A couple of afternoons a week I volunteered at Toynbee Hall, a settlement in the East End that offered education, cultural activities and advice, including legal help for those who couldn't afford a lawyer. Occasionally at Toynbee there'd been a burst of joyous camaraderie with other idealistic postgraduates: Ambrose Applebee, the MP Clement Attlee and Carrie Morrison, a friend from Girton with whom I learned a great deal about the law concerning rent arrears, employment rights and death duties. On the whole, though, it was a lonely time, haunted by the knowledge that the lawyer in the family should have been James, not me; that if James were alive his path would have been smoothed by a combination of his own talents and father's connections. The obstructive legal world became, in my mind, associated with guilt.

But at Toynbee I made a vital though tenuous connection. A name mentioned often by Carrie as a champion of the poor was

Daniel Breen, and one day from the public benches of Bow Street Magistrates' Court I witnessed a performance by the man himself.

The defendant was a woman wearing threadbare overalls, dishevelled after a night in the cells. From her appearance, one would judge that she could not have afforded a cup of tea let alone a solicitor to speak for her and yet she was represented by a smartly dressed, sharp-eyed lawyer who berated the police for imprisoning a woman overnight merely because she had stolen a second-hand scarf from a dealer in the Old Kent Road. '*Second hand*,' he said, glowering at the bench, and I noted that his vowels were not quite as polished as my own, 'worth a farthing at most, I'd say. Of course the police were only doing their duty in arresting her: we can't have an *honest* second-hand-clothes dealer stripped of his assets' (a raised eyebrow, a glint in the eye inviting the bench to share the joke), 'but what's wrong with a caution? Admittedly my client has numerous previous convictions for like offences, but the temperature yesterday afternoon was below freezing, and she has only the clothes she stands up in. Small wonder she was tempted by a scrap of moth-eaten wool. If I were addressing a less experienced bench, I might despair, but you, with your considerable knowledge of these cases, will seek not just to punish but to reform. Now I have found her a place in a hostel for . . .'

Breen thereby alternately hectored and flattered the magistrates until they were so full of compassion and largesse that the defendant, who had appeared dozens of times in the courts and was surely due for a lengthy spell of imprisonment, was given half a crown from the poor box and sentenced to a night in the cells, deemed to be have already been served.

Afterwards I pursued Breen, who scurried out of court so fast that I could scarcely keep up with him. 'I was wondering, sir, do you need a clerk?' He stood stock still and regarded me, his head on one side, like a blackbird. 'I heard your name mentioned at Toynbee Hall and I have been looking out for you. I'm a bachelor of law and I need to be given a chance. Nobody will take me on because I am a woman. But you, sir, I think you might.'

His best features were his fiery eyes and exceptionally fine skin; otherwise he was unremarkable, perhaps forty years old, blunt-nosed, balding but with a frizz of wild hair above his ears, and barely an inch taller than me. 'You know nothing about me.'

'I know you by reputation. My friend Carrie Morrison speaks highly of you. And I saw you in court today. I guessed you would at least listen to me.'

'Put it in writing. I can't stop now.' And he was off, clapping his trilby low on his brow as he hurried down the court-room steps. But I had noted a flash of interest, and knew he wouldn't forget me, so I found out his address from an usher and within an hour had written my letter.

Later I discovered that my application to Breen could hardly have failed, given that the source of his immense energy was a passion for proving everyone else wrong, and it was therefore a characteristically Machiavellian move to take on a female. The fact that I had been turned down by dozens of firms with partners educated at public school and Oxbridge, rather than at grammar school and London like himself, inflamed Breen further.

However, his championing of my cause had not so far extended beyond accepting one hundred and fifty pounds by way of a fee (a crippling amount which drained the entire fund my father had set aside for my dowry) and allocating to me sad and unsavoury cases usually involving women with marital difficulties, a mountain of paperwork such as the copying out of wills and writs, and a very unpleasant space in which to conduct my business.

Breen & Balcombe occupied the ground floor and basement of a sixty-year-old terraced house in Arbery Street off the Euston Road, where I had a so-called office in what was once the basement kitchen. No sunlight ever penetrated there and the room was still equipped with a greasy range and a wooden rack on a pulley for drying washing, which I sometimes employed as an extra shelf for documents. Over the past twenty or so years the former kitchen had become the last resting place for files, so I worked in a gloomy nest of paper and cardboard that harboured a host of black beetles.

Aside from Breen and his partner, Theo Wolfe (the Balcombe half of the partnership was never mentioned and I believe had died out several generations back), the only other employee was Miss Drake, the secretary, a thin-haired woman who had perfected the art of speaking without moving her lips, and who viewed me as a traitor to her sex. She therefore contrived not to communicate directly with me at all. On my first morning Miss Drake, instructed to give me a guided tour of the premises, had done so without once looking me in the eye and had ended by showing me a cupboard in the kitchen housing a stinky mop and stiffened dusters, as if to suggest that my true vocation actually resided there.

Nevertheless, when I pushed open the door from the street and descended to my fusty office, I usually felt relieved to be out of reach of the clinging tentacles of home. Even on the Monday my nephew exploded into my life, when part of me longed to run back and reassure myself that the boy really was asleep with his mother in the spare room, I was glad not to be a part of the inevitably tortuous conversation between the females of Clivedon Hall Gardens and the interloper Meredith over the toast and marmalade. Though the events of the past twelve hours hung about my consciousness like black drapes and my eyes stung from lack of sleep, I tucked my chair up close to my pitted desk, dipped my pen, pulled a spike holding a pile of bills awaiting payment towards me and began writing the first of a series of polite but firm reminders.

So James had fathered a son. James, my lovely, soft-haired younger brother, had embarked on a love affair. (I scrunched up a page spoiled by too many errors and hid it in my pocket – among Breen's many pet hates was a wastage of paper.) James was always so careful, so intact. James had deliberated every action before embarking upon it. James, as my father always said after a whisky or two, would have made a wonderful lawyer because he relished order. (Another sheet of paper wasted.)

The telephone rang in Miss Drake's office on the floor above. She liked to maintain the myth that her fingers were worked to the bone, so she never answered until the ninth or tenth bell and my nerves jangled as the vibrations trilled through the thin ceiling. In the end I decided to answer it myself and was halfway up the basement stairs before she picked up the receiver. 'Breen & Balcombe ... Mr Breen is not expected back from his holidays until later today ... Mr Wolfe is at a meeting ...'

Long silence as a voice spoke on the other end of the line.

'Well, there is no one else here,' drawled Miss Drake, then added, after a significant pause, 'unless you're prepared to have Miss Gifford ... Articled clerk ... I presume she's qualified ... Yes, you heard correctly, she is female. Capable of taking notes, I believe ... Well, if you're sure ... Yes, I can leave her a message. If you want ...'

Five minutes later a typewritten note was pushed under my door. *Telephone Shoreditch police station. 447. A lawyer is needed. Case of kidnapping.*

I was still novice enough to be awed by the responsibility of representing a client, and that Monday in particular, my nerves jumping from the impact of Meredith's arrival, I would almost rather have stayed hidden in my basement. On the other hand, I could not help marvelling, as I clapped on my hat, that Evelyn Gifford had been called on to deal with a crime so sensational.

At the police station I braced myself for the tedious business of convincing the duty officer that I was indeed a qualified advocate.

'But you're a woman.' His pink-rimmed eyes were insolent.

'I believe the secretary at Breen & Balcombe mentioned that I would be attending the case.'

'I've never seen a woman lawyer before. Are you sure you'll be of use?'

'I presume you know Mr Breen? He trusts me completely.'

'It was Mr Breen the prisoner was after.'

'Mr Breen is away.'

The officer raised his brows, made a note in his ledger and allowed me through the smoky back office to the narrow flight of steps leading to the cells. In the antechamber a plump jailer manned a small desk, his stomach so vast that his short arms could barely reach to write in the ledger. 'So you're the lady they said was coming from Breen & Balcombe. Well, madam, I hope you're ready for this.'

Hauling himself up, he led me to the last cell in the row. There, he opened the wicket and showed me a woman called Leah Marchant who was dressed in an assortment of skirts, blouses and shawls, her feet shoved into men's shoes, hair falling about her face, her complexion deathly white and her eyes red from weeping. She stood with her back to the wall opposite the door.

'Please open the door,' I said.

'She's not fit to be let out, I warn you.'

'I cannot speak to a client through bars.'

'On your head be it.'

When the door was thrown open Leah Marchant stared at me for a moment. I tried to smile back, to offer my hand as Breen would have done, but too late I sensed her implacable rage. Springing forward with a kind of hoarse roar she fell on me with such force that I was driven back against the jailer and felt the full weight of her chest on mine and the flailing of her muscular arms across my head and shoulders. She tore at my jacket collar, then my hat, which went flying despite the pin, allowing her to grab a fistful of hair so that I yelped with pain. Her breath was damp and fumy with alcohol. 'Fuck off. Fuck off an' all. Give me my fuckin' baby. Where is he now? Give 'im back, you whore. Ain't you got no babies of your own?'

The noise in so confined a space was ear-piercing; the woman clung like a cat, and I ducked my head just in time to avoid her fingernails, which fortunately scraped my cheek rather than my eye. I was rescued by the jailer, who tore her off me and dumped her back in the cell. 'Maybe come back later when she's calmed down,' he said. 'Or fetch Mr Breen. She insisted she would only see Mr Breen. It's probably because you're a lady.'

'Did she say how she knew Mr Breen?' I fumbled in my bag for a handkerchief to staunch the trickle of blood.

'Met him once years ago when she was charring for some couple in Marylebone. He was a regular visitor to the house and kind to her. She's never forgotten his name, apparently. Begged us to have him fetched here.'

I sat bolt upright on a bench, prodded a strand of hair back into its coil, put on my hat and pressed the handkerchief to my torn cheek. My first battle wound, I thought grimly.

The jailer disappeared so I was left alone with the locked door separating me from the woman in the cell, her fury pulsing through the walls. After ten minutes or so it was quiet on the other side of the door, so I went to the jailer and asked if I might approach Leah Marchant again. When we peeked through the wicket, the woman had subsided onto the bed with her head in her hands.

'I am here to help you, Mrs Marchant,' I called. 'The police asked me to come. I am a lawyer. I work with Mr Breen.'

'I don't want you; I want Mr Breen.'

'Mr Breen is away, I'm afraid. He'll be back tomorrow. So can I help until then?'

'Fuck off. I don't need no 'elp. I jus' wants my baby.'

'*Your* baby? But you are charged with kidnapping.'

'My baby. My baby. Mine. Mine,' she sobbed.

'Mrs Marchant, if you would only calm down and tell me . . .'

'Don't tell me to be calm. I won't be calm no more.'

'I am here to listen. I'll not go away until you've told me the whole story.'

'I'm not tellin' you nothing.'

'Very well. But I shall sit here and wait, nonetheless.'

I seemed to have won over the jailer because a few minutes later he set a tray on the bench beside me and handed me a sheaf of papers. 'A sup of tea might soften her up,' he said. 'It's a terrible case. They've brought down the notes at last. Her own baby. It was put with a foster mother and she couldn't get it back by legal means so she snatched it while it was left outside a butcher's. Bet you've never come across anything like this before.'

I read the notes and sipped my tea. Then I called through the wicket, 'Mrs Marchant. Please let me help you.'

This time she said nothing at all so the jailer opened the door and passed in an enamel mug of tea. Then I went in and sat beside her on the bed while the jailer leaned on the door frame. 'I gather that Charlie is your own baby, Mrs Marchant, and has been placed with a foster mother. And your two daughters are in a children's home, is that right?' She took a slurp of tea and ran the back of her hand across her eyes.

'Can you tell me why the children are in a home, Mrs Marchant?'

'Because I took 'em there. I used to pass it when I worked the buses and I thought it looked like a kind place. I had nothing to give 'em to eat. I'd borrowed till I couldn't borrow no more. I thought if I gave 'em up for a bit, I could get work. Nights. Anything.'

'Is your husband alive, Mrs Marchant?'

Mirthless laugh. 'Gone to sea.'

'Does he send you money?'

This, apparently, was an inappropriate question. The mug went flying across the cell, hit the wall, ricocheted against Mrs Marchant's foot and was given a kick for good measure.

I sprang up and the jailer ushered me out, slamming the door behind us. 'That's quite enough for one day,' he said.

Chapter Three

It was six thirty by the time I reached Clivedon Hall Gardens but my pace slowed as I came to our railings, where the Monday smell of reheated roast crept up from the basement. As on every other evening, I climbed the front steps reluctantly and my hand faltered as I inserted the key in the lock. And yes, here it came, the familiar tremor of apprehension because this was the same action – the unlocking of the front door – that had begun the series of events leading up to the news of James's death.

On 21 November 1917, I had arrived home just after half past seven, chilled by freezing smog and sore-eyed from too much close reading at the censorship office. I stuffed my gloves in a pocket, hung my hat and coat on the stand, gave James's panama a flick for good luck and threw open the drawing-room door. Grandmother urged me to sit by the fire and mother poured tea as they plied me with questions about my journey and workmates, taking care not to delve further; my task of reading hundreds of postcards a day was grindingly humdrum but they were impressed because it was top secret. Mother said she had been busy at the church hall, packing relief parcels for war widows and orphans. She was wearing a gauzy evening blouse under a long bottle-green cardigan knitted by grandmother – whose sight was much better in those days – fastened at the bosom by two iridescent mother-of-pearl buttons.

We were fragile still from the news a month ago that James had been injured and we treated each other with great care as if we were all convalescing from a dangerous illness. There was also a slight air of self-congratulation among us because we had come safely through a crisis and thought we had behaved well. At one point we'd been informed that James's injuries were so severe he would be sent home, then that he was being treated in a military hospital and would soon return to the front. All in all it had been a tumultuous time but we had convinced ourselves that he was now immune from harm.

I leaned towards the fire, took hold of the toasting fork and wondered if it was too close to supper to ring for a couple of slices of bread. My mouth watered at the prospect of buttered toast. There was a knock on the front door.

I threw down the fork and crossed the drawing room, calling over my shoulder, 'I expect it's father, forgotten his key. How many times must we tell him the girls hate being disturbed when they're in the middle of mashing potatoes …?' then I was in the hall, my hand was on the latch and, all unsuspecting, I was throwing open the front door.

The telegram was succeeded, a couple of weeks later, by a letter from James's company commander: … *sad duty to give you details of how Captain Gifford died … climbed from the trench in full view of enemy snipers in order to rescue one of his men who was trapped in deep mud … exceptional courage … Mentioned in dispatches …*

I was not satisfied. The picture was too vague, the choice James had made too extreme. In my mind I roamed across a sea of mud searching for him, convinced that he was not dead.

I wrote letters to everyone I could think of and in the end extracted the truth from an officer friend of James who had been invalided home after Christmas. *The story I heard was that one of Gifford's men, or rather a boy not yet eighteen, had been wounded in no-man's-land and was crying out. It was a frosty night and therefore murderously clear but in the end Gifford simply climbed out of the trench and clambered the hundred yards or so to the boy. Miss Gifford, you ask me specifically about his injuries, you tell me not to spare you. He lost an eye and was severely wounded in the right shoulder. Though he was still alive when they finally reached him the next night, he died when they tried to move him.*

Night after night I stood in the fusty gloom of the dugout, listened to the boy crying in the mud, and tried to fathom my brother's decision to climb out of the trench and die. What absurd, feckless, reprehensible courage. I used every possible argument to change his mind but out he went, again and again, under a clear sky. Try as I might, I could not preserve him.

When I showed the letter to my father he said we should keep the details to ourselves. Meanwhile grandmother shrank into a corner of the sofa and knitted endless pairs of socks, mother took to her bed, father the bottle and I continued as usual. Two months after James's death, on the last Sunday of January, I found myself with an unexpected opportunity to be alone. The girls were to spend the afternoon with an ancient aunt in Tooting and we had been invited to lunch with Prudence, who at that time was still living in Buckinghamshire. As soon as the trip was mooted, I knew I wouldn't go – 'Mother, I'm feeling under the weather. Please explain to father. The time of the month . . .' – even though I had an inkling of what would happen once the house was empty.

And how right I was. The instant they drove away and I closed the front door, the absolute quiet surged back and I was alone with James's hat and summer blazer.

I was seized by anguish that twisted my guts so that I choked and retched, and slumped down onto the brick-red and yellow tiles of the hall floor, voiceless and gaping. The only words that formed in my mind were, I want him back. I saw him, instead of the smart youth in the photograph, lying in a swamp of gore and mud with his shoulder shot through and an eyeball hanging from its bloody socket.

When I got up at last to wash my face, I was a hundred years old.

But by the time my parents and grandmother came back I had composed myself. Rose served us hot milk, which we drank together before bed, father's laced with a stiff whisky. My parents reported that Prudence's hens weren't laying, presumably the time of year, and that her cottage was ridiculously chilly because although father ensured she was well provided for, she would not spend money on creature comforts. I sipped my milk between occasional shuddering breaths and realised with an unexpected pang of regret that my opportunity for mourning was over.

These memories never went away: each time I returned to the house I was reminded: the toasting fork, the telegram, the frantic letter-writing, the prostration on the hall floor. But on the evening after Meredith's arrival and the interview with Leah Marchant I was distracted the instant I stepped through the front door because a well-travelled trunk was placed in front of the potted fern, along with various other items of luggage, including a hatbox with racy stripes. Even before I'd removed my hat, mother had shot out of the drawing room, gripped me by the wrist, ushered me inside and closed the door.

Everything was much as ever: Prudence was seated at the writing desk with her back to the room in a pose of frigid restraint, and grandmother was perched at the very far end of the sofa, holding her crochet up to the dim light that filtered through the thick lace curtains. There was no sign of our visitors.

'She's still here,' whispered mother, hands on hips.

'Of course. She would be.'

'For heaven's sake, Evelyn, what have you done to your face?'

'It's nothing.'

Mother looked baffled but continued: 'Anyway, she's unpacked.'

'She must wear clean clothes, I suppose.'

'She left the boy with us for hours while she went out. She said we needed to become better acquainted with him though I can hardly bear to look at him. He's so like ...' She dabbed her eyes and added, 'We couldn't think what to give him for lunch. Prudence said the girls couldn't be expected to provide different meals for a child. If we had a house full of servants, like we had before the war, but we're so overstretched ...'

'Didn't you ask Edmund what he'd like?' I asked, eager to prevent a well-rehearsed complaint about the servants.

'He was very vague, just said, "No tomatoes," and you know it's mean of me but I thought, She's told him to say that because James – oh my darling boy – never liked tomatoes. In the end Rose boiled an egg. I couldn't go to bridge and leave him with mother and Prudence; it wouldn't have been fair.'

'Well I should think not.'

Prudence suddenly turned round, pen suspended in mid-air. She had a habit of staring when she spoke and her light grey eyes were full of disapproval beneath their drooping lids. At times she reminded me of a basset hound. Her voice was too loud for the dimensions of the room. 'I said he ought to eat tomatoes. Boys should eat plenty of fruit and vegetables.'

'It was the way his mother just left him without even saying where she was going or asking if we minded. I can't *stand* her,' said mother. 'And as for the letter she's supposed to have sent telling us she was coming, I've seen no sign of it.'

'Where is Meredith now?'

'Upstairs with the boy.'

'I'll go to her.'

'Be very careful what you say. She makes no bones about it: she's short of money. She wants the boy to have an education and she wants to live here, in this house, presumably rent free. Oh, good God, I wish your father were alive.'

But it was father who landed us in this situation, I thought. Mother's habit of idolising the dead was infuriating, especially as the full extent of father's failure to insure his family against unpleasant shocks came to light. 'Since there is no question that Edmund is James's son,' I said, 'we must take some responsibility for him, as I'm sure father would have wished.'

Mother would not meet my eye. 'She might want a lot of money – which we don't have. It's one thing to believe we're related to the boy, but can we be sure she's really the mother?'

'You've presumably had plenty of opportunity to question her.'

'She tells me that she was a nurse in the hospital to which he was sent when he was wounded, but what does that prove? He can't have been there long. A couple of weeks later he was ...'

'What else did she say about James?'

Mother flinched. Over the years his name had become a word almost too sacred to utter. A shiver trembled across the muffled surfaces of the drawing room, the layers of wool and lace and linen among which we women moved with slippered feet, the arrangements of dead birds and foliage under glass domes, the china figures, the photograph frames – James in his rugby shirt, James as a fat baby in a perambulator.

'Some questions one simply cannot ask,' said Prudence.

'Did father never speak about it to either of you? He obviously knew of Edmund's existence.'

Silence. I had placed Prudence in a dilemma to which she

responded by pressing her shapely lips together and folding her hands. If she admitted father had confided in her she would be guilty of having withheld vital information from me. If she hadn't known about Edmund, her position as father's chief adviser, adopted since her arrival in the house in 1919, would be diminished. She therefore wished me to believe that of course father had confided in her but had bound her to secrecy. I suspected she had never been told.

Mother put her hand to her forehead in a gesture that in pre-war days she'd used to great effect in Christmas charades but was now usually a precursor to tears.

'He might have mentioned something. It was all too terrible, so soon after James was killed. You can't expect me to remember ...'

'You *must* remember, mother. If father made her promises, we should honour them.'

'Oh, he would never have done that. He was much too careful.'

Grandmother now made one of her unexpectedly apposite interventions into the conversation. 'He's a nice little boy. I like him.'

'Mrs Melville was very patient with him, weren't you, dear,' enunciated Prudence. 'Showed him all your cards and buttons.'

I hovered for a moment longer by the window, clutching my elbows, head down, then, braced to meet Meredith and the boy again, I left the room and took the stairs two at a time. When I reached the second floor I was shocked to see that the door to James's room had been flung open so that light from its un-shuttered window poured onto the landing. I hesitated for a moment, taking in the deep red curtains, the crimson and green and blue in his rug, the faded red of his bedspread. Usually this room was visited only by mother, who made a daily pilgrimage. Until today James, had he miraculously returned, would have found nothing changed: his books in order, his shirts and socks folded neatly in the drawers, the seam of wallpaper near his pillow peeled back where he had picked at it during a bout of measles, his plaid slippers still thrust under the bed.

Now, the sudden violation of hallowed territory took my breath away. The sash had been thrown up so that noises from the street burst in, the quilt was rumpled and James's childhood books tossed about on the carpet. Mother and son sat on the bed passing my brother's kaleidoscope between them as if they were unsure what it was. Edmund's legs were swinging and Meredith was wearing a light green frock that revealed her round arms and slender ankles. It seemed to me that James's room had been reconstituted, its dull, breathless parts raked over to reveal their shiny sides, like glowing coals.

Meredith's eyes, when she glanced up, were abnormally large in her kittenish face and bright with relief. I could not help recognising the dreary day she must have spent in our house among hostile women and I softened a little, despite this desecration.

'Well hello there, Evelyn,' she exclaimed and, leaping off the bed, she seized my wrists, raised herself on tiptoe and kissed my cheek. 'You look very hot. And oh my Lord, what happened to your face?'

'Nothing, it's nothing.'

'It looks to me like a nasty scratch.' Her cool fingertips touched the wound inflicted by Leah and I smelled the floral perfume on her wrist. 'I have some lotion in my room. Let me fetch it.'

'Please. Leave it. Oh be careful with that, Edmund; James was very fond of it.' The boy was shaking the kaleidoscope and holding it to his ear. 'Bring it over to the window and you'll see how it works.'

I took the toy from him, put it to my eye and glimpsed the chips of coloured glass reforming into patterns I could no longer bear to see. When Edmund stood shyly beside me I covered his left eye with my palm and told him to look into the tube. 'I see colours,' he cried, 'I see them change. Mommy, won't you take a look at this?'

His tousled head was waist-high to me and he had a distinctive fragrance like fresh greens. His eyelashes fluttered against my hand and I noted, as he twisted the kaleidoscope, that his finger-nails were grubby and needed cutting. Until he was eleven I had been James's nail-cutter; after that fingers and toes had become his own responsibility and I was wordlessly excluded from another intimate ritual. The back of Edmund's head from crown to nape was so endearingly steep-angled that I had to resist the urge to cup it in my hand.

Meredith gripped her son's shoulder and dropped a kiss on his hair. Then she took the kaleidoscope and peered through it. My heart gave a lurch of recognition because there, prominently displayed on her middle finger, was the silver signet ring engraved with James's initials – *JHG* – bought by me for his eighteenth birthday the day before he went away. The trip to the shop was still vivid in my mind, the glass cases of engagement rings winking their hard eyes, James turning his smooth, slim hand back and forth to admire the new ring.

'Are you sure it's not too girlish?' he said.

'You must have something to remember me by. I'll drop straight out of your head otherwise.'

'Absolutely, you're right. I'd never think of you again.'

I couldn't help myself. I reached out and touched the ring on Meredith's finger.

'I'd always assumed it must have been buried with him.'

She pulled it off and dropped it into my palm with such alacrity that I realised the exposure of the ring had been quite deliberate. It had been fitted with a clip because it was too big for her. I wanted to close my fist around it, this morsel of my brother, but Meredith took it and slipped it back on her finger. 'Actually I wear it for Edmund's sake, as a reminder of his father.' Then she added briskly, 'I am so grateful for your kindness last night, by the way. I admire the way you took it all in your stride.'

'Hardly. It's just so extraordinary for us to meet you both.'

I told them supper would be served in five minutes, then left them in my brother's bedroom because I couldn't bear to linger another moment. In my own room I locked the door. My face, pale except for an inch-long gash on the cheek, stared back from the dressing-table mirror. 'Where *did* you get that chin?' mother used to ask. Her own was soft with a shallow dimple, a 'lady's' chin. Mine, she said, was a sign of my intractability, like my mass of untameable hair. 'James has all the looks,' mother would add, 'the best of both families: your father's intellectual brow and good nose, my mouth and cheekbones. One day he will break hearts.'

There were snippets of James in my room too, the hopelessly inappropriate gifts he'd bought with his pocket money: a powder puff, a small china doll, a notebook too small to write in. And a tin box of letters kept in my bottom drawer alongside winter cardigans – notes from boarding school, from the seaside when he visited a friend, from France.

Snatching the pins from my hair I dragged at the tangles with my fingers. Meredith's hair was cut so short that the pink tips of her ears and twisty little earrings were exposed. With savage sweeps of the brush I set to work, coiling and jabbing until my hair was neat and prim as a Victorian governess's. I had longed and longed for James to come back but not like this, under the wing of a spiky little Canadian with guileless eyes and flawless teeth. What had she taken away from me, in exchange for the gift of her son?

Monday dinner was always cold roast made over as a pie or fricassée. We stood behind our chairs, mother at the head of the table, grandmother at the foot, Prudence on one side, me on the other, awaiting our visitors. The electric light did nothing to soften that sombre room with its maroon flocked wallpaper and Gothic furniture, including a sideboard as hefty as a church coffer. Despite the plainness of the food the table was laid with exquisite care: white damask cloth, second-best oak mats, napkins in polished silver rings, bone-handled cutlery including cheese knives though there was never a cheese course. The girls loved any job that harked back to our family's glory days.

At last we heard light footfall on the stairs and mother and child appeared, very spruce with combed hair, Meredith wearing a glittering jet necklace. She had changed into a crushed-velvet evening dress with a draped neckline and wrap-over skirt and looked as dainty as a fashion plate. The rest of us wore evening blouses tucked into our serviceable skirts.

'Oh good Lord, I hope we haven't kept you waiting,' she cried.

Edmund took one look at the empty places beside or opposite Prudence, seized his mother's hand, and wailed, 'I want to sit next to mommy.'

We weren't used to howling children at Clivedon Hall Gardens and Prudence glowered at him.

'He's not normally shy,' said Meredith. 'I expect he's still tired from the journey.'

'Of course, I'll sit next to Prudence,' I said, moving round the table. We then watched as our visitors sat down without saying grace and unfolded their napkins. Behind grandmother's head in full view of Meredith was the large, framed photograph of James in army uniform with just a hint in his frank eyes that he couldn't take it all too seriously – the uniform, the war, his rank as officer. Perhaps only I noticed the shake of Meredith's head when she glimpsed him. After that she seized her spoon and worked her way ravenously through a bowl of tepid mushroom soup. Meanwhile I was conscious of a tussle within Prudence between piety and good manners. The latter won, though after she was seated she folded her hands in her lap and mouthed a quick prayer.

With her spoon suspended between bowl and mouth, Meredith asked brightly, 'So, tell me, Aunt Prudence – do you mind me calling you that, you are Edmund's great-auntie, after all – how long did you say you have been living in this house?'

Prudence, whose neck was supported by the dozen or so rows of pin tucks in her collar, drew her elbows tightly against her sides and made a great show of laying down her spoon and dabbing her lips before speaking. 'Five years.'

'And before that?' asked Meredith.

'Before that,' I intervened, sensing that antagonism had already sprung up between the two women, 'Prudence lived in Bucking-hamshire. After the war, when money was short, it became uneconomical to keep up both this house and her cottage, so she let the cottage and moved in with us. We were – are – very grateful for her company.'

'Well it seems very convenient for you all. And you,' Meredith added, addressing grandmother, 'Mrs Melville, have you ever lived in the country?'

Grandmother didn't hear the question until I had repeated it three times. 'Certainly not. It would be far too quiet for me.'

'Grandmother has always loved London,' I explained. 'She knows it intimately. She used to be an actress, you know, before she was married. She's performed in some of the great theatres.'

Mother sniffed; we should not be disclosing our somewhat disreputable family history to a stranger. Nonetheless, I ploughed on: 'And she marched through most of London's streets, before the war.'

'Did you, Mrs Melville? What was your cause? Personally, I have always been a very keen suffragist.'

But Prudence interrupted: 'It was a great sacrifice for me, leaving the country.'

'I'm sure it was.'

'I had a cottage with half an acre. I kept chickens. I was known by everyone in the village. My brother, Edmund's grandfather, had been more than generous in supporting me, but after the war I knew that the family finances could not sustain two establishments.' This was presumably a thinly veiled reminder to Meredith that Gifford money was tight and she ought to show some consideration. 'When I left, a special service was held in the church. I was given a eulogy – it can only be described as such – for my services to the congregation. I'd taught Sunday school for nearly forty years and I supervised the flowers. And there was a tribute to James because he was my nephew and a great favourite.'

Meredith, who had been staring wide-eyed during this outburst, laid down her spoon. 'Do you know, I'm hoping the next course will be served soon. This boy is so sleepy his head is almost hitting the bowl. And yet he must eat. I don't believe he's had a proper meal since we left Toronto, and although you've tried with your soup, haven't you Edmund, mushrooms are not his favourite.'

'I'm afraid we are not used to fussy eaters,' said mother with a nervous glance at Prudence.

'Oh now, it's only that he's never cared for soup,' Meredith replied.

'Canada must be a very profligate country, if small boys are allowed to dictate the menu,' observed Prudence.

'He's bound to like the fricassée,' said mother. 'Rose always manages to come up with something tasty.'

But I never did discover what Edmund thought of Rose's fricassée because at that moment the final drama of that momentous day began to unfold. There was a commotion in the hall, the door burst open, Min's red face appeared, full of self-importance, and I was summoned outside. There in our hall was Mr Breen, hat in hands, eyes ablaze with excitement.

'I've been called out,' he said in the casual tones he adopted when most agitated, 'to Buckinghamshire, where an old acquaintance of mine, an insurance clerk, has been arrested on suspicion of murder. You must come. Wolfe is out of town and I may need someone to take notes. Besides, you won't get many opportunities like this. On with your hat and off we go.'

Chapter Four

I sat beside Breen in the cab, too stunned to do more than watch the familiar villas and terraces of Kilburn roll by. We stop-started past shuttered shop windows and locked yard gates, overtook omnibuses and horse-drawn carts, then ground to a halt behind a delivery lorry. On the pavements a straggle of tradesmen and office clerks in crumpled suits and trilbies headed home. When we set off again the horizon beyond the cab window began to expand: walls were replaced by fences, fences by hedgerows bordering lush suburban gardens, gardens by farmland.

The moment we cleared the London traffic, Breen opened his briefcase and worked through a mountain of mail accumulated during his holiday, filing the contents into different categories to be examined the next day by Miss Drake, who would cut out and save every square inch of blank paper; the rest she would consign either to the stove or to the buff folders containing clients' records.

But despite the intensity with which Breen seemed to peruse each document, I sensed he was so fired up that if we had to stop at another crossroads he would surely leap from the cab and run ahead to let other traffic know that this was an emergency. It seemed to me I could still smell the Highlands on him, a whiff of heather and soft rain that clung to his wiry hair and the fibres of his clothes. I, on the other hand, was feeling increasingly displaced, unable to comprehend how I had been wrenched suddenly from the dining room at Clivedon Hall Gardens to find myself inside a cab with Mr Breen, and still reeling from the shock of seeing my dead brother's mistress and child eating soup in our dining room.

'Did you have a pleasant holiday, sir?' I asked, in the vague hope that if I observed the niceties, the evening might not slip even further out of control.

His head snapped up. '*Pleasant*. What kind of a tepid word is that? But yes, I had a good holiday, thank you. I walked. I strode out. I breathed pure air. You should try it some time.' He addressed me, as he often addressed a bench, with biting irony. I thought he must be referring obliquely to the stuffy environment of Clivedon Hall Gardens.

Yet, despite his mood, opportunities for a tête-à-tête with Breen were so rare that I thought I should not waste this chance. 'Sir, I'd like to speak to you about a case that will be in court tomorrow, a woman called Leah Marchant. She is accused of kidnapping her own child. She wanted you to represent her because years ago, when she was a servant, you were kind to her.'

As I'd anticipated, Breen found this flattering portrait of himself irresistible. 'You say she *was* a servant. What is she now?'

'Destitute. She was abandoned by her husband, who's a sailor – he was last seen more than two years ago. She has been accused of child abduction although the baby is her own. After Christmas, according to the notes, she was faced with starvation having fraudulently claimed poor relief – she was earning a few shillings a week and hadn't declared it. When the relief was withdrawn she surrendered the children, two little girls and a baby of one year, voluntarily to the care of a children's home. Then she worked for a month or two and scrabbled together enough money to provide for them. But the home refuses to hand them back on the grounds that she is not a fit parent. They say she drinks, that there is no father or other family member offering financial or moral help, and that she therefore has no means to support the children in the long term.'

'So this kidnap?'

'Mrs Marchant discovered the address of the baby's foster mother and followed her until the perambulator was left outside a butcher's shop. Then she simply plucked the baby out of the carriage and ran off. She had held him in her arms for only about two minutes before she was captured.'

Breen picked up a letter, studied it with an extravagantly furrowed brow then thrust it aside. 'Well certainly she should have bail if it is her own child. She's hardly a threat to the public at large.'

'The police say there's a danger she'll go after him again. They say she's in a poor mental state. There's no surety and she's as good as homeless.'

'What do you mean *as good as*?'

'That's what the police are saying.'

'Never go by what the police say. She's either homeless or she's not. Have you tried to find her a hostel?'

'I haven't had—'

'We can't have our clients languishing in prison unnecessarily. It's highly unlikely that a reasonable judge will imprison her for the offence of kidnapping her own child. She must have bail.'

'There is no certainty that she'll be able to get the child back legally. That's why I don't think the court will grant bail. I've studied the 1891 act which gives the courts the right not to grant custody to unfit parents—'

'At the moment I'm not interested in legal rights. The woman must be got off this ridiculous charge. We'll go to court in the morning and have her bailed. Then you can put her in touch with some organisation that will help her to earn money while we write to the prosecution. Good Lord, Miss Gifford, I took you on because I thought you'd be resourceful – I didn't expect you to fall at the first hurdle. What about your friends at Toynbee? Miss Morrison. Have you talked to her? I'm sure she'll have some ideas.'

'Yes, I could consult—'

'Well do consult. Explore every avenue. Think through and round the problem, Miss Gifford. Use your contacts, limited though they may be. I thought you women were good at talking. Nurture your acquaintances; you never know when you might need them. The accused in this case of murder, for example, is an old acquaintance of mine and suddenly he needs me all right. Stephen Wheeler and I were brought up more or less round the corner from each other. We attended the same elementary school. The victim is his wife, shot in the breast at close range. Apparently they were on a *picnic*.' He spoke this last word with utter incredulity, as he might have said a *high wire*, and certainly I could not imagine the purposeful Mr Breen, for whom the outdoors was territory to be mapped and traversed, indulging in anything as frivolous as a picnic. 'Such a stroke of luck that when I got off the train at King's Cross I called in at the office to pick up my post. While I was there, the telephone call came about Stephen Wheeler. Of all people. The least offensive soul in the world. At school he was one of those stolid children who never step out of line.'

'What proof is there that he did it?'

'His army revolver and gloves were found buried near the body. There is a match between the bullet that killed her and his gun. That's all I know.'

He resumed his reading and I was left to watch the twilit countryside: a timber-framed farmhouse, a shaggy haystack and hedgerows blowsy with cow parsley. At the police station we swept through a cluster of onlookers, including a couple of reporters with notebooks, and spoke to the officer on the desk, who was breathless with self-importance. In a few minutes we were ushered through to a cramped back office, where the investigating sergeant sat behind a heap of papers, sipping from a mug of tea.

'Wheeler's not speaking,' he told us. 'If only he'd help himself. He was full of words yesterday morning, apparently, when he came here to report her missing. But since we arrested him, nothing except your name and details, Mr Breen. I was hoping I'd have a full statement by now.'

'I'm very pleased he's said nothing. As far as I'm concerned a client shows excellent sense in refusing to speak except in the presence of his lawyer. May we see him at once?'

Wheeler was slumped in his cell with his head in his hands. He was a stocky, soft-fleshed man of around forty with a surprisingly heavy beard for an insurance clerk and ungainly hands, the heels of which he ground into his eye sockets so that I could not help wondering what image he was attempting to blot out.

Breen was transformed when with a client: the hurry went out of him and his voice grew tender. But with Stephen Wheeler not even these strategies were successful. His head sank further and he wouldn't speak. My notebook and pencil were redundant.

Only once, when Breen asked, 'Tell me, Stephen, about the last time you saw your wife,' did Wheeler look up and allow us to see the expression of utter hopelessness in his eyes. Then his head went down again.

After quarter of an hour or so Wheeler was handcuffed between two policemen and escorted down a narrow corridor to a stifling interview room where space was so limited that I, being the most insignificant person present, had to stand with one foot in the passage. And there, beneath the grimy light of a single bulb, Wheeler was subjected to question after question, none of which he answered, not even to give his name or date of birth. By the time he was charged with murder, his head was so low that he could have been asleep except that occasionally a tear fell into his lap or he ran his sleeve under his nose.

An hour later we left the police station with nothing achieved except an agreement that Breen would represent Wheeler when he appeared at Amersham Magistrates' Court in the morning – which meant that, unless Wolfe re-materialised in time, I would have to deal with Leah Marchant's bail proceedings single-handed.

What we did have, however, was a duplicate résumé of Wheeler's war record and a copy of the police statement, which Breen passed to me one page at a time so that I could read them, at great cost to my equilibrium, as the taxicab lurched back towards London.

Chapter Five

Stephen Arthur Wheeler. DOB: 14 September 1888
Occupation: insurance clerk
2nd Battalion London Rifles
Rifleman S.A. Wheeler: 289351 2/5 London Regiment
Trained Haywards Heath, Crowborough, Jarris Brook
Served trenches of Ploegsteert sector
Invalided – gas poisoning – 2nd Battle of Ypres, 23 April 1915
Spell at Birkenhead – recruiting duties
Promoted lance corporal, August 1915
Loos – 25 September 1915
Commended (Military Medal) – Somme (Gommecourt,) 1 July 1916
Promoted corporal, November 1916
Commended (bar to the medal), Cambrai 1917
Commended (bar to the medal), 21 March 1918 (wounded)
Light duties, London.

The alleged facts of the Wheeler murder case were as follows:

On Sunday, 18 May 1924, at about seven thirty in the morning, Police Constable Scrivener, asleep with his wife in Chesham's police house, was roused by a violent knocking on the door. There in the porch was the defendant, Stephen Wheeler (a clerk working for Imperial Insurance). He was dishevelled, out of breath and holding on to a bicycle. He told PC Scrivener that his wife of three weeks, Stella – aged twenty-two years and formerly a waitress at a Lyons tea shop in Regent Street, central London – had gone missing, and that he'd last seen her at about one thirty the previous afternoon, when they had sat together on the hill above the church at Chesham eating corned beef and pickle sandwiches.

As he spoke of the picnic Wheeler had sobbed uncontrollably.

'I wish I'd stayed with her,' he said, 'but I had a thirst on me and fancied a beer. We'd had an argument, and she told me I could go to the pub on my own. I said I wasn't bothered if I did. I'd just go down for a quick one and be straight back, then I left her lying on the blanket in the shade.'

Wheeler had duly gone down to the Queen's Head, where the landlord was somewhat lax about opening hours, so that it was nearly half past three when Wheeler, having drunk no more than a couple of pints, finally returned to the picnic spot to find the blanket and the basket exactly where he'd left them, but no sign of Stella apart from her hat.

Wheeler was not overly worried at first. In fact he thought his wife must have wandered off for a little stroll, so he lay down and had a nap. When he woke an hour or so later with a blistering headache due to the shade having moved, exposing his forehead to the full heat of the sun, she still wasn't back, so he roamed about the hillside and nearby woodland, calling her name. Next he ran back to the town to see if he'd somehow missed her and she'd gone shopping on Chesham High Street. When he returned to the picnic spot, at about six, he reluctantly decided that she must have taken it upon herself to go home without him. So he packed up the rug, the sandwich wrappers and the hat and made his lonely way back through town to Chesham station, where he waited forty minutes for the little steam shuttle to return from Chalfont and Latimer, then took another train back to Harrow-on-the-Hill, whence he had to walk a mile or so to his home in Wealdstone. As he approached the house his spirits rose because he thought that Stella was bound to be there; to his despair he found the door locked and the spare key still in its place under a loose brick in the backyard.

At this point he had no idea what to do next. Though he had known Stella since she was a child – she was some sixteen years his junior – the couple were too recently wed for him to understand all her moods and he thought that perhaps she had been so offended by their argument that she had taken it upon herself to go home to her mother. So the exhausted man set off again, this time by bicycle to Acton. But when he got to his in-laws he found no Stella. Afraid of alarming her parents, he told them that he

37

happened to be passing after a day's fishing with his mates from work. Though they offered him a mug of cocoa and cheese on toast, he said he must get back.

Even then, at midnight, he still hoped that when he turned the corner of the street he would see lights burning in the house, but it was in darkness.

Early next morning, after a sleepless night, he bicycled back to Chesham. First he went to the picnic site. A light rain had fallen but otherwise the area was as he remembered, the grass still crushed from the weight of their bodies on the blanket. Convinced now that something terrible had happened, he ran down the hill and hammered on the door of the police house, hence the note made in the incident book at 7.30 a.m. on Sunday, 18 May.

Officer Scrivener said he would report the woman missing, and as soon as possible summon a couple of men from Amersham station to take a look at the picnic site – it being Sunday, of course, there would be only a skeleton staff. Whilst registering Wheeler's distress, Scrivener had the distinct impression that there were marital difficulties between husband and wife – Wheeler had seemed nervous when describing his last conversation with his wife. However, when Scrivener suggested that perhaps Stella might have run away, Wheeler had become agitated and insisted that she would do nothing of the kind and that he trusted her with his life. When asked what he intended to do next, Wheeler said that he would have another look round the hillside and Chesham town before returning home in the hope that Stella would turn up there.

It was not known how Wheeler spent the rest of Sunday but in the meantime a couple of policemen went up the hill and had a look about. They found nothing suspicious and the search was duly logged in the incident book. However, on Monday morning a dog walker let her mongrel, Caspar, off its leash in woodland about three quarters of a mile from the Wheeler picnic spot. The dog disappeared for several minutes into the trees and failed to re-emerge. When its owner went in after it, calling its name, the dog suddenly sprang out with a woman's shoe in its mouth. Urged on by the creature's insistent yapping, the intrepid owner investigated further and discovered that the shoe had been attached to the foot of a young woman who was buried under a few inches of leaf mould and a pile of bracken. She'd been shot in the heart at close range. Later a pair of army gloves and a revolver, again lightly covered with soil, were found nearby. The police, after rapid checks on Stephen Wheeler, discovered that he was an ex-army man. They went immediately to his house to arrest him. He was not at home, but Scrivener had made a note of Wheeler's occupation and place of work. Unlikely though it seemed that a man whose wife had just disappeared would choose to go the office as usual, when they reached Imperial Insurance in Far-ringdon, there was Wheeler, at his desk. He was duly arrested on suspicion of murder. Wheeler's colleagues viewed the proceedings with disbelief, their consternation shared by the management, including the company director, Sir David Hardynge, who hap-pened to be in the building at the time.

Having read the statement I rolled down the window and took gasps of the evening air in an effort to cure my motion sickness. Breen, unusually, was silent until we turned into Clivedon Hall Gardens. As I stepped from the cab he said, 'Don't be making too harsh or quick a judgement of Stephen Wheeler.'

'I had no intention—'

'He was a good person when I knew him. Heaven knows what the war did to him. I only drove ambulances for a couple of years and still I came home with my nerves shot to pieces. Wheeler stuck it out almost for the duration. You keep an open mind until we find out the truth.'

'My mind is open, Mr Breen.'

'Good, make sure it stays that way.'

A light had been left burning in the porch but the rest of the house was in darkness. However, when I opened the door to my own room, I was startled by the sight of Meredith perched on the windowsill, knees tucked up to her chest and wearing a flowing robe drawn tight at the waist. 'I thought I'd wait up for you. Did you see him? Did you see the murderer?'

I switched on the bedside light, flustered, even annoyed by her intrusion into my room. 'I saw our client, Stephen Wheeler. He's not been found guilty of murder yet.'

'What was he like?'

'Sad. Very.'

'What will happen next?'

'In the morning he'll be brought to court. He won't be granted bail. Then, when the police are ready, he'll be arraigned the indictment will be read.'

'The indictment?'

'Charge. Then, if he pleads not guilty, a trial date will be fixed.'

'And what will you do in the meantime?'

'I'll probably have nothing more to do with the case, except perhaps to shadow Mr Breen.'

'It's all so exciting. You are lucky.'

'I suppose I am. Wheeler isn't, though.'

She studied me for a moment then asked, 'And tomorrow. What are you doing tomorrow?'

'Tomorrow I shall be working as usual.'

'I would like the opportunity to talk to you alone, away from this house. Might I buy you lunch?'

'I'm afraid I never take a lunch break.'

'But just this once, surely? I passed a department store on the bus today, Peter Jones. I'll bet that has a restaurant. What do you say? One o'clock?'

Elfin in her flowing robe, with her head to one side and her eyes fixed pleadingly on mine, Meredith was a strange addition to my bedroom. After all, it was rather touching that she'd stayed up for me. In any case I was too tired to argue. It was now nearly twenty-four hours since I had slept, and in the midst of yearning for my bed and dreading the next morning's court appearance on behalf of Leah Marchant, I found myself agreeing to meet her punctually at one.

Chapter Six

The following morning I travelled to Shoreditch to represent Leah Marchant. Once more I visited her in the cells; once more she refused to cooperate with me because I was not Mr Breen. Half an hour later her case was called and she appeared in the dock cuffed to a woman jailer and looking even more dishevelled than she had the previous afternoon. Her case was sufficiently unusual to have attracted a straggle of spectators and I was conscious of a frisson of interest as I took my place in an advocates' pew, facing the bench.

Months spent observing from the public galleries had familiarised me with the magistrates' courts: the smell of polish, freshly mixed ink and clashing body odours, defendants brought up from the cells with only hands and face washed, magistrates and lawyers scented with hair oil and shaving soap; the dim light filtering through windows set high up lest a prisoner be tempted to jump dock; the somewhat languid atmosphere generated by the constant toing and froing of ushers, the swinging of the court doors and the inattention of lawyers lolling about waiting for their own cases to be called. Today the bench was occupied by a single stipendiary magistrate I judged to be in his late sixties. The clerk, meanwhile, was a round fellow with owlish spectacles through which he appeared to see very little.

My client was told to identify herself, and it was established that she was Leah Joan Marchant, born 4 May 1896, aged 28, address, 9 Caractacus Court, Haggerston.

'Leah Joan Marchant, you are charged with the offence of child abduction; namely that on Monday, 19 May 1924, you unlawfully and without reasonable excuse snatched a baby, Charles Marchant, aged sixteen months, who had been left in his perambulator by his foster carer outside a butcher's shop ... And you are represented, Mrs Marchant, by ah ...?'

The usher handed up a slip of paper on which was written my name: Miss E. Gifford, Breen & Balcombe. As I rose to my feet my knees shook under the mercifully heavy fabric of my skirt. This was only the third time I'd addressed a bench, the first being to request the extension of a licence to sell alcohol in a church hall, the second, under the eagle eye of Mr Breen, to ask for an adjournment for prosecution papers to be served in a case of stealing a loaf of bread. The court went very still when I said in a voice that sounded surprisingly confident but unquestionably feminine, 'I appear for Mrs Marchant, Your Worship.'

There was a murmur of surprise. I was aware that the court doors had creaked open to admit another observer. The clerk's myopic eyes crinkled into an unconvincing smile. 'So, you are Miss Gifford and you represent the defendant. Are we now ready for a plea to be taken, Miss Gifford?'

'Not yet,' I said. 'The case is a complex one, as you are probably aware, because it involves Mrs Marchant's own child. Might my client be seated?'

The magistrate, a trim individual with very white teeth, gave me a long stare. 'Remind me again in what capacity you are appearing in this court, Miss er ...'

'My name is Miss Gifford. I am Mrs Marchant's legal representative.'

'Working for which firm?'

'Breen & Balcombe.'

'Ah, Breen. Now all becomes clear. And where is Mr Breen today?'

'Is this relevant, Your Worship? I am here to represent—'

'Are you *qualified*, Miss er ...'

The clerk jumped up and held a whispered conversation with the magistrate. There followed a guffaw of laughter, raised eyebrows, then a deep sigh from the bench. 'Well, Madam Lawyer, do proceed and tell us on what grounds you are asking for an adjournment.'

'As I've said, this is not a straightforward case, Your Worship. The defendant is accused of taking her own child. I am asking for one week's adjournment so that all the facts can be made known to the defence.'

'And what will you do with these facts, when they are known?'

'They may affect the plea, Your Worship.'

'I see. Or is it that Mr Breen, who clearly believes this court is so lowly that it can be used as the playground in which ladies may conduct a flirtation with the law, is just too busy to appear before us in person today, so is adopting one of his notorious stalling tactics.'

'Your Worship, this is an unusual case. There is no question that my client attempted to take her baby, but her motives, her understanding of what she was doing, must be fully explored before we can enter a plea.'

Another whispered conversation ensued. 'Very well,' said the magistrate as if humouring a spoilt child. 'I'll adjourn the case for one week, after which pleas will be taken. I presume, Miss Gifford, you don't intend asking for bail because you'll be wasting your time.'

By now the palms of my hands were sweating. The audience in the public gallery tittered.

'With respect, Your Worship—'

'No, with respect to you, Miss Gifford, I have given you quite enough of my time. There is no question of bail. You tell your Mr Breen that if he wants bail for his clients, he should come to court himself.'

'Your Worship, you cannot refuse bail on the grounds that you don't approve of the person representing the defendant. That is unlawful ...'

The clerk rose to his feet and said smoothly, 'Your Worship, police bail was refused on the grounds that the woman, in her desperate state, is likely to attempt to take the child again.'

'Quite so. I'll remand the prisoner in custody for—'

'At least let me speak for my client,' I cried.

'When have I ever been able to prevent a woman from speaking, if she has a mind to?' the magistrate asked, raising one eyebrow at the spectators in the public gallery, who roared with laughter.

'I should like it to be put on the record that my client was not given a fair hearing today, and that comments prejudicial to her case were made in open court such as: "I presume you don't intend asking for bail because you'll be wasting your time ...'"

There was now silence in the courtroom as the magistrate twiddled his thumbs. I glanced at Leah Marchant, who had thrown back her head and was looking at the cracks in the ceiling as if utterly disassociated from the proceedings.

'Ah,' said the magistrate at last, 'I'm glad that your determination to teach us how to do our jobs extends not only to me but to the learned justices' clerk, who has, let me see, is it thirty years' experience in his current position? What a relief that a young lady has joined the ranks of advocates so that we may all learn how to proceed. You may take the prisoner down.' He clicked his fingers at the jailer.

Gathering papers and briefcase I headed for the door, which the usher made an elaborate play of opening for me, bowing from the waist. In the foyer a group of lawyers went quiet and fixed me with cold stares before resuming their conversation. I went down to the cells to see Leah but was told she didn't want to speak to me.

All this time I had been fighting back tears. I wanted to escape this scene of humiliation, but as I ran down the court steps I heard someone call my name and then a hand fell lightly on my arm. Startled, I glimpsed long fingers, shapely nails, a starched cuff under a pinstriped sleeve. 'Miss Gifford,' a cultivated voice murmured in my ear, 'admirably done. We absolutely cannot allow behaviour of that kind by these magisterial despots.'

A stranger's face was inclined close to mine: amused eyes, youthful lips under a glossy moustache, deep forehead and a scent of cologne. 'One tip, if I may be so bold. Your worst crime is not that you're a lady – though that's bad enough, as I'm sure you're aware – but that you interrupted the magistrate. My advice: never interrupt a magistrate or judge whatever nonsense they speak. Makes 'em mad. Hear 'em out, agree, ignore. That's the trick.'

I withdrew my arm. 'Thank you, but I don't believe I asked for advice.' I marched away, thinking that to be patronised by this smooth-tongued barrister was the final straw.

*

44

I arrived in Sloane Square with ten minutes to spare. Meredith, on the other hand, was nearly a quarter of an hour late, which at least gave me the opportunity to gather my wits. It seemed to me, after the debacle of the Marchant hearing, that I had no choice but to offer my resignation. It was one thing to harbour an ambition to be a lawyer, quite another to see clients suffer as a result.

Having made this self-sacrificial and momentous decision, I wanted to act on it immediately and grew irritated by Meredith's tardiness. Punctuality was one of the absolutes by which we lived at Clivedon Hall Gardens. When at last she appeared, decked out in a lilac frock with a triple-layered skirt and matching hat, she apologised profusely, saying she'd got all mixed up with the omnibuses. Seizing my hands as if we were sisters or best friends she kissed me on either cheek. This collision of flesh, the waft of perfume, her 'Oh it is such a joy to see you', threw me off balance after the hostility of the courtroom so that for the second time in an hour I felt tears pricking.

As we entered the store she bestowed a dazzling smile on the doorman, who snapped to attention.

'Where is Edmund?' I asked.

'Your grandmother is keeping him company. They have found a shared interest in collecting things: your brother's stamp collection, her albums of theatre programmes, Edmund's foreign coins – the few I allowed him to bring – her box of buttons, out they have all come.'

'Grandmother will enjoy that.'

Meredith paused beside a counter of white fluff, glanced winsomely at a shop assistant, and flung a stole round her neck. 'What do you think? Do you like it?' She drew up her shoulders and snuggled her face into the fur, which settled fetchingly against her pale skin and auburn hair. 'You try it, go on, Evelyn.'

'I'd rather not.'

'Well, how about this pink scarf? I would like to buy you something. I should so like to see you in a colour.'

'I have plenty of clothes, thank you.' But the next moment I was manoeuvred in front of a mirror and found myself unexpectedly transformed by a wisp of pink chiffon. My jaw and complexion were softened and the harsh lines of my jacket broken by the drift of silk.

'You see. I knew it would suit you. Those wonderful bones need something delicate to show them at their best. Oh do say you'll wear it.'

'But it's so expensive. I wear dark clothes for work, so it would be wasted. We should go upstairs; I have very little time and we may not get a table.' I put the scarf firmly aside; it was so frivolous, so costly, nearly half a week's housekeeping, and yet so lovely that I yearned to touch it again.

In the restaurant Meredith made circumstances adapt to her requirements with startling ease. Although there was no empty table she persuaded the waitress to look about for a couple of ladies who might soon be leaving. 'We don't want a nasty tucked away table; we want one with a view,' she said. In a few minutes we were facing each other across a fresh cloth. 'Tell me what you've been doing this morning. I want to know every last detail,' said Meredith.

'I represented a defendant who was remanded in custody.'

'But how marvellous. You mean you actually stood up in a court full of people? I wish I'd been there.'

'I'm very glad you weren't.'

'Why so?'

'I'm not well received in court, as a woman.'

'Well of course not. How could you expect it to be otherwise? Back home in Canada the argument is largely won but there are still those who refuse to regard women as *persons*, and since only *persons* can be lawyers . . .'

'We're always envious of the progress female lawyers have made across the Atlantic.'

'I heard Annie Langstaff speak at a University Women's Club lecture when she demolished the argument about separate spheres. Quite brilliant.'

'If only we didn't have to get involved with such arguments. If only we could prove ourselves by the quality of our work. I simply want to be left in peace.'

'Or do you mean isolation?' Meredith gave my arm a playful squeeze as if to soften this last, rather disturbing remark. She then

46

smiled up at the waitress, who made a maternal fuss setting our table with milk jug, tea strainer, napkins and cutlery.

Meredith cupped her chin in her hand, gazing about like a wondering child, her big, dark-lashed eyes (did she use some form of make-up and if so whatever would Prudence say?) fixing first on one diner then the next with such intensity that occasionally she attracted a shy glance or smile. I saw the restaurant mostly in monochrome, waitresses in black dresses, silver cutlery and condiments, white napkins and aprons. Only Meredith, in her lilac dress, was brightly tinted at that moment. An artful curl peeped from either side of her hat and I sensed that everything she did was planned, including her spontaneity.

'I expect you're dying to ask me questions,' she said, knotting her fingers under her chin like a Kate Greenaway illustration.

'I'm sure you'll tell me exactly as much or as little as you want,' I replied. She had ordered a ham salad, I, poached egg as the cheapest choice on the menu. It turned out to be tepid and I thought anxiously of the cost of this meal compared to my usual lunch of a cheese sandwich brought from home.

'No, no. I don't want to foist information on you,' she said, sprinkling oil on her lettuce. 'After all, there may be some things you don't wish to hear.'

'What troubles me most is that I didn't know of Edmund's existence until yesterday.'

'That must have been your father's choice. I admit I thought it odd that Edmund never heard from his Auntie Evelyn or indeed his grandmother.'

'When did you tell father about Edmund?'

'Let me see. I would have written to your father in the early spring of 1918 to let him know I was coming to London, and why. We met for luncheon in a very smart hotel – or so I thought at the time – called Brown's, though I remember the beef was tough. I was pregnant of course, and a fastidious eater. That's when we reached our agreement. He thought it best that I return to my family in Canada but he promised I would have a monthly allowance. For a while he sent me regular cheques, then more erratically until about eighteen months ago, when they dried up completely. I wrote but received no answer.'

'When father died last April he left us in very poor financial circumstances.'

'But as I had Edmund, in the end I had no choice but to come here and throw myself on your mercy. To be truthful, Evelyn, these years have not been easy. Can you imagine how your family might have reacted if you'd appeared back home six months pregnant by an unknown, and incidentally dead, serviceman? My family was far from pleased, I can tell you. They are Roman Catholics and live in a small village outside Toronto where everyone talks. Relations between us since Edmund's arrival have not been easy, especially when the money from England dried up. And I was surrounded by siblings and cousins who had done the right thing – got married, even been widowed, some of them – as opposed to bearing a child out of wedlock. Besides, nursing in the war had given me a taste for independence. I felt stifled at home, and once I'd thought of travelling to London I couldn't resist the idea, so here I am.'

'But weren't you taking an enormous risk, coming all this way and not knowing how you'd be received?'

'I didn't think so. I'd met your father, and James of course, so I knew what type of family you were. I expected you to be charitable.'

Was there just a hint of irony in that word *charitable*? I noted that she had not said welcoming or even merciful. Apparently she'd got the measure of us already.

Around us lady diners wagged their heads so that collective feathers waved and nodded, and from the next table came a trill of laughter as a couple of young women leaned their heads together over a cigarette lighter. The air was warmly scented with food and perfume and smoke.

'When I went through father's papers after his death,' I said, 'I found nothing about you and Edmund, otherwise of course I would have written.' How typical of father to have kept this secret from me. He would simply have deemed it none of my business, unless he chose to make it so. But it must have been on his mind as he sat late at his club or, on the rare occasions he dined at home, in lonely splendour at the end of the dining-room table while we ladies yawned over tea in the drawing room, watching the door. 'Did you have a formal contract of any kind? I need to know what is due to you.'

'I can tell what you're thinking,' Meredith said after a pause. 'You think that I may be an impostor of some kind, posing as Edmund's mother. Well, I have this ring. And your father was convinced right away. He was very generous. But then I think he had to be, don't you? After all, there's Edmund.'

You think I may be an impostor. It cut me deeply that she had given voice to such an idea so crudely. But then perhaps I was shocked because her judgement was so unerringly accurate. I wanted Edmund to be real, but not Meredith. Until now, James had been the shining heroic boy, entirely ours, a young brother grown so tall he could hook me under his arm and rest his chin in my hair, whose great feet thundered on the stairs, who used to burst into my bedroom and project himself head first across my bed: 'I swear I will throttle father if he tells me one more time I'm throwing away any prospect of success if I don't go into partnership with him.' I thought I had known him, inside and out. Even when he died he was still mine; sometimes it felt as if the best part of me had followed him down to the cold, still place he'd found.

'Perhaps, if you don't mind, you should tell me a little of what happened between you and James,' I said stiffly. 'You were a nurse and he was your patient.'

'That's it. I was posted for a while to a hospital near the Belgian border. Men not so badly wounded were sent back to us to be patched up and returned to the front. James, as you probably know, sustained a severe injury to his upper arm. He was with us for about three weeks.' She was watching me across the rim of her teacup, which she held daintily, as if it were porcelain. 'A week or so after he'd been sent back, I heard he was dead.'

She was so much closer to him than I, had more recent knowledge. It was as if a new fragment of my brother was being dangled before me. 'Three weeks,' I murmured, 'you knew him for just three weeks.'

'That's all. A lot can happen in three weeks, in a war.'

I reached for my briefcase, finding this last, softly spoken remark too intimate to bear.

49

'You said you wanted to talk to me alone,' I continued. 'Was there something else before I go?'

'Evelyn, I want you to be on my side. I want a life here. You have achieved so much. Will you help me do the same? And I want to see Edmund settled in a school. He must have at least as good an education as his father's, don't you think?'

James's old school? The idea was clearly impossible – we could never afford it and they would surely not accept Edmund (the word *bastard* flashed through my mind and I felt a protective pang of indignation on his behalf). But also it dawned on me that Meredith was regarding her stay at Clivedon Hall Gardens not as a visit but as a permanent arrangement. Things were moving much too fast.

'We'll talk again. I must get back. I have so much to do.'

She caught my hand. 'You work too hard. Really you do. I should like to see you have a little fun. How would it be if you came to the seaside with me and Edmund one Saturday? I feel as if he must catch up on his English heritage and surely a trip to the beach must be part of that?'

'Thank you for asking, but I'm afraid I have to work most Saturdays. I am very behind, as I've said.'

She seemed to have forgotten her offer to pay for lunch and made no effort to reach into her handbag. In just one hour I had squandered nearly a fortnight's spending money.

Chapter Seven

When I reached Arbery Street I found the door to Breen & Balcombe ajar and even at a distance could hear that Breen was in one of his rages. 'And where is that blasted boy?' I heard him shout. Muted reply from Miss Drake.

I crept into the hallway thinking that I would retreat to my basement office, write up the Leah Marchant notes and prepare a letter of resignation. Breen's office door was wide open. 'The partnership will be bankrupt,' he yelled as a pile of papers was slapped down on the desk. 'Nobody has earned a penny since I left for my holiday – my first break in six years, note – and the moment I turn my back ... Where is Gifford; what excuse has she for deserting a sinking ship?'

'She appears to be taking a very long lunch break,' observed Miss Drake slyly.

'I'm here,' I said.

What had formerly been the front parlour of a family house was now Breen's office: sunlit, dusty and furnished with ancient Victorian pieces passed down through generations of Breen & Balcombes. The room had a maverick quality and could change as fast as its owner's moods. Sometimes the shelves of ancient tomes and box files seemed to dominate, creating a fusty, legalistic atmosphere, but on others, such as winter afternoons when there was a fire in the hearth and Breen was happily engaged in dashing off one of his devastating tirades against the police or a government department responsible for victimising a client, the room was as inviting as a Christmas card. Today the desk was littered with ledgers and a window was open, causing a billowing of documents and curtains so that it was as though Breen were on board ship, surging through a backlog of paperwork. Miss Drake sat demurely in a chair, notepad at the ready, striped blouse crisply pressed.

'Ah, Miss Gifford, I've been searching for last month's invoices. Where are they?' said Breen, as if genuinely bemused.

'I placed them in the tray as usual.'

'These?' He held up a few wisps of paper. 'They come to ten shillings and ninepence. Your ragtag of clients scarcely pays a bean, Miss Gifford; you have turned this partnership into a charitable institution.' There was no point protesting that my clients were allocated by Breen himself; best allow the storm to pass over. 'What about your new case – Marchant – I suppose it's too much to expect that you managed to get her bail?'

'If I may, sir, I'd like to talk to you in private about Mrs Marchant.' I glanced at Miss Drake, who hung over her notepad, feet firmly planted in anticipation of witnessing a delicious row.

'You can tell me on the way. I've been waiting for you. We're off to Wheeler's house to collect a few personal items for his use while he's in prison. I need a female eye – see if you can notice anything the police might have missed.'

'Mr Breen, there is so much … I must talk to you …'

He gave me a piercing stare: 'If you'll excuse us, Miss Drake.'

Miss Drake displayed an excess of feeling by a reduction in her expression rather than the reverse. Gathering up her things, she gave Breen a tightly professional smile and closed the door sharply behind her.

After she'd gone I said, 'Mr Breen, I should like to offer my resignation with immediate effect.' Even to my own ears I sounded melodramatic, a trait that Breen could not abide in others.

He flung down his pen and I was conscious of a slight creaking of the floorboards in the passage outside the door. 'It's for me to dismiss you, not for you to resign.' He picked up the next document to signal that the conversation was at an end.

'I am doing damage, sir. This morning, in the case of Leah Marchant, I made us look ridiculous – the defendant, myself, even you, because of your association with me. She is charged with a very serious offence and must have proper representation.'

'She has it.'

'No. She won't even look at me, let alone trust me.'

'Is that your only complaint? Stephen Wheeler won't speak to me but that doesn't mean I'm going to drop his case.'

'The magistrate made such a fool of me there was no point even trying to argue for bail. Sir, you're the one she needs, though I warn you she's got no money whatever to pay your fees. Don't you think she's disadvantaged enough without me representing her?'

'You found her, you keep her. And as for the fees, I've no doubt we can twist the arm of some journalist or other to pay us a few bob for the exclusive rights to her story.' He glanced at his watch. 'I said we'd be at the Wheeler house by four.'

I felt better. How could I not when I was marching along dusty pavements in the wake of Mr Breen whilst above us clouds passed swiftly over the sun so that one moment there was dense shade, the next vibrant heat? As our train puffed its way out of Euston, I told myself that a thousand ladies at this moment fidgeting over afternoon tea trays would give their eye teeth to be Evelyn Gifford, articled clerk. My face was reflected in the dirty windowpane; wonderful bones, Meredith had said.

And as we passed through Queen's Park and Willesden, amidst grubby factories and terraces backing on to the railway line, I glimpsed the lives of other women. Prudence said that when and how people hung their washing was a sure indicator of breeding and it was certainly the case that, it being Tuesday, only grey remnants of laundry remained in certain backyards. I saw a woman sitting on a step as she minded a clutch of children and poultry and another washing her scullery window.

During the journey Breen immersed himself in back copies of the *Times Law Reports* but occasionally favoured me with a spurt of information, the most momentous being that Stephen Wheeler had not entered a plea (or indeed uttered any other words) that morning in court when the charge was read out, and that committal proceedings were already under way. The police regarded the case as cut and dried and expected it to be heard at the Aylesbury Assizes in July. After all, the circumstantial evidence fitted: Wheeler and his wife had been alone on the hill above the church for several hours, and the weapon and gloves were his. The police had even fixed on a motive, scornfully outlined by Breen.

A fortnight before he was married, Wheeler had taken out life insurance for himself and his wife to the tune of ten thousand pounds each. 'The police say this is suspicious,' said Breen, 'but what man, cautious by nature and working in an insurance office, would not be tempted by his company's special rates for employees? His wife was not earning – she'd been a waitress at Lyons but of course had stopped working when she was married. He was wise to take out insurance, I'd suggest.'

'And an insurance company wouldn't pay out in a case where there had been such obvious foul play,' I said. 'How could Wheeler hope to get away with it?'

'Exactly my thought. Wheeler, as I recall, was hardly the brightest boy in the class, but he wasn't a complete idiot. The police have come up with another theory. They say it was purely by chance that Stella Wheeler's body was found – after all, it took a particularly tenacious dog owner to unearth it. They say that it was probably Wheeler's intention to go back, remove the gun and gloves and bury her more thoroughly, having raised a hue and cry to make it seem as if she was genuinely missing.'

'Has Wheeler said anything about all this?'

'As I said, Wheeler is still not speaking. He weeps and shakes his head and turns his face to the wall. I suspect he's still in shock, though the prosecution will say it looks like guilt. I'm very concerned about the health both of his body and mind. Next time I visit I shall take a doctor with me.'

'Given the gun and the gloves, and Wheeler's silence, isn't it likely the police are right and he did kill her? Who else would it be?'

Breen raised the newspaper higher to shut me out. 'At this point I have no idea. And the killer could indeed be Wheeler, although I make a point of never believing a client of mine is guilty until he tells me so himself or a jury decides for me. But unless we take action, that man will be in and out of the dock and hung by the neck before anyone has time to get near the truth of the matter.'

In Wealdstone we walked along streets milling with children released from school. Girls sat cross-legged in a circle by the kerb intent on a game of fives, their summer frocks pulled up over bony knees, whilst a crowd of a dozen or so boys kicked a battered leather ball from gutter to gutter. A baby howled in its pram and waved frantic fists, and a couple of toddlers earnestly collected a pile of cinders whilst their mothers leaned together, deep in conversation. I heard the name Mrs Wheeler and realised that by now news of Stella's death would be on everyone's lips.

As we neared the Wheelers' street we discovered that the atmosphere was indeed charged; there was a distinct frisson of excitement, and as strangers we were watched with more than usual interest. At the coal merchant's on the High Street we turned left and then immediately right on to Byron Street, which consisted of two rows of terraced houses, a chosen few, including number 7, distinguished by the fact that they had bay windows on the ground floor. Later, as I built a mental image of Stella Wheeler, I realised that having that superior bay window would have meant a great deal to her.

A policeman was waiting on the doorstep, very hot and self-conscious, surrounded by a small crowd that was clamouring for information. Though Stephen Wheeler had paid a deposit on this house a couple of months before his marriage, its faded paintwork suggested that it had not been much cared for since. Even before I set foot across the threshold, Prudence's strictures on the art of good housekeeping (until now largely ignored) were echoing through my mind. Stella Wheeler had not been an ideal housewife: her front step had collected more than just a few days' litter and her net curtains were grimy.

The policeman removed his hat, revealing a rash of pimples on his youthful forehead, and let us into a narrow hall. Pushier members of the crowd had to be discouraged from clustering in after us. There was a strong smell of damp, and the linoleum on the floor was so well trodden that in places the pattern had completely worn away. Though the house had only been shut up for a couple of days there was a hopeless quality to the stale air, as if even the bricks and mortar knew that the Wheelers were not coming back.

Prudence would have had a field day; there was grit along the skirting and dado, torn wallpaper and grease marks round the door handles. The front parlour was furnished with a couple of ugly chairs, probably passed on by relatives of the newly married pair, and the hearth was ornamented with unlovely china – a floral vase with a yellow rim and base, and a matching ashtray.

The back room was a little more inviting. On the dresser a dainty tea set was arranged with great precision, its gilt-edged cups polished, its saucers stood on their sides to show off the pattern. Inside the jug was a little card with a printed bouquet of flowers at one corner: *On your Wedding Day. From All Your Friends at Lyons*. In the scullery beyond, preparations for the picnic were still evident (more proof of Stella's slovenliness): it looked as if mice had got at the heel of a loaf of bread and a pickle jar had been left open, attracting the attention of flies.

I had rarely felt as uncomfortable as I did then, on the verge of those other, ruined lives. And the stillness of the air, the way in which everything was suspended at the moment the couple had set forth to catch the Metropolitan Line train to Chesham, the knife flung across the breadboard and the dishcloth trailing over the side of the sink, half in and half out of the scummy washing-up water, reminded me of how time becomes warped in moments of trauma, so that physical surroundings seem out of step with the lives that inhabit them. I remembered how Clivedon Hall Gardens, the instant that I flung open the front door and saw an envelope in the hand of a telegraph boy, had become frozen in time, so that it was not until the next morning that the toasting fork was hung back on its hook by the hearth or the tea tray was carried down to the kitchen. Until then grandmother's crochet remained in a heap on the floor, my coat and hat flung untidily across the hallstand, my satchel on the bottom stair.

I was reminded of this, fleetingly, by the sight of Stella Wheeler's little scullery with its half-dozen flies buzzing at the window. She had presumably expected, as she left the house for the picnic, to return and continue where she had left off.

'The prisoner's things will be upstairs in the wardrobe,' said the policeman, suddenly officious. 'I was told nothing else should be disturbed.' We climbed the stairs with their strip of diamond-patterned carpet and found two rooms, the back pitifully unused, with a spare bed covered by a blanket and a few incongruous household items including a brand new cast-iron boot scraper in the form of a hedgehog, and a pitcher and basin in pink ceramic. I edged past a heap of packing cases and a chair with a broken cane seat to peer out of the window onto a small backyard containing a privy, a shed and a couple of pots of dying geraniums. Beyond and on either side were more yards, in one of which a trio of women stood with folded arms, staring up at me. My appearance at the window would presumably cause yet more sensation in the neighbourhood.

As we left that bleak room, I saw a picture propped facing the wall. Expecting a wedding portrait – I had seen none so far – I turned it round, but it was in fact a photograph of two soldiers, one scarcely more than a child, full-lipped and with a pimple between his brows, the other a beardless Stephen Wheeler. Then, as now, Wheeler's eyes were his best features, steady and solemn. Both men had signed their names underneath: *Paul Christopher Fox. Stephen Anthony Wheeler.* I thought it the saddest thing in the house; not the photograph itself but the fact that it had been set aside.

We went through to the front bedroom and here at last the figure of Stella Wheeler became more vivid to me. I understood that although she loathed housework, a great deal of time had been lavished on her own appearance. This room was entirely hers; there was even no sign that she was married, other than the man's plaid dressing gown hanging on the back of the door. The bed was covered in patchwork shades of pink, and the surface of the dressing table spread with lace mats upon which were arranged bottles, brushes and pots of lotion. A flighty satin nightdress was folded on the left-hand pillow, great care having been taken to smooth it flat and keep the elaborate embroidery on the bodice exposed, and fluffy pink slippers of the kind also favoured by Meredith peeped from under the chair by the dressing table.

Fortunately there was hardly room for the policeman to enter – he had obviously been instructed to keep us in his sight – so instead he had to stoop under the lintel and crane to see what was going on as Breen made a great show of slamming drawers and throwing open wardrobe doors in search of Wheeler's underwear. Meanwhile I did as I had been instructed and attempted to uncover Stella's secrets, which included a drawer full of surprisingly

57

expensive-looking undergarments, all far more glamorous than my own: a bust flattener, a flesh-coloured rubber girdle, a white broderie anglaise petticoat, satin knickers with fine lace trim, meticulously rolled silk stockings (I had one pair, Stella three). The dressing table had a shelf under the mirror and two small, additional drawers on either side. One contained a few items of costume jewellery, the other her sponge bag, which smelled of damp toothbrush. Presumably, in the absence of a bathroom, Stella carried this bag down to the scullery each morning and night.

'So have you got everything?' asked the policeman.

'That's it,' said Breen. 'Handkerchiefs, underwear. Good. Do you want to check them, officer? Anything else catch your eye that you think the poor man might need, Miss Gifford?'

I had found nothing startling; everything fitted the portrait I had been building of a youthful wife with a taste for finery and not much interest in her domestic surroundings. When I glanced inside the wardrobe I thought the allocation of space very telling – Stella's pastel frocks and coats occupied two thirds of the rail while Stephen's two suits were crushed at one end. But as we waited for the policeman to make a note in his book of the items we'd removed, I took another look at the sponge bag, it being the most personal item in the room. It contained toothbrush and paste, face cream, tweezers, rouge, a lipstick. Nothing else. Except that there was a tear in the oilskin lining and slipped inside, between the inner and outer shell, was a scrap of mushroom-coloured paper, folded very small. I felt a stab of excitement thinking this might be it, whatever it was we were looking for, but when I smoothed it out I found that it was just a cloakroom ticket, number 437. I showed it to Breen then slipped it into my pocket.

When I returned that evening, late again, to Clivedon Hall Gardens, the aura of the Wheeler house and its abandoned contents still clung about me, mingling with those other, more powerful images of my own loss. But as I unlocked the front door, all other thought was driven from my head by the sound of music – *jazz*, of all things – coming from the drawing room, and then the trill of Meredith's laughter. As I hung up my hat I was amused to catch myself patting my hair into place in the mirror. Just because Meredith said she admired you at lunchtime, I told myself, suddenly you've grown vain. I pushed open the drawing-room door.

Meredith sat in grandmother's usual place at the end of the sofa by the open French window, the curtain blowing against her shoulder and a glass of what looked like whisky in her hand as she mouthed the words of the song. Prudence was at the writing desk as if to disassociate herself from the scene. A whole clutch of unwritten rules was being broken: no strong alcoholic beverage to be drunk by women unless in extreme circumstances such as Christmas, influenza or death; no music in the drawing room, where, since James's death, the piano had been shut up tight.

'It Had to Be You' floated on the air. Another unwritten rule of post-war Clivedon Hall Gardens: no discussion of relations between the sexes, unless in the pages of an Ethel M. Dell novel sneaked up to her bedroom by Prudence and discovered quite by chance one day when Min brought it to me, supposing it must be mine. It had got caught up in a mound of sheets taken down to be laundered. After reading the first page and the last I was never able to view Prudence in quite the same light: 'You are the prince of my heart – for ever. I love you as – as I never thought it was humanly possible to love.'

Poor Prudence, had there been a prince of her heart? Did she have, beneath that rigid corset, a needy, romantic side? James would have loved to know that Prudence read Ethel M. Dell beneath the covers – he and I would have succumbed to fits of laughter – but alone I was more compassionate. While she was occupied downstairs I had returned the book to her room, slipping it into her dressing-gown pocket. Now I imagined from the set of her shoulders that she was yearning towards the music as she yearned towards the sentiments of Ethel M. Dell, but would not let herself weaken.

Mother, on the other hand, was weeping, and after another moment I understood why.

Edmund was dancing with grandmother; she barely a head taller than him, her little feet in their buttoned shoes occasionally tangling with his, her half-blind eyes gazing over the top of his head as they held each other by the hand and upper arm. The

59

little boy was too young to be self-conscious about dancing with an old lady, and allowed himself to be manoeuvred back and forth in a cross between a waltz and something more modern, grandmother's approximation to jazz. She was utterly absorbed, leaning into the music, grinning, whisking her small partner around the room, swinging him back and forth as much as her stiff limbs would allow.

And as for Edmund, no wonder mother was weeping. He was dressed quaintly in pale blue trousers and a loose cotton shirt with a girlishly rounded collar, his brows drawn together by the concentration required to keep in step. And in his expressions, posture, determination he was James, our little man, returned to us as his beloved, six-year-old self. But at the same time he was patently not James, and therefore not ours. I caught Meredith's eyes above the rim of her tumbler and saw that they were soft with love.

When the gramophone wound down, the record was left fizzing on the turntable. Nobody spoke until mother said, wiping her eyes, 'Well, I understand that you and Meredith are taking the boy to the seaside next Saturday, Evelyn. I'm very surprised you've managed to find the time, given that the other day you said you couldn't spare two hours to come with me to St Mark's fete.' The spell was broken; grandmother sank into a chair, Prudence took up her pen and Edmund retreated on his mother's knee. I said nothing, since if I did I was bound to give offence to someone.

Chapter Eight

On Thursday morning, obedient to Mr Breen, I trekked across London to investigate Leah Marchant's former lodgings in a tenement off Gosset Street in Haggerston, half a mile or so from my old stamping ground of Toynbee Hall in Commercial Street. Alighting from the second omnibus I was pursued by swarms of ill-clad children, some of whom shouted abuse after I had emptied my purse of coppers and said I had nothing else to give them. Despite all my good intentions, I never could quite overcome my fear of the poor. I wanted to help but didn't know how to cross the divide or stop myself recoiling from the dirt and brashness even of those innocent children. Perhaps there was more than a streak of Aunt Prudence in me. According to her, there were no ills that could not be set right by hard work. To compensate I tried to engage one little girl in a conversation about school. 'Can't go to school,' she said, 'till ma gets me shoes.'

Another little boy winked so naughtily that I couldn't resist giving him sixpence though it nearly started a riot among his friends. Edmund was responsible for this flash of generosity; since his arrival I'd developed a renewed susceptibility to small boys with shapely heads and inquisitive eyes.

Meanwhile the sun blazed down remorselessly and the smell of privies was, in places, overwhelming. When I reached number 9 Caractacus Court I found that its front step was much better scrubbed than the late Mrs Wheeler's had been and the woman who answered the door was wearing a clean pinafore, her hair neatly controlled by a dozen or so grips. Her manner, however, was hostile. 'Are you an 'ealth visitor?'

'No. Most definitely not.'

'Then what are you?'

'My name is Miss Gifford. I am here on business concerning Mrs Leah Marchant. Are you Mrs Sanders? Mrs Marchant gave the police this address and said that a Mrs Sanders was her landlady.'

Impasse. The woman didn't move a muscle. She had tired eyes and a forlorn mouth. Behind her was a dank cave of a hallway and from the floors above came a racket of children's voices. 'I'm a lawyer,' I added desperately.

The woman's expression changed from suspicion to cynical amusement. 'You and 'oo else?'

'I'm acting on Mrs Marchant's behalf. As you perhaps know, she is in trouble, arrested on a charge of kidnapping. We need to find her a bail address so I want to know is there still a room available for her here?'

Mrs Sanders acknowledged this speech with an infinitesimal shifting of weight. 'She 'ain't paid no rent for months. I'm not obliged to keep 'er a room.'

'Are her things still here?'

'Might be.'

'May I go up and have a look?'

'At what?'

'As I said, we need to find accommodation for Mrs Marchant. I want to see if her old room is suitable and, if not, collect her things.'

'You're takin' nothin'. Like I say, she owes me rent.'

'I'm sure we can come to an agreement if you'll show me her room.'

At last, after scrutinising papers headed Breen & Balcombe with a good show of actually being able to read them, Mrs Sanders said, 'Well I s'pose I can't stop you. Third floor, door on the right. I'll unlock it for you.'

The house was similar in plan to Clivedon Hall Gardens, but whereas noise in the Gifford establishment was muffled by fabrics and the weight of furniture, this house, bare-boarded and uncurtained, echoed like a drum and the banister shook under my hand. From behind a half-closed door on the first-floor landing a baby yelled; there was a sharp slap, then a woman's raised voice and a bellow of outrage from the child. The higher we climbed, the

62

hotter and more rank the atmosphere became, saturated with the smell of old cooking and damp clothes. At last we reached a door that was horribly splintered at the bottom, presumably by somebody's boot; Mrs Sanders unlocked it with a key selected from a set worthy of Holloway.

Fortunately my weeks among the insect life in the basement of Breen & Balcombe had prepared me for the scuffling that followed our intrusion into the room. There was one single bed from which all the blankets had been stripped, leaving a mattress stained with what looked like blood, and worse. The only other furniture was a table covered with newspapers, assorted broken chairs, an empty hearth and a dented kettle. Arranged on shelves were various bits of crockery, and poked behind the mantel was a photograph of a young man wearing a sailor's uniform and a rakish smile: Mr Marchant, perhaps. I disliked him on sight. He had light hair, prominent ears and a swanky way of cocking his head to one side and looking boldly into the lens.

There were very few signs of the children except for a couple of indefinable garments hanging from the bed frame, the remains of a slate and a worn-out packing case from which poked the earless head of a teddy bear. The window was high, small and greasy, and a moth was trapped behind the glass.

'Thing is,' said Mrs Sanders suddenly, 'I'm 'er friend. I've got a loyalty to 'er. We was on the trams together. We knew we'd be turned off at the end of the war and rather than go back into service she takes the first man that comes along – '*im*. How could she live with 'is boozin' and whatnot? Turns out 'e's even worse than I thought. Comes back once in a blue moon wantin' money, gets 'er pregnant, then disappears. Ain't seen him for more 'n two years. And if 'e were to crop up, it would be the same as before, the drinkin' an' draggin' 'er down with 'im. She can't resist, soft as putty when 'e's about. But when 'e's gone she sobers up, gets a grip of 'erself.'

'Would you have her back here?' I asked quite calmly, though all this talk of children impetuously conceived was painfully near the knuckle.

'I'd 'ave 'er back. Trouble is the authorities would be down on me like a ton o' bricks if she brought the children 'ere. The minute that lot's involved everything gets inspected, and afore you knows it you're in all kinds of trouble.'

'If the rent was paid and a little extra given to you, could the room be painted and furnished? Might there even be other, adjoining rooms? We could try to find her somewhere else but if you're her friend and she was happy here ...'

'Who would pay the rent?'

'I don't know yet. We'd see.'

'If the rent was paid that would be a start. But I can't 'ave her goin' out all day and leavin' them kids again. The oldest is not six and she left her mindin' the baby. Worried me to death, I can't always be bringin' 'em down to me.'

'Might you even, if necessary, be prepared to come to court and vouch for her good character?'

She gave me another expressionless stare. 'If it got 'er out of prison, I'd 'ave to.'

As we went downstairs I wondered whether I ought to offer payment but when I took out my purse Mrs Sanders waved her hand angrily and ushered me out of the door.

I was far too hot, my spirits were depressed after my clumsy departure from Caractacus Court – it seemed to me that once lost Mrs Sanders' respect would be difficult to regain – and I was a little unsure of my direction. My plan was to call at Toynbee Hall to see my friend Carrie Morrison, as Mr Breen had suggested, and ask her opinion of the Leah Marchant case. Carrie would do me good, she would never allow herself to become mired by the kind of emotional sludge in which I currently wallowed as her private and professional lives were bound to be kept firmly apart, and there was a chance she would know, through her close connection with Toynbee, of the best help available to a woman in Leah's position.

In another five minutes I found myself in Commercial Street and there ahead of me, in that long rackety road crammed with shops and traffic, was a familiar clump of greenery and a plaque on a high wall engraved with the words TOYNBEE HALL. From the open doors came music, a Brahms quartet, and I realised that a Thursday lunchtime concert must be in progress.

Had it not been for Meredith I might have shunned the music altogether, abandoned the idea of seeing Carrie and gone back to the office, but a door in my soul, closed for years, had been left ajar by the sight of grandmother and Edmund dancing in the drawing room. So I marched up the path that led past a patch of struggling lawn and into the hall, which was flooded in sunlight. A soft draught blew along the floor and ahead, through another doorway, the little auditorium was crammed with chairs.

The woman on the door recognised me from the old days. Waving aside my offer of payment she pointed to a vacant seat at the end of a row. Sitting down, I let my hands fall into my lap, closed my eyes and gave myself up to the torrent of music. From the street outside, beneath the rumble of carts, came the distant clatter of Spitalfields Market, barely a quarter of a mile away. I knew, without opening my eyes, that the light would be splintered into shards of colour by the stained-glass arch of each window, and that the audience would consist largely of unemployed labourers and clerks in collarless shirts and frayed waistcoats, but that amongst them would be plainly dressed young men, university educated, the latest batch of idealists come to help out.

Of course it was foolish of me to have ventured inside; quite apart from the music, merely being in that place rubbed me raw because the smells of beeswax, bodies, books and soup were redolent of the months of near-despair when I was looking for work. And then the music took me deeper still into the past. Perhaps I had known it would and that was why I couldn't keep away. The previous night, as I watched grandmother and Edmund dancing, and Meredith so absorbed by love for her boy, I had wanted to feel something deeply too. I thought I could take the risk; surely enough time had gone by? So I let myself be touched, for a moment, by the rusty emotions generated by two stillborn love affairs.

Peter Shaw and I had first exchanged friendly words when I visited father's office before the war. Decked out in picture hats and swishing skirts, mother and I were supposed to dispense charm and encouragement to junior employees at our bimonthly tea parties. Mother was an expert; I slouched in my chair and envied the young men their enthusiasm. But Peter always looked out for me and drew me into conversation whenever he could. His eyes were a melting brown and his gaze clung to mine, tearing a little rip in my composure. I lay awake at night, replaying snippets of conversation in search of inner meaning, dreaming of the toffee-brown of his eyes. After the Christmas party in 1914, which as usual took place in the drawing room at Clivedon Hall Gardens with the carpets rolled up and furniture pushed back, candlelight, sherry, music (one of the senior partners had a limited repertoire on the violin), we stepped outside into the smoky late-afternoon air and ran away, panting and giggling, I in my party dress and thin shoes, until we came to the shelter of a canal bridge, where he kissed me until my mind popped with shock and fear and delight.

But what a wasted opportunity that kiss had been. I couldn't concentrate for wondering: Yes, but do I really love Peter Shaw or is it just that he's available and going away in the New Year? If I'd known that his might be the only kiss that would ever be granted me I'd have drawn him into the darkness, abandoned my Clivedon Hall Gardens principles altogether and let him make love to me, à la Ethel M. Dell. Because as soon as he went away, even before he got himself shot or shelled or whatever it was that provoked the word 'missing' on the telegram home, in my imagination he became taller, bolder, more beautiful, an ideal boy in fact, with Byronic hair and features, full of wit.

The music was an opportunity to lose myself again to his touch, to snatch more forbidden moments in the shadow of the bridge, to remember his three letters, each of which closed with the phrase *You have been on my mind* (into which I read a restrained but passionate yearning), to smell his alien young male scent, to feel his fingertip playing secretly along the veins on the underside of my wrist as we sat side by side at the Clivedon Hall Garden dining table the night before he went away.

The second affair, nearly four years later when I was twenty-five, had been more tortured still. It was enough to recall a bowl of red glass cupped in the hand of a uniformed man to make my blood shudder with the anticipated shock of lovemaking.

The music ended and I opened my eyes to find that I was being scrutinised from across the room by a man I recognised but at first couldn't place. Then I remembered that he was the barrister who had caught hold of me on the steps of Shoreditch Magistrates' Court after the humiliation of Leah Marchant's bail proceedings. Not wishing to be reminded of that morning I looked hastily for Carrie, but seeing no sign of her, I headed for the door.

'Miss Gifford.'

Surely I was mistaken; he would not bother to follow me into Commercial Street and was hardly likely to have remembered my name. But though I didn't pause, he called again and actually came abreast of me. 'Miss Gifford.'

I shielded my eyes from the sun to look into his face as he offered his hand. 'Nicholas Thorne,' he said. 'Last time we met I'm afraid there was no time for introductions – do you remember – Marlborough Street Police Court or some other godforsaken hole?'

You don't deceive me, I thought as I withdrew my hand from his clasp, you remember exactly where we met. I walked on, wondering what on earth he wanted with me.

'Did you enjoy the concert, Miss Gifford?' he asked, falling into step beside me.

'Very much.'

'Although I think you missed all but the last piece. I saw you come in towards the end. Such a shame. We had Gluck, and Handel's G minor sonata. Do you know that particular work? It happens to be one of my favourites. I've not seen you at the Toynbee concerts – is this a first for you? It's like old times for me, quite a nostalgia trip because I was here just after the war offering a bit of legal advice and a spot of lecturing in psychology and French. Sanest thing I'd done for years.'

There were many reasons for my reluctance to be drawn into conversation with this man, the foremost being that I could see no reason why he should wish to talk to me other than to bait me. I had encountered plenty of embryonic barristers at Cambridge and recognised the educated drawl, disarming smile and acute memory. Yet he was such a gentleman in the way he manoeuvred himself to ensure that he was on the outside of the pavement, and his smile was so engaging – barely a muscle was disturbed in his lip or cheek but his eyes were warm – that I could not be completely immune. He was a beautiful, intact, youngish man, and therefore a rarity indeed. And of course I was still in the grip of that wretched music.

At last I said, 'I used to go to Toynbee Hall last year. I worked on the poor man's law scheme too.'

'Actually I assumed you used to frequent Toynbee.'

'Why?'

'You work for Breen. Everybody knows the work Breen did at Toynbee. There was bound to be a connection. Did you enjoy your work there, Miss Gifford?'

'It gave me a degree of purpose. Unlike you, I suspect, I worked there not out of altruism but necessity. Nobody else would take me. It was the only way I could gain any experience in the law at all.'

'Has it been a very rough ride for you, Miss Gifford? Do you know, I'm absolutely fascinated. A couple of ladies have recently been called to the bar, possibly you're acquainted with them, Williams and Normanton. Such stalwarts. So fierce and determined. One has to admire them. Look, I'm absolutely parched. I know of a cracking little tea shop near here, could you bear to take tea with me? You probably won't believe this, but I have been hoping to run into you these past couple of days.'

I was so startled I actually stopped dead. 'I'm afraid I have to get back to the office.'

He threw back his head and laughed. 'Tea, Miss Gifford, is all I'm suggesting. Ten minutes of your time. Don't look so horrified.'

But I had grown hotter still, this time with anger. I knew his game all right. Let's charm that frightful bluestocking Miss Gifford into pouring out her would-be legal heart and then cut her down to size. It had happened before: 'I've often wondered, Miss Gifford, perhaps you'd give me your opinion – do you think that tokenism is better than nothing at all? How does it feel to be a token, Miss Gifford?'

A cart had slipped a sack of coal and the cloud of dust was stifling. Before I knew it Thorne had seized my briefcase. 'You are as white as a sheet. I think you'll find the place I have in mind is rather cool, and it will barely take you a step out of your way.'

He strode along swinging my case, and short of wrenching it from his hand what could I do but trot alongside him as he scattered remarks like a bird feeder dispensing corn? 'Extraordinary friendships forged at Toynbee ... Missed your Breen by a couple of years but knew of him by reputation ... Opportunity to share one's education with those who ...' We reached the café, where the door stood open. Inside the edges of the checked tablecloths were ruffled by an electric ceiling fan. He chose a corner table and took my jacket, pulled out a chair for me and then folded himself into another – his long legs would not fit under the table. 'The truth is I was very impressed when I saw you in court the other day. Less impressed by the magistrate, I might add, who I thought treated you appallingly. For the first time, when I heard you pleading for your client, I saw the case for women in court. I realised there might be sympathy between a woman in trouble and a female lawyer.'

An urn hissed behind the counter while a woman in a flowered overall came forward to take our order. I gathered my wits. 'No,' I said firmly.

'Miss Gifford?'

'That's not why I trained, to help only women. No, I wish to serve all people. I don't want to become part of some lesser branch of the law, as I think has happened to some extent with women in medicine.'

'I didn't mean *lesser.*'

'I think you probably did. I have heard the argument before numerous times. Would you consider yourself to be an effective barrister if you were only allowed to practise with one half of the population?'

'You have a point, Miss Gifford, but you must allow me to take one step at a time. Before I met you I had an entirely different viewpoint: I didn't see the need for lady lawyers at all.' He paused to bestow a smile on the waitress as she set out the cups, ran his fingers through his damp hair to slick it back from his forehead and rested his arm along the table. 'I couldn't imagine doing battle with a lady across the courtroom. It would be like sparring with my mother or fiancée, something that, as a well-brought-up young man, I simply couldn't do.'

69

'Forgive me, but I believe that to be a wholly unconvincing argument. Are you suggesting that gentlemen politicians will find themselves unable to argue with female members of parliament or county councillors? Are you telling me you never argued with your sister? What you mean, I believe, is that women aren't worth arguing with because they'll never be able to withstand your mental and verbal dexterity.'

His laugh had the most perverse effect on me, like a finger drawn across my breastbone. 'I don't have a sister, Miss Gifford, so I can't answer the first part of your argument. Later I'll examine my conscience and judge whether you have, in fact, found me out with the second.'

Everything about him was leisurely, as if there was a lag between thought and deed so that his smile dawned at the back of his eye and only after a second or so reached the corner of his lip. It was the same with his gestures. When at one point he hitched up his trouser leg, the movement was a slow lifting of first hand, then knee. He removed the teapot lid, stirred, took the strainer and poured the tea expertly. As he handed me a cup he glanced into my face and must have seen my absorption. 'Do you not approve of my method, Miss Gifford? I have a Lancashire grandmother who taught us to put the milk in last.'

'I'm sure it will be very good tea.'

'Thing is, I'd better come clean. It was a stroke of luck meeting you. I'd been due to pay a visit to Breen & Balcombe on behalf of a client of mine who happens to employ a client of yours, Stephen Wheeler. I've been asked to keep a friendly eye on the case, see if there is anything we can do to help out. So when I saw you today . . .'

'Stephen Wheeler is Mr Breen's client, not mine.'

'But Mr Breen wasn't in Toynbee Hall and you were, so I thought I'd have a word. Miss Gifford, my client, Sir David Hardynge, is concerned about the reputation of his company. It's all over the press that Wheeler killed his wife for the insurance payout, which we find hard to believe.'

'You can hardly expect me to—'

'Of course you can't discuss the case, but I wanted to offer you my assistance, should it be required. Obviously I can't represent

Wheeler due to a conflict of interests. I am very closely connected to Hardynge, served with his son – we've been friends since boyhood in fact – and I'm engaged to his daughter Sylvia, but if I can advise . . .'

'Thank you. I shall tell Mr Breen about this conversation. And now, if you'll excuse me . . .' I pushed my cup aside.

'You seem taken aback. Perhaps I've handled this badly. I'm simply speaking on behalf of a concerned employer. Hardynge cares about all his men, particularly those who served in the war, to whom he shows almost paternal indulgence. He telephoned me on the afternoon of Wheeler's arrest and asked me what could be done. All in all I'd say he's a most enlightened employer.'

'I don't doubt Sir David Hardynge's good intentions and I'm sure Mr Breen will be most grateful.' I signalled to the waitress to bring my jacket, then, without pausing to fasten the buttons or adjust my hat, I picked up my case and held out my hand. 'Thank you for the tea, Mr Thorne.'

'I'll give you my card.'

'As I've said, any correspondence should be with Mr Breen.'

'Miss Gifford . . .' Instead of releasing my hand he held it within his own. 'You look upset. What is it? Please don't dash away.'

'I must, I'm afraid. I feel it's quite inappropriate to discuss the Wheeler case any further.'

'Then we'll talk of other things.'

'Really, no, thank you.'

I left him at the table, one hand in his pocket as he reached for change, a bemused smile on his face but otherwise unruffled.

I, on the other hand, walked away at great speed, muttering to myself: 'What were you thinking of? You made an utter fool of yourself. Why else would he want to buy you tea except to gain information? Engaged to Sir David Hardynge's daughter. Fool. Fool. And you thought he was impressed, attracted to you, even. That's why you're upset. You thought he'd singled you out.'

In our last week at Girton one of our sternest lecturers, a woman in her fifties dressed in the regulation soft-collared blouse, belted cardigan and ankle-length skirt, had proposed the motion in a debate entitled 'The future, my dear, must perforce be female.' Until Miss Lang spoke the atmosphere had been light-hearted. Examinations were over and we were about to graduate. Our only objection to the debate was that the subject was so tediously familiar it could hold no surprises. But we had overlooked the fact that Miss Lang had no qualms about uttering the unutterable.

'You are the first generation of young women that has ever faced a future in which you will not depend on men. This will give you extraordinary freedom and extraordinary responsibility.' We smiled and nodded, and felt rather proud. 'For most of you this will not be a choice but a fact of life. We are missing nearly a million men, who were, as you are painfully aware, your contemporaries. I don't want to dwell on the agony of loss – not a woman among us is unmarked. But I would argue that you are the lucky ones because all of you have brains and some of you a private income. Pity the poor girls who have neither. I urge you, my dear young ladies, don't waste your youth seeking out a husband who in all probability is lying in an unmarked grave somewhere in northern France. Instead, seize the opportunity of your unique status to change the world.'

I had always hated prophetic statements; I suspected that the ones that struck home were the ones we knew in our hearts to be true. We'd read the statistics and the evidence lay in the empty bedrooms in our family homes, the widows' weeds in church, the cripples on the street corners, the newly built war memorials. But I can't have been alone in thinking, It may be true for some but it won't apply to me.

Because of that debate, the last week at Cambridge was tainted. Until then we had been studying because that was the path we'd chosen. We regarded ourselves as exceptionally clever girls with an insatiable appetite to prove ourselves capable of all that our brothers could do and more. We looked down on our mothers and their friends and neighbours, the ladies in the grand houses and the housewives in their terraces, because we thought their lives were hollow. Most of us envisaged that we would have a career, yes, but we wanted to be loved as well. And now this wretched Miss Lang had said that we wouldn't marry. 'This is it, girls, the years of expectation are over. We are sisters, and on our sisters and ourselves we must rely or we shall face a future filled with pointless yearning.'

So while some had gone into medicine, teaching or research, Carrie Morrison and I had entered the law, where, ironically enough, we met nothing but men: the aged, the avuncular, the damaged, the very youthful, the very fortunate, the quick-footed. But on the whole these men wanted nothing to do with us. While they were fighting they had yearned for their civilised chambers, offices and courtrooms, and what most of them had hoped was that on their return nothing would have changed. We educated women were the symbol of an outcome they hadn't sought. They certainly would never have considered *marrying* a dowdy legal woman when they had their pick of soft-skinned girls in translucent frocks who would grace their hearths and refrain from asking awkward questions.

The fact was, until Edmund turned up on my doorstep and Thorne touched my arm at Shoreditch Magistrates' Court, I had convinced myself that the one thing I really did not need in my life was a man. I had no intention of sacrificing years of hard work for the sake of a sickly, lascivious, fortune-hunting or cradle-snatching type such as mother occasionally insinuated into my way after church. I thought I was immune. I don't believe I even saw Breen and Wolfe as men so much as accessible outposts of the law. And then Edmund turned up and I wanted a child, and Thorne poured my tea, adjusted the cup on the saucer, glanced at me with unexpected deliberation, and I wanted a lover.

Chapter Nine

Before leaving Clivedon Hall Gardens for our trip to Eastbourne we were cautioned to take umbrellas, spare woollens, gaberdines, even the address of a distant cousin of Prudence who lived in Polegate and might be persuaded to put us up should we be stranded for the night.

'Stranded?' exclaimed Meredith.

'You never know with trains,' said Prudence, 'they can be extremely unreliable,' as if each locomotive had a wicked will of its own.

'If we're stranded,' said Meredith, 'we shall bivouac on the beach. Wouldn't that be something, Edmund?'

So I found myself on yet another unaccustomed journey, steaming through blowsy late-May fields, first Surrey, then Sussex. It was hard to leave behind the *shoulds*, the most pressing of which was that I should have been with mother. Although it was never stated it was understood by the inmates of Clivedon Hall Gardens (with the exception of myself and possibly grandmother) that my work was a matter of self-indulgence and I should be very grateful that I was allowed to do it. The fact that I worked because somebody must was too painful to voice, so Saturdays with mother were therefore my penance for indulging my whim during the rest of the week. Sometimes we went to a gallery, sometimes I endured a tea party or an afternoon's gardening.

And if mother happened not to need me, I should have been reading up on the law regarding the custody of children and preparing a bail argument for Leah Marchant. Above all I should not be spending yet more money, this time on a day out by the sea.

My perception of Meredith kept shifting. In the area of money, for instance, I had no idea of her true situation. She claimed to be poor but when Edmund said he couldn't find his bathing drawers she told him airily that she would buy him a new pair in a shop by the seaside: 'I can't believe there won't be mountains of bathing costumes in Eastbourne.' And he was promised a bucket and spade and an ice cream. So many treats.

Then there was the question of her clothes, which were neither practical nor cheap. Perhaps the illicit rifling through Stella Wheeler's bedroom had sensitised me a little to the nuances of women's fashion. Stella's clothes, I suspected, with the exception of the nightgown, undergarments and stockings, had been cheaply bought. The dyes had been saccharine, the fabrics creased. Most of the items in my own wardrobe could best be described as sturdy; skirts and jackets made to measure by my mother's quavery pre-war dressmaker Miss Pouncett, the rest off the rail at Debenham and Freebody. All Clivedon Hall Gardens clothes were expected to last season after season. Prudence was proud to claim that she still wore boots bought in 1906, resoled three times by a favoured cobbler in Buckingham but otherwise good as new.

Meredith's wardrobe, on the other hand, was exquisite. The shades were subtle, the accessories carefully matched. Today she wore another low-waisted frock and knitted jacket, a straw hat, yellow (of all colours) gloves and matching bag. Prudence would never have recommended yellow. The principle by which we abided in Clivedon Hall Gardens was that each garment should match every other, so navy, beige and especially black and grey were staples.

But the biggest mystery of all regarding Meredith was exactly what she was after, as mother put it. How much money did she need to fulfil her plans? Where did she intend to live in the long term? Had she tickets booked for a return voyage to Canada? I had been told to find answers to all these questions but on the train journey, as we watched fields of cow parsley crushed by overnight rain, a herd of cows each angled precisely in line with the others to face the railway line, farms tucked like models into their yards, towns and villages nestled into valleys exactly as described by a guidebook about the British countryside (according to Meredith), the sudden emergence of the sun between banks of cloud, and then the wide open plain and steeply rising downs before the sea, we talked only of neutral subjects.

'Tell me about Prudence,' said Meredith. 'What is her story?'

'There is no story. She is my father's only sister. My grandfather was a widower so she was obliged to care for him, and when he died and the family house was sold, she moved into the cottage that used to be the gardener's. Prudence loved that cottage but when father's money went her allowance had to be reduced so eventually she came to live with us.'

'How did he lose his money?'

'Bad investments. After James died he grew reckless, although I think he was trying to secure our future.'

'Poor Prudence, losing her home,' said Meredith. 'Poor you.'

'Oh, we rub along quite well.'

'But why do you put up with it? Why do you let her dominate those dreadful meals?'

'Does she dominate? I find her amusing, really. I'm very fond of her. She's company for mother; they're roughly the same age.'

'It doesn't seem to me as if they like each other much.'

'They make the best of their circumstances.'

'Oh dear. What a way to go on.' Meredith turned to the window, as if I was somehow culpable. 'Everyone lives so meagrely in your house. Your lives seem so constrained.'

I was silent. Meredith was surely not being deliberately obtuse but there she sat in her buttercup-coloured lambskin gloves, eyes wide with concern, apparently oblivious to the irony that part of the cause for the Giffords' financial distress was sitting only inches away with his nose pressed to the window, watching out for a first glimpse of the sea.

'What I have noticed about your house,' she added, 'is that everything in it is not only old but brown. Why is that, do you suppose? You live among sepia tones. I wonder, is that why everyone seems so low in spirits?'

After a pause I murmured, 'Everything was different before James died. We cannot seem to recover from that.'

As I had anticipated, the conversation ended abruptly. Meredith put her arm round her son and said, 'Look, darling, look at all the back gardens full of roses. This is Eastbourne, I feel sure. We must be nearly there.'

Meanwhile I reflected that perhaps she was right and Clivedon Hall Gardens really did have a pervasive brownish hue. Only in odd little patches did the house show a flash of colour: a new pink soap in the bathroom (mother's birthday present from a well-to-do bridge partner), lovely crimson in the kitchen, where Rose was knitting a daring tea cosy in red and royal blue, grandmother's collection of theatrical memorabilia, confined to her room to conceal the shameful fact that she'd once been an actress, a fistful of early sweet peas, grown by Prudence, hanging over the edge of their vase like the lilac, cream and coral frocks of dancers. And of course, James's closed-off bedroom.

In Eastbourne I hovered in the doorway of a shop crammed with mainly pointless seaside items while Meredith bought her son blue and green striped swimming drawers, and a bucket and spade. Her method of spending money was a revelation. Out came a little purse in matching yellow leather, and from it a fistful of change, offered to the assistant to select and sort. 'I still can't manage these farthings and threepences and whatnot; take what you need.' How careless it seemed not even to count what was given in change. Then at last we were safely away from the shops and high up on the promenade. 'Of course there is water and to spare back home,' said Meredith, 'but this is proper seaside. This is what I was hoping for.'

'It's pebbles,' said Edmund, scanning the row of breakwaters. 'No sand.'

'When the tide goes out there might be sand,' I replied. He dashed ahead, down the winding path to the sea, and I felt a lightening of the heart as the breeze caught my hat and the air was suddenly full of salt and memories of more than a dozen childhood holidays in Cornwall. Not that those had been filled with unalloyed pleasure. There had been so many unconquerable tensions. Mother was always too cold or too hot and had to keep shifting her deckchair, while father grew impatient sitting on the beach, having no function other than to bark injunctions at James and me, so disappeared on long, mysterious walks, thereby making mother even more restless and leaving us all with a vague sense of failure that we had not proved interesting enough.

This day, on the other hand, promised a less precarious kind of pleasure. Meredith had the knack simply of accepting things as they came, whether it was that the sun was now shining so warmly and steadily that the few remaining clouds were melting away, or that the tide was timed to perfection, on the way out and revealing a bit of sand amidst the pebbles, which allowed Edmund to build a shallow trench down to the water. Even the picnic was perfect because Meredith had bought a few little extras from the baker and given a substantial tip to the servants for their trouble. 'She will *ruin* those girls,' said Prudence. 'They are overpaid as it is.'

After lunch, indifferent to the fact that she was revealing an eye-catching stretch of lower leg, Meredith lay on the pebbles with her jacket behind her head. Edmund was befriended by a bossy girl a couple of years younger whose frilled skirt was tucked firmly into her knickers and who insisted he help her create a gigantic face, complete with moustache and eyebrows made of pebbles and seaweed. I too lay back, closed my eyes and let the tumultuous week draw away from me, in the waves rising and falling, the shocks and journeys and the new faces of demanding people, Leah Marchant, Meredith herself, poor Stephen Wheeler in his prison cell and Nicholas Thorne, curse him, whose smile hovered in my inner eye like the Cheshire cat's, even he was fading and mingling with the call of seagulls.

I felt a fly tickling my throat and then the back of my hand – no, not a fly, Meredith, fluttering a stalk of dried seaweed over my skin. 'Tell me about the murder scene,' she said. Her face shadowed mine but behind her the sky was a vibrant blue. She had removed her hat so that her fine hair was blown around in wisps of reddish gold.

At first I couldn't think what she meant and my voice was slurred with drowsiness. 'Murder scene? I've never visited a murder scene.'

'But you went to the dead woman's house.'

'To collect the defendant's clothes.'

Meredith was propped on her elbow so close to me I couldn't move. Her eyes, huge and inquisitive, trapped me.

'What was it like, to be in that poor woman's house?'

'Sad.'

We stared at each other. I could see each individual lash and, yes, I'm sure hers were painted. 'And what else?'

'Bleak. You know, hopeless.'

'Why hopeless?'

'Well obviously, the marriage came to an awful end.'

'But things are not usually hopeless. Things are just things. Anyway, did you find any clues?'

'We weren't looking for clues.'

'Oh yes you were, I'll bet you were. I've read my detective novels; I know the score.'

So there I was, literally breast to breast with Meredith, and there was the dead Stella Wheeler with her dank kitchen and seductive nightdress. And behind Mr and Mrs Wheeler were other, even more uncomfortable associations with their tragedy, not least the encounter outside Toynbee Hall, the fan swinging round and round in the café, Nicholas Thorne adjusting the fabric at the knee of his trousers.

'We shouldn't talk about the Wheeler case,' I murmured. 'For a start, I don't know much about it and anyway this is the weekend. I don't want to think about work.'

'But it's in all the papers. I'm fascinated that the instant we arrive in London Edmund's auntie gets caught up in a murder inquiry. Surely you can tell me what's going to happen next.'

'I don't know. Nothing, according to the police. They seem to think it's cut and dried.'

'Do *you* think it's cut and dried?'

'Mr Breen is not satisfied. He says there is no motive. We are to pursue our own investigations alongside the police as he thinks they won't do a thorough job because they believe the evidence against Wheeler is overwhelming. I'm to visit the place where Stella worked as a waitress, and Theo Wolfe, who also works for Mr Breen, will talk to Stephen Wheeler's colleagues. Wheeler himself still hasn't said a word.'

'That doesn't surprise me. Quite the reverse. In the war, I saw quite a few men who couldn't or wouldn't speak because of what they'd seen or done. You can't blame me for being interested.

What you deal with is so vital, don't you see? And it fascinates me how the intensely private, the circumstances of the dead girl's marriage, becomes a public matter because of a crime. It was the same for me when I worked in hospitals. Although sickness is a very intimate state, it makes a person public property. I never could get used to the mix of the extremely personal and the fact that everything went on in full view of dozens of people. After all, that was how I came to know your brother James.'

His name jolted me wide awake. Meredith was still hanging over me and there was a gleam in her eye, perhaps in anticipation of my reaction. I was tempted to reach out my hand and push her aside, as if it was just her body that blocked my view of him. 'Tell me,' I whispered, 'when you knew him, what was he like?'

'What was he like?' she repeated lightly, as if discussing the cut of a frock. 'Why, he was like all the others, I suppose. Ill. Sick of the war.'

'Describe him to me, please, as you knew him.'

'Well, let's see now. I didn't know him for long. You, on the other hand, were his sister all his life.' She had clasped her hands between her breasts but still knelt with her face only inches from mine. 'So I'll trade you, Evelyn. First you tell me what he was like as a little boy.' Then she flung herself on her back, spread her arms wide and closed her eyes.

In a flash of irritation – she was toying with me, surely; she must know how much this conversation meant to me – I sat up so suddenly that I felt dizzy. Colours melded together in a bewildering soup of sparkle and glare until at last, by pulling the brim of my hat firmly across my brow, I could focus on Edmund, who was making a laborious journey up from the sea with his bucket.

'I want Edmund to have a father,' said Meredith, tapping my forearm softly with her fist. 'That's partly why I'm here. I want him to have a past as well as a future. So conjure up the young James.'

'He was like Edmund to look at though perhaps a little plumper in the face and taller for his age. Very determined, single-minded, affectionate.'

'Yes, that's Edmund exactly. What else?'

'I was thinking when we first came down to the sea today that I remember James very clearly – Jamie, he was then – on our seaside holidays. He always was a perfectionist. We holidayed each year in Cornwall, near Padstow, and he loved to build sand-castles, but woe betide us if the sea came in too suddenly or a dog leapt on his creation. He couldn't stand it.'

'And when he couldn't stand something what did he do?'

She folded her hands behind her head so that her slight body arched and I could see her ribs and the outline of her breasts through the gauzy fabric of her frock. And again I was disturbed by the memory of Stella Wheeler's underwear drawer, the too-dainty knickers and the unseemly bust-flattener that had once defined the shape of her upper body. A pulse throbbed softly at Meredith's throat and her jaw and cheekbones were so fine and small that she appeared fragile. I chose my words with great care, as I had already learned to do with Meredith.

'He got angry, I suppose, like most children. Shouted. It never took long to calm him down. Overall he was a sweet-tempered boy.'

'On the other hand, I can't imagine that *you* ever made a fuss about anything, even when you were little.'

But I would not be put off any longer. 'Now, please, tell me about James when you met him.'

She didn't open her eyes. 'Well, you'll be glad to hear that he bore his injury well. There had been talk at first of amputation and when he heard his arm would heal he pretended to be relieved, but I saw in his eyes what I'd seen in others – that even losing a limb would have been a small price to pay for being sent home for good. But he soon covered that up. And when he was better ...'

I found that I had gripped her hand. 'Yes ...'

'He was quite noisy – loud with his fellow officers – but it was touching too, the way he'd sit by the beds of the men and read letters to them or write for them, awkwardly, with his uninjured hand.'

I saw him so clearly: his head bent, that beautiful inclination of the neck, his bottom lip pushed forward. But I was not allowed to dwell on this image because Meredith leapt to her feet, picked up her hat and said, 'I'm off to explore this *authentic* seaside town. Keep an eye on Edmund, will you,' and, with a scrunch of pebbles, she was gone.

I couldn't fathom her. One moment we were exchanging confidences, the next she had deserted me so suddenly that I felt abused, as if she'd helped me up with one hand and knocked me down with the other. As so often with her, I had the distinct impression that she had taken a good deal from me but given little in return.

At that moment Edmund came running up to say that his new friend, Moira, was going to bathe and he wanted to as well. Tearing off his shirt and sun hat he raced away as fast as the pebbles would permit and was soon at the water's edge with Moira, who was barefoot but otherwise fully clothed. I called after him to wait for me but he didn't or wouldn't hear. Moira's parents were snoozing in deckchairs so I seized my bag, pushed my feet into my shoes and ran after him muttering to myself, 'This is absurd, he shouldn't paddle so soon after lunch. Where is Meredith? She should be here to look after him.' And then I decided with horror that I was turning into Prudence – in fact I must surely look like her in my city shoes and flapping dark skirt on that sun-struck Sussex beach.

Back I went to the picnic blanket and removed, with great difficulty, shoes, stockings and my hat, then I hitched up my skirts and staggered over the stones. My feet looked like beached water creatures and my progress was very slow because my hair kept blowing across my eyes, and I stubbed my toes. The next moment I had caught up with Edmund and Moira and was holding each by their cold wet hands as we jumped the waves. Moira instantly pulled away and announced she was going back to her mother. Edmund, gratifyingly, stayed with me.

'I used to jump the waves with your daddy when we were children,' I said. 'We loved the sea.'

'I don't have to hold your hand. Mommy lets me paddle without holding her hand.'

'But I feel I must, Edmund, because I remember I lost your daddy once, when he was a little boy. I wouldn't want to lose you.'

'How did you lose him?'

'He was angry with me and he walked away when I wasn't looking. We found him back at the guest house, on his bed, reading an annual. By then half the town was searching for him, even the police.'

'Why was he angry with you?'

'He was bored, I think that was it.'

'Well I'm not bored.' He plunged forward and ducked his shoulders under the water then rose up, flapping his thin arms, stamping his feet. 'It's freezing,' he shouted. 'It's lovely. It's so cold.'

Suddenly, like a new wave breaking, I was happy; my purest moment of happiness since James's death − no, since war was declared and we knew he would have to go away. The only times that had come anywhere close were my graduation and the news that I was to be taken on by Breen, but both these events had been tempered by my family's ambivalence to them. It was the collision of water, sun and memory, the blue horizon, the sudden bond with my new-found nephew, the touch of his wet hand, the way he had flashed me a delighted smile as he emerged from the water, his prancing figure. And beyond Edmund, the context of that day felt promising, the fact that my work, awaiting me like a sleeping beast, seemed full of fascination and complexity. And at the back of all, an illicit twitch on the far edge of my consciousness, was Thorne. I had an absurd wish that he might see me like this, with my hair blowing around me and my feet bare.

And perhaps I was happy to be in the present because I'd remembered so vividly the pain of the past as I took Edmund's hand: the lying on my stomach in the sand reading *Great Expectations* and my mother's sleepy question 'Where's Jamie, Evie, can you see him?' Then the search, escalating to a frantic trawl of the beach, my father's return from his walk. 'What do you mean he's lost? I thought you were keeping an eye on him.' Father had stood in his cravat, panama and blazer, one hand on the small of his back, the other shielding his eyes as he renewed the hunt. We had to begin from the beginning because he couldn't believe we had looked properly in the first place.

In the end I was sent up to the guest house half a mile or so from the beach, just to check that Jamie wasn't there, and I was

83

so panicky that I could scarcely breathe. In the last few minutes before I discovered him, keeping a nervous lookout for me over the top of *The Boy's Own Annual*, I had a glimpse into a future without him, and I saw that my family would become a husk and that I would spend the rest of my days forever running uphill in an attempt to find him.

Now, for the first time, with chill waves lapping my toes and this other little boy boldly doggy-paddling between breaking waves, I had a sense that even though James was gone, my life was full enough.

Meredith's mood had been further altered by her walk. It was now I who bustled about collecting our things while she looked on. She said we would take the omnibus to Beachy Head and look at the lighthouse, and when Edmund moaned about getting dressed and then the sand in his stockings she said: 'That's enough, Edmund', so harshly that he fell silent.

'What did you think of the town?' I asked.

'I didn't see much of it; I visited a church.'

I tried not to show my surprise.

'Actually I got homesick,' she added. 'Isn't that absurd? Twenty-nine years old and missing my sisters and mother and a remote village by a lake.'

'Why wouldn't you miss them?'

'Because I fought so hard to get away,' she said so fiercely that I decided not to probe any further.

We walked on the upper promenade with Edmund hanging over the railing to watch the band in the stand below play a military march. All we could see was the flash of brass and the conductor's epaulettes. 'Can we go down?' he asked.

'You'd be bored,' said Meredith. 'You'd have to sit on a deckchair and listen to the music without saying a word, just like those other people who've paid for their tickets. We're better off here.'

Edmund studied the occupants of the deckchairs, who sat in the concrete bowl of the arena: elderly couples, invalids, ladies with handbags gripped in their laps. One segment of the auditorium was devoted to wheelchairs in which sat youngish men who were missing one or both legs. During the war people used to say you could hear the guns thundering in France from the promenades of the south coast, and at that moment I recoiled from the band's cloying military cheer, the wounded soldiers and the quiescent ladies with their handbags.

Meredith wrenched Edmund away to catch the bus but it was not until we were safely on the top deck and riding out of town above a promenade punctuated by stumpy Martello towers that she spoke to me again. 'Edmund and I may not be taking meals with your family in future.'

'I don't understand.'

'Prudence said yesterday that she thought Edmund should eat apart from the grown-ups. I won't have that.'

'It's not for Prudence to decide. If you wish Edmund to sit up with us, then he shall.'

'I do wish it. I'm not used to being separated unnecessarily from my son. And there are other things you should know. One of the reasons I came to Europe was that I want to learn to paint. I have been looking about and have found a class on Tuesday evenings that might suit me. I'm hoping I can rely on Edmund being cared for. He will need to be bathed and put to bed. He always has a story.'

'Well, certain—'

'And there's the question of work. Father was very generous and I saved up to travel here, but that money is fast running out. I'm hoping I can come to an arrangement with your family, that you will perhaps settle some money on me, but it won't be enough, I'm sure. So I shall have to look for work, but that will mean Edmund has to be taken to and from school by someone else.'

'What sort of work do you have in mind? Will you nurse?'

'Not necessarily. I have an appointment to see Dr Marie Stopes tomorrow morning.'

'Marie Stopes.'

She looked me directly in the eye. 'Do you know her?'

'Not personally. But of course I know that she has a clinic in Holloway and I'm aware of the type of work she does.' I spoke low so that we would not be overheard by Edmund, but Meredith's voice was ringing.

'Don't tell me you disapprove of that too. I feel very strongly that women should be able to make choices about conception. If I can get work as a nurse in such a clinic I would be pleased.'

I did not rise to the bait and point out that she could have chosen nothing more likely to dismay the ladies of Clivedon Hall Gardens. Instead we rode in silence while I contemplated her latest demands. Was she being unfair? Certainly she was very direct, something to which we were not accustomed. Elaborate rituals ought to be gone through in the asking and granting of favours. And Marie Stopes. I was conscious that my reaction was tempered with something very close to chagrin. *I* was the rebel in Clivedon Hall Gardens. If boundaries were to be pushed back, it should be by me.

'You'd like to make your home with us then,' I said.

'I would never let Edmund stay somewhere he wasn't welcome.'

'You are welcome, of course you are. But Meredith, you must see that if you intend to live with us we will have to make arrangements.'

'What kind of arrangements? You talk so coldly. This is your nephew, your mother's grandchild. We are family. At least, I was hoping we might be regarded as such.' She looked away, biting her lower lip.

I felt ashamed. 'We still haven't had time to work out where we stand.'

'Is it so difficult?'

'Not difficult. Strange.'

On the cliff top the wind was strong and quite cool, a kite-flyer was winding the spool of a diamond-shaped speck in the sky, and a skylark bounced higher and higher on the air currents. Near the edge of the cliff I hovered behind Edmund's shoulder, ready to grab him should he take a spring forward.

'Look, Edmund,' cried his mother, pointing beyond the blade of white cliff, 'look at the lighthouse. Don't you think it's marvellous? I love lighthouses, I really do, because they are a sign of the good that men can do for each other. Imagine the danger of taking a boat out to the lighthouse amidst those rocks in bad weather. And the lamp is never allowed to go out at night, whatever the circumstances.'

For me, that moment was forever to be associated with primary colours, the red and white striped lighthouse, the blue sea, the yellow of Meredith's glove. Because, after a gust of wind had knocked us all a pace or so nearer the cliff edge, she turned to me and spoke vehemently but so quietly that her son could not possibly have heard: 'You think I venerate your brother's memory, as you do. Well, you're quite wrong. I hate to think of him. The very last place I'd choose to be is with his family if it weren't a necessity. If I could tear him from my being, I would. But I cannot, because of Edmund. Come Edmund,' she added sharply. 'It's time to go home.' Dragging at the boy's hand, she marched him away towards the bus stop.

I stared at the lighthouse and tried to comprehend what she had just told me. I had imagined, until then, that she had been angling to become a rather ill-tuned member of our sombre chorus of women in mourning for James. Instead, it was as if she had scrunched my image of him into a tight ball that was reopening slowly in the palm of her hand, creased, worn, different.

And perhaps it was true that she didn't really want to be with us after all. Barely had I got used to the idea of Meredith and Edmund as plaintiffs than she had turned the tables and placed me, abruptly, in the position of need. I needed her and Edmund to stay.

Chapter Ten

I hadn't been long at Breen & Balcombe before I decided that Theo Wolfe was more decorative than useful. At first I couldn't fathom why Breen put up with him and thought perhaps it was because a family connection had given Wolfe an introduction to the firm. In fact I sensed that Breen, despite his well-aired leanings towards the Labour Party, was a little in awe of the Wolfe lineage and was content to nurture Theo, despite his extreme laziness, because he enjoyed looking at him, liked to hear scandalous anecdotes about his years at a prestigious public school and had the lower middle class's grudging awe of the upper. Furthermore, while Breen was in some areas a spartan, in others his taste was expensive, even exotic. He loved good whisky and one of his favourite possessions was a mahogany corner cabinet housing a pair of exquisite cut-glass tumblers and a decanter. Late on chill Friday afternoons he and Wolfe were to be found snugly seated before the fire, savouring the malt. Wolfe, in Breen's eyes, had the same function as the Liberty print silk handkerchief that adorned his breast pocket on festive occasions. By anyone's standards a beautiful young man, he was roughly my own age, a little heavy about the stomach and with floppy hair, an irresistibly boyish smile and a talent for avoiding strenuous work of any kind. A tendency to asthma had ensured a wartime spent pen-pushing in the Ministry of Munitions, and on foggy days he didn't turn up in the office at all, but allegedly lay at home gasping.

Had Breen employed a more useful junior partner, his own hefty workload would have been reduced and the firm's income correspondingly enhanced. On the other hand, Wolfe definitely had his moments. He was, for instance, excellent at hobnobbing with the opposition and was often given five shillings from the

Breen & Balcombe petty cash box to take a police prosecutor out to lunch. I had not witnessed him in operation but could imagine the affable passing of the wine bottle, the sharing of somewhat off-colour legal anecdotes ('Did you hear that Judge Michael Fitch's wife has left him? Small wonder given his well-known predilection for touring the backstreets of Soho in search of a delectable ...'), the skilful segue of the conversation from the subject of whose star was in the ascendant to whether the police prosecutor thought there might be any room for negotiation in a certain case dear to the heart of B & B.

It was by such means that we learned there was considerable irritation amongst all concerned with prosecuting the Marchant case because the *Daily Mail* (courtesy of Wolfe, none other) had got hold of the story and was vilifying the pernicious authorities who, not satisfied with separating a mother from her innocent children, had locked her up despite the fact that her only crime was to show a maternal desire to hold her own baby.

The day before Leah Marchant's next court hearing, Wolfe lunched with his pal Wotherspoon, who worked directly to the divisional superintendent, and the result of their conversation was relayed to me by Breen on the courthouse steps.

'So,' said he, whipping off his trilby and brushing its crown with his sleeve, 'we're in luck. The police are willing to drop the charge – not a sniff of a committal, nothing.'

'This is excellent news,' I said, though I couldn't help feeling a little disappointed, armed as I was with a lengthy bail argument and Mrs Sanders as character witness.

'My thoughts exactly. So when we meet with Mrs Marchant, tell her to plead guilty.'

'Guilty?'

He resettled his hat. 'Ready, then?'

'Mr Breen. She's not guilty. She's a mother. It was her own child.'

'Legally, she was guilty.'

'Perhaps legally. But all she did was hold her own baby.'

'Miss Gifford, if Mrs Marchant pleads guilty, the police, who as you know have endured a good deal of adverse publicity over this affair, have agreed to a conditional discharge. They will cite as reasons Marchant's previously good character and the fact she has already served a spell on remand in Holloway.'

'If the police don't like the adverse publicity they should drop the charge.'

'Can't do that. Can't be seen to be bowing to the pressure of the gutter press.'

'Nor should we make our client plead guilty to something she didn't do. She'll have a criminal record.'

'Will it make one iota of difference to anyone if your Leah Marchant has a criminal record?'

'It will to her. Surely it will make it harder for her to win her children back. And what about her prospects of employment?'

'She's a char, I believe, not a nanny. All her employers will care about is whether she's honest. We can get someone to write her a testimonial to that effect. In fact I'll write one myself.'

'Well I won't suggest that she plead guilty. It feels utterly wrong.'

Now that I had crossed him Breen's face seemed gaunt and severe. 'I wasn't aware that your feelings were at issue here, Miss Gifford.'

'My feelings have nothing to do with it, obviously. But is it fair of us to ask Leah to plead guilty to holding her own child?'

'Fairness is hardly the question. Miss Gifford, you and I are paid to work within the constraints of the law, and in the eyes of the law Mrs Marchant is guilty. If you're unable to accept this simple fact, tell me at once and I shall deal with the case myself.'

He knew I was trapped. How could I back down from this, my first significant case? And I was far too junior to go out on a limb, although his pragmatism dismayed me. We went down to the cells in time to hold a brief interview with Leah, who was subdued by her week in Holloway. She looked considerably tamer in a clean though over-tight frock, I suspect lent by the loyal Mrs Sanders, with her hair scraped back in a bun. In fact I could detect a glimmer, in her round forehead and full lips, of the girl who had caught the eye of Breen as she polished the grates of his elderly client and later attracted the attentions of that feckless seaman Marchant.

As soon as she saw Breen, Leah seized his hand and kissed it. 'I knew you'd come. Now I shall be free.'

Breen responded to her relief and delight like a cat caressed beneath its chin. 'My dear Mrs Marchant, I am touched that you remember me after so many years.'

'I wouldn't forget you, Mr Breen. And now I've seen you I know for sure that me an' the kids is safe.'

Breen perched on the edge of the plank that passed for a bed and patted the space beside him as if offering Leah a velvet sofa. 'Your case is being dealt with by Miss Gifford here, who has left no stone unturned to ensure that you will be freed. I want you to listen very carefully to her.'

The jailer brought a chair for me and I sat facing the pair of them in that tiny cell, upright and lofty as a maiden aunt. Leah gave me a disdainful look and pushed her hand into Breen's. 'I want you to represent me, Mr Breen.'

'Well I shall, in a manner of speaking, because Miss Gifford and I work together, but once a lawyer has taken on a case it's most irregular to hand it over to someone else. You are fortunate because you will have the benefit of Miss Gifford's advice as well as my own.'

Throughout this conversation, the argument with Breen had been continuing in my head. Could I defy him? Must I do as he said? I wondered what James would have done in my place. Father would certainly have chosen the most expedient route, but James? His life had stopped when he was barely twenty, before he'd had time to develop into a moral touchstone.

In the end, deference got the better of me. I owed Breen this much, surely. He had taken me on against all the odds.

'I have visited Caractacus Court, Mrs Marchant,' I said briskly. 'Your friend Mrs Sanders will appear in court this morning to offer a character reference and an undertaking that you can have your old room back, should such information be required. We're hopeful that proceedings can be completed today and you will be released.'

'Eh? I was expecting a trial. How can that be?' Again she addressed Breen, who nodded towards me.

'We suggest that you plead guilty to the charge of child abduction. I will then give the mitigation – the reason why you did it – and afterwards we expect the magistrate to accept your reasons and to agree to a conditional discharge, which means that you will be free.'

'You mean plead guilty to somethin' I didn't do?'

'Not exactly, as I—'

'Never.'

'You see, you did take the child, Leah.'

'What does she mean, *the child*?' she demanded of Breen, whose hand she still clasped. 'Does she mean my own son Charlie? 'Ow can that be abduction? I never 'eard such rubbish. No, I won't say such a wicked thing, that I was a criminal in takin' my own child. Don't make me, Mr Breen.'

I ploughed on. 'If proceedings are concluded today we will be able to arrange for you to visit the children, or at least the girls. I have already written to the home.'

'What does she mean, visit 'em? I don't want to visit my own children; I want 'em back. I'm not listening to 'er any longer, Mr Breen. It seems to me she don't make no sense. All I want is me own kids back. Oh Mr Breen, I beg you, please set 'em free for me.' Tears ran down her newly washed face.

I suspected that Breen was relishing every moment of this interview. Squeezing Leah's fingers he removed a handkerchief – plain linen – from his pocket and handed it to her. Meanwhile precious time was passing; we were due in court in ten minutes and we'd received no indication from Leah as to how she would plead.

'So may I repeat, Leah,' I said, 'that our considered advice is that you should plead guilty to this offence. If you do we very much hope that you will be free within half an hour.'

'Oh yeah, and what if it don't turn out as you say? What if they says, "Ho, guilty are you? Then 'ave six months inside." I know what 'appens to people like me when they're in the 'ands of people like them.'

'It's a risk . . .' I began, but Breen stood, adjusted his necktie and picked up his bag.

'Miss Gifford has given you the benefit of our advice, Mrs Marchant. If you don't choose to take it, that's up to you. We shall do our best for you, whatever the circumstances, but I can make you no promises. We shall see you in court.'

'Don't go, Mr Breen. Oh I beg you. And don't make me plead guilty to somethin' I ain't done.'

'You've heard what Miss Gifford said: we are suggesting that you plead guilty to something you *have* done.' And so saying he swept out of the cell, leaving Mrs Marchant staring at me with burning resentment as if his unwelcome advice were all my fault.

Catching up with Breen on the cramped staircase I whispered, 'What will we do if she persists in pleading not guilty?'

'You will have to make a plea in open court for the case to be dropped. After all, we know it's what the prosecution wants. Failing that, you will have to get her bail. But let's hope she'll do as we told her. I suspect she might.' It did not occur to Breen to hold the door for me so I had to prop it open with my shoulder. In all my years as a law student, nothing had prepared me for the state of inner turmoil in which I entered that courtroom. I hardly knew whether to hope that Leah would follow our instructions and plead guilty or not.

This time when Leah Marchant's case was called the courtroom was relatively crowded. In addition to Mrs Sanders, who was dressed from head to toe in black, and a handful of other spectators, a couple of reporters lounged on the public benches, and beside me, in a supervisory role, sat Breen, though he feigned a complete lack of interest by filling in *The Times* crossword with one hand and leafing through the pages of a file with the other.

Also present was Meredith, who had insisted on being told the date and time of my next appearance in court. 'If I don't see you in action, you'll never make me believe you are nearly a lawyer,' she had said. She was a distraction. I neither trusted nor understood her; the words she had spoken above Beachy Head lighthouse were scorched into my consciousness and I feared what new surprises might be sprung on me. I had not been told the result of her interview with Dr Stopes.

The same magistrate, Shillitoe, presided. When Leah was brought up to the dock he made a show of shooting his cuffs and wiping his pen before peering first at her, then at Breen, over the top of his spectacles. 'Mr Breen?'

'Huh,' said Breen, as if awoken from sleep.

'I presume this is your case.'

'This is Miss Gifford's case.'

'Then why are you here, Mr Breen?'

Breen's right eyebrow arched and he did not trouble to rise more than a few inches from his seat. 'Forgive me, I presumed this was a public court of law.'

The magistrate gave him an irritable look but said nothing more.

The charge was read by the clerk and the police prosecutor began: 'Your Worship, as you know, the case is an unusual one because it concerns Mrs Marchant's attempt to kidnap her own baby. The 1891 Custody of Children Act gives the court the right to refuse Mrs Marchant custody of her children, if she be proved incapable, and her own rights to custody having been voluntarily relinquished by Mrs Marchant when she gave the children into the charge of the Good Samaritan Home, Hammersmith, section 3 of the act gives the court a duty to decide whether it ought to restore said children—'

'I just took 'em into that blasted 'ome in the first place because I couldn't manage. Nobody told me I wouldn't get 'em back,' yelled Leah from the dock. 'Nobody told me what I was signin' my name to. If I 'adn't of taken 'em in, if I'd kept 'em, then I wouldn't be 'ere now. I curse myself for tryin' to care for my own—'

'Mrs Marchant, kindly do not intervene in these proceedings unless you are invited so to do,' said the magistrate.

'But they're me own bloody kids.'

'Excuse me, Your Worship,' I said, 'might I have a word with my client?' I hurried to the dock, where I used its high oak sides to hoist myself up on tiptoe, and whispered, 'Leah. You must be quiet. Above all don't swear or you will find yourself in contempt of court.'

She glowered but said nothing more. As I swung round to face the bench I caught a glimpse of Meredith, who was watching with such intense interest that it would have been no surprise to me if she had leapt to her feet and berated the magistrate.

'Are we now ready for pleas to be taken?' asked the clerk. 'Leah Marchant. Do you plead guilty to the offence of child abduction?'

The dock was behind me so I couldn't see Leah's face. Breen entered another answer on his crossword. At last she murmured, 'I might.'

The magistrate's eyes widened. '*Might?* That's no reply. Guilty or not guilty?'

'They told me to plead guilty, even though I'm not.'

'Mrs Marchant—' began Shillitoe.

Meanwhile, I remembered but chose to ignore Thorne's advice about not interrupting a judge.

'Your Worship, we advised our client to plead guilty; we did not tell her to do so. I would ask that the charge be put again.'

The magistrate raised his hand to quell me. 'Sit down, Miss um … Mrs Marchant, I want you to listen very carefully to what I have to say. You are charged with a very serious offence indeed. If you plead guilty, you may face many months of imprisonment so you should think very hard before giving your answer. Under no circumstances should you blindly obey the dictates of your lawyer … legal adviser, if you don't agree with her.'

I clasped my hands in my lap and gazed straight ahead at a point above the clerk's bald patch. Breen swivelled round and stared long and hard at Leah.

'Guilty then,' she said sulkily.

'I beg your pardon?'

'I plead guilty.'

'Are you sure?'

'How many more times do I 'ave to—'

'Mrs Marchant, please be aware that you are addressing a court of law. I don't like your tone.'

'Now that we have a plea, perhaps the prosecution can give us the facts of the case,' the clerk said soothingly.

The prosecutor, as if reading from a script prepared by Theo Wolfe and his lunch chum, outlined the facts and stated that although on the face of it there could be few offences more serious than child abduction, in this particular instance the prosecution was well aware that there were many mitigating factors, as would doubtless be outlined by the defence, which was why the case had, exceptionally, in view of its seriousness, not been sent to a higher court, and certainly, if a lenient sentence, for instance a conditional discharge were, on this occasion, to be passed, the prosecution would not object.

It was my turn. 'Your Worship, I would support what the learned police prosecutor—'

'Then there's nothing more to be said, is there?' said the magistrate in a quiet and measured voice. 'I have the full picture.'

Breen threw down his pen, sat up straight and folded his arms.

I gathered my wits. 'On the contrary, Your Worship. I of course want to be sure that you give due consideration to my client's circumstances before you sentence her, even though I am grateful for the police prosecutor's compassionate view of her offence. Her landlady Mrs Sanders is here to vouch for her good character and devotion to her children. Would you like to hear her speak, Your Worship?'

'I would not.'

The courtroom was so still that I could hear Leah's uneven breathing in the dock behind me. The magistrate had me on the end of a wire and I recognised that this was not a matter of professional dislike or suspicion, as I had previously assumed, but of mortal outrage. He saw me as an aberration, an enemy of the Establishment, and I had no hope at all of reaching him.

'Are you minded then to go along with the police—' I said shakily.

'I am minded to sentence this woman as I see fit, Miss Gifford. I won't be dictated to by you or anybody else.' He smiled, showing his small white teeth.

Too late I heard Leah's sucking intake of breath. 'I told you so. I told you what would 'appen when we was down in that fuckin' cell. Oh my Gawd, he's goin' to lock me up and I ain't never goin' to see my kids again.'

'Silence, Mrs Marchant.'

Leah lurched at the door of the dock but one jailer seized her wrist, the other whipped out handcuffs and held her while she writhed and yelled, 'I ain't never goin' to listen to no one again. You're all bastards. You don't give a damn for me an' my kids. I'm not waitin' 'ere any longer—'

The magistrate intoned, 'Leah Marchant, for the offence of

child abduction I commit you to three months' imprisonment, that is penal servitude, with hard labour, plus another month, to run consecutively, for contempt of court. Four months in all. You may take her down.'

The courtroom was suddenly abuzz and my own voice rang out: 'Your Worship, you cannot commit a defendant to imprisonment of any but the First Division for Contempt of Court.'

'I'll do what I damn well like in my own courtroom. Take her down.'

Breen uncrossed his legs, stood up and lightly drummed on the desk while he waited for silence to fall. His mouth was arranged into an incredulous smile and when he spoke his tone was jocular, as if he were conducting a conversation with a close but misguided friend. 'Your Worship, this is quite unlawful. Imprisonment with hard labour cannot be imposed for contempt. We will appeal.'

'Do so, Breen, by all means. Mr Clerk, is the next case ready?'

I made a play of gathering and sorting my papers, then crushed them into my bag. Breen leaned across, screwed the lid onto my pen and handed it to me, presumably to signal that he was firmly on my side. Meanwhile Leah was sobbing violently and shouting abuse as she was led down to the cells. A young lawyer, waiting for his own case to be heard, sniggered in the benches behind me. I sensed that Meredith's passionate gaze was on my face but couldn't bring myself to look at her. The inside of my head was dark apart from one thought, white and hard as a pebble, so that when Breen took me by the elbow, steered me across the foyer, ushered me into a cramped interview room and closed the door I could not prevent myself from saying in a choked voice, 'You should not have intervened.'

He had perhaps intended to utter a few bracing words of advice; at any rate he was fired up, ready to leap into action with his customary zeal and knock the British justice system into shape on behalf of the two victims of this disaster, Leah and myself. Therefore my words were like a blow to the cheek. I had never seen him so taken aback: he visibly stiffened and his eyes went cold. 'I do beg your pardon.'

'You made me look a fool ... even more of a fool. It's bad enough that Leah is now facing months of prison. I was wrong

97

on two counts. First I allowed my ambition to stand up in court to take precedence over a client's best interests. As was clear to all, that magistrate had no intention of giving a woman advocate a fair hearing. Then I went against my own judgement in persuading Leah to plead guilty. But at least I did it by myself; at least I was seen to be handling the case from start to finish, however badly. But then you stepped in. It was on the tip of my tongue to say we'd appeal but you didn't give me the chance. Mr Breen, have you considered how you would feel if I were to stand up in the middle of one of your cases and intervene with a point of law?'

He had a child's tendency to show that he was wounded by jutting out his lower lip. Settling his hat firmly onto his unruly hair he bowed slightly and said, 'Forgive me, I shall try to be more circumspect in future.'

Now my heart ached in the knowledge that I had spurned a loyal and influential colleague. 'Mr Breen, this afternoon, if you remember, I am visiting Stella Wheeler's workplace, Lyons. Will I see you afterwards, in the office?' But he was gone and the door had slammed shut.

Alone in that nasty little room, I stared at the frosted glass window and drew a long breath. In my mind's eye the goldfish bowl of the courthouse seemed to shrink and enclose me, and I felt I would never be able to get out. *You should not have intervened.* With that outburst I glimpsed, again, that the end of endurance would mean an end to self-control. After all, I knew what it was to peer over the edge of reason into an abyss where images of the dead howled along vacant passages of my consciousness. Last time I had ended up face down on the hall floor, scarcely able to draw breath, my fists squeezed tight as they drummed the cold tiles.

Not here, not now, Evelyn, no self-recriminations yet. First you must act.

So I planned my next moves with the precision of a military operation: I would tidy my hair, adjust my hat, open the door and cross the foyer to the usher's desk. There I would lodge our appeal. I would speak to Mrs Sanders and explain what had happened. Then I would go down to the cells and face Leah. If Meredith was waiting for me, I would send her away. Under the circumstances I did not think I could stand her pity or indignation.

What I would not allow myself to do, for the time being, was dwell on the disgraceful behaviour of the magistrate or my impulsive criticism of Breen. And I would put off until later consideration of the awful truth that, largely because of me, Leah was even further from release.

When at last I emerged from that evil-smelling interview room there was no sign of Meredith. I filled in a lengthy form and delivered it in person to a senior clerk; still no Meredith. I went down to the cells and conducted a pitifully short interview with Leah Marchant, who turned her face to the wall. When I re-emerged, by now longing for a little companionship, no Meredith. How typical of her to do the one thing guaranteed to disturb me most – in this case, witness the fiasco of Leah Marchant's hearing then disappear without a word.

Chapter Eleven

By two o'clock I was walking down Regent Street in search of Stella Wheeler's tea shop. For once abandoning Prudence's dress code, I wore neither hat nor jacket, both of which were stuffed into the top of my briefcase. No wonder I drew curious glances. The day was dull and cool for the end of May, but I rolled up my sleeves and occasionally a fierce gust of wind ripped a strand of hair from its pins so that when I glimpsed my reflection in a shop window I saw a madwoman, white-faced and Medusa-haired. Although the pavements were packed with lunchtime shoppers, the crowds parted before me.

I marched on amidst office workers who dived in and out of shops or plunged across the road. London heaved and churned, billboards and summer frocks and omnibuses, but that afternoon I couldn't for the life of me see the point. Nor could I stand the churning faces, in and outside my head: the way Meredith, Leah, Thorne, Breen and Stephen Wheeler spun round and round in the maelstrom of my mind.

'For heaven's sake, have some consideration,' said an elderly lady as I barged into her, and she grabbed my arm to hold herself steady. The encounter calmed me. I apologised profusely and waited patiently as she bent down to tie her shoelace. Being useful, after all, was safe territory; it had been my vocation since birth.

Here it was, Lyons tea shop. The door stood open and inside was the familiar counter stacked with Eccles cakes, doughnuts, iced buns and sausage rolls – upon one of which a bluebottle feasted. Beyond the counter was the restaurant with its green and brown patterned linoleum floor covered with rows of tables and bentwood chairs. Swing doors at the back led to the kitchen and beside them a vast dresser was piled with crockery and napkins.

Although it was not quite the end of the lunch period, business was slack and I might have chosen any one of a dozen empty tables. In the end I sat under the clock, facing the room. To my left, across the counter, I could see onto the street.

Because it was a cool day the ceiling fans were still, though when I looked up I was reminded of the breeze that had wafted onto my face when I had tea with Nicholas Thorne. Thank God he had not been in court today to witness my shame.

The table needed a wipe: sugar was sprinkled across its top and a fly landed again and again to feed. I didn't mind. At least I was alone, anonymous. I closed my eyes to the clink of crockery, the ebb and flow of other people's conversations, the roar of the traffic on the street beyond.

A tea shop. How many thousand conversations about everything and nothing had been conducted here? How many love affairs begun and ended? I remembered Thorne's shapely hand moving among the tea things inches from my own, which had been primly clasped on the edge of the table – Prudence maintained that hands, particularly those belonging to children, should be constantly in view. I smelled tea and sweet pastry, and a faint trace of the disinfectant they must use to swab the floor. When I opened my eyes, the restaurant was spread before me, Stella Wheeler's premarital world, where she'd worked for nearly seven years after leaving school. It was as if the remnants of a pea-souper lingered in the room, a translucent pall of old cigarette smoke, bacon rinds and coffee grounds. Despite the precision with which the tables and chairs had been arranged there was an impression of untidiness, something to do perhaps with the dingy floor and lassitude of the waiting staff. I was surprised that a girl with a taste for finery like Stella should have been content with such a humble workplace.

A waitress approached, languidly swaying her hips. She held a tiny notepad and raised her eyebrows uninterestedly to take my order. I picked up the menu card and out of habit asked for a poached egg and a pot of tea, both considerably cheaper than they had been at the Peter Jones department store. But in any case, I decided, for once I shall be like Theo Wolfe and make a claim on Breen & Balcombe's petty cash box. If I am to be dismissed by Mr Breen for insolence, at least I should not be out of pocket.

When the girl came back with my pot of tea – the egg would take longer as it had to be put *fresh on* – she also brought a dishcloth with which to swipe the sugar granules onto the floor. 'I was wondering,' I said, 'if I might speak to the manager. It's about someone who used to work here, Mrs Stella Wheeler.'

The girl had exquisite skin but irregular features including a beaky, high-bridged nose and close-set eyes. Beneath the unwieldy cap her hair hung lank and dead straight. When she heard Stella's name she clenched the dishcloth and pressed her pale lips together. 'You knew Stella, then?' I said.

'She was Stella Hobhouse when she was here.'

'I realise that. But you did know her?'

'Course I did.'

'Do you think you might be able to help me? I have a few questions.' The girl took a step back but hovered. Her eyelids were pink as if from recent tears or sleepless nights. 'I'm a lawyer, you see. This is a very difficult question but I'm assuming you know what happened to Stella?'

'Of course. The police come in and asked us all questions.'

'What did they tell you about her?'

'That she was dead. That she was shot.'

'What did they want to know from you?'

She backed a little further and said, 'I should fetch my manager,' but continued to watch me with her light eyes.

'The thing is, we need to make sure that the police have collected all the necessary information,' I told her.

'They said Stephen probably done it. They was asking if we knew how he treated her when they was together.'

'I suppose that's partly what I want to know too. And I would also like to learn more about Stella.'

'Why don't you ask the police?'

'We think they've made up their minds about Stephen and might miss something. We want to do our best for him so we thought we'd look into things ourselves.'

'Did Stephen do it?'

'I don't know.'

'Did he say he didn't do it?'

'He hasn't said anything. He can't, or won't, speak.'

She was even paler now and her large eyes were fixed, though not focused, on my face. 'I knew him. I knew them both. I was at their wedding. Stell and me was mates.'

'Can we talk then?'

'I should get my manager,' she repeated, this time with even less conviction.

'Don't do or say anything that makes you uncomfortable. Take your time to decide whether or not you'd like to talk to me.'

We exchanged names – hers was Carole Mangan – then she disappeared to fetch my egg, which was cooked to perfection and piping hot, and when she'd unloaded her tray she darted away to serve a couple of ladies who had come in laden with shopping and wearing hats that were surely far too heavy for the season. They dropped into their chairs, scattering bags about their feet, and exclaimed how *exhausted* they were and how they had spent far too much but never mind. Carole, in her well-worn shoes, stood patiently by, waiting to take their order.

I wondered how proficient a waitress Stella Wheeler had been. Given her fastidious taste in underwear, I presumed she would have noticed the unsuitability of those hats, especially the one with dark brown velvet ribbons. And how had she endured the uniform, the calf-length sack of a dress and nurse's apron with its bib rising to chest height then split to cross the shoulders in wide bands? Had Stella worn her hair short or long? Short, I guessed; there had been no dish containing hairpins on her dressing table. And with a stab of excitement very far from my earlier despair I realised that Carole would know every one of these details. If they'd worked together for years, they must have had oceans of time to share intimacies.

I sensed that Carole was aware of me even as she took the latest order through to the kitchen, and that although she was nervous, she was interested in me. When I'd finished my lunch she came close again. 'If you'll let me know the truth about what's going on, I'll talk to you in my tea break. Our manager doesn't tell us nothing. It's not fair.'

'When is your tea break?'

'Half an hour.'

I waited, at first fretfully, then more calmly. There were any number of uses to which I might have put that half-hour. Prudence's birthday, for instance, was imminent and I might have shopped for handkerchiefs or some equally unimaginative gift. Prudence was impossible to please because she had so many negative opinions. There were bookshops nearby in which I could have looked up the latest legal publication or even found some little treat for Edmund. I could have taken a walk. Instead I remained at the table sipping tepid over-brewed tea and accustoming myself to Stella Wheeler's world. An older waitress stood listlessly in the doorway, arms folded, watching the street. Her cap was neater than Carole's but her hair had been badly cut and sat unevenly on her collar. She adjusted her weight from one leg to the other, as if to relieve pain.

An elderly woman came in with a couple of children a little younger than Edmund, who spent a painful length of time choosing between chocolate and banana milkshakes. Which would Edmund prefer? I wondered. Perhaps one day he would come with me to a tea shop. My heart ached at the thought of his short legs swinging from the chair opposite. James had gone for chocolate every time. Carole reappeared with a trolley and began systematically clearing and wiping tables. I heard the hands on the clock above my head shift a notch and somebody drop a bit of china in the kitchen. What an uncomplicated job a waitress's must be, I thought – skimming the surface of other people's lives, their moments of celebration, exhaustion or simple thirst a matter of complete indifference. In my own work I was expected to meddle, and look where that had got me.

Promptly, at a quarter past three Carole again emerged from the kitchen, this time without apron or cap and with the top button of her dress undone. She wore a pink cardigan and a straw hat, making her ashen skin seem rosier. When we were outside I heard her inhale sharply and it was true that even the air in the street, reeking of manure and motor fumes, was fresh after the fug of the tea shop. She walked ploddingly with her handbag clasped in both hands and told me that she worked until six and then caught the bus home to Balham. It was a long day, ten hours, and she didn't half miss Stella and couldn't believe what had happened to her.

'We was mates,' she said. 'We used to get the giggles terribly, you know, about some of the customers. There's no one to have a laugh with now.'

'Can you describe her for me?'

'She was quite moody. Liked getting her own way. But she was very pretty and always hugged you after she'd been mean, or bought a bit of chocolate, so you had to forgive her. And she was hard-working and would always cover for you if you was tired or sick. I think in all the years I knew her she was hardly ever off ill or late even.'

'How long is it since you last saw her?'

'A couple of weeks. Like I said, I went to her wedding in April and then she came into town after work one day and we had a drink. I can't bear to think that was the last time I'll ever see her. I'll try and go to the funeral, though the manager says we can't all have time off. As far as he's concerned one person is more than enough, and it'll probably be him.' Her skin was so fine that I thought the tears might seep through it rather than gather on the edge of her lids.

'Tell me about the wedding.'

'Well of course because she was getting married she had to stop work, and she was excited about that, but then sad at the end, I think. We had a party on the Friday, and we'd had a collection, even head office chipped in, and we gave her this tea service she wanted from Lawleys – she and I were always walking past the windows and she had her eye on one set in particular – and on the Saturday we went to the wedding she looked beautiful, but then she always did. It took her weeks to choose a frock, creamy-yellow, all floaty at the back. It suited her lovely because she was thin and it showed her ankles. But she said it wasn't to be so fancy she couldn't wear it afterwards.'

'Did you like Stephen Wheeler?'

It had dawned on me that I must not underestimate Carole – her responses were carefully weighed. 'Does it matter if I liked him?'

'The thing is, I don't know either of them. We are having to defend Stephen based on very little information because as I said he's not talking to us yet, though we hope that might change.'

'But his gun was there.'

'It was. His gun and his gloves.'

'He was nice,' Carole said, taking the plunge suddenly. '*I* would have married him if he'd asked.'

We smiled though the expression in her eyes was raw and pitiful. 'He was quite a bit older, wasn't he?' I asked gently.

'Much older – sixteen years or so. But he seemed so kind even though Stell said the war changed him, made him heavy-hearted sometimes. Whenever we met he'd shake my hand and give me ever such a lovely smile. And when he wasn't smiling he'd look sad again but I thought, Lucky old Stell to have a man like that, who you could bring round easy enough, I would suppose, by taking care of him and treating him very softly. I used to be so jealous of her, the way he'd be there after work with his hat off, waiting for her. I thought she took him an awful lot for granted.'

'And after she was married, do you think he was still kind to her? Were they happy?'

This drew a very sharp look indeed. 'I don't know much about that,' she said. She broke off suddenly. 'Do you have a watch? I only have quarter of an hour for tea.'

'Your time is almost up.' We hurried back along Hanover Street while I decided which of a dozen questions was the most important. 'What did you talk about that evening in the pub after work?'

'Mostly about Lyons, and the manager, and customers she remembered. She said she sometimes even wished she was still working, which we all thought was mad because she'd been champing at the bit to get out.'

'So she was slightly bored but otherwise all right. There was no suggestion that she was frightened or anything?'

'No. Definitely not. Just restless as usual, always looking around. There was a sort of spark in her eye that I'd not seen before. She said we should go for tea at her house one Sunday afternoon when she'd got it all nice but she couldn't fix on a date for the time being.'

We were on Regent Street again where the noise of cabs and carts was almost too intrusive for speech. 'Miss Mangan, is there anything else you can think of that might help me? Any reason Stephen would suddenly turn on her? Nothing she might do to make him angry or jealous?'

'Jealous?'

'For instance, was she ever keen on anyone else?'

'The police asked me that.'

'What was your reply?'

'We all have our admirers, even me. I gave them a list of men who used to ask for Stella.'

'But there was no one special?'

'Not that I know of.'

'Could I have a copy of that list?' We were at the doorway of the tea shop. 'And, Miss Mangan, might you have a photograph of Stella?'

'A wedding photo, yes.'

'I'll call back then, shall I?' She nodded and gave me one of her shyly acute glances. Then she stepped across the threshold to an interior which had grown more crowded in the short time we'd been away.

Chapter Twelve

I dreaded my return to the office, where I would have to face Breen, but although I was back by four thirty, a time when Wolfe was generally taking tea and Breen rattling off dictation, I found Arbery Street deserted save for Miss Drake, who was jabbing at the keys of her typewriter. I placed the Lyons receipt in her in tray, bade her good afternoon and descended to my basement, where I made a note of my discussion with Carole Mangan and wrote up Leah Marchant's disastrous bail hearing.

Periodically, as I recalled the painful events of the morning, I glanced up at the corroded bars on the window, the lime-stained sink and teetering stacks of files, thinking how ironic it was that after Leah's first hearing I had offered my resignation, whereas after her second I faced dismissal. At six o'clock I heard familiar movements overhead presaging Miss Drake's departure: the whisk and clatter of a typewriter being closed down for the night, the washing of cups in the new scullery, the upending of chairs so that the floor would be properly swept tomorrow morning. Next I heard her reluctant footfall on the basement stairs and a note was pushed under my door, typed on the inside of a thrice-used envelope. 'Mr Breen says you're to attend Wheeler's bail hearing with him in Amersham. Ten thirty sharp tomorrow morning. And afterwards an appointment has been made with Chesham Constabulary for a visit to the crime scene. Mr Breen insists you wear sensible shoes.'

Another slip of paper followed – my receipt from Lyons. On the back Miss Drake had written in her famously regular copperplate, *Application refused. All expenditure pertaining to company business must be authorised before its incurrence.*

*

The atmosphere in Clivedon Hall Gardens, when I arrived home, was even more frigid than it had been at Breen & Balcombe, and with some cause: I was late for dinner, everyone was hungry; Meredith had gone out and Edmund was misbehaving, sitting on the bottom stair and refusing point blank to go to bed. His thumb was stuck deep in his mouth and he glowered at Prudence, to whom thumb sucking was anathema. Min was hovering exasperatedly at the top of the basement stairs. Had she been left in charge, in the old days when James and I were children, she would have brooked no such nonsense.

'I've promised him a story,' said mother, trying to take hold of his free hand, which he snatched away and pushed under his thigh, 'but he says no. He's being very naughty. He hardly touched his supper. We had no idea when you were coming back so we insisted he ate his.'

'But Meredith and I had agreed he would eat with the grown-ups,' I said.

Faced with an intransigent boy, none of us knew what to do. Mother, it seemed, had forgotten all she ever knew about handling children, though if my memory was accurate it had always been her preferred style to float downstairs in a mist of lace and rose water ready to dine out or watch a play, rather than stay in and put us to bed.

'It's no use his being hungry now,' said Prudence. 'He should have eaten when he had the chance.'

The little boy pressed his knees together and pattered his fingers on the side of his nose.

'Oh dear, are you hungry, Edmund?' asked mother, and I knew she was terrified lest he was because what could she do about it? She could scarcely defy Prudence.

Rather than reply, he lowered his eyelids so that his cheeks were shadowed by his long lashes. I admired his obstinacy. 'Why don't you and Prudence keep grandmother company?' I said to mother. 'I'll put Edmund to bed.'

'But what if he won't go? We've all tried. Mother even offered to take him up one of her collections.'

My heart ached for Edmund with his downcast eyes and wedged-in thumb; he must be very miserable. But I also knew that this had become a battle in which we were all joined. If I failed to get Edmund to bed it would be a triumph for Prudence, who was now bound to be willing him to stay put.

Once Edmund and I were alone I attempted to stroke his head but he flinched. Had this been the six-year-old James, and such behaviour of Edmund's was uncannily like his father's, I would have tickled, cajoled and joked until I had persuaded him to race me up the stairs. But I was no longer nine and I had forgotten how to tease a small boy without hurting his pride; instead I found myself addressing him as if we were in a court of law. 'It seems to me you have three choices, Edmund. You can either stay here until your mother comes home, though I think you'll be very tired, or you can sit at table with us, which as you know is pretty dull, or you can come up with me and we'll have a story, and you can wait for your mother in bed. The latter seems by far the most advisable course of action, but it's up to you.'

Having waited a moment for the counter-argument, which was not forthcoming, I offered my hand. When he made no move I climbed the stairs anyway, very slowly. His will stretched against mine and I knew that he wanted to come to bed but was unable to rescue himself. In the end I hung over the banister and whispered his name repeatedly until I saw the glimmer of a reluctant smile. This time when I reached for him he allowed himself to be lifted into my arms. I picked him up clumsily, surprised by his sudden, willing weight, and had to manoeuvre him until his legs were properly hooked around my waist. And it was like Eastbourne again, the waves breaking, the sun shining. His chest was pressed to mine, his arms clasped firmly about my neck so that his breath was in my hair as he twisted a loose strand absentmindedly round his finger. The smell of him, the green, lovely perfume of Edmund, James's child, sang in my blood.

When we reached the room he shared with Meredith I set him down and helped him to undress, folding his still-warm clothes but resisting the temptation to press his shirt to my face, and protecting his modesty by bustling across the landing to run water into the basin. After he had washed his hands, he nestled into the crook of my arm, as Jamie used to, while I read to him from the Brothers Grimm, the copy won by me at Sunday school in

December 1902 and so well thumbed that the back cover had nearly dropped away from the spine. In went the thumb again, Edmund's head fell back against my shoulder and I read into the fluff of his hair. Once, towards the end, I kissed him, though he didn't seem to notice. It seemed to me that my lips had been starved of kisses all these years and that as I read I felt my lost self unfurling a little more, not just the sister but the mother I had never been, though my voice didn't falter: 'And when the wolf came to the brook he stooped down to drink, and the heavy stones made him lose his balance, so that he fell, and sank beneath the water . . .'

I would have sat like that, though the awkward angle made my back ache, until Meredith's return or longer, until morning. Forever. But Edmund curled gratefully onto his side when the story was over then rolled back and murmured, 'We never said any prayers.'

'Does your mother say prayers?'

'Oh yes, we say prayers every night.'

'What kind of prayers?'

'She has beads and we touch them. We always pray for my father. We ask Jesus to look after all the young men who died in the war.'

So Meredith was a Roman Catholic like her parents, on top of everything else. In any event, I did not feel equal to praying with Edmund since my worship these days was limited to occasional attendance at church, where I raged at the banality of addressing a God who patently didn't listen.

'Shall we leave it for tonight, as it's so late?' I stooped to kiss his hairline.

'Mommy says we must never be too tired to pray because God is probably never too tired to listen to us.'

I noted the 'probably' and smiled. Trust Meredith to put in a caveat. However, I pressed my hands together, bowed my head and dutifully recited the Our Father, which seemed to satisfy him.

Then I kissed his forehead again, switched off the lamp and went downstairs, my feet sprung with joy and triumph, only to find that a bowl of tepid celery soup awaited me in the dining room, where the others sat before their already empty bowls.

'We couldn't wait any longer,' said mother, glancing nervously at Prudence.

'I'm afraid I had to point out once again that it is unhealthy for a household to be dictated to by the whim of a spoilt child,' said Prudence, adjusting her knife and fork on either side of her mat.

Min was already at the door bearing a tray laden with the next course. Nobody spoke while she cleared the bowls and laid out the casserole dishes. Grandmother, as usual, seemed largely oblivious to the poisoned atmosphere, though she occasionally raised her head as if to catch the currents in the air. I helped myself to potatoes and waited for the next salvo.

'She goes out without a word of explanation,' hissed mother the instant Min was gone. 'No wonder the child is upset. His mother would give no indication of what time she'd be back. And she's asked me for money. She says she has nothing to live on and must have an allowance.' I ate a few mouthfuls, hungry despite the significance of the occasion – money being discussed at mealtimes. 'Prudence and I agree that she is quite impossible. It's as if she's come with the deliberate intention of living on us. Well, there's no more money – no matter how deserving she is – and that's that.'

Mother, when roused to anger, tended towards petulance rather than effectiveness. She was better suited to acquiescence. In her heyday she had charmed most comers, especially male, with her upward glances and winsome smiles. She could meet a dozen of father's colleagues in an evening and remember every one of their names, enquire as if she knew them intimately after their wives and daughters, suggest birthday gifts, give witty critiques of concerts and plays and leave not a heart untouched by her tenderness. Mother, after all, was the daughter of a successful and rather daring actress: Ibsen was often mentioned in the same breath as Clara Fielding – grandmother's stage name. This somewhat risqué fact was overlooked, perhaps even envied, by father's colleagues because mother was beautiful and had a white, pillowy bosom.

But now the men were no longer here and there was no one to save her except that poor substitute for husband and son, me. 'Prudence says this has all gone on long enough. Meredith seems to be running rings round us,' she added. 'I know she was

James's ... and we must ... But her expectations are entirely disproportionate.'

Prudence cut a cube of braised steak into quarters and raised a segment to her lips without bending her spine a notch to meet it. 'In my view, her sudden arrival is very irregular. I suspect she has something to hide.'

'But don't you love Edmund?' I cried. 'Don't you want to keep him here with us? I would pay any amount to make that possible.' Grandmother's neck shot forward as she craned to hear what had roused me. 'Grandmother,' I enunciated, 'don't you love Edmund being here?'

'Oh, I do. He's a dear little boy. So intelligent and polite.'

'No,' said mother suddenly. 'I won't put up with that woman just because she's Edmund's mother, whatever anyone says. It would be different if it was just the boy – I accept we have a duty towards him – but I cannot manage with her in the house.'

It was on the tip of my tongue to ask *Manage what?* but Prudence said, 'I fear for your mother's health, I really do. In my view this is putting intolerable strain upon us all.'

'Will you speak to her, Evelyn? Tell her we have no money.'

I ate a meagre bowl of semolina pudding and jam whilst pondering my next move. The situation was complicated by the memories of Saturday's conversation with Meredith on Beachy Head, and Edmund's arms about my neck as we climbed the stairs.

When Meredith came home I was already preparing for bed, but with a brisk knock she burst into my room decked out in strings of red beads and a long coat embroidered with multicoloured flowers. She reeked of smoke and alcohol, her eyes were shining and she dropped a bulging carpet bag in the doorway. Her slender ankles were exposed and her shoes were pointed, with wide straps. I, on the other hand, was wearing an ancient nightgown so well washed that it was grey rather than white and my large feet were bare.

'Look at you,' cried Meredith, 'straight out of a painting by Millais or Rossetti. You ought to be floating in water with your hands pressed together on your breast. If that judge could see you now, a voluptuous nymph rather than a bluestocking in a grey jacket, how surprised he'd be. But, you were a sensation in court this morning. Everyone was talking about you in the foyer afterwards. Were your ears burning? I was so proud to know you.'

'I was horrified by what happened, actually,' I said.

'Horrified? But why? You were lancing a boil. Don't you see, that beast of a man was exposed for the senseless bigot he really is.' She kicked off her shoes, jumped onto my bed, and fell back on the pillows as if fully intending to stay awhile.

'That poor woman, Leah Marchant, is in prison tonight because of me,' I said, dragging my hairbrush through tangles with such force that the hair crackled.

'Oh yes, but I don't suppose it matters that much. I was talking to a friend of hers called Mrs Sanders and she said at least being locked up would keep Mrs Marchant away from the bottle – since she lost her children she's been drinking heavily apparently. Your ears must have been burning. We both said how much we admired you and how brave you were. Do you know, as I was watching you I really thought to myself, This is an historic occasion – I am witnessing practically the first time that a woman in England has stood as an advocate in court. But listen, you are not the only one breaking new ground – this evening I attended my very first art class.'

She sprang up and unpacked various items from her bag. 'I went along to the art school in Chelsea and they had no vacancies, at least not for beginners, but they did have a noticeboard filled with cards written by teachers offering classes and I found one in Bloomsbury. The teacher, who's called Hadley Waters, was gassed so he's very thin and wheezy but he studied at the Slade and has his own studio where the classes take place. He happened to be holding one this evening so he invited me to join it as a tryout. He didn't even charge me and his class turns out to be just what I'm looking for. There are five other pupils with very mixed experience, including another beginner like me. We experimented with perspective and the human form. I'm so happy.'

A clutter of paints, brushes and boxes piled up on the floor-boards until finally a sketch pad emerged which Meredith held to her chest with both hands. Thus displayed was a drawing of a female nude seated on an upright chair with her back to the artist but her head turned, as if her name had suddenly been called. Thankfully all but the side of her breast and the cleft of her buttocks was hidden from view.

Though I knew virtually nothing about art I could tell that Meredith had flair. With minimal strokes of charcoal she had depicted living curves, not to mention a distinctly hoydenish glint in the model's eye. 'It's because he worked at the Slade that Hadley Waters has the confidence to allow a mixed class to tackle nudes. I'm so relieved. The last thing I need is to spend months drawing flowers or some such. I particularly wanted bodies, whole, healthy bodies, having been a nurse, you know.'

She perched on the side of the bed and held the drawing at arm's length, then darted across the room, propped it against the wall and gave it further scrutiny. Her ability to confound me was quite extraordinary. Somehow the fact that she had made such a proficient drawing of a strange woman wearing no clothes made it impossible for me to raise the subject of funds.

And then she cried, 'I forgot the most important thing of all. We have been invited to a party. You and me. In Kew, wherever that is. It's on the river, Hadley says. Can you imagine? I go to one art class and come home with a party invitation. Hadley says we must go because he thinks everyone will be there, including Augustus John, and that the house where the party is to be held is itself a work of art.'

'A party? We can't go to a party given by strangers. We won't know a soul.'

'We'll know each other. You can be quite sure that I only agreed to go if you were invited too. It's a fortnight on Thursday.'

'Oh dear. I'm sorry but I think there's a concert at the church that night which mother would like me to attend.'

'That's all right, we'll go on to the party afterwards. It probably won't start until terribly late. I can't tell you how thrilled I am – it was my dream back in Canada to find a world of culture in London and now I have, and so easily. Hmmm, would you smell the inside of my bag? Don't you just love it, oils and linseed? I feel like an artist already. I'm sorry I had to rush off this morning, by the way, before I had a chance to tell you how brilliantly you performed, but I had so much shopping to do.'

'Meredith. Forgive me for asking, but how are you able to afford all this?'

She sat back on her heels and gazed up at me. 'I still have a little of the money my father gave me. He was very generous.'

'Mother says you spoke to her today and asked for an allowance.'

'Oh yes. I did. Perhaps I should have waited until you were home but I'm eaten up with anxiety about how Edmund and I are to manage and I thought the best way would be to bring it all out in the open. Unfortunately the job I went for yesterday was not quite right so I shall have to try elsewhere. I found Dr Stopes surprisingly conservative on some matters, notably the question of marriage. She and I didn't exactly see eye to eye. So until I do get work, I must have some money to live on.'

'The thing is, as I've told you before, we can barely make ends meet here. We are quite ready to house you and Edmund for as long as you like but none of us has a specific allowance. Prudence has some savings, I believe, but very little. We're all having to scrimp and make do.'

Her eyes hardened. 'Well, I'm afraid I am not prepared to go on like that. I have been making do since Edmund was born and I cannot stand it any longer.' She piled her things back into the bag and I felt sorry that her pleasure in them had been tainted by our conversation. But I was also aware that her movements were a little clumsy and wondered if alcohol was behind her shrillness.

'Shall we speak again tomorrow,' I asked, 'when we're not both tired?'

'Tomorrow you'll be out again, in your wonderful world where you are significant, Evelyn, and I shall be cooped up here in these terrible rooms. I must have some money. I'm not asking for much. Twenty pounds a month is what your father used to send me but I don't expect anything like that. Half would do.'

'That is still a huge amount, almost as much as we pay the girls.'

'Then I have come to a new prison, worse than being at home. Have you any idea how it feels to be so confined? Perhaps I should find other lodgings; in fact it's possible there may be a room in Hadley Waters' house.'

'I should be very sorry if you were to take Edmund away. That's not what I want.'

'Evelyn, it's not for me to tell you how to run your affairs but I've been thinking, couldn't you raise money on this house?' She had changed tack again and now spoke more softly. 'Perhaps you could borrow money against its value or let a room.' Her voice did not falter although we both knew the only empty room was James's. 'And it's beyond me why your mother pays for two women to cook and clean when she and Prudence sit around all day and complain about the cost of everything.'

'It's what they were brought up to. They don't know any other way. It would be cruel to expect them, or indeed Min and Rose, to change now.'

She was watching me, and my heart beat faster because I knew she was weighing something up in her mind. Sure enough, 'I have something to show you,' she said, and she opened the door, crossed the landing and disappeared into her own room while I picked up the nude, who had an overbite and a weak chin, and wondered what new blow was about to fall.

When Meredith came back she stood so close to me that I could pick out the individual strands of embroidery silk on her coat. From a little leather wallet she withdrew a scrap of paper, stained and soft, which she handled with her fingertips and cradled in her palm lest it break apart at the creases. She passed it to me as if it were a fragile living thing, a wounded butterfly, and I began to weep.

'He wrote it while he was dying,' she said. 'They found it in his hand when they recovered his body and brought it to me.'

On the paper was one word, very faint, scrawled with a blunt pencil and smeared with dirt. I knew the writing, I would have known it in any circumstances. The word was in fact a name: 'Meredith'.

Chapter Thirteen

The next morning I obediently took the train to Amersham in good time for Stephen Wheeler's hearing. Much to my relief I was an hour ahead of Prudence, who was travelling along the same line later that day, on an annual birthday visit to her old home.

It was a haunted journey. From a smeary window identical to this Stella Wheeler had gazed at the lanes and hay fields of Middlesex with, I suspected, no great interest in the bucolic pleasures they offered. Everything I had learned of her so far suggested a girl who preferred the city to the country: her family home had been in the suburb of Acton and she had chosen to work in central London. I guessed (though I'd seen no details) that the costume she'd worn for the fateful picnic would probably have been planned in accordance with some fashion-book fantasy of what ladies might wear in the country rather than with a mind for practicality. And I imagined that Stella would have sat opposite her husband instead of beside him, with the picnic basket on the floor between them. Perhaps Carole's wistful, 'I would have married him,' and the implication that Stella had taken her suitor somewhat for granted had convinced me that the affection between the Wheelers had been rather greater on his side than hers.

And as for Wheeler, what had been in his mind as he journeyed to the furthest reaches of the Metropolitan Line? Murderous thoughts? Or perhaps, despite all the evidence to the contrary, he'd simply anticipated a picnic with his new bride, a pint or two in a country pub and a return in the late afternoon, refreshed and sunburnt, for a night of marital harmony – I shunned the word 'passion' as being too Ethel M. Dell – at home in Harrow and Wealdstone.

Unlike the other ladies on the train, I had to uphold the pretence that I was an articled clerk with a future before her, so somewhat self-consciously I opened my briefcase – inherited from father – and removed my notes from the day before. Perhaps I could use the fact that I had won Carole Mangan's trust to buy more time in Breen's employ. I had no idea how deeply I had hurt Breen but I imagined that he was the sort never to forget a slight. And because I felt unable to apologise I was in a double bind: I wanted to work for him but at what cost? Must it be always on his terms, regardless of any conflict with my conscience or the damage he might choose to inflict on my dignity as a lawyer?

The Lyons tea shop notes occupied me for a while but my mind kept straying to the previous night. It was almost as if Meredith had stage-managed the sequence of events: the child on the bottom stair, his head on my shoulder, her renewed request for money and the subsequent suggestion that she might leave. I couldn't possibly let Edmund go now he'd allowed me to put him to bed. And surely to do so would be a betrayal of James. My brother's torturous death was a raw wound still, the pain made more acute by the addition of one small detail, the scrap of paper unspeakably stained. What had it cost him, with his one good arm, to extract the paper and pencil from his pocket and scrawl her name? Only hers.

Later, when I reached the courthouse door, I expected the usual chilly reception from staff and fellow lawyers but instead an usher actually smiled. 'Miss Gifford, I presume? I have a message for you, ma'am. Mr Breen says if you would be so kind, could you join him downstairs in the cells?' At least this man was courteous as he led the way, although he was unable to resist a conspiratorial twinkle as if he were playing a parlour game.

Downstairs in the interview room I discovered that the firm of Breen & Balcombe had turned out in force, while a police officer stood in one corner, hands folded, staring straight ahead like a parody of himself. Breen was seated at one side of a small, square table, left arm hooked over the back of his chair as he gazed piercingly at Wheeler, whose head was again in his hands. He was wearing the jacket in which he'd been arrested and a clean shirt, presumably one collected by Breen during our trip to the house in Byron Street. Wolfe was note-taker. I had never seen him sit full-square on a chair; he always contrived to balance on one buttock with the other leg thrown across his thigh or extended before him, a posture which conveyed the message that while everyone else might be taking these proceedings seriously, he really could not. I imagined that he had been lolling thus on the fringe of events since he was at school.

When I was introduced by the usher, Wheeler made no move but Breen snapped to his feet and pulled out the fourth chair from the table while even Wolfe half rose and made a gesture, as if toasting me, with his pen.

'Miss Gifford,' said Breen, handing me into the chair with disturbing ceremony. 'Stephen, this is the third member of our firm, Miss Gifford. She will be working on this case alongside me. Miss Gifford, you should know that Mr Wheeler's recollection is now clear and that he denies the charge of murder.'

My heart pounded with relief. I was not to be dismissed or cold-shouldered then; in fact I was now to be included in the most exacting proceedings handled by Breen & Balcombe in living history. It was as if yesterday had been a triumph for me rather than a fiasco.

'So, Stephen, I'll ask you again, was there anyone else you can think of in Stella's life who could have had a motive for killing her?' Breen said.

Wheeler shook his close-cropped head, upon which the hair grew dense as fur.

'As far as you were concerned, on the morning of her murder everything was as usual between you?'

'Yes.'

'And I know you've told the police already, but when was the last time you saw the gun and the gloves?'

'They was in my shed. To be honest I'd forgotten they was there. I moved into the house in January, to get it ready for Stell, and I didn't really know what to do with all that military stuff.' Wheeler's voice was as dismal as his bearing and I doubted whether, even when times were good, he had spoken vigorously.

'Did Stella know about them?'

'Of course. I showed them to her when I took her round the

house after I moved in. That was the last time I seen them.'

'Stephen, I know this is a very personal question, but would you have said you and Stella were happy together?'

Breen spoke the word 'happy' tentatively, as if it were in slightly poor taste. By way of reply Wheeler huffed air through his nostrils and nodded three times, slowly. I thought I understood him well enough: since the start of war the notion of happiness had seemed a distant thing, like a flash of sunlight in a dark wood. But I could not help thinking that, even setting aside the ten days of imprisonment, accused of murder, Wheeler hardly cut a romantic figure, or one who was cut out to be a promising husband for a wayward girl-bride. His body was bulky and round-shouldered, his neck short and his face, though regular-featured, too fleshy to be striking. Hair grew thickly down past his wrists and up his throat and his left hand was badly disfigured, having lost all but the thumb and index finger.

'Miss Gifford, do you have any questions for Mr Wheeler?' asked Breen.

'I have one question.' My female voice must have struck a chord with Wheeler because he looked me full in the face for the first time, revealing eyes of a touchingly liquid grey. I drew a sharp breath because I was reminded suddenly of other eyes, as desolate as Wheeler's. James, towards the end of his last leave, had become increasingly detached, a-quiver, like an unshelled mollusc, with the anticipation of going back. 'Mr Wheeler, what did Stella do all day while you were at work?' I asked softly.

'Looked after the house. Did the shopping and washing and things like that. What else would she do?' It was clear that he hadn't liked the question and he stared at me defiantly.

'Mr Wolfe?' said Breen. 'Anything else?'

Wolfe, in between doodling in the margins, had been dashing down notes in handwriting that would later have Miss Drake tut-tutting as she attempted to type them up. 'The hat,' he said, in his asthmatic drawl, 'I think your wife was wearing a hat on the picnic?'

'Of course.'

'Did she wear a hat most of the time or was she inclined to take it off whenever she could?'

'She didn't like the sun on her face, if that's what you mean.'

'I believe her hat was found with the picnic basket. We've seen it in the box of exhibits.'

'I don't know what you're talking about.'

'I mean, when you left her to go off for a drink, do you recall whether or not she was wearing her hat?'

'She was lying in the shade. She had her hands on her chest and she was holding the hat between them.' Wheeler's mouth contorted at the memory and he bowed his head.

The hearing was due to begin in ten minutes so we shook Wheeler's too-soft hand and went upstairs to courtroom I, which was crowded with press and spectators amongst whom our arrival caused quite a stir. I found myself sandwiched between Breen and Wolfe and realised that a conversation must have taken place between them to ensure my inclusion and protection. Though I did not look directly to my left, I glimpsed a number of women's hats and realised that Wheeler's family was probably present, perhaps Stella's too. And then any further consideration of the Wheelers was pushed from of my head because I caught sight of the black-clad figure folded into a lawyer's bench behind me: Nicholas Thorne.

Before I could recover, Breen turned, gave him a nod then whispered to me, 'I understand you've met Thorne already. We've arranged a meeting after this hearing. Incidentally, Wheeler's boss, Thorne's prospective father-in-law, is also in court – over there to the left. Sir David Hardynge. It will do the case no harm if Imperial Insurance is prepared to supply Wheeler with a character reference. There's even talk of them paying his costs.'

After a decent interval I glanced across at the gentleman in the frock coat and pinstripes, very dapper with thick silvery hair and a glossy moustache meticulously combed, his fingers folded lightly over the handle of a cane. His bright, curious gaze was partially concealed by the thick lenses of his spectacles but as he glanced at the dock in anticipation of Wheeler's appearance, he caught my eye and gave me the brisk, appraising stare of a powerful man.

The court was ordered to rise and the bench of three magistrates entered, self-important with the prospect of dealing with a murder rather than the watering-down of milk by a local farmer, the next case on the list. Wheeler, handcuffed between two policemen, was led into the dock and there was a frisson among the observers, a scratching of pencils on paper as the press sprang into action. I heard a sob. When I glanced round again Wheeler's eyes were wet because he'd seen his family and Hardynge, who smiled with great kindness. I turned back hastily to avoid meeting Thorne's eye.

I was actually trembling, and the side of my body nearest him, which he might have reached out and touched, ached. In fact the entire proceedings were thrown into sharp relief by my disproportionate and ungovernable reaction to Thorne. I regarded the tragedy of Stella Wheeler and her workaday husband in the light of what was happening to me as I stood in front of Thorne, a man whom I had met only twice but who had the power to change the colour of the air.

Meanwhile the hearing proceeded. The defendant was identified as Stephen Anthony Wheeler, date of birth 12 September 1886, aged thirty-eight. The indictment was read out: that on 17 May 1924, at approximately three o'clock in the afternoon, the defendant Stephen Anthony Wheeler had, with malice aforethought, murdered his wife, Stella Jane Wheeler, formerly Hobhouse, by shooting her once in the breast with a single bullet, at close range, from his revolver.

Dead silence in the courtroom.

'Are we ready to take a plea, Mr Breen?'

'We are, Mr Clerk.'

'Stephen Anthony Wheeler, to the offence of murder with malice aforethought, do you plead guilty or not guilty?'

'Not guilty.' Another ripple of excitement as the legal machine rolled on. An early date was set for committal proceedings to the Aylesbury Assizes, and bail was refused. A woman sobbed in the public gallery. 'No, no, no,' she moaned, 'it can't be true.' In less than ten minutes the prisoner had been removed to the cells – he did not look again at the public gallery – and the hearing was over. There was a bustle in the courtroom as the spectators and press filed out. Thorne crossed to Hardynge's side, held open the door for him and they left the courtroom together.

'Very well,' said Breen. 'Divide and rule. Wolfe, you and Miss

Gifford are to speak to the Hobhouse clan; I'll deal with the Wheelers. And at eleven thirty we're to meet with Thorne in the King's Arms.'

Wolfe and I drew Stella's parents aside and interviewed them in a little room reserved for the use of victims. The mother, pale and tremulous, was slender, barely forty, with hair neatly cropped under a heavy hat. Her elegant mourning clothes showed considerable attention to detail: the gloves fastened from wrist to thumb with a dozen buttons; a handkerchief edged with black clasped in her fist and her slim shoes immaculately polished. The father was much less fine-featured, slight of build, and a chauffeur by profession. He turned his hat round and round and said that he might lose his job over all this, he'd already had three days off work, today was the fourth, and there was the funeral still to come.

Also present was a married daughter, Julie Leamington, who was three years older than Stella, and for the first time I glimpsed what the dead girl might have looked like. Julie was a dressmaker and, like her mother, impeccably turned out, though she had inherited her father's prominent nose, small mouth and wide-set pondering eyes so that her appearance, in the uncertain light of the witness room, was Madonna-like. She was very slender with a long, delicate neck and fine hands. Unlike her parents, who were so engrossed by their tragedy they seemed not to notice that I was a woman, Julie regarded me with considerable curiosity and suspicion.

Wolfe, who proceeded to impress me with his handling of the interview, did not act so much with tact as with the easy-going indifference of the well born. When offering his condolences his detachment contrived to be professional rather than offensive – I suspect he bestowed the same degree of sympathy on these parents bereft of a daughter as he might on a friend who'd lost a bet. The effect was to quell any potential outbursts of emotion, at least at first. His frame was comfortingly large, his smile amiable, though at the same time it managed to convey that he was communicating with the Hobhouse family across a considerable social divide.

'I expect the police have been asking you all sorts,' he said.

They nodded.

'You must feel utterly bemused by it all, as are we. But we need to get the bottom of this case so we can account for the dreadful thing that happened to your daughter. So if you don't mind, we'll try to put a few pieces of the jigsaw in place. Is that all right?' They nodded again. 'Very well, can we just clarify one or two things. I think Mr Wheeler rolled up at your place on the Saturday night? How did he seem to you?'

Mrs Hobhouse pressed her handkerchief to her mouth and spoke through the cloth. 'We welcomed him. I can't bear to think of it. We could tell he was out of sorts. Panting, you know, flushed after his bicycle ride. We wondered afterwards if he was the worse for drink. Turns out he'd come to us fresh from murdering our child.'

My pitying respect for Mrs Hobhouse was growing by the minute. I saw her as a woman jolted out of a quiet existence by this violent event, but determined to play her part well. Her bearing suggested a conscious desire to be dignified in her grief, as if she was an actress thrust before an audience despite being somewhat unsure of her lines.

'Mr Wheeler denies that he killed her, Mrs Hobhouse,' said Wolfe. 'We mustn't lose sight of that. I was wondering, is there anything more you could tell us about Stella, the type of girl she was?'

Hobhouse, who I had decided was the weaker partner, spoke emphatically. 'She were a lovely girl. Quiet. Worked hard at that restaurant of hers. Loved to dance. Couldn't wait to be married.'

'She was a child, I believe, when she first knew Stephen.'

'He used to come over and play with her when she was no more than a babe,' said Mrs Hobhouse, 'take her for rides in a go-cart, which was a thing she loved. Our families were bound up together through church connections. Stephen adored our Stell. He wrote to her all through the war. I didn't think it was right, her being so young, but it was wartime so I hadn't the heart to stop her sending letters back. And she stayed loyal to him afterwards, even though I always thought she could have done better. She had several admirers – not all of them fit for marriage, it's true, but she didn't need to marry *him*. She wasn't desperate.'

'Any admirer in particular?'

'None special, as I told the police.'

'Do you think Stella was happy?'

'Happy? In what way?'

'Her choice, you know, her marriage.'

'Oh, she was happy enough. Our Stell was the type of girl who had to be wed. She was restless at home. I just wanted her to be sure in her own mind. I asked her a few times, the last was on the night before her wedding. I said, "Are you sure, Stell?" and she was cross with me, she said what did I think she was putting us to all that trouble and expense for, if she wasn't sure? She was very fierce when she'd fixed her mind on something.'

'Mrs Hobhouse, the way you're talking makes me think you had your doubts about the wisdom of your daughter's marriage?'

'I thought she was very young and he was quite old by comparison, but she had set her heart on it and that was that.'

'She was lucky to have him,' the sister said suddenly. An odd remark, I thought – though the waitress Carole Mangan had said much the same – given that Stella was now dead, apparently by her husband's hand. 'At least he was alive with only three fingers missing. Had the luck of the devil in that war, he did. I lost first one fiancé then another.'

'You're happy enough with Michael though, aren't you, Julie?' said her mother.

'He wasn't my first choice.'

I noticed that Julie was resting her palm on her stomach and wondered if she was expecting a child.

'Yes, but Michael isn't moody like Stephen was,' said Mrs Hobhouse. 'Stephen did have awfully bad moods.'

There was a pause.

'That's frightfully interesting, Mrs Hobhouse,' said Wolfe, examining his nib. 'Mr Wheeler was moody, you say?'

'Only since the war and very rarely even then. He was the sweetest-natured boy before that. Far too soft for our Stell, I sometimes thought. She was a girl who needed keeping in line. But I do blame the war for the fact he got very low from time to time, our Stell said. I believe he could have opted for home duties, you know, after he was gassed, but no, he would go back. I used to think they should pass a law that took a man out of the trenches once he'd survived for a couple of years.'

'What form did his moods take?' Wolfe asked.

'Oh you mustn't make so much of a small thing,' cried the mother. 'The fact is he killed our Stell. And that's not what you do when you get low, is it? Just because he went quiet sometimes doesn't give him an excuse to kill her.'

'What about finances? Do you think the couple had any money worries?'

'I doubt it. They were short, of course, but Stephen was very careful with his money. It's one of the reasons it took him so long to marry her – he was saving up.'

'Mrs Hobhouse,' I said, 'could you tell us when you last saw Stella?'

Tears spilled down her cheeks. 'She came for tea and to fetch the picnic basket the week before she died. She was excited about the picnic, poor soul. I offered to go over to hers and help her get the house nice but she didn't seem to want that. She said she'd like to come home and go upstairs to her room and look at her old things, and I thought, Why not? After all she's still a child.'

'What kind of things did she keep in her room?'

'Oh you know. Dolls. Old clothes. We never got round to clearing it after she was married. We didn't have time.'

'Would you mind,' I asked, 'if I came and had a look at her bedroom some time?' The mother nodded. 'I went to see where Stella worked, you know, at Lyons. Apparently she had a wonderful record, never ill, never late. You must have been proud of her.'

'She was a very good girl. But we brought up both the girls to be hard workers.'

'Good job,' said Julie sullenly. 'Looks like I'll be slaving away till the end of my days. *He'll* never get off his backside and find work.'

'Julie,' said her mother sharply.

'I talked to Stella's friend at work and she told me Stella had hardly been late once in all the years she'd worked there,' I said. 'That's an outstanding record.'

'Oh I should think that's an exaggeration,' said Mr Hobhouse. 'The buses and trams aren't that reliable. You was always shouting at her to get up in the morning,' he reminded his wife.

'She was a very good girl,' insisted the mother. 'I always knew where I was with Stell.'

'Come off it, mum,' said Julie. 'She was no saint. What about the night when she never came back at all because she'd missed the last train? Dancing down the Trocadero with her friends from work, she was. You were worried sick.'

'When was that, I wonder?' asked Wolfe, adding tiny leaves to a drawing of a weeping willow.

'Lord, I can't remember. Some time in April, a couple of weeks before she were married.'

'Was Stephen with her?'

'Not that I know of. She was out dancing, is all, having a last fling. He knew she loved dancing. He liked to watch her when they were some place together, being flat-footed himself.'

'Stell said not to tell him when she went down to the Trocadero,' said Julie. 'She knew he'd get into one of his states. He didn't like her going down there.'

Now that the Hobhouses' hitherto united front had fractured, the atmosphere in the room grew sour. Nevertheless, their acquiescence thus far had surprised me. I tried to imagine how we would have reacted, a few days after the news of James's death, had we been confronted by a barrage of questions from those trying to exonerate the German who had fired the shell. The Hobhouse family had responded meekly to our probing, I guessed, because they had been schooled all their lives to do as they were told by professional people.

Half an hour later the firm of Breen & Balcombe met Nicholas Thorne over morning coffee in an upstairs private room at the King's Arms, where Thorne achieved the difficult balancing act of showing deference to Breen's reputation and experience whilst not in any way diminishing his own status. Nor did he reveal that he and I had parted on a strained note the previous week, and I was conscious that a bond was created between us by the very fact that we chose not to share details of our meeting with the others. He sat in an easy chair, legs stretched before him, a diminutive coffee cup and saucer in his hand, indulging with Wolfe in the kind of male joshing that never failed to annoy me. In a rapid exchange, they established a network of common experience and acquaintance. Radley, was it? Ah no, Rugby man myself. Then Christ Church. Did you know Saint, Rentoul, Marshall Hall? Either Wolfe or Thorne had dined with the first, scouted for another, knew a friend of a friend whose sister had married a second cousin of the third. Their talk then drifted on again. Poor old Jeffries . . . Colossal promise, brilliant career ahead of him . . . Last days of the war . . . The brother survived. Not half so sharp . . .

Breen was between them, spaniel-like, smiling his grammar-school-boy smile as famous legal names were tossed about as easily as bonbons. I, on the other hand, sipped my tepid coffee and tried to assume an expression of tolerant disdain. My heart told me Thorne was perfect; my head already knew that he was not. What a shame to find him guilty of being so tediously true to type.

Even so, he moved me so that the air around him seemed to oscillate with colour like a shattered rainbow. Surely I was not so shallow as to be stirred by spotless cuffs, knife-sharp creases or fineness of cloth? So what was it? Perhaps he reminded me a little of the dead boys I had known, my brother and his friends, Peter Shaw who had kissed me under the canal bridge. Like them Thorne bore himself eagerly, as one anticipating an ever more interesting future. Like them he had a boyish laugh and the ability to switch moods from banal to solemn in a flash. He was undoubtedly the most beautiful man I had seen in years, not so much for the regularity of his features and the cleanness of his limbs as for the openness of his gaze, his slow but momentous smile, the particular tilt of his head when he was listening. And I loved to hear his voice, which was clipped, bright and full of easy laughter. I wondered what kind of war he'd had, that it could have left him apparently so unscathed.

'To business,' he said at last, drawing himself upright and unaccountably managing to wrong-foot us, as if only we had been indulging in idle chat whilst Wheeler suffered.

'Sir David has decided that Imperial Insurance will fund Wheeler's defence, he's very cut up over this case, thinks the least we can do is make sure we get the very best man for the job. Wheeler has been with the company since he was sixteen – his position was kept open during the war, of course. Had it not been for the slight conflict of interest I might have worked on the case myself.' His smile was self-deprecating but we were left in little doubt that his days of working on briefs in a junior capacity were all but over. 'We are somewhat embarrassed by the police assumption that the motive was an insurance claim and find it hard to believe Wheeler would be so misguided as to think he could get away with it. After all he, more than any man on earth, will have been very clear about the terms and conditions under which life insurance is bought – he will have explained them himself to numerous clients. But one way or another, under the circumstances I can only help and advise, and perhaps suggest whom we might instruct. Marshall Hall would have been ideal but he's taking on less work these days. There's Burton Wainwright.'

'Could we afford him?' Breen asked.

'Money is not at issue here. We want to do the right thing by Wheeler.'

'Then Wainwright would certainly have my confidence,' said Breen. 'You'll be aware that the evidence against Wheeler is very strong except for the matter of a plausible motive. I would like to believe he's innocent but at present there is not a single scrap of evidence to suggest another culprit. We are therefore pursuing a parallel line of defence, at least for the time being: that Wheeler is not in his right mind, whether or not he committed the murder. Had he maintained his silence I would have gone for a fitness-to-plead hearing but he now speaks very coherently indeed. The fact remains that Wheeler served nearly four years in the trenches, the crime is insanely unsubtle and his response when arrested was that of a broken-spirited and bewildered man. Burton Wainwright has, I believe, dealt with other such cases and would therefore be an excellent choice.'

'Stella's family told us that Wheeler has been moody since the war, something Miss Gifford's waitress at Lyons mentioned too,' said Wolfe. 'Breen, you spoke to the Wheeler clan. What had they to say on the subject?'

'That he was often withdrawn, not himself.'

'Any money problems?'

'They thought not. But he had a terrible war. Refused to rest, even when he was offered the chance. Saw countless slaughtered. Was finally sent home with half a hand missing just months before the ceasefire. Who would not be damaged by such experiences?'

'Who indeed?' said Thorne. 'But I'm afraid the counter-argument to shell shock as mitigation is very powerful. The prosecutor will ask where would we be if every ex-soldier whose nerves had been shot to pieces took to killing his wife?'

'And the murder was hardly unpremeditated,' I said, and found myself abruptly the centre of attention.

'That doesn't mean a thing,' said Breen. 'The mad have their own logic.'

'It seems to me,' I added, 'that his plan was both ridiculously ill-conceived and meticulously well worked out. If Wheeler really killed his wife and hoped to get away with it, why did he hide the gun and gloves next to her body? And why didn't he take the opportunity to bury her properly, given that he had most of the weekend? Besides . . .'

'Besides?' Breen prompted.

'Besides, Wheeler says he didn't kill his wife, and I believe him,' I said.

'What makes him different to every other murderer who pleads not guilty in our courts?'

'He was trusted. I met a friend of Stella's who knew him quite well, and today her sister – they both trusted Wheeler.'

Thorne smiled. 'I'm afraid most murderers are trusted by those who know them well.'

I could scarcely add: And I would defend Wheeler with the last atom of my being because he reminds me of James, not for his appearance or demeanour of course; Wheeler was nothing like my slender, straight-backed brother. It was the way the war had swallowed these hopeful young men and spat them out as strangers. I remembered the soiled scrap of paper upon which James had scrawled Meredith's name. He had marched to war one person and died another, just as Stephen Wheeler had returned moody and sorrowful, and was now engulfed in this new tragedy. In my book, he should be cherished and protected if for no other reason than that he had been treated with such abject lack of humanity in the past. 'If he'd done it,' I said weakly, 'I think Wheeler would not lie about it.'

Breen said with surprising warmth, 'Well, Miss Gifford, you

have the makings of an excellent defence lawyer. You speak of our client's innocence with conviction, which is exactly what we need.'

All this time I'd barely looked at Thorne, but as we prepared to leave that small upper room where the smell of spilled beer and old cigar smoke lingered in the dust, Breen said, 'I was wondering, Miss Gifford, if we might instruct Thorne on the Leah Marchant appeal. It's up to you, of course. I wouldn't dream of interfering but it seems a good opportunity to me. I have to watch my step with Miss Gifford,' he added to Thorne. 'She can be very fierce.'

'I'm well aware.' Thorne shook my hand and looked directly into my eyes. In the street below two dogs were rivalling each other in barks. A window was open behind him and a patch of sunlight fell, a parallelogram, onto the intricate pattern of the rug. It seemed to me I could smell that sunbeam, a hint of bonfire.

'Drop me a note at my chambers,' he said, 'if you so wish.' Then he released my hand and gave me his card.

I picked up my father's briefcase, passed through the low doorway ahead of him and went down the crooked stairs to the public bar. 'I saw Thorndike's *St Joan*,' he said as we emerged onto the street. 'Did you, by any chance?'

I nodded. He smiled. 'I thought you would have done.'

'We're off to visit the crime scene, Thorne,' called Wolfe. 'Care to join us? We could just about squeeze you in.'

He laughed. 'Thanks. I'll have to give it a miss. Con at two.'

And I tried to dislike him again, for being so busy, for using the slang of his chambers to such crushingly exclusive effect. But with what terrifying speed he was becoming enmeshed in my life, and at what risk to my equilibrium? I did not watch his departing form as he strode off towards the station; instead I turned resolutely away and threw back my head, pretending to crave the sun.

Chapter Fourteen

Wolfe's blue Austin tourer lurched and spluttered jauntily along the Chesham Road. Breen sat in the front with his hat off, his hair like a dandelion clock round his bald patch, while I twisted sideways in the back seat to accommodate my legs and prayed that the journey would not last long enough to make me sick. My eyes were alternately blinded and dazzled as we flashed in and out of dense shade, first deep woodland then high hedgerows. Due to the engine noise I couldn't participate in conversation so I was mercifully free to pursue my own thoughts.

I was lecturing myself. You have seen Nicholas Thorne three times, Evelyn. You know him to be arrogant, ambitious and engaged to an heiress. Do not behave like a lovesick girl. Put him out of your head at once. And so he was in my mind all the way to Chesham as I relived the walk on sun-baked cobbles from Toynbee Hall to the tea room, the way he had swung my father's briefcase back and forth, the competence of his hands among the teacups, his voice today in the upstairs room, gentle, cultured, full of laughter.

He was still with me as the car jolted to a halt by a wall near the church, where a policeman, detailed to accompany us to the crime scene, was waiting in the shade of the lychgate. As we followed the track through the churchyard and on up the hill, Thorne was at my shoulder. Breen, in his element, took off his jacket and walked in his shirtsleeves with his waistcoat undone and his striped braces exposed. Wolfe, far less fit, panted behind us complaining of the seed heads, pollen, wild flowers, the *smell*, all sure to lay him low. And ahead of us ambled the policeman, heavy hipped in his sweltering uniform.

It was a near-perfect day – a light breeze, a few puffs of cloud, the track shaded – only the company was wrong. The air was filled with birdsong and the whirr of insects. Cow parsley and ragwort clustered in the hedgerows, and cattle dozed in a field nearby. We came to a stile by a copse and beyond it a gap in the hedge and on the other side an uncut meadow dense with colour. Prudence could have named every flower but I was only able to identify campion with some misgivings, poppies with certainty.

Near the hedge out of sight of the path a square-ish patch of grass had been trampled down. 'This is where the picnic was held,' said the policeman, 'according to our man Wheeler, although by the time we comes up here on Sunday morning, he's removed all the evidence and taken it home so we have only his word for it. It's true the grass was crushed and my colleague found a bit of gristle that might have been corned beef, but that's all we got.'

It was a dreamy, isolated spot, only twenty minutes' walk from the town yet absolutely cut off from it. The Wheelers could have got up to anything here but I imagined a languid Stella lying back on her elbows and telling her husband to keep off – someone might come along.

'The poor young girl was wearing pink,' said the constable, who had been present when they'd retrieved the body.

What had she been feeling? Restless, bored, sleepy? And Stephen, according to his own version of events, would have been aching for a pint whilst trying to entertain his flighty young bride with his plodding conversation. Or was his heart pounding and his hands shaking because of what he had in mind?

'Of course she weren't shot here,' said the policeman. 'That much we do know, even though he denies until he's blue in the face knowing of the place where she was buried or how to get there from here. We think they must have walked half a mile or so to them woods across the valley.'

'Only one witness has come forward who saw them making their way up the hill from Chesham at twelve,' said Breen. 'Isn't that extraordinary? We're within a stone's throw of the town.'

'You could spend hours out here and never see a soul, especially at weekends,' the policeman said. 'I can take you to where she was shot and buried, if you like. Shouldn't be more than half an hour or so, there and back.'

Wolfe said he would wait for us in his automobile on account of his asthma, then the constable went ahead as before, followed by Breen and finally me. The path sloped quite steeply down to a dry valley and up the other side so that the view was constantly changing. Meredith would have dubbed the countryside quintessentially English; that is well managed, its wildness confined to patches. We walked in silence for a while, as if out of respect for Stella, who had been a few minutes from death as she swished through these grasses. But with Breen ahead of me and not a word said about our argument after the Leah Marchant hearing I could not be quiet for long. 'Mr Breen, yesterday I was hasty. I—'

He gave a bark of laughter and put up his hand to silence me. 'I knew that would be on your mind, Miss Gifford. Never undermine a good argument by backtracking. You were right and you know it, at least on the question of my intervention over the appeal. Learn to stand your ground without self-recrimination.'

On we went along the side of the hill with a cluster of farm buildings ahead and a soft breeze funnelling down the valley.

Nothing else was said, but I smiled at the back of Breen's head and loved him.

'We think this is the way they must have come,' said the policeman as we approached a coppice. 'It's the most direct, though again we've found no evidence. But there's a number of routes Wheeler could have taken, once he'd killed her, to cut back to the picnic spot and then on down to the town. We think he must have done it before he had his drink – there was no sign of a revolver in the pub and why would any girl hang about for an hour or more on a hillside waiting for her husband to drag her further away from town and shoot her? Which means he was sitting in the Queen's Head, supping his pint in full view of other customers, even though he'd just killed his wife. See, there's a matter of nearly three hours between when they were sighted walking up to the picnic spot and when Wheeler had his pint. Definitely time for all kinds of murders to be committed. And of course Wheeler knew this area well, on account of his being a bit of a fisherman and coming out here to fish in the Chess since he were a young boy. It goes without saying, by the way, that neither the Wheelers nor the woman who found the body come to that, should have been in these woods, strictly speaking. They're private.'

Stella had been discovered deep inside a pheasant covert with a picket fence surrounding it to contain the birds. The gate had been padlocked by the police. Inside, the woods were cool and dim, the tracks thick with leaf mould and quiet except for the pheasants who occasionally clattered shockingly among the trees. We came to a clearing pungent with the smell of cut bracken where there were signs of heavy-booted trampling.

The policeman spoke lower and lower as we drew closer to where Stella had been found: 'We think it's likely he prepared the ground in advance. Shallow as it was, two feet, if that, the grave was a neat affair, probably all ready and waiting for her.'

What had induced Stella to enter these woods? I felt a soft lurch, as if a bird had taken flight within me, because I thought it could only have been sex. There will be shadows, she must have been told, and a bed among the bracken. No one will see us, only the pheasants. Perhaps she had lain down willingly on her green mattress, all unknowing of the fact that a few feet away a trench had been dug to receive her body. And perhaps, after the shot had been fired, she had time to stare up through a blood-red haze to the glittering leaf canopy and to hear, after the affront of gunfire, the hush of the breeze through young birch leaves. Perhaps she had thought of the old days in the tea shop with its menu cards and tin trays and hideous caps as her memories unwound from their spool until she was a child again in Acton. Perhaps, if I stared hard enough, I might see a trace of her, a wisp of Stella Wheeler. But no, there was nothing.

My father and I visited my brother's grave in 1921, on Valentine's Day. As we approached the graveyard near Arras the sun came out so that the landscape, which had hitherto been shades of grey, as in all the photographs, was tinged with pale green and yellow. New buds simmered beneath the surface of bare twigs. At first we saw farmland and villages clustered round unbroken churches but gradually the landscape sickened: no hedges or trees, the ground pitted and deeply furrowed though furred with early spring growth. Rusty heaps of metal and wire littered the edge of the road. Houses were under construction amidst heaps of rubble.

We were members of a group of mourners invited by the regiment, who deemed the graveyard just about fit to be visited, though only temporary wooden markers had been placed at the heads of the graves and the entire field, as far as the eye could see, was criss-crossed by duckboards. Once there, father and I walked in single file. Throughout the journey I had avoided touching him because I knew that instead of comforting me he would expose me to his grief, obscenely raw so that his face had become a mask of suffering and his eyes refused to recognise me. He repeated, 'My son, my son, my son,' as if he were in a movie and the subtitles had to be kept simple.

As I studied the impossible field of graves, I could not fathom that each represented a man or that a place so orderly had been the scene of thousands of violent deaths. The symmetry of it made me recoil. How dare you take more care of the dead, I thought, than of the living? I despised the soldiers who accompanied us and even the men who lay dead under earth. It is men, I thought, with their unassailable conviction that half the population is more stupid than they are, who have done this.

Stretching out my gloved hands to the sunshine, I tried to reach my brother, who was lying under the soil of this plot 386 and who had died, we were assured, only yards from here. Of course I wanted to know details. Where exactly had he climbed from the trench? What about the boy stranded in no-man's-land, where would that have been? The officer, embarrassed, answered vaguely and edged away. So the only true image I had was the mud. The duckboards lay over acres of mud. One of our party lost his footing, floundered and only by grasping another man's arm was he able to drag his foot free. I realised then that we had sent my brother to live and die in mud, like an animal.

Still, I thought, I must surely be able to pass through time to him, that it was only time, that wretchedly impenetrable fourth dimension, that held me back because here I was on the very spot where he had last been alive. But he seemed further from me than ever in that French place, on French farmland, a few feet under the newly sown lawn of the cemetery. I had no sense of him at all as I looked at his name on the plaque: LIEUTENANT JAMES

CARTWRIGHT GIFFORD, 13642, 15TH LONDON REGIMENT, or the date relating to his curtailed life: 20 NOVEMBER 1917, AGED 20. These digits had nothing to do with him.

But later we passed out of the temporary gate, walked down a lane edged on either side with broken ditches and came to the remnants of a stone barn with walls three feet thick that must have stood for centuries before it was mown down in an hour by shell and rocket fire. Only a corner was left, but a resourceful farmer was once more using the building for straw and had rigged a tarpaulin to protect it from the rain. I felt a little consoled, to see the building thus reclaimed for its proper use.

And I knew, as I laid my hand on the stone and closed my eyes to the glare of the low sun, that my brother had sheltered here. I felt it as a shock to the arm. Meanwhile father walked on, all unknowing, absorbed in the dead and regardless of me, his living girl.

Chapter Fifteen

That evening I was again greeted by music on my return to Clivedon Hall Gardens and the entrance hall was an altogether unfamiliar place. Sunlight had got in through the open door of the drawing room and I saw our commonplace red tiles as colour traps, their little yellow scrolls like tender signatures. The smell of cake-baking wafted from the kitchen so that it was as if the house had been sprayed with an essence called Home. Meredith was throwing a birthday party for Prudence.

'My goodness,' she had cried, 'don't tell me you never even celebrate birthdays properly in this house? We can't have that, can we, Edmund? Edmund and I are very fond of birthdays. In fact we are experts at birthdays. You shall have a party, Prudence, whether you like it or not.'

Normally birthdays in Clivedon Hall Gardens were marked by the opening of cards at breakfast and presents after dinner. Before the meal we drank a small glass of sherry. We called our gifts 'tokens'. I had bought a posy of anemones for Prudence from a florist near the station and a pin cushion with felt petals, like a rose, from a shop in Amersham. Neither of these offerings seemed sufficiently open-handed in the light of Meredith's celebration.

In the first place Rose had been induced to bake a special cake, which was now being served in the drawing room even though it was six o'clock and barely an hour before supper, thereby putting everyone's – but especially Edmund's – appetite at risk. The surface was bedecked with shop-bought flowers, roses and freesias spilling out of vases and nodding in the breeze from the open French window. There was – surely not – champagne – and there were candles on the cake. 'Just five, Prudence, I'm guessing one per decade?' Prudence, flattered despite herself, put her hand to her breast and tried to look fifty.

Meanwhile Marcia Freer and Henry Burr crooned 'What'll I Do' from the gramophone. Prudence's cheeks were very pink, but then she'd spent the day in Buckinghamshire and had caught the sun whilst in the garden of her friend Miss Lord, who had provided a generous lunch consisting of chicken in some kind of jelly and shaped into a loaf ('It sounds very unusual but I can assure you it was delicious. Miss Lord's girl is a very imaginative cook') and strawberries. All four of Prudence's intimate circle had been present and emphasised, as always, that their lives just weren't the same without her.

So perhaps she was mellower than usual because she'd had a dose of church gossip – the organist was the chief concern, being too arthritic to hit all the right notes, which was particularly distressing at funerals. Furthermore Prudence had taken the opportunity to visit her old cottage, though here a slight shadow had been cast. The current tenants were keen to keep the cottage on but had travelled to Scotland for the summer, which meant that the rooms were vulnerable to damp. 'Miss Lord says she will go in to air it regularly but I feel it's a great imposition.'

Or perhaps Prudence was rosy-cheeked because even she could not resist the pleasures of a party despite the fact that Rose had been exceptionally heavy-handed with the cochineal in icing the cake, which was now the colour of beetroot stain. Prudence took a delicate sip of wine before turning to the small pile of presents, which included one from Miss Lord, *The Essays of Elia*, bound in calfskin and rewrapped in its tissue paper so that Prudence could have the pleasure of opening it again in front of us.

Mother was wearing her second-best blouse and attempting to participate whole-heartedly in the festivities although I could tell from her frequent glances at the flowers that she was wondering how on earth all this had been paid for. She took angry little sips of champagne as if by drinking it faster she would make it cost less. Fortunately I provided an outlet for her irritation. 'What's that dirt on the hem of your skirt, Evelyn? Could you not make some small effort?'

I fled to my room, threw off my work clothes and stood for a moment in a slip as the draught from the open window soothed my skin. Then I dressed in my one summer frock, bought a year ago – in unexceptional cotton voile with what mother had declared a *hideous* line; it had a broad sash tied at the hip and a pleated skirt. Glancing in the mirror I thought of Nicholas Thorne as he stood on the pavement and asked me about *Saint Joan*. Of course now I scrutinised my reflection for signs that I was like her, or her theatrical representation, because surely that had been his message? I too had caught the sun even though I'd worn a hat, and my eyes were unusually bright. But perhaps Thorne, noticing what James used to call my furious jaw, saw me as a fanatical trail-blazer rather than a passionate, utterly compelling girl-saint.

I smiled at myself and there I was, simply a woman who was no longer young enough in a pale frock, with a touch of wistful excitement in her eyes. God help me.

'At last,' said Meredith when I reappeared downstairs. 'Now the party can begin.'

We sang 'Happy Birthday' lustily, especially grandmother, who was tone deaf, and Edmund, who had an enthusiastic treble. Then Prudence blew out all five candles with one breath.

'Did you wish?' cried Meredith.

'Of course.' What would Prudence have wished for? A return to her cottage, money, a man (even this might be possible to a devotee of Ethel M.), a resolution to the Meredith problem?

Then the presents were opened. Mother had bought a novel by Dorothy L. Sayers entitled *Whose Body?* which Prudence set aside hastily because she was not used to murder stories and was probably unsure whether they should be cast in the forbidden category of light fiction. My pin cushion was received with restrained enthusiasm. Grandmother had crocheted a set of mats for Prudence's dressing table – I seemed to remember a similar gift being offered the previous year – and Edmund's present was also home-made, a representation of Aunt Prudence herself with stuck-on buttons for eyes and nose, one of which fell off as Prudence presented the picture to us for inspection. Fortunately Prudence's good manners did not fail and she thanked him gravely.

'And now mine,' said Meredith, 'also artistic, I'm afraid. Like mother, like son.' And she presented a scroll tied with a blue ribbon. Having unfurled it, Prudence rotated it a couple of times then held it at arm's length and squinted before turning it outwards to us so that we could all see. It was a piece of stiffened fabric with unbound edges, linen perhaps, painted with an abstract design in strong shades of red, orange and brown: spots, zigzags and stripes which contrived to form some kind of unified whole that could, by a stretch of the imagination, be a face framed by symmetrical locks of hair, or perhaps it was something else entirely, a crest of some kind or nothing at all.

'I found it in a market,' said Meredith. 'Don't you think it's stunning? I believe it's from Guiana. Whatever, it's a completely original design. I thought it would be perfect in your room.'

Prudence's bedroom in Clivedon Hall Gardens was as near a reproduction as she could manage of her old room at the cottage: sprigged wallpaper and white-work cloths. The picture rails were hung with a cross-stitch design behind glass depicting a cottage garden, a couple of faded photographs of our stiffly Victorian Gifford forebears and a reproduction of Constable's *The Haywain*. This new work of art, if such it was, would be glaringly out of place.

'Let me see,' said grandmother, removing her spectacles and holding the fabric half an inch from her eyeballs. 'Oh, the beautiful colours. And what a clear pattern.'

Prudence and mother were in agreement on the subject of modern art. In order to qualify, a great painting had to be representational and worked with invisible brushstrokes. Ideally a moral should be drawn from it, which made Holman Hunt's *The Light of the World* probably the most perfect picture in existence. Modern art was therefore summarily dismissed as lacking in skill and crude, the latter being a heinous crime only surpassed by lateness and blasphemy. However, this was her birthday; Meredith had given her a present (I think Prudence shared my suspicion that the gift had been chosen to perplex rather than please); and she must be thanked.

'And will you put it up in your room?' demanded Meredith with the eagerness of a child. 'Do you have a frame?'

'Perhaps I shall find one among some of my stored items in the attic,' said Prudence, setting the fabric aside. But she could not quite leave it alone, and I saw her glance at it again and even stroke it while we waited for the dinner gong. Her head tilted and her lips pursed as she tried to decide whether or not she was being duped. When we filed into the dining room – mother firmly gripping the half-full champagne bottle in case the girls got hold of it – Prudence left the painting behind on the arm of her chair but then, as we crossed the hall, she went back to fetch it, saying that if we didn't mind she would hang it over the edge of the sideboard so that she could look at it during the meal.

'When is the next birthday?' asked Edmund, who was excused soup these days. 'Mine's on July the thirty-first.'

'And after that it will be Evelyn's, on August the fourteenth,' said mother, who had recklessly poured another glass for herself and Prudence but just a thimbleful for grandmother, Meredith and me as if we were all underage.

'And how old will she be?' Edmund asked.

'Goodness,' said Prudence. 'We never ask a lady her age.'

'I shall be thirty-one,' I said.

There was a painful silence. 'That means you're older than mommy,' he said.

'But only by two years,' added Meredith. 'And the thing about Evelyn is that she has crammed so much into her life already.'

Mother, at the end of the table, finished her soup and Min came forward to remove the bowls. We were in dangerous territory, so I waded in to change the subject. 'You'll never guess where I've been today.'

'Oh good Lord, I forgot. You've been to the murder scene. How fascinating,' cried Meredith.

'We won't want to hear about it at table, I think,' said mother, wiping her mouth.

The silence was filled by grandmother. 'By the time I was thirty I had finished with the stage and was expecting you,' she told mother.

'That's it,' said Meredith. 'This room is filled with exceptional women. I am in awe of you all.' Nobody else seemed to notice the irony of this remark being made by a woman who had crossed the Atlantic to nurse behind the front lines and who had conceived a child out of wedlock.

'I've always missed it,' said grandmother. 'There's nothing quite like the fear of that curtain going up and having to encounter the dark space on the other side. Now that's what I call being alive, a lit stage and an audience in darkness. One is so aware of oneself, quivering in the footlights, and nothing else matters except that first word, which will decide the fate of actor and audience. I was someone who always had to be in the light.'

'Which was your favourite part, would you say?' Meredith asked.

'That would be Nora in *The Doll's House*, which I played in Manchester.'

'And you wore such stunning costumes. Edmund loves the picture of you as Titania ...'

'It was a very long time ago,' said mother. 'Why bring up the past? You have not acted in years, mother.' Tears were brimming and she put her hand to her head and pushed back her chair. 'I'm so sorry, Prudence, on your birthday ... My head. It's the heat. Forgive me.' Then she was gone from the room and we heard the rush of her feet on the stairs.

Edmund was wide-eyed for a moment but soon tucked into his mashed potato. Meanwhile Meredith said, 'Prudence and I are off to the Tate Gallery tomorrow. While you were upstairs getting changed, Evelyn, I made her promise to come. It's such a pity you're not free too.'

'I've never been to the Tate,' said Prudence. 'One ought to make the most of being in London.'

'Of course it's work for me,' said Meredith. 'I have to prepare for my next class with Hadley Waters and at the moment there's no plumbing the depths of my ignorance.'

'I don't expect I shall like everything in it,' said Prudence, 'but one has to keep an open mind.'

Suddenly, across the table, I met Meredith's eyes and I was eleven again, sitting at the back of the class with my best friend Margaret Bagshott, struck by an agonising fit of the giggles. Meredith and I tried to suppress our laughter; we put our hands to our mouths and dabbed away our tears while Prudence looked from one to the other of us, smiling uncertainly. 'What have I said?'

Mother was not laughing when I went upstairs half an hour later; she was at her dressing table, still with tears in her eyes. Despite the season, the windows were shut tight, the curtains drawn, the lamps lit and there was a leather-bound album open on her lap containing photographs of James and myself as children – solemn figures in intricate clothes posed in the garden or a studio, the arm of the lanky girl invariably flung round the neck of her sturdy little brother. In one James sat on my knee, his legs so short that they stuck out dead straight, a coil of my hair falling onto his fist. He stared as if mesmerised into the camera. I was watching him.

Keeping my distance, I perched on the edge of the bed and said briskly, 'It was so good of Meredith to arrange a party.'

'You know I can't stand birthdays. I cannot bear to count the passing years. Evelyn, it's for your sake I feel so unhappy tonight.'

'Oh mother.' I took her cold hand and squeezed it. 'Don't be unhappy on my account.'

'You have missed out on so much. I do wish you'd marry.'

She could have no idea how that night especially her lament touched a raw nerve. Springing to my feet I said abruptly, 'On the other hand, I have had a fascinating day, one such as few women, I think, have ever experienced. If I had a husband to care for and a clutch of babies I doubt if such a day would have been possible.'

She put aside the album and turned on me with equal force, very pale but with a gleam in her eye that may have been due to the unaccustomed champagne. 'I don't want to hear any more about your grubby life. You are wilful and cruel because you insist on talking about your work all the time, even though you know I can't bear it. You have abandoned me. My life is in ruins and you will not help me.'

'What could I do to help, mother?'

'You could be *here*. You could try to behave like a proper daughter. You could save me from having to deal with that terrible woman, day in day out.'

'At least I shall soon be earning money.'

'I would sacrifice the money tomorrow if it meant I wouldn't be so alone.'

'You have Prudence. You have grandmother and the girls, and

your bridge parties. Now you even have a grandchild, Edmund. You are better off than most when it comes to company.'

'I didn't choose any of this. My life is nothing compared to what it used to be before the war. Can't you see? All this has been thrust upon me against my wishes. And all that I loved, all that I strived for, has been torn from me. Oh, if only James had lived . . . Instead he ruined everything.'

'What do you mean, he ruined everything? Mother, he was killed; he could hardly help that.'

She shot me a strange look, half-angry, half-frightened, then seemed to recover herself a little. 'Of course. What I mean is – I can't help it, Evelyn – I sometimes think you have taken his place; you have used his death to get what you want.'

She had never voiced her resentment so explicitly before and I think we were both shocked.

'Or perhaps I'm keeping something of him alive,' I said shakily.

By way of an apology perhaps, she put out her hand and I pressed it reluctantly. Her lace sleeve came to a point on her knuckle and had tiny buttons along the cuff. As a child it was considered one of my privileges to be called down to her bedroom to help with fastenings before she went out, but I was always sulky because the task brought me up close to the side of her that was forever pulling away. Now she had allowed her hair to fall from its pins so that it tumbled down her back. From this angle, in this light, she might have been younger than me. For a moment we watched each other, neither of us moving, neither of us able to break the silence. I felt dreary to my soul that this conversation, like so many others, had ended with us locked into positions of mutual disappointment, each incapable of being what the other wanted.

Chapter Sixteen

Leah Marchant's appeal was scheduled for a ten thirty hearing on Friday morning before Recorder Martin Hestlethwaite. I arrived early but found no sign of Thorne or indeed the defendant, who was to be brought there by prison van. The wait was torture for me because I would not listen to the voice of reason within my head: You sent Thorne the papers. He has the facts of the case and that's all he wants from you. Apart from that, you are nothing to him.

At ten o'clock precisely Thorne strode in, immaculately turned out and ineffably calm, though perhaps a little warm after a brisk walk. Removing his hat, he ruffled his hair in a gesture I had come to anticipate. 'How was the trip to the crime scene, Miss Gifford? I was so sorry not to see it for myself. Perhaps I'll wander up there next week. Could you spare the time to show me, do you think?'

Was he seriously proposing so intimate an expedition as a walk in the Chesham fields?

'It's late,' I replied. 'We should go down and see Leah Marchant at once. She should be here by now.'

'Lead the way.'

He followed so close behind me that I distinctly felt his knee brush my skirt as we went downstairs. Fortunately, when we reached the cells I had only to stand by and watch as the machine clicked into action for Leah Marchant's benefit. And there displayed were all the tricks he'd used on me: the frank smile, the eyes suffused with sympathy, the hearty handshake, the inclination of the head as he commiserated with her on the appalling treatment she had received thus far at the hands of the judiciary. 'I promise that I shall do my level best, Mrs Marchant, to ensure that you walk free this very morning.'

Neither Leah nor I was required to speak. She was of course

dazzled by the gloss of the man. To her the authoritative voice, the tailored clothes, the scent of him must have been unutterably alien, and she behaved as though star-struck, whispering mono-syllabic responses and never taking her eyes from his face. Thorne showed a detailed knowledge of the case, including the names and ages of her children, although he'd probably not read my notes until minutes previously. The interview ended in yet another prolonged handshake, and moments later I was seated behind Thorne in court, mesmerised by the way the neat tag of his wig nestled at the back of his neck.

It was immediately obvious that Thorne and the recorder, Hestlethwaite, were more than nodding acquaintances. When introduced by the clerk they acknowledged each other formally but an underlying familiarity was indicated by a flicker in the judge's eye. In the presence of Thorne and Hestlethwaite, the police prosecutor was apologetic. The last hearing, he inferred, had been an aberration. Even though the police had felt there was considerable mitigation, events in court had persuaded the magistrate, in his wisdom, that only a custodial penalty would do.

Mrs Marchant, who was again supported by her friend Mrs Sanders, never took her adoring eyes from Thorne. A tear trickled down her left cheek. When allusion was made to her unfortunate attitude in court during the last hearing, Thorne glanced at her incredulously as if struggling to understand how any judge could possibly have taken offence at such a sweet-natured woman.

Thorne rose to his feet, and it seemed to me that others in the courtroom held their breath at the unfolding of his great height. His delivery was restrained, that of a rational man barely having to exercise his wits in order to steady a minor wobble in the British justice system. 'At any point, Your Honour, do stop me if you think I've gone far enough. I'm sure you will be as dismayed as I am that this case has come thus far and that the woman before you has now served weeks in prison. Your Honour, in the third decade of the twentieth century I for one am appalled to find myself representing a mother cut off from her own children not for loving them too little but for loving them too much.'

We emerged from the courtroom ten minutes later with Leah's sentence remitted to six months' conditional discharge and a letter from Hestlethwaite instructing the matron of the Good Samaritan Home for Destitute Children in Hammersmith to allow Mrs Marchant an interview with her two oldest children at the earliest opportunity. In another five minutes we all met in a private room, together with a *Daily Mail* reporter who made enthusiastic notes as Leah gabbled her gratitude to Thorne.

'Mrs Marchant,' I interrupted, and received a resentful glare. 'I shall write to the home and accompany you there. The *Daily Mail* has very kindly agreed to fund your case until your children have been released to you.'

'Can't Mr Breen come with me or Mr Thorne?'

'I am your legal representative.'

'How does it feel, Mrs Marchant, to be represented by one of our first lady lawyers?' asked the reporter wolfishly.

Leah chose not to answer but instead vowed that she would henceforth be working twenty hours a day in order to provide a decent home for her children.

'Don't make promises you can't keep,' said Mrs Sanders, who'd been talking to Thorne about landmarks near Toynbee Hall familiar to both. 'I've only got the promise of ten hours' work a week for you so far.'

Thorne sat on the table edge, arms folded, apparently enjoying the aftermath of his success. Was it fair of me to question his motives? Surely his interest in Mrs Sanders was genuine rather than to make a point of displaying the egalitarian leanings acquired at Toynbee.

When the two women were ready to go he rose and bade them farewell as if this had been a social event rather than an appeal. Afterwards the empty room seemed strikingly intimate though the door stood ajar. While I packed my papers he loosened his bands and ran his fingers across his scalp to release hair flattened by his wig. At last I said stiffly, 'Thank you, Mr Thorne. You made that seem very easy.'

'It's always easy when there has been an insane judgement such as the one passed on your Mrs Marchant. I do have some faith that justice, or in this case plain common sense, will assert itself where necessary. You were treated unfairly at the last hearing, Miss Gifford. I have given you much thought since we met and, believe me, I do understand the great mountain you have to climb. It's hard enough to get a toehold in this profession when one is male and has friends.'

'The trouble is I must cut my teeth on real clients. It is they who suffer.'

'Beginnings are always tricky and I cannot think of an institution more entrenched in its own traditions than the law, excepting of course the Roman Catholic Church. After all, both depend on tradition for validity, to some extent. I suspect that what you must come up against all the time is our collective resistance to change. I confess I'm guilty of that sin too, as you did not hesitate to point out when we first met.'

'Why would anyone who loves justice resist change if it is necessary?'

'Ah, but you see, my brothers in the law don't see that change *is* necessary. They believe that we perform perfectly adequately without women. And of course you're a threat.'

'But they should be interested in justice.' The strain of exchanging ideas with a man whose image had haunted me night and day made me speak more harshly than I should have done. 'Why do they want things to remain the same? Was the past so perfect? Was it fair?'

'Steady on, Miss Gifford. I wasn't trying to defend the past, merely to explain the present.'

'Isn't it convenient that you are able to dismiss the past instead of admitting that perhaps it doesn't bear scrutiny?' I said.

'To which particular aspect of the past are you alluding, Miss Gifford? I do feel it's always safer to deal in specifics.'

'I'm surprised you have to ask. Is there an adult alive who could look back over the last decade with any degree of gratification?'

Too late I saw the conversation hurtling away from me, and only afterwards did I have time to analyse the real cause of my anger. While the argument was actually taking place I blamed my loss of bearings on Thorne's insufferable self-satisfaction. Later I realised that his earlier reference to our tea together, his acknowledgement of a connection that I had tried to convince myself meant nothing to him, had thrown me entirely off balance.

He was no longer smiling. 'It seems to me, Miss Gifford, that you are perfectly right in holding my unfortunate sex largely responsible for the war and all that followed. But surely you weaken your case by seeing us as a collective. By herding us together you remove responsibility from the individual. I like to consider my sex and yours as comprising separate human beings, each of whom has free will.'

'Generally, I think you'll agree, women have not been seen by lawmakers or society as individuals. Women are always banded together as the weaker sex, if we are allowed to have any characteristic at all.'

'So you're a suffragist, Miss Gifford?'

'Don't categorise me. I don't want to be put in a box any more than you do.'

We stood, one on either side of the table, as if the air had developed a viscosity that trapped us. I would not be the one to look away. It seemed that his eyes had a different light in them today; a spread light like a candle behind glass. I think, for a moment, my body actually leaned towards his before I came to my senses.

'If you will excuse me, I have a luncheon appointment.'

'Perhaps we are walking the same way.'

'I shall be taking an omnibus.'

'You are still angry with me. I have done nothing to convince you that I am on your side.'

'It ought not to be a question of sides. It ought to be a matter of justice. Good day, Mr Thorne.'

Then he did something very odd: he reached out as if to push the door open wider for me but instead raised his hand to cover his eyes. As I passed him he said, 'Miss Gifford, I wish you well, I really do. But forgive me for saying that I also wish with all my heart that I had never clapped eyes on you.'

How I caught the right omnibus for Holborn or found the correct change I have no idea. When the conductor moved away I sat with closed eyes, stifled by the stench of diesel, while the earth recovered its equilibrium and I my wits. His last words echoed in my mind, over and over.

Every couple of months or so I met other women lawyers at the Law Society, where we ordered lunch, made a point of lingering over coffee and entered the date of our next rendezvous in our diaries before leaving. There were many cheaper and nicer places to go but one of our unspoken motives was to assert our right to use the building now that we were members and had forced the issue of facilities so that a ladies' cloakroom had been installed for us, at vast expense (they said), in what had formerly been a coal hole in the basement. We considered it our duty to make our presence felt where we could (we were not admitted to the reading room) in case anyone forgot us or thought we would fade away.

Generally I anticipated these meetings with a passionate sense of pride that here we were, the ground-breakers, still going strong four years after we had first gained access to the society, still full of verve and hope. As I climbed the steps between grandiose white pillars I thought I knew how grandmother must have felt making her entrance on stage, into the limelight.

When I met with Carrie and the rest it was usually a relief that, after weeks of maintaining an air of unassailable determination in our daily work amidst male colleagues, we could let down our guard and vent our feelings. There was always a little verbal jostling as to who should go first, but on the whole we listened attentively, rejoiced in each other's triumphs and offered advice and commiseration over setbacks. Rivalries which had surfaced in the battle to find work were now suppressed by our joint resolve to overcome the iniquities of the professional world. United, we presented a much more formidable front against the pinstriped brigade who rustled their newspapers and lowered their voices when we were near.

But that Friday as I nodded to the porter, I felt apprehensive at the prospect of meeting my friends. There they were, assembled under a portrait of Edward Leigh-Pemberton, president in the mid-nineteenth century and therefore spared the horrors of dealing with women lawyers, four ladies in dark colours and last summer's hats, their voices light and fluid in that austere setting. Last time we had discussed whether our new-formed association of women solicitors had played into the hands of the male Establishment by setting us apart, and the debate was scheduled to continue today, but I had so little appetite·for the discussion that I almost turned tail. I couldn't imagine any of them would understand how I felt and I expected no sympathy because I thought I had betrayed them by falling in love.

Carrie greeted me with her customary appraising stare then, before I had time to shake hands or draw up a chair, she cried, 'Evelyn, I saw you. I saw you last week at Toynbee Hall. You came into the concert late, and at the end I tried to fight my way over to you but you'd gone.'

To hide the sudden heat in my face I ducked my head and began unbuttoning my jacket. 'I shouldn't have been at Toynbee in the first place. I was due back at the office but I was passing that way and couldn't resist the music. Afterwards I had to dash.'

'It was a wonderful concert, one of the best we've put on, I think. But surely you must have known I'd be there? Why didn't you look out for me?'

'I was so hot. I . . .'

'Well, not to worry. We've been talking about Toynbee, actually. They're giving me more work. I intend to specialise in family law. I don't mind what comes my way really, but it seems a good field to choose because so little is being done to improve the rights of married women. It's not fashionable or lucrative, but it matters.'

I settled deep into an armchair, pretended to follow the conversation and even managed to order a bowl of soup. In this company it was quite acceptable to acknowledge that one was short of money. And then Carrie suddenly embarked on a subject that was entirely pertinent to me and therefore set my nerves jangling. She was in love, though being Carrie, her love was straightforward. She was engaged to a solicitor who, according to her, was as radical and ambitious as she. Of course she loved him unequivocally and of course her love was reciprocated. Such was her confidence none of us dared suggest that marriage might prove detrimental to her career or that engagement to a successful lawyer might be seen as compromising our ideal of achieving success and recognition through our own merits. Her good fortune in finding not only a healthy man but one in sympathy with her ambitions was so extraordinary that we felt awe rather than jealousy.

Which made my own pathetic state all the more absurd. There was no question of my confiding in these women. So you've fallen in love too, they'd say incredulously. It must be catching all of a sudden. Who is he?

And some of them, on hearing the name Nicholas Thorne, would be even more disbelieving. But he's already engaged to marry Sylvia Hardygne. He's bound to be a silk one day. What *are* you thinking of?

Thankfully their conversation had moved from love to the more pressing subject of money. Our current rates of pay, those of us who received any fees at all, were untenable. Why should we be paid so much less than our male colleagues for doing the same work, usually in half the time? Maud, the most committed suffragist among us, was so vexed by the question that she had canvassed her MP and brought it up at a political rally. 'It's the only way. We have to make our presence felt with every element in society but especially those in public office. We have to keep challenging the norm or they'll think they can get away with it. They pay us pin money in the expectation that we'll be grateful for anything, as indeed I'm afraid we are.'

'There isn't time to do battle on too many fronts,' said Carrie. 'My own feeling is that we should concentrate on the law. We have to prove ourselves as lawyers and we don't want our cause to be tainted by association with shrill women who are simply looking for a cause, any cause.'

I was thinking: What if Carrie had reached me that day in Toynbee after the concert and insisted I took tea with her? What if there'd been no rush along the hot pavement, no Thorne carrying my briefcase, no argument in the tea shop? What if I'd not seen him between the day of Leah's first court appearance, when he touched my arm and gave unwanted advice, and Stephen Wheeler's bail hearing in Chesham this week? Perhaps his impact would have faded, leaving only the faintest scorch mark instead of an indelible scar.

Carrie said, 'Once we have expertise in a certain field of the law we are uncrushable because we are needed. If we're too generalist, we are dispensable. I said to Ambrose ...'

Nonsense, I told myself. You're not in love. How would you know what being in love is? It's so long since you felt anything for a man that you think the faintest spark of interest, a raising of the pulse, is love. You don't even know Thorne.

So I set the thought of him aside and heard myself talk quite calmly about the Wheeler case – which they'd read about in the newspapers – the fact that we had our own line of enquiry, and that I was to visit Stella's house on Monday. Then we discussed Leah Marchant's predicament and Carrie had much to say concerning the iniquities of a law which would probably ensure that Leah never recovered her children. 'You do realise how much money she'll need before they are released. Each day they're in the home will cost her more because in order to get them back she'll have to recompense the charity for their board and lodging. And then she'll have to show that she can provide for their moral and financial needs. I mean, the authorities might conclude that the children are better off in an institution – have you thought of that?'

'I've never seen Leah Marchant with her children or visited the Good Samaritan Home so cannot make a judgement. But given she surrendered them voluntarily in the first place, this all seems very unjust.'

'She will have been told the rules when she placed them in the home but was probably so desperate to get away that she won't have listened. How could a woman, forced to surrender her children, think rationally? Did she sign a document? Can she read? But you should visit the home. It's possible you might be pleasantly surprised. Is it one which sends children to the colonies?'

'What do you mean?'

'One thing you'll need to check is where the home stands on child migration. I don't expect you want the children mixed up in that.'

'I don't understand.'

'Surely you know that this country ships hundreds of children to the colonies every year, particularly Canada and Australia. It's government policy, has been for years, to support charities in sending unwanted children overseas to underpopulated outposts of the Empire. After all, there are hundreds of perfectly good homes for them out there, people crying out to adopt a child.'

Maud said, 'For some that must surely be an excellent solution. I heard of a boy who was given his own land in Canada and is now a prosperous farmer.'

'Yes but I also know critics of the scheme,' said Carrie. 'Some of the children they send abroad are very young. And I don't know what checks are made, once they're out there.'

'But what has this to do with the Marchant children?' I asked. 'You're surely talking about a scheme for orphans. The Marchant children have one if not two parents.'

'I'm just warning you to be vigilant. At Toynbee all kinds of things come to light. I recently dealt with the case of a woman who'd conceived a child when she was sixteen and given it up after her father turned her out, but who now wanted it back because she'd married a good man, prepared to bring up her illegitimate child as his own. But when they made enquiries they were told the child had been adopted and was enjoying a comfortable life with a well-to-do family in the West Country. I've written numerous letters but the only response from the charity is that they feel it's important for the child not to be contacted by its natural mother at this late stage. The mother is adamant she never agreed to the child being adopted and the charity is refusing to show me the papers they say she signed. If it's all above board, why the secrecy? The only way forward might be for me to take the charity to court and let them prove they went through a due process and that the child is still in this country and hasn't been sent to some far-flung outpost of the empire.'

'Surely no child could be sent abroad without the mother's permission?'

'Hopefully not. But it seems to me that charities are being overzealous about having children adopted and rather coy about admitting what form these adoptions might take. If the Marchant children are healthy and personable, they would be considered ideal candidates for Canada. It's such a cheap, neat option.'

Before I left, very troubled, I arranged to call on Carrie in her offices to look at papers she had collected on the welfare of children taken into care. I was cursing myself for not having consulted her earlier. If only I hadn't been distracted by Thorne that day at Toynbee I would have acted with greater urgency. Carrie had pulled me so firmly back into line that the turmoil of the morning now seemed an aberration. My vocation was clear: to rescue the Marchant children from the abyss into which it appeared they might have fallen.

Chapter Seventeen

On Monday I visited Stella Wheeler's childhood home, 83 Manchester Street, in a grid of mid-Victorian terraces off Horn Lane in Acton. The house was substantial compared to Stella's and was set back a few feet from the street behind a low wall that shielded a diminutive garden with a rose bush in the centre and borders crammed with lobelia.

The front step was swept, the door had recently been washed and the hall smelled of baking. Mrs Hobhouse greeted me with the words: 'I've been cooking for the funeral. They say her body will be released early next week. Of course for now I can only do things that will keep. Dundee cake.' She showed me into the front parlour, which was stuffy from lack of use and into which had been crammed a collection of oversized furniture, presumably passed down from previous generations. Mrs Hobhouse's housekeeping, unlike her daughter's, was decidedly up to scratch. Even the fire irons, I noted, had been dusted, and the antimacassars were newly starched.

'I'll fetch the tea,' she said. 'Will you be all right in here for a moment?'

The parlour spoke volumes for Mrs Hobhouse's respect for good-quality old things coupled with a love of what was new and fashionable. The sideboard, for instance, was Victorian oak but on it was arranged a modern tea service with a stylishly inconvenient pot – probably a bad pourer – patterned in orange and green. In the middle of the mantel was a black and white vase with Egyptian figures and at either end were framed wedding photographs, one for each of the Hobhouse girls.

Julie's was on the left. Her unfortunate groom, Michael, had an awkward posture and his bride, in an ethereal lace frock, looked impatient as she held herself rigid whilst supporting him on her arm.

In the other, identically framed photograph, I at last met the younger daughter Stella, standing beside her new husband in a church doorway. One glance confirmed my belief that the Wheeler marriage had been a mismatch. Stephen's feet were planted too far apart, his shoulders rounded, teeth showing through his beard, trilby clutched to his soft belly with one hand, the other resting on his new wife's slender hip. She had a girlish form and was evidently well aware of her beauty; her pose and restrained smile suggested that she was holding herself carefully, as if she were modelling her clothes rather than participating in a wedding. She wore her hair in a dainty bob and her headdress had two small earpieces – artificial flowers clasping the veil on either side of her forehead. Her face had the regular beauty of an illustration from a women's magazine, except that her nose was perhaps a little too broad. Her eyes, like her sister's, were wide-set but she had a prettier mouth and was altogether much more fine-featured than Julie. Though her frock had a demurely square neckline there was a heaviness in her eyelids that was somehow affiliated to Wheeler's hand on her hip, bunching the fabric of her skirt. A bouquet of lilies was clasped to her breast.

'I can hardly bear to look at that,' said Mrs Hobhouse, who had brought in a tray of tea.

'What was the date of the wedding?'

'April the twenty-sixth. They'd not been wed three weeks when she ...' Tea was poured and I was provided with napkin, plate, knife and rock bun, but it was clear, despite this hospitality, that Mrs Hobhouse was not comfortable with my visit. She treated me with reserve and once or twice gave me a slightly hostile glance. The house, save for the ticking of a clock, was silent, and I thought of the hours she must spend alone in it now that her daughters were gone.

'You must be wondering why I'm here,' I said. 'Forgive me if it seems intrusive but I wanted to see Stella's room, just in case there was anything the police had missed, something that might give us a clue as to why she died.'

'Do you think I haven't been through it a thousand times?

There's nothing in her room, I can tell you. I can't help thinking, Miss Gifford, that it's his things you should be looking at, not hers. He's the one who did it.'

'I understand how you must be feeling and I'm sorry. I won't stay, if you'd rather I didn't. It's just that the police are so sure of Stephen's guilt that they are going to set an early trial date. Just supposing Stephen isn't the right man, and it was someone else?'

'But it was his gun.'

'Mrs Hobhouse, there's no motive. And it's just possible someone else could have used Stephen's gun. Anyone could have got into their backyard. The shed wasn't locked.'

She was momentarily startled by this idea, then slumped back in a gesture of total exhaustion. With her mouth slack and her eyes closed her face aged twenty years. 'I've thought this through. In my view there's no doubt Stephen did it. He wasn't right in the head, I can see that now, and I reproach myself for not taking more notice before. Our Stell was scared about staying too long when she came here that last time, lest she wasn't home when he got back.'

'What was she afraid of, exactly? Did he lose his temper with her, do you think?'

'She never gave details. I think he could be unpleasant, you know, go silent. I don't think he hurt her, if that's what you're getting at. But even when they were engaged the fact he kept such a close eye on her caused friction. His jealousy could have provoked her into being difficult.'

'Can you explain what you mean by difficult?'

'Sulky. She was always a bit of a sulker. And I expect if he asked her questions she didn't like, she wouldn't give him straight answers on principle.'

'But do you think, aside from that, she ever gave him cause to be jealous?'

'You're talking about the dancing that Julie was going on about. He didn't really mind that. But you see this terrible thing has happened and what's on my mind is that Stella may have played up, deliberately, not realising he was far more dangerous in one of his moods than any of us realised, and what he might do to her in the end.'

She led me upstairs to Stella's bedroom at the back of the house. It overlooked a symmetrical garden with vegetables and fruit bushes, and smelled of clean bed linen and the fruitcake that was baking below. There was a narrow bed against one wall, a space where a dressing table had once stood – the rug was dented with castor marks and there was a pale oval patch on the wallpaper – a wardrobe and a chest of drawers. The only incongruous item was a dressmaker's dummy with a half-made black skirt pinned to its waist. The surfaces were painfully bare.

'I miss her terribly,' said Mrs Hobhouse. 'The last time my Stell slept here, it was the night before her wedding.'

'Do you mind if I open the drawers?'

'Do what you like. The police have been through it all anyway. I don't feel anything's private any more. But you won't find anything.'

I recognised the room's appalling sense of abandonment. Everything in it, so familiar to Stella, was disconnected and cheapened without her. I opened a few drawers but the contents were so sorrowful that I closed them hastily: clothes too unloved to be moved to the bride's new home, a child's prayer book, a doll with a wonky eye, and a waitress's cap and apron presumably from her days at Lyons.

'In the top of the wardrobe are some wooden bricks and such I was keeping for grandchildren,' said Mrs Hobhouse.

I held an irrational belief that whatever I was looking for would never be found with Stella's mother present. In the end I asked if she could perhaps find me paper and pencil, since I had foolishly forgotten my own. This did the trick: she backed away and left me. Very softly, so as not to offend Mrs Hobhouse, I closed the door and something swung against me, a cotton robe with frilled edging and a faded design of roses. With some reluctance, I brought the cuff to my face. The fabric smelled of the room and of a sweet perfume I remembered from Stella's wardrobe in her new house. The pockets were empty.

Other than that, the room at first yielded no secrets. The rails at either end of the bed could have done with a fresh coat of paint and I imagined Stella's damp stockings hung there to dry overnight. In the narrow wardrobe was a child's woollen coat with a velvet collar and, on the shelf above, a sun hat and a collection of toys in battered cardboard boxes.

I shut the wardrobe door and looked into the mirror. On the eve of her wedding Stella would surely have tried on her dress one last time and paraded here, turned sideways to examine her profile, contorted herself to get a glimpse of the back view. She must have sat on the bed, crossing and re-crossing her legs to inspect her ankles in the glass which now reflected only my pale face, framed by the dark rim of my hat.

I hoped Stella had enjoyed her dancing days while she had the chance.

I used to be invited to parties even before Meredith arrived to shake us all up, though generally I didn't go; experience had taught me that church socials and gatherings organised by former school friends, now married, would unfailingly disappoint. But I remembered a time, before the war, when I had sat thus before a mirror and lifted the hair from my neck because I was nearly an adult and had acquired a slender throat and a rather intriguing set of curves between chin, breast, waist and hip. I remembered, on the evening of a party, believing that I was on the verge of everything and that life was a precipice over which I longed to fling myself.

And today, gripping the edge of Stella Wheeler's mattress, I felt the same as during the concert at Toynbee Hall. Love, love was what I wanted. I saw reflected a thirty-year-old virgin with creases on her brow and a frown between the eyes, and I recalled the hopeful girl I had once been, the girl who had got herself kissed under the canal bridge. The ghost of the murdered Stella Wheeler clung to the robe hanging on the back of the door and whispered, You could have had more. You had the chance to find out more and you didn't take it. Well more fool you.

The man in question was of such a high rank that I had to fall back against the wall when he passed me in the corridor. We women were mostly employed in the bone-cold rooms of the censorship office, crammed so close that our elbows collided. Our days were spent dipping our pens in black ink and scrubbing out dates, times and places from the back of a hundred thousand postcards. After my brother's death I worked like an automaton because it seemed to me that every postcard must in any case be from a dead boy; the last product of his pen a spattering of unoriginal words many of which I ruthlessly crossed out. Sometimes I was tempted to stuff a sackful under my blouse and burn them to spare the families the hope, on seeing his handwriting, that a beloved boy was alive.

We all assumed that any woman in the building not engaged in the censorship office must be doing something much more interesting. There were some locked rooms we didn't go near because the work that was done inside was so secret that only the cleverest women who could also type or knew languages were admitted. So I persuaded my father to bring a typewriter home from his office and in the small hours taught myself to touch-type (amidst complaints from the girls, who slept in the rooms above mine) and successfully applied for a transfer to a much snugger office in a grander building, where I typed up decoded messages about the movements of German troops. Nobody ever discussed the information we passed on but amongst us, in that office, there was a warm and unspoken camaraderie, founded on pride.

One officer, a colonel, noticed me, and I sensed that when he entered the room he sought me out and took pleasure in seeing me there. He was quietly spoken, reserved, and had been injured in the left arm. The spring and summer following my brother's death felt cold and I was cocooned in layers of wool and grief so that the world held few connections for me except the keys of my typewriter. This unassuming man, though, occasionally caught my eye and smiled.

A few weeks before the armistice there was a party after work to celebrate a birthday. As I was leaving, the officer approached me with a stunningly straightforward invitation. 'It's Miss Gifford, isn't it? Would you have dinner with me tonight?'

It must have cost him dear to ask. I knew that he was married with a family in Dorset and I suspected he was not an habitual philanderer. So I agreed at once, touched by his interest, flattered and too numbed by grief to know what my true feelings were.

The streets were wet and a light drizzle was falling. He was gentlemanly, shielding me from the traffic and adjusting his pace to mine. Dinner was in a discreet restaurant, subterranean, with tables pushed into little alcoves so that we were more or less alone. It occurred to me, when I realised the intimacy of the place, that he was perhaps more accustomed to clandestine suppers than I had imagined. I made a safe choice from the menu, thinking that Rose could have managed much better leek and potato soup than this. He drank several glasses of wine to my one and talked about the first year of the war when he'd seen active service at Aisne and Ypres, where his arm had been wounded. He considered himself much better suited to intelligence work than combat. 'I'm indecisive, a poor quality in a military officer but in many ways excellent for someone working in intelligence. I can be relied on not to do anything rash. It has taken me three months to get round to inviting you to dinner even though you are the most attractive woman I have seen in a long time. Ah, you look surprised, which I suspect is typical of you. You seem to me quite unaware of your own power.'

Smiling, he lowered his eyelids as if pursuing a private thought, and I knew that he would want to make love to me, and that I would let him. I was curious, after all, and found him intriguing even though he seemed not to find any incongruity in talking to me about his wife, who bred dogs, or his three sons, two of whom, thank God, were too young to serve in France. I was required to disclose nothing about myself.

He had a quiet apartment near the restaurant, full of beautiful pieces of porcelain and glass. 'I'm a collector,' he told me. 'Even in France I found time to seek out bits and pieces. I can't resist them,' and he gave me a globe of hollowed out glass that filled my hand with crimson.

I never could stand the truth of colour. At that moment I wished he had been less kind, less tentative, because now that I liked him more I wanted him to make love to me less. I couldn't imagine how it would come to pass that we would remove our clothes and lie on his bed.

He took the bowl from me and put it down. 'You have beautiful hands,' he said. 'It was the first thing I noticed about you. But I have some advice. After the war, never let on that you can type unless you have no other choice. I think you are much too clever a woman to spend your life typing up other people's letters.'

I smiled cautiously. He was holding my elbow as he looked down at my hand and I made out the shape of his skull under his thinning hair. His thumb moved from my arm and began stroking my breast. The trouble was that, in the end, I was quite incapable of losing myself in his touch and therefore could not stand the thought of the mechanical act ahead. He was too polite, I too indifferent.

I took a step back and withdrew my arm. 'I'll go now,' I said.

His face closed and the corner of his lip, under the moustache, tightened. In the neat space of his apartment my movements were calm as I collected my gloves and bag from the hall and let myself out. But during the long walk home I cursed myself, not for accepting his invitation to dinner, but for failing to take the opportunity which had been offered.

I glanced again into Stella's mirror and it was then that I saw her, almost concealed from view behind books on a shelf above the bed, with just one foot peeping out from behind a copy of *Little Women*. Pushing aside the book I discovered a statuette, so small that it would almost have been covered by my fist, of a naked girl connected to a plinth by one tiny foot. She was running, hair flying back, hands raised above her head, small-breasted, every detail distinct, even the fuzz of pubic hair and her little toes. I knew practically nothing of art, still less about sculpture. But I knew that this little bronze, suggestive but exquisite, was entirely out of a place in a bedroom where no other item had cost more than a guinea.

When Mrs Hobhouse returned we made an inventory, beginning with the dressmaker's dummy (modelling her half-made dress for Stella's funeral), the robe behind the door, and the bed, and continuing with the contents of the wardrobe and drawers. We even took out the box of toys, noted the farm animals and counted the bricks. In a further box was a collection of doll's house furniture, roughly made but with working doors and drawers. 'My husband used to make it for her. She loved small things when she was a child,' said Mrs Hobhouse, beginning to weep.

I opened each miniature drawer. Inside were trinkets, a windmill from a charm bracelet, a tiny shell and an odd assortment of dried-up things such as one might find on a nature table in school: an acorn in its cup, a sycamore key and a conker case.

'Funny girl,' said Mrs Hobhouse. 'She will have kept those for her dolls.' I didn't contradict her but the horse chestnut, although discoloured, was quite soft and its smell too distinctive to be anything but last season's.

Last of all I went to the bookcase and took down the bronze dancer. 'Oh that,' said Mrs Hobhouse. 'I didn't know she kept that here.'

'Where did it come from?'

'She bought it herself. I hate the thing.'

'Mrs Hobhouse, might I borrow it, if I take great care of it?'

'Whatever for?'

'I want to show it to Mr Breen. It seems rather unusual to me.'

Her eyes were fixed on the statue, and I realised that it was asking a great deal to take away something of Stella's.

'I'll write you out a receipt,' I said. 'I won't keep it long.'

Afterwards she followed me downstairs. 'Well, that was a waste of your time. I'm sorry.'

'Not wasted,' I said. 'I wanted to know more about Stella and now I do.'

'Such as what? What do you know?'

'Why, that she was much loved, Mrs Hobhouse.'

Perhaps it was this last remark that made her finally trust me because as I left she put her hand on my arm. 'I'm worried that there won't be hardly anyone at the funeral. Will you come?'

Chapter Eighteen

On the night of the art party I had agreed to attend the first half of the concert at St Mark's, though such an arrangement was in direct defiance of Prudence's maxim that a task done half-heartedly is best not done at all. The next day I was to visit the Good Samaritan Home with Leah Marchant so I worked late in preparation and then went straight to the church. The approach to the hall was through an overcrowded graveyard and a dim entrance where Mrs Gillespie sat at a trestle table upon which were displayed a small pile of handwritten programmes and a wooden bowl of change. A brown envelope had been left for me, inscribed with the information that Miss Prudence Gifford had reserved a ticket for Miss Evelyn Gifford but that the ticket was so far not paid for. Admission to the concert cost one and sixpence, programme and refreshments included, all proceeds to the Church Bell Restoration Fund.

It required extraordinary willpower to cross the threshold from the golden light of a mellow June evening and enter the gloomy hall with its smell of bare feet – an 'expressive' dance class was held on Thursday afternoons – and floor polish. There I was confronted by a dozen or so ladies in second-best hats, a handful of gentlemen spread out across five rows, the choir assembled at the front in their frilled white blouses, and mother twisting round on the lookout for me.

As I edged my way into the vacant seat beside her she murmured in a low voice reserved for the interior of ecclesiastical buildings, 'You're not still intending to go to this wretched party, are you? She's turned the house upside down. She intends to wear *trousers*, did you know? I doubt if we shall ever get the boy to sleep while you're both out.'

Mother's breath smelled of tea as she huffed through the veil she had worn outside the home ever since James's death, its black spots a dreadful plague on her skin. As the choir launched into 'An English Country Garden' I found myself longing to be at home with Meredith. At this moment Edmund would be perched on her bed, offering advice while she dressed. The art party had turned out – horror of horrors – to be fancy dress, on the theme of the sea, and Edmund had revealed a disturbing (Prudence's word) aptitude for rifling through grandmother's chests of old clothes and producing just the right garment. 'However,' Prudence had added, 'I think you should be more graceful about the party, Evelyn. After all, you might meet some proper artists there.' Now that she had been to the Tate and was in possession of a scrap of painted linen from Guiana she considered that she had a toe in the modern art world and was therefore licensed to criticise those of us reluctant to engage with it.

Perhaps it was the experience of having been in Stella's bedroom, or even the witchery of the bronze dancer, but I wanted urgently to be with Meredith and Edmund, decked out in my summer frock and the sheath of blue satin that was to transform me into a sea nymph. I wanted to pick Edmund up in my arms and bury my face in his neck while I tickled him, a new ritual we had.

The choir had now launched into a Gabrieli madrigal. Mid-song, I whispered to mother, 'I'm sorry, I have to go ... I don't want to be late ...' and then, surprising even myself, I clambered past three pairs of unyielding knees. The doors had been left open and beyond the porch was the path leading to the gate, the grass and yew tree bathed in slanting sunlight, and the head of an angel with long stone tresses hanging over the grave of a child.

Before we left for the party I showed Meredith the bronze dancer, fearful that, out of the context of Stella's bedroom, the statue might seem less exceptional, but she stood on my palm as exquisite as before, light pooling in the hollow of her throat.

'My, my,' said Meredith. 'Where did you find this?' She took the dancer to the windowsill, where the figure's soft curves and strong legs glowed darkly against the muslin curtains.

'Do you think she's valuable? She belonged to the dead girl, Stella Wheeler.'

'Did she now?' Meredith put her hand to her mouth. 'So Stella held her too ... Doesn't that just bring us so close to a murder victim?'

'What do you think?'

'I think she's lovely and probably worth a small fortune. She's quite modern, I'd say. I swear I saw something like this in a gallery in Toronto.'

I persuaded Meredith that we should travel to Kew by bus since we had hired a cab for the return journey, which was likely to be very costly. We attracted considerable attention from other passengers, given that she was indeed wearing green trousers under a diaphanous tunic, a costume adapted from Titania's found by Edmund in one of grandmother's boxes. He had suggested that I should tie my hair loosely with a blue ribbon. I thanked God that mother and Prudence were safely interred in the church hall and had not witnessed me leaving the house.

Our hostess, Lady Jane Carr (no mention was made of a husband), owned a red-brick villa that backed on to the river, and as we approached we heard jazz, perhaps being played in the garden at the rear. The front door was opened by a bored-looking woman holding a cocktail glass and wearing a clicking necklace made of wooden fishes. She neither took our names nor introduced herself to us. Instead she drifted upstairs, weaving between a mermaid and an octopus who supped beer directly from the bottle.

The first-floor drawing room ran the width of the house with a door at each end and a row of windows reaching floor to ceiling that overlooked the garden, where people were dancing wildly to the jazz band. Meanwhile in the drawing room, which was decked out with balloons and streamers, a man and woman sat in one corner, he playing the guitar, she the banjo, both severely dressed and intently watching each other's fingers, so that to see the jazz dancers below in their flashing colours and to hear the passionately rhythmic music in this room was to be in a dreamlike state of dissonance.

Guests had arranged themselves about the furniture and a group of devotees hung over the musicians with rapt expressions. Some were in extravagant costumes, others simply wore a symbolic badge or sash, but there were too many colours, the blues and greens confused me, what with the dizzying music and the women's painted faces. Too often lately I had found myself in situations where I didn't know myself and now here I was in the midst of the Bohemian set, my companion the unreliable Meredith, who was utterly transfixed by the party and stood beside me wide-eyed and speechless. Seizing a couple of cocktail glasses from a tray held by a waiter dressed as a sailor, she thrust one into my hand. 'Hadley said there'd be absinthe. Maybe later.'

Apparently nobody here knew the Clivedon Hall Gardens rules of behaviour. They dressed differently, talked differently, touched each other differently. I couldn't categorise them socially or work out how much money they had. I even grew sentimental about my mother, who in her heyday had been an expert hostess and on seeing strangers would surge up to them with a string of pleas-antries designed to make them feel they were very special to her, and a proposal to introduce them to people they would *absolutely* adore.

There was no sign of Meredith's teacher Hadley Waters or of the promised Augustus John (surely one would recognise him), and as far as I could tell from snippets of conversation not a single person was talking about art. However, after another few sips of whatever it was in the glass, my perceptions changed and I liked the room and the people in it a little better. The house was indeed a work of art. The walls themselves had been treated as canvases and were covered by primitive, two-dimensional paintings of furniture, and there was even a painted window with a painted woman's face, thick-nosed and heavy-browed like the banjo player's, peering in. Along the door frames were drooping tendrils of painted ivy.

Meredith cried, 'How marvellous. Do you think your mother would mind if I decorated my bedroom like this? Only joking, really. Hadley hasn't taught us how to draw flowers yet. But let's go outside and find him. There's no one in here.'

We went down, stepping over the loungers on the stairs. A passage led through the house to a glass door opening on to the garden. There was no sunlight left and cool air was blowing from the river so some women had picked up blankets from the grass and draped them round their shoulders. 'Look,' said Meredith, 'over there. I think he's famous.' She pointed to a man who could certainly be someone. 'Epstein or Kramer, I can't decide which.'

The band, which had been resting, was tuning up once more in its arbour and there were shrieks of laughter as a girl in a fringed skirt tried to blow into a trumpet. A long-faced woman with hair cut at right angles, dressed in masses of blue drapery and smoking a black cigarette in a jet holder, moved away from a nearby group and introduced herself as Jane Carr, our hostess, and were we having a lovely party? Did we know Carrington and dear Ralph, who had promised to call if they happened to be in town …? Almost at the same moment Meredith was greeted by a thin man in a pirate's outfit complete with red headscarf, gold earring, cardboard dagger and eyepatch. Hadley Waters.

'But Hadley,' exclaimed Lady Carr, 'you will never convince me that you are *dangerous*.'

Hadley, who was willowy-framed and long-haired, had two women in tow. The first I recognised as the model in Meredith's picture of a nude; there was no mistaking those hare-like eyes and protruding teeth or even the droop of her unbound breasts under the fabric of a clinging jersey dressing gown, which she wore over a knitted bathing costume. 'You'll know Margot,' Hadley said, and she and Meredith kissed extravagantly, 'and this is another regular at my Tuesday class, Sylvia Hardynge.'

The other woman held out a cool white hand first to Meredith, then to me. I managed to meet her eyes, which were remarkable – dark grey and with an alluring internal sparkle – and I even smiled, but it was as if sound and movement had been sucked violently from the party and there was just this other woman – Thorne's fiancée – and me, and somewhere else, waiting inevitably to reveal himself, Nicholas Thorne.

Sylvia's beauty was such that it was hard to look away. Her abundant black hair fell in tendrils and she was draped in some kind of white, Grecian robe which she said was an attempt at Atargatis, sea goddess. The gown revealed the pearly skin of her shoulders and the perfect lines of her long body. Even as something in me died at meeting this lovely creature, I registered that her laughter at her own incompetence with the paintbrush was infectious and her voice had a pleasing, slightly sardonic confidence. Then I saw that she wore a sapphire ring on the third finger of her left hand.

'I believe I know your fiancé,' I said.

'Oh?' Her lovely eyes were full of curiosity.

'I work for a firm of solicitors. I met him, Mr Thorne, in connection with a murder enquiry.'

She was enthralled. 'He mentioned you. Said he'd been upbraided by a woman lawyer for being too old-fashioned and stick-in-the-mud. Good for you. I'm delighted to meet you. Anyone who pulls my Nicholas down a peg or two ...'

'What about you?' I asked. 'Have you an interest in the law?'

She didn't quite like the question. 'I have no intention of studying the law, if that's what you mean. Daddy's not keen on women having careers as such. But I am getting myself embroiled in politics. Daddy's standing for parliament at the next election. I have a feeling that might turn out to be my thing too.'

'Do you go to political meetings?' cried Meredith. 'Could I join you? I keep meaning to go but haven't yet.'

'But would you be in my party?' And there, again, was that throaty laugh. 'I'm with Tom Mosley. I follow him slavishly, from right to left. Daddy's appalled, but there it is.'

'How could I know which party to be in until I've tried them all?' Meredith said.

'"Somebody Stole my Gal",' said Hadley, cocking his ear to the band. 'Shall we dance?' And he led his harem of three aspiring artists onto the dance floor, which was a platform of wooden boards set up on the grass. I hung back and as soon as they'd forgotten me went on and on, retreating until I was among the trees.

Lanterns had been strung across the dance floor so that light reflected off the sequins and rhinestones on dresses and headbands. The band played faster and faster and Sylvia Hardynge threw back her head so that her long white throat gleamed. She was laughing down at little Meredith.

He would come. There was no escaping the pain. I wanted his meeting with Sylvia to be over so that I might watch them together from this safe distance and lay the ghost of my own non-existent love affair. And there, sure enough, was Nicholas, a latecomer in boater and blazer, kissing Lady Carr on both cheeks then standing with folded arms beside her and surveying the garden in the uneven light from the lanterns and an extraordinary crescent moon which had, in the last few minutes, risen above the river, with the old moon burdening its lap like a fat round cushion.

I merged myself deeper into the trees. The pain was such that I rubbed the old wound on my cheek against a trunk in an effort to divert sensation elsewhere than my heart. And at that moment I saw Sylvia detach herself from Hadley Waters' flailing embrace and spring off the dance floor towards Nicholas. Seizing his arm she raised herself on tiptoe and kissed his cheek and lips then gave his boater a teasing nudge so that it tilted over his forehead. Perhaps she complained she was chilly because the next moment they set off towards the house, she clinging to his arm, the trailing hem of her robe a pool of ivory, her hair a swathe of black silk.

By midnight the garden was so cold I was numb and the long-awaited absinthe had almost run dry. My soul had shrivelled and my thoughts were bitter morsels of complaint. I wanted to be at home in my bed. Unlike every other woman at the party I had to get up for work the next morning. I wanted to sleep and never wake. I was hungry. I was a fool. I was pitiable. I should have known better.

Hadley Waters, on the other hand, had grown damp-eyed and sentimental. 'We should take a boat out on the river,' he said. 'Might I have the pleasure of rowing you ladies?'

By now the band was improvising somewhat melancholy themes, which wafted across the water to where people floated in cushioned rowing boats with lanterns swinging from hooks on the prows, like illustrations from *The Twelve Dancing Princesses*. Hadley claimed to be an expert oarsman and Margot and Meredith were both keen. I couldn't imagine anything less inviting than the Thames at this hour but thought when it was over it might be one thirty, time for the cab, and if I let Meredith disappear in the boat without me there was no telling how long I'd be left on the bank waiting for her.

Margot sat in the prow facing Hadley, who had the oars, and Meredith and I were side by side in the stern. Drink had loosened Meredith's tongue and she talked in a high, fast voice, her accent much stronger than usual: 'How wide the river is here. You know, it makes me homesick for Canada, where the rivers run so fast and clear. Your Aunt Prudence was very impressed by the Turners in the Tate, by the way. Water, she said, is difficult to paint but he managed wonderfully. Why is it that even when Prudence pays a compliment, it sounds like a decree? You Maida Vale ladies have everything sewn up, don't you? No room for doubt.'

I recognised wearily that she wanted to pick a fight so I trailed my hand in the water and changed the subject. 'I was talking about Canada the other day, incidentally. I'm told that our country sends hundreds of orphans out there each year. Do you know anything about that?'

'Of course. Not that we want all of them. You're only supposed to send us perfect children and instead you fob us off with defective ones. If a child is already half-witted it's not nearly so much fun for a farmer out on the plains to knock the living daylights out of him.'

'Meredith, what are you saying? I was given to understand that our children go to good homes.'

'Oh I'm sure some do, Evelyn, if that's what you'd like to believe.'

'It's not a matter of belief. I'd rather get at the truth.'

'Truthfully, then. I have worked in hospitals where your migrant English children, your rejects, or home children as we call them, have turned up riddled with sexual diseases or mentally defective.'

'I didn't know. I . . .'

'Did the news not reach you here of little Charles Bulpitt, who hung himself in a barn, he was so abused by his master? Oh it's a common sight, when you visit a Canadian farmstead, to see a ragged home child leading in the cattle or some such. Mother's cousin had one as a housemaid. That was all right, I think; she was a good worker.'

'How could I not have known about this?'

'On the other hand, I'm sure your Aunt Prudence would applaud the scheme. If a child is to be destitute due to the improvidence of its parents, at least let it be useful.'

It grew colder despite the cushions and even a rug thoughtfully provided by Lady Carr. The river, poisoned by my conversation with Meredith, seemed horribly dense between little puddles of light cast by the lanterns. Behind us Lady Carr's garden was like a painted film set. Then Meredith's mood changed entirely as she tucked herself up closer to me crying, 'Isn't it cold?' Reaching both her arms round my waist she rested her head on my shoulder and kissed me under the chin. 'Glad you changed your mind? Happy to be here?'

That night she wore an exotic fragrance, musky, and the heat of her tense little body transferred itself to mine so that despite the shock of intimacy, I welcomed her closeness. A bottle was passed among us and I took a reckless swig, mesmerised by the sight of Hadley Waters' oars dipping in and out of the river, the fall of a few drops of water as the blades hovered then sliced the surface tension with deliciously tiny plops.

He and Margot were planning an exhibition. 'But I don't think we should restrict it just to paintings,' he said. 'I think we should go foraging in the flea markets for anything we consider to be art – jugs, radiators even, all welcome as long as they have lovely shapes.'

'I like the idea of an exhibition of things,' said Meredith. 'Evelyn's Aunt Prudence and I are going to the British Empire Exhibition next week to see what *things* there might be to look at from those far-flung places. Prudence says that primitive art is fine if it is done by primitive peoples. But you know, I love all beautiful things. I don't care if they're useful or not, as long as they're good to look at. That's why I've acquired Evelyn as my very best friend. She's a bit useful, I suppose, but more than that she's very beautiful, though she doesn't know it.'

The bottle was passed again and the conversation drifted. Hadley's knees were touching Margot's and eventually slotted between them. There was a lot of jiggling of the boat as they began a series of long, closed-eyed kisses that made my heart beat hard and uneven until at last I forced myself to look away.

Meredith, who had been drinking steadily, snuggled deeper

beside me under the rug and buried her face in my lap. 'I love you,' she said. 'I love you and I hate you, did you know that? I love you because you're Evelyn, and one minute you're stiff and starchy as Prudence, and the next you're this bold, amazing woman, braver than almost anyone I know. And I hate you because you're the sister of James and your eyes are tight shut.' She paused.

I saw the coming revelation rather as I might have watched a demolition ball hurtling towards me; there was no possibility of ducking or interrupting its momentum. Alcohol and cold had disempowered me so that it was easier to lie still beneath the blanket and wait than to offer any resistance. Besides, wasn't I always greedy for information about James, anything that would return him a little more solidly to me? Meanwhile Margot had shifted and she and Hadley, now side by side, drew in the oars and ran their hands over each other instead.

Meredith stroked my neck. 'I've wondered for years whether I would ever tell your family the truth about what happened. Part of me wants to keep it a secret, to protect you, I suppose. Part of me wants to tell you, so that you have the full picture. Which is the path I should follow? Tell me, do. I'll leave it to you to decide for me.'

I looked up at the stars. 'You know I want to know more about James.'

She adjusted her weight so that her head lay on my shoulder and her breath, full of spirits, fell on my neck. With her finger she traced my features: nose, jaw, breastbone. 'I'm too drunk to know what I'm saying, almost. I only know that it's now or never, here on the river, where the boundaries are all gone. If I leave it any longer it will be too late and you'll be striding out of my life again, as you do each morning, leaving me to boil with frustration in the house.'

I lay like a sacrificial victim, arms by my side. It was as if Meredith, the obsidian river and that bright bowl of a moon had enchanted me. She took a strand of my hair and wound it round and round her finger, held it up as if to examine it in the light, cast it aside and picked up another. 'You see we were a religious order, nursing in a general hospital quite a way behind the lines. By the time the men got to us they'd been patched up to some extent or their wounds were sufficiently minor that they'd been brought straight to us – by minor I mean frostbite, gas, suchlike. The lucky ones, and there weren't so many of them, were sick enough to be sent home but not so ill that they wouldn't recover in the end. The unlucky ones would be maimed for life. The unluckiest of all, we nurses used to say amongst ourselves, made speedy recoveries and were sent back post haste. Your brother fell into the latter category.'

It was as if she had brought me up close to a window and James was on the other side. My nose was pressed to the glass; yes, if I looked deeper, if I strained my eyes, I would see him. I caught hold of her hand and held tight.

'We have no idea about his last days,' I said. 'We hadn't seen him for months before he died. He wrote from the hospital, said he was injured. We knew that. Tell me, please, what did he look like? How was he, in himself?'

Her eyes were huge in the dim light. 'To me he was just an ordinary boy.'

Ordinary? James? No. Beautiful, ambitious, funny, quick-tempered, impetuous, but ordinary? No. No.

'He was very young,' Meredith was saying, 'his skin was young, like so many of those boys. He was exhausted when he arrived and his wound was in a bad state, quite a slash to the upper arm, severe loss of blood, though it mended quickly. His voice was unusual, with a throaty quality to it and similar intonations to yours. Were you aware that both you and he slice off each sentence at the end, as if you are in too much of a hurry to linger on the final word? Then, as he got better, he grew mischievous and childlike, reckless, as many of them did. It was the release of being away from the lines for a while. We had to put up with all kinds of pranks, I can tell you. Your brother was a ringleader, a practical joker, not that there was much scope in the hospital. But they got access to a typewriter and sent round a directive to bed-bound patients that only those reduced to one limb out of four were henceforth to be sent home; the rest would be considered fit for duty, trenches widened to accommodate wheelchairs and ramps provided alongside fire steps. Most took the letter in good part but some men wept.'

'It seems a cruel thing to do. James wasn't cruel.'

'You don't think so? Perhaps it was just that, like so many of them, he had gone beyond knowing what was reasonable.'

'His values would not have deserted him, even in those conditions.'

'Oh, is that what you think, my dear Evelyn? How saintly you are with your strong bones and your pioneering spirit. You think the world operates in black and white, don't you, and if there are grey areas then the law will sort them out. I think it remarkable that you have reached the ripe old age of thirty and still believe there is clarity about what is right and what isn't.'

I didn't know what I had done to rile her. 'We ought not to talk any more,' I said, 'in case we say something we regret. We have both drunk far too much. Please.'

She lay watching me, one dainty arm crooked behind her head. 'I've weighed up what I want to say. I know that if I do tell you, something will be broken for ever. Bizarrely there's a part of me that wants to preserve your memories of him. You are all so frail, creeping about in your old museum of a house. Why, I can see the imprint of your father's head in a cushion on a drawing-room chair and I swear that James's boater hangs at a certain angle in the hall because that's how he left it. I've done an experiment, pushed it another way, but half an hour later it's always back in the same position. It's as if you all took a deep breath when you heard that he was killed and you've never let it out again. Now what if I break this spell, I think, and tell the truth about their precious boy? What then?'

'Nothing could make me love or miss him less.'

'Oh, that's never been my intention. No, we all need to love as much as we can. Perhaps a whiff of human frailty might make you love him more. Well, the truth is this. James fell in love with me, like so many of them did. We were ministering angels, after all, in our white veils and aprons. Those men emerged from the pain and the horror to find that we had created order and had quiet voices and gentle hands. We were women. But unlike the others your brother was greedy. It wasn't enough to look – he had to touch too. He grew hungrier and hungrier, pursued me, wouldn't leave me alone, refused to take no for an answer, found out my routine until, on the evening before he was due to go back, he came looking for me with just one idea in his head.'

I watched the candle within the lantern flicker as it swung back and forth. Dimly I was aware that the lovers had settled into the bottom of the boat, murmuring and nuzzling.

'Say something,' she said.

I was silent.

'Do you understand what I'm telling you?'

'Of course I understand. There's Edmund.'

Her voice came in stabs. 'Ah no, you don't understand. I'm telling you that he forced himself on me.'

I said not a word.

'Well?' she said.

'Please, no. Don't.'

'I was ready for denial. I know you'll say it wasn't rape. I couldn't understand your brother until I met your father, and now that I've met you too I have an even clearer picture of why he did it. Oh, James was brought up decently all right, but there was a kind of stranglehold on his emotions, a point where he simply went blind and gave in to desire because he didn't recognise desire for what it was. He thought that desire had to be satiated, like hunger or thirst. There was no stopping him; he would not listen to me or I suspect the voices of all you others in his head.' She looped her arm round my neck and pulled herself up so that her mouth was actually on my ear. 'Let me tell you one more thing,' she whispered. 'Then you'll believe me, perhaps. You see, I wasn't just any nurse. Like I say, I was with a Roman Catholic order. I was training to be a nun. I had taken vows. You didn't ask where it was I went at night, to be alone, where he found me. Can't you guess?'

I thrust her away with such force that my elbow flew back and cracked against the side of the boat. 'I don't believe you. Why do you want to hurt me like this?'

'I don't want to hurt you. It's the truth. I'm telling you the truth because I want my life back. I did not choose Edmund. I love him, though I thought I never would – he had done such damage to what I was. But when he was born I felt this tug at my heart and I could not help but embrace him. But why should that one moment define my life? I didn't sin yet I find myself with no vocation, no future and hardly any money, forced to love the child conceived in a moment of struggle and fear. And, because of Edmund, I have to relive that moment again and again, the fact that though my mouth opened no sound would come, that I felt so little and powerless, in such pain and shock, not just my body but my soul, my own self, all I wanted to be, violated. In the end I couldn't live with the imbalance of that, of knowing you were all here, oblivious to the damage he'd done.'

It was impossible to follow what she'd said. Instead I was scrabbling to recover my old images of James: James in uniform, the hardness of his warm cheek when I kissed him, James mortally wounded and innocent. 'Did you make this allegation about James to my father?'

'No. I did not.'

'Why not, if it's true?'

'I took pity on him.'

The pair in front had emerged from their embrace and in a clumsy effort to regain their seat, tipped the boat so furiously that one of the oars fell into the river. Margot gave a little scream, stood up, clutched hold of the side and tried to reach it. Too late I saw what was happening; the next moment she had tumbled in after the oar with a wild cry and a great splash. She surfaced, shrieking with laughter, hair plastered to her face.

'Never mind the oar,' shouted Hadley, a little more sober. 'It's floated too far away. Work your way round to the front and hold on to the prow ...'

Meredith and I sat side by side, not touching. My face was set in a travesty of a grin, as if I thought that was the correct response to losing an oar and a passenger, and I discovered that I was wet through. The bottom of the boat was inches deep in river water and Margot had splashed us all. Meanwhile, the commotion had attracted the attention of other boats, a few of which came pitching or gliding downriver, depending on the oarsman's skill or degree of inebriation. 'Are you all right?' 'Is everyone safe?' came voices across the water.

'We've lost an oar,' called Hadley, hauling Margot back into the boat, where she slithered in her trailing robe like an ungainly fish.

'Hard to find it in the dark,' someone said after a few minutes.

'I tell you what, grab hold of our painter and we'll tow you in.'

By now we had drifted a long way downstream, but at last our boat made uneven progress back to Lady Carr's jetty. Margot was shaking violently under the sodden blanket. I thought perhaps Nurse Meredith would spring into action, but she said nothing and I couldn't bring myself to look at her. As we neared the jetty we saw that quite a crowd had formed, including Lady Carr, whose jet beads glinted in the moonlight. And there too, with the inevitability of all the events of that fateful night, I saw Sylvia Hardynge, shrouded in a shawl and hopping from foot to foot, and beside her Thorne. I looked away to the far bank, which was mercifully dark, and then closed my eyes as the boat drifted with surprising speed to its mooring.

Everyone was shrieking instructions to Margot, who had to be helped out of the boat, swathed in a dry blanket and rushed up to the house. Arms reached down to Meredith and me. I allowed my hand to rest briefly in a warm male clasp, then stood shakily upright, though I could scarcely feel my hands and feet. My dress clung to me, the blue satin sheath drooped from my shoulder, and my hair was matted against my cheek. I walked through the crowd, still with that polite smile stuck to my lips, looking to neither right nor left. Meredith was ahead. And now I was on the lawn, feet squelching in wet shoes, the strip of blue satin knotted round my thighs, and I was past the empty dance floor, and the arbour where the band had been. I had almost reached the gate at the side of the house. I would walk straight home, I thought, anything to get away. But it was too late. I heard his voice behind me full of incredulous laughter: 'Miss Gifford, Sylvia said you were here but I thought she must be mistaken. What an extraordinary coincidence.'

I stood stock still in my sodden clothes, aware that my frock clung to me, was perhaps even translucent, and that my hair was in rat's tails. Half turning my head I murmured, 'Forgive me for not stopping, Mr Thorne. I am very wet. If you'll excuse me.'

But he came closer and put the back of his finger to my arm. 'You are freezing cold. Can I offer you my jacket. No? How are you travelling home? Sylvia and I could take you ...'

'Thank you. We have a cab.' I moved on. From the corner of

my eye I had seen the group who'd thronged the jetty hurrying towards us, led by Sylvia and Lady Carr. Then at last I was at the side of the house and out on the street, where miraculously a cab was waiting with Meredith already crammed into the far corner of the back seat. For a moment I wondered whether I could bring myself to get in with her. Then I thought of Edmund, of work in the morning, and of Thorne, who was staring after me.

We did not speak on the journey home, though from time to time one or other of us shivered violently. At Clivedon Hall Gardens I paid the cab-driver and unlocked the front door while Meredith waited wordlessly on the step. Once inside she slipped away and ran upstairs.

Rather than follow, I waited until there was no further movement overhead then went into the dining room, where I drew back the curtain. Moonlight fell on the table set for breakfast, on the looming furniture.

I sat in my customary chair from which I could see the portraits of father and James. My brother's eyes were shadowed in the inadequate light but the lines of his cap and shoulder were clear as ever. I went up close and drew my fingertips over the glass. Never had I wanted him back so badly.

But my father. Even now I could smell the whisky on him, a sickening whiff of hair pomade and spirits. At night sometimes, after the war, I had woken in the small hours and known that he was still up. When I crept downstairs I found him at the table, a tumbler pushed among the breakfast things, the decanter un-stoppered, his head sunk low. Sometimes, if I could bear it, I sat with him.

Once he did speak, weeping unrestrainedly so that tears and saliva dribbled onto a plate. 'I killed him,' he said, 'my son.' And he glanced at me with cowed eyes to see if I would offer any comfort. 'I could have kept him back. I could have pulled strings and got him a safe posting. Instead I forced him to sign up early. I envied him. I thought the war would be glorious and swift and that it would be better for the firm if he volunteered. I told him he was a coward when he admitted to being afraid.'

I could not even bring myself to reach out and touch his hand. I did not trust those whisky-fed tears or know how to forgive him.

But now I had words all right. 'Why, on top of everything else, did you not tell me about Meredith and Edmund, father? It's too much for me to bear.' I knew why. Father had preferred to wallow in the death of an innocent boy. To have acknowledged that James had darker urges, had loved a woman, would have sullied the process of grieving, complicated the guilt. And so he had kept James's memory simple, like a martyr's.

I did not believe Meredith. I loathed her. But she had altered my image of James for ever. Desire hung about the polished surfaces of that room. I felt it twitch and mutter even within the tightly folded and rolled napkins.

Chapter Nineteen

When I arrived at Caractacus Court at ten o'clock the next morning, or rather the same morning, in yet another cab, courtesy this time of the *Daily Mail* fund, I was greeted by Mrs Sanders, who invited me to go up and view the transformation to the Marchant living accommodation. She told me that Leah had been scrubbing floors both in her own house and other people's since her release, and had already saved five shillings. Leah stood at the entrance to her room, arms folded as if to say, I told you so, wearing a jaunty hat and well-brushed jacket and skirt. Thanks again to the newspaper, her debts to Mrs Sanders had been paid and her old room refurnished with a couple of beds and four dining chairs. There was even a rug to go before the fire and a cradle for the baby when she got him back, though I doubted that an eighteen-month-old child would fit into so small a bed. Less promisingly, I distinctly smelled alcohol on Leah's breath.

Once in the cab neither of us spoke. Leah was pent up, clutching a canvas bag containing gifts for the children, as stipulated in a letter from the home – grapes and coloured chalks. Apparently she still regarded me as her worst enemy because she turned her face to the window and refused to engage with me. And I, reeling from the events of the previous night, was in no mood to speak to her. My eyelids stung and my pulse raced – I had slept for perhaps an hour and a half. Poor Leah, engaged in the mission to save her children, could have no idea how remote she seemed to me or how unfit I was at that moment to be her legal representative. But then, as rain slashed against the window, she suddenly said, 'You tell 'em to let my kids come 'ome with me and I'll give 'em such a treat of fish an' chips. Mrs Sanders'll mind them evenin's, when

183

I go cleanin' them banks. Mr Breen give me a reference so I shall have no trouble gettin' as much work as I like.'

'Mrs Marchant, please don't raise your hopes. There is no question of the children coming home with us today. This is simply a visit in which we must begin the process of convincing the authorities that you are a fit parent. So of course we shall tell them the good news about your work and you will be allowed a brief interview with your children – fifteen minutes, they said – but that is all.'

'D'you think I can bear to see my children and then leave 'em again? I thought they was comin' 'ome.'

'It was explained to you very clearly after court that the judge had ordered that you have a visit. Nothing was said about the children coming home. There is a long legal progress to be gone through first.' I spoke sharply and she said nothing more but stared sullenly out of the window.

The home was set behind a pair of gates bearing a sign in wrought iron: GOOD SAMARITAN HOME FOR DESTITUTE CHILDREN. There was a yard with hopscotch marked out before a grey-brick building with high windows and double front doors set in a Gothic-style frame and painted green. 'That's why I chose this place,' said Leah, 'because I seen the hopscotch.'

We sat in the entrance hall, where a flight of stairs rose dead centre, divided on a little landing and then continued to left and right. The unplastered walls were painted dark green to shoulder height, cream above, and there was a smell of antiseptic covering up something less palatable. Although the building was quiet there was a definite atmosphere of lives held in abeyance.

The matron kept us waiting for several minutes, which I thought ill-advised. Leah could not sit still but crept again and again to the foot of the stairs, peering up as if expecting her daughters to come running down from the landing. The quiet was punctuated by the occasional distant closing of a door or the echo of a woman's voice. Sometimes Leah fiddled with her hair and twitched at her skirts or glared accusingly into my face. Thanks to my father I was all too familiar with the symptoms of one overfond of alcohol but deprived of the bottle. By the time we were summoned into the office Leah was wild and my heart was in my boots.

The matron, Miss Buckley, was dressed in a formidable costume of pale grey linen with a silver badge on the lapel: an engraving of the home complete with its cathedral-like doors and the Latin motto '*Ut prosim*' above it. Her hair, cut in a chin-length bob, was brushed into a shiny grey helmet. Considerable effort had therefore gone into her appearance and yet she had achieved what most women would strive to avoid – an air of utter restraint, which betokened a kind of negative vanity. I sensed that she would be rigid.

When she opened her mouth I knew we were doomed. Her voice was too high and girlish for a woman well into her forties, and though she smiled a good deal, her eyes were hard. Her desk was completely empty except for one closed file, and she indicated that we should sit on two wooden chairs opposite. I thought with surprising nostalgia of my basement office stuffed with files and papers, which at least showed that for decades Breen & Balcombe had been grappling with human transactions. Surely this room ought to have some sign that its business was children? The only obvious reference was a pious painting of a child at prayer beneath a crucifix on which a lurid figure of Christ hung with blood dripping from brow, hands and feet.

For a moment I was distracted by the memory of Meredith's drunken disclosures about her vocation and had an absurd urge to laugh – today she and Prudence were off to the British Empire Exhibition. Did Prudence really not know that Meredith was a Roman Catholic, and therefore a viper? Once again I was flooded with dread. She sickened me utterly, the way she had insinuated herself, used her son to win our trust and then attempted to destroy my brother's memory.

'I think it's wonderful, Mrs Marchant, that you have come to visit your little ones. You'll find them in very good spirits,' said Miss Buckley.

Leah nodded eagerly, setting a pair of ornamental cherries wagging on her new hat. For the time being she was composed in her dark clothes, but her hands were folded tightly on her bag as if it contained her excitement.

'There are just one or two things I need to say,' added Miss Buckley in her over-soft, over-modulated voice, 'before I bring the girls in.'

'I'll see them alone – we'll be private, won't we?' said Leah.

Miss Buckley acknowledged the interruption with a slight lift of an eyebrow. 'No, not this time. As I was about to say, we have very strict rules about visits from parents. It can be upsetting for our little ones to see their mothers, and your two, Mrs Marchant, have only just started to settle. In some ways they're coming on beautifully – you'll see that Ellen has completed her first sampler and dear little Cathy is learning her alphabet. We think she's very clever.'

'She is clever,' said Leah. 'They both are. I want 'em home.'

'Shall we talk about that afterwards?' said Miss Buckley quietly.

'I think it would help Mrs Marchant to accept the current situation if there was some hope.' My voice, abused by last night's unaccustomed alcohol and lack of sleep, sounded rusty. 'Perhaps you can explain the process to her?'

'She will need to show that she can provide a good home for the children, of course. Where is the husband?'

'We are attempting to contact him. He is at sea.' So far we had sent three letters to shipping companies enquiring after Sam Marchant, all of which had been sent back with the words '*Not known*'. 'But even if he is unavailable, I think we will be able to prove that Mrs Marchant has provided the children with a comfortable home and we are checking to see that there are places for the girls at a local school.'

'That all helps. We have to be sure that we are returning our children to safe homes where they will be cared for as well, if not better, than here. But for the time being, I want you to listen to me very carefully, Mrs Marchant. You shall have fifteen minutes precisely with the children. We are very strict about a first visit. Miss Gifford and I will be with you at all times. It's appropriate to give them a little present, if you have one, and ask them about their studies. When they come in you may shake hands and later you may kiss them goodbye, but otherwise we discourage physical contact because the children find it too disturbing. And I must warn you that if you fail to keep to any of these very easy rules, we shall be forced to end the interview early and the board will be notified. As I said, we have learned from painful experience, the shorter the better at first.'

Leah said nothing more but sat with her head back and her bottom lip clenched between her teeth. I felt nauseous. Miss Buckley rang the bell, there was a few minutes of silence, and then the door opened and two little girls were ushered in by a mistress who was dressed from head to toe in beige.

The children were aged perhaps seven and five and wore identical grey frocks and white pinafores. The younger had brown hair pulled into a tight tail at the back, the elder's fine, near-white hair was parted at the centre and worn in two thin plaits. In her right hand was a scrap of canvas. Both had huge greenish eyes. At the sight of their mother, they stood absolutely still, hand in hand.

'Oh my Gawd. Oh my precious girls,' breathed Leah.

The girls didn't move but the younger turned her solemn eyes towards the matron, who nodded. 'I've been telling your mother that you know your ABC, Cathy. She's very pleased.'

The child watched her silently.

'Give mother your ABC.'

Both little girls were frozen to the spot, hands tightly clasped.

'Cathy,' said Miss Buckley in her soft, sweet voice, 'do as I say.'

Nothing. Finally the matron said, 'You may shake hands with your mother then, if you can't remember your ABC, and with Miss Gifford.'

The older girl's gaze flickered to me and my lips managed a frail smile. The child was an inch or so shorter than Edmund, but whereas his eyes were trusting and inquisitive, this little girl was expressionless as she came up to me, sister in tow. One after another, I felt their small hands in mine. Both were cold and neither returned the pressure of my fingers.

'I believe your mother has brought you a present,' said Miss Buckley.

Leah produced the bag of grapes, squashed so that the juice had bled into the brown paper, and the chalks in a little cardboard box.

'The girls will be allowed to share with their friends after tea,' said Miss Buckley. 'And now I think, as nobody has anything to say, our time is almost up so ...'

One of the children gasped, as if she had been holding her breath all this time; at the same moment Leah's spine seemed to collapse and she held out her arms. The spell broken, the children hurled themselves at her and all three were knotted together, their heads pressed close.

'Very well,' said Miss Buckley. 'It's time to part now.'

They were sobbing, covering each other with kisses, arms wound tightly together.

'Come, Ellen,' ordered Miss Buckley. 'Bring your sister away.'

The group tightened, the sobs grew louder. I pushed aside my chair and backed to the wall. Had Leah not been between me and the door I believe that I would have walked out of the home into the cab rather than face that scene. The matron marched up and tried to pull one of the girls away but she stuck fast. 'Help me,' Miss Buckley commanded, and when I didn't move, she opened the door and called sharply, 'Miss Hands.'

'Oh good God,' I cried, 'this is inhuman. Could she not have five minutes alone with her children?'

'It's because I am human that I won't allow it. The judge promised in his letter that the mother would behave herself. Have you any idea how long it will be now until these girls settle again? Night after night the older one soils her sheets.'

The other woman came in and there followed a nightmarish attempt to wrench the children from their mother. Their fingers were unpeeled one at a time from their grip on her clothes and hair, and their eyes were wild as they felt themselves torn away, struggling, howling, writhing. At the last moment Cathy, the younger, got hold of her mother's skirt again and the pair once more clung to each other.

At long last, and much too belatedly, something in me broke. 'No,' I shouted. 'No. This cannot be right. Miss Buckley, if you will leave us alone, I undertake to return these children to your care in five minutes.'

The matron's immaculate hair had come adrift, her collar was askew. She stared at me venomously and returned to her task.

'I shall report you to the board for cruelty to these children,'

I said, very quietly now. 'You are perhaps unaware that we have powerful friends.'

'We have rules.'

'Yes. You have rules, but in extreme cases I believe rules have to be bent. Even I, a lawyer, believe that.'

Miss Hands, the minion, had given up the struggle and was looking at her fingernails as if to detach herself from the proceedings. Leah now had both girls on her lap, and the grapes were a sodden purple mass on the floor beside her foot.

And then the matron abruptly gave up and left the room, followed by Miss Hands. I closed the door. 'Leah. You have five minutes. Five minutes. If you don't let the children go after that, I can guarantee that you will never get them back. Do you understand me?' She was whispering into their hair, showering them with kisses. Their crying quietened.

I went to the window overlooking the yard and the treacherous hopscotch. Again I remembered the conversation in the boat with Meredith and I recognised the danger – because of what had happened at the art party, I was a different woman this morning and there was no telling what I might do next.

As if in proof, I now began to look around the room. In one corner sat Leah. The youngest child was telling her about Sunday tea, at which they had jam and sponge cake. And in the morning was church. According to Cathy, the service was at least three hours long. My hand rested on Miss Buckley's empty desk with its inkstand and ledger complete with fresh blotting paper. Behind it was a filing cabinet. On one wall was the crucifix, on another a further very bad painting in oils, presumably of the Good Samaritan at work. And to the left of the window was a noticeboard with a dozen or so typed or handwritten lists and memoranda pinned to it.

Three minutes had gone by. Somewhere upstairs a handbell was rung and then carried along a passage, still jangling relentlessly. The girls were attentive as rabbits to a dog's bark. 'Playtime,' said Cathy. 'We go out to play now.'

'Hopscotch?' asked Leah.

'Skipping. We skip.'

When I have read every notice on this board, I thought, I will tell Leah that it is time to go. There were details of the local doctor and hospital in case of emergency, a list of board members, weekday and weekend timetables (two visits to church on Sunday: morning and evening), and the dates when a nurse would come to inspect the children for nits. And pinned to the bottom right corner was a handwritten page:

The Metagama
Date of Sailing, 22nd September, 1924.
150 children. Aged 8 and above.
Placements various, domestic, agricultural.
Fee £13.00 per child.
Submissions by 11th August 1924.

I looked from the notice to Leah and her children and remembered Carrie Morrison's warning and, in the boat last night, Meredith's scathing judgement of the government's emigration policy. Was this to be the fate of these children? What if Leah could not resist the bottle and her drunken husband was never found?

The filing cabinet was not locked, and when I peered inside I found that the partitions were neatly labelled: ACCOUNTS, MEDICAL, BOARD MEETINGS, CHILDREN ADMITTED 1920, 1921. In the third drawer I found what I was looking for, MIGRATION, and in a folder:

Canadian Outfits for Girls:
1 warm overcoat
1 hat
2 sets warm underwear . . .
1 comb
1 prayer book . . .

I crushed the page into my pocket. My time was almost up. Frantic, I scanned the noticeboard again and found the somewhat yellowed sheet:

Board of Trustees, January 1923
Bishop Ogilvie
Reverend Hawkin . . .

Other names: Thurrock, Curren, Smythe-Engleby, Carlyle . . .

Ten names in all. I unpinned the notice, folded it up small and put it in my pocket. Then I told Leah, 'It will look much better if you surrender the children now rather than be forced.'

A gush of endearments followed. The children, I noticed, were more stoical than their mother; the younger, Cathy, clutching the chalks, the older, Ellen, again holding tight to her sister's hand. They were now keen for the moment of parting to be got over while Leah was too wrapped up in the drama to help make it happen. When I opened the door Miss Hands was in the passage, looking frightened. The children were hugged violently by their mother, then surrendered. I was relieved to see that Miss Hands smiled down at them kindly, and that they took her hands fearlessly. Then they were whisked away with merciful speed.

'We should wait for the matron to come back,' I said. 'We should apologise for the earlier scene.'

'She's the one what ought to be sorry.'

'Leah, she holds all the cards. Don't you understand? She could report you to the board and they could forbid further visits.'

But after quarter of an hour or so it became clear that Miss Buckley would not return to her office. Her absence was the last word and I realised that she was even more formidable than I had thought.

Chapter Twenty

After depositing Leah at Caractacus Court I made my way by omnibus to Arbery Street, where I intended to tell Mr Breen about the disastrous episode at the children's home. He was not about, however, so I sat in the basement and wrote a verbatim account. At one point I went upstairs to make tea, offering Miss Drake a cup as usual, today more than ever for the sake of companionship.

'Thank you, no. I shall have my tea at a quarter past four.'

'I can wait.'

'I wouldn't dream of putting you to the trouble.'

I tried to catch her eye, I so longed for a little warmth, but she went on hammering at the keys.

By the time I let myself into Clivedon Hall Gardens that evening the family was at supper and Meredith's voice rang clearly through the half-open dining-room door.

'There were wonderful artefacts from Africa. Prudence was very taken with them, weren't you, Prudence?'

'Certainly. I have a great fondness for colour. The exhibition gave one a sense of one's place at the centre of an empire teeming with opportunity and inspiration. My criticism is that there was too much to see in one day. Far too much. I shall have to go back. The silks from India . . .'

'And of course I could not keep away from the Canada Hall even though I knew it would make me a touch homesick,' said Meredith. 'They insisted that our chief claim to fame is that we make good butter. Can you imagine? When we have so much richness . . .'

I was determined not to sit at the same table as Meredith and had actually reached the foot of the stairs when Min appeared from the basement with a tray of liver and onions. 'Are you going straight in to dinner then, Miss Gifford? I imagine you won't be wanting soup.'

So I sat next to Prudence, managed a few mouthfuls and after a while began to register a disturbing change, which in the circumstances had a macabre irony, as if the Fates were laughing at me. Surely I must be imagining it, but no, absurd though it seemed, Prudence too was in danger of falling a little in love. There was Meredith with her huge eyes and darkened lashes, cutting Edmund's liver into slivers, some of which she slipped onto her own plate so he wouldn't have to eat it all. And there was Prudence, alert to every move, no longer huffy with disapproval but teasing, posting remarks across the table as if daring to see how they might be received.

'No, Meredith, I did not like that Aboriginal shield. On the contrary, I found it horrific. You always seem to prefer items connected with blood, I notice; whereas I liked the more domestic artefacts, the—'

'Blood and death,' said Meredith, with her mouth full. 'Even you cannot deny their existence, Prudence. My art teacher, Mr Waters, instructs that they are common themes in art. Oh, and love of course.' Here she looked Prudence full in the eye and I felt the poor woman quiver beside me. 'You show me a great painting, Prudence, and I'll show you . . .'

'In Hunt, for example, *The Light*—'

'Hunt is not a great painter. It's time you came to terms with that. He's great with his brush. He's great at telling a story, but he's not a great painter. He does not push back the boundaries of our understanding; he is insipid.'

'How can you say that . . .?'

The rest of us were excluded. Mother interrupted from time to time with an admonition to Edmund to keep his elbows off the table or eat up his nice liver but she'd been defeated at bridge that afternoon and consequently had a headache. Grandmother, who was fond of liver, ate with her usual dedication to the task and for once did not bother to pick up snippets of the conversation. Only I, it seemed, spotted the danger to Prudence's peace of mind.

The subject of the party came up over the blancmange.

'Meredith tells me you had a lovely time,' said mother a little resentfully, 'but that you nearly drowned in the river.'

'Hardly.'

I would not meet Meredith's eye though she exclaimed, 'Oh, it was so good to see Evelyn having fun for a change. You should have seen her knocking back the absinthe.'

There was an awful silence. 'Absinthe,' said mother faintly.

'Not in front of Edmund,' said Prudence.

'Why not? What is absinthe?' he asked.

'A poisonous drink. So poisonous that it's against the law,' mother said.

'And mommy drank it?'

Meredith hugged him. 'And so did Auntie Evelyn, and look, we're both still alive. It's not poison, Edmund, unless taken in great quantities.'

'All alcohol is a form of poison,' said mother. 'It's a poison to children, Edmund, and to some adults who don't know when enough is enough. But absinthe. I'm surprised at you, Evelyn. Your father always used to say that if, as a lawyer, he was ever found dabbling in illegal substances, he would expect to be struck off.'

Meredith laughed. 'Absinthe, like all drink, is delicious, Edmund, and don't let anyone round this table tell you otherwise. Your father, as I recall, was especially fond of spirits.' I flinched at this reference to James, which was accompanied by a sideways glance at me as if to say, Remember what I told you. 'What your grandmother means is that like so many grown-up things, drink has to be treated with respect. Why, I bet you've drunk plenty of absinthe in your time, haven't you?' she asked grandmother, who was sucking blancmange through her remaining teeth.

'We got hold of some once for a first-night party – the play was a Sheridan, I believe. This was before the ban, of course. I have never been so sick. But afterwards I dreamed that I was a ballerina. I've never forgotten that dream. So vivid. So lovely to float through the air and then leap clean off the stage.'

Meredith helped herself to more blancmange; she had a very sweet tooth and was undaunted even by Rose's lumpy milk puddings. I broke in hurriedly with an offer to take Edmund upstairs for a bedtime story, and to my relief he came willingly, holding my hand as if we were old friends. I had visions, as I got up from the table, of his performing the same trick as the Marchant girls and clinging to his mother's skirts. He chose the story of Briar Rose, the abused girl whose fate was decided by the whim of a couple of wise women and whose only other claim to distinction was that she slept for a hundred years.

Afterwards he lay against me full of questions. 'But she'd be a hundred and fifteen when she woke up. How would she be able to stand?'

I thought of those little Marchant girls trapped in a place they hadn't chosen and my anger grew, like the wise woman's in the story, until when Meredith came up to help Edmund with his prayers I was in a furious state. Wicked, wicked woman for slandering my brother. And now she'd compounded the wrong by seeking to corrupt his son with talk of absinthe.

After Meredith had kissed Edmund on the forehead he curled up on his side, ready for sleep. I took her pointy little elbow, pushed her into my own bedroom and shut the door behind us. 'I can't bear it, what you said about my brother. Admit you were lying.'

'Evelyn, aren't you tired after our late night? I am.' She did look exhausted, sunken-eyed.

But the counter-arguments had been building in my head all day. I would take her story apart until there was nothing left but the lurid shreds of her twisted imagination. 'You know what bothers me most of all: that you said you were training to be a nun, that you would lie even about that. You love clothes, beautiful things, art, pleasure. Forgive me, but I see nothing of the nun in you.'

'Oh,' she said wearily, her hands loose on her lap and her head bent, 'and what is your image of a nun, I wonder? I wanted to be a nun because I loved God, it was that straightforward. I was a fool, I guess. I had such a clear sense of what I would do, it was bound to go wrong. I would devote myself to God and I would nurse. And then in the war, in those hospitals, my faith – I guess that's what you'd call it though it doesn't fully explain what I felt – at first grew even stronger. I could do what was required of me.

I could love those men, those pitiable men; I could love our enemy, who sometimes came to us in a pulpy mess as prisoners; even the profiteers and the politicians and generals who had sent men to their deaths in such monstrous numbers. I didn't become angry or rebellious or resigned because I had sacrificed my will to another's. What I *thought* was irrelevant after that, what I *did* and believed was all that mattered. Yes, I had surrendered, and it was a good feeling. I let go. I did my work. And then your brother came along.' She glanced at me and her eyes were sober, as if she were struggling to be entirely truthful, but I didn't trust her. I thought her a consummate actress and this gravity just another ploy. 'He saw me as a challenge, something to break through to. He wanted me, all of me, body and soul, my full attention. He couldn't stomach the fact that I might actually have something else, someone else on my mind.'

'My brother did not rape you. He was incapable of hurting anyone. He was kind and respectful. He wouldn't do that to any woman because he loved *me*. He would think of it happening to me.'

She lay back on my pillow and drew her knees up to her chest, watching me. 'It's not my intention to make you think too harshly of him. I understood him and perhaps in some ways I wanted him. I had wanted so many others. I wanted to be held and kissed and made love to. I wanted oblivion. Of course I did. But don't you see? I had wanted it but given it up. I had turned my back on that kind of comfort and he violated the choice I had made. That was the worst thing he did, almost worse than forcibly entering my body.'

'But if you wanted him, you must have given him a signal?'

'What signal, exactly? That I found him handsome and amusing? That I felt sympathy for him? That I rejoiced in his recovery and was so sad because he had to go back? Yes, I felt all those things. Is that what you mean, Evelyn?'

'I think he must have believed—'

'You were about to say he must have believed that when I resisted him I was just play-acting? Then you think as your brother chose to. You are no better than him. I might have known. God, you British middle classes, you cannot be in the wrong, can you, especially not if you want something you can't have? He regarded my resistance as an obstacle, simply, to overcome.' She rolled up from the bed and stood so close that we almost touched. I could see every detail of her small throat and her moist mouth and her hair falling in feathery wisps across her forehead.

'He raped me, Evelyn. Believe it. Accept it, please, so that we can put it behind us. So that we can be on the same side.'

Her eyes were pleading and ardent, turned up towards me like a saint's at the foot of the cross in a cheap painting. Perhaps it was fatigue, the lingering nightmare of the party or the visit to the Good Samaritan Home; perhaps it was the unwanted intimacy of that moment or that she seemed so false, so determined to act out her part, but I couldn't stop myself. My hand came up and I struck her on the right cheek, not hard but enough to shunt that piteous look from her eyes.

'I don't believe it. I used to think I would help you, that we should accommodate you for the sake of Edmund. If you want us to care for him, we will. He shall be ours. But I want nothing to do with you and your lies and your wickedness. I want you out of my life.'

She was still for a moment, not reacting even by putting her hand to her reddening cheek. Then she closed her eyes briefly, drew a deep breath and left the room.

Chapter Twenty-One

It rained sporadically all the way through Stella's funeral. We had to prop up our umbrellas in the church porch, where they were so numerous that I wondered if I would ever recognise mine again. Trickles ran across the flagstones and collected in a puddle by the step. Inside, the church smelled of wet fabric and lilies, and I was confronted by rows of black-clad backs and heavy hats. Stella's mother, Mrs Hobhouse, had feared that there would be a lack of mourners but instead there were rather too many and I saw her glance round in bewilderment at the crowd of strangers: reporters, voyeurs and police officers. The coffin, in lonely splendour on plush-covered trestles, was decorated with a single wreath of roses.

In between hymns we heard the wind bluster against the windows and a sudden spatter of hail. It was fitting, somehow, that a girl who had died violently in sunshine should be laid to rest in rain. Since the war all churchgoing had seemed to me inexorably connected with death rather than resurrection. My brother's memorial service, held in the church we'd attended all our lives, had left me untouched, even faintly bored, and I was outraged when later I saw his name inscribed on the plaque in the side chapel among the other war dead. How dare they confirm something I didn't believe to be true? My father's death, on the other hand, had been marked by the kind of bombast that featured in most aspects of his latter years. He was buried with considerable ceremony, mourned by a congregation of senior legal colleagues in their tailored coats and top hats. The address from the pulpit was by an archdeacon because our vicar didn't consider himself to be quite grand enough, and the wake had been held in the gloomy parlour of a hotel near Baker Street. What I remembered most was the smell, at midday, of the previous night's whisky and cigarettes.

They formed a sorry parade in my mind – brother, father, Stella, and behind them a million others. Waste, waste. I stared at the coffin and willed that girl to rise up and tell me the truth. What happened, Stella? Why did someone believe you needed to die?

A couple of pews ahead of me an older man and a young woman stood a little apart from each other. I recognised Carole Mangan, the waitress at Lyons, by her bony shoulders in a black coat that was too large, and her fine blonde hair sticking out from under her hat. Stella's family was clustered together, except for the husband of the disdainful sister, Julie. He had been consigned to the pew behind and remained seated throughout. The hymns were so conventional that they could only have been chosen by people who rarely went to church, and the vicar gave a brief, embarrassed address about a young girl's life cut off in its prime by a wicked act, presumably a deranged mind ... So much killing and death already this century, you'd think we'd had enough bloodshed ... In the end his voice trailed away as if he was worn out by the futility of his own words.

And then we all trooped out, jostled in the porch to retrieve our umbrellas and straggled down a path under a yew tree towards a square of land that had been newly annexed to form an extension to the cemetery. Poor Stella had again been short-changed. If it were me, I would much rather have lain among the snugly lichened or half-fallen gravestones in the old churchyard than in a bit of virgin earth that had hitherto been wasteland.

I stood well back from the other mourners, feeling more than ever an intruder, and wondered if any of them knew secrets about Stella, notably how she had come by the bronze dancer which was even now weighing down my briefcase. If Meredith was right about its value, no one here was moneyed enough to have given her the statue as a present – worn shoes, uneven hems, ill-fitting coats and greasy hat-brims all betokened shortage of funds – except perhaps the elderly gent who had accompanied Carole Mangan, a senior figure from Lyons who wasted no opportunity to point out to the press the showy wreath sent by the company as a mark of respect. He then shook Mr Hobhouse heartily by the hand and drove off in a waiting taxi, far too important to linger.

After he'd gone, Miss Mangan, who had been standing at the edge of the grave, glanced over her shoulder and shifted surreptitiously towards me, as if afraid of drawing attention to herself. Rain had reddened the end of her nose and her skin was made sallow by her black costume. She had brought me a wedding photograph, different to the one on Mrs Hobhouse's mantel because this was of the bride and groom and all the guests, including Carole herself wearing a pale shapeless dress and a hat with a turned-up brim. Stella's smile, as in the other photograph, was like a model's in a fashion plate.

'Do you know who everyone is?' I asked.

'Stella went through it with me but I don't remember them all, no. Most were family friends. There were three of us from work. You can borrow it if you like.'

'Can you spare a moment to talk to me?'

'I have to be back in the restaurant by one.'

'May I travel with you some of the way perhaps? Are you going by bus?'

We said goodbye to Mrs Hobhouse, who wore a dazed smile and scarcely seemed to know who we were, then set off through the now half-hearted fall of rain towards the omnibus stop.

'I have the list you asked for as well,' Carole said as soon as we were alone, and withdrew a sheet of paper from her bag. 'We did our best, me and the other girls. We argued over some. Number three, for instance, we was never quite sure if he came to look at Stell or Jeannie – Jeannie left about the same time. And seven is so poor he hardly seemed worth mentioning. She'd never have bothered with him.'

'Do any of these men still come to the tea shop?'

'A few. The wheelchair boy sometimes. Before she left, or at least before they found out she was getting married, they was all regulars.'

'Did the police ask about any of these men?'

'Obviously. I gave them the same list, but I just told them, didn't write the names down. They didn't seem that interested after I said Stella had never gone out with any of them.'

'How did you know? How could you be sure?'

'Stephen met her most days after work. I don't see how she could have kept another man hidden from him, or me, for that matter.'

'There must have been some occasions when Stephen wasn't able to meet her. What about her lunch breaks or days off?'

She shrugged. 'We had few enough days off and I presume she spent most of them with Stephen. At lunchtime we often get less than half an hour. Of course I don't know what she did with every minute. I only know what she told me, and it was pretty ordinary stuff. For the past few months it was mostly errands to do with the wedding. Sometimes I would go with her at the last minute – she never minded, so I doubt she was having secret meetings.'

'The thing is, Carole, there are one or two things I've found that don't quite fit with the picture I have of Stella. For instance, when I was in her house I couldn't help noticing she had beautiful clothes, especially underwear.'

Carole blushed. 'She loved clothes. She'd have starved to save for a pair of silk stockings.'

The omnibus came and we sat side by side on the top deck, I with the umbrella propped between my knees. It took several minutes for the conductor to reach us but I waited until we'd paid for our tickets before I showed Carole the scrap of paper I'd found in Stella's sponge bag. 'Do you know where this ticket is from?'

'No idea. It's nothing to do with Lyons, I can tell you that.'

'And here's something else I want you to see.' I opened my case again and showed her the dancer lying in its nest of tissue. 'I found it in Stella's old bedroom, in Acton. I think it might be worth quite a lot of money.'

She peered into the case. 'Never seen it in my life.'

'You don't think the manager, for instance, that man who was at the funeral, might have given it to her as a wedding present.'

'Are you joking? We had a whip-round for the tea set, like I said, but the manager didn't chip in. We had to plead with him to let us have a bob or two for her leaving party.'

'What about someone from your list?'

She shook her head then gave me a sidelong glance. 'There is something that I should mention, while I have the chance, though it's probably nothing much. Do you remember I told you that

Stella was nearly always on time? It's been on my mind ever since because one day in April, a couple of weeks before her wedding, she come in at about ten o'clock, two hours late, with mud on her shoes and her dress all crumpled, and it was obvious she hadn't been home all night.'

'Her sister thought she'd stayed out dancing at the Trocadero one night and missed the last bus home.'

'She hadn't been dancing that night – she wasn't wearing dancing shoes. When I asked her why she was late she just said she'd overslept and missed the bus. But I knew she was lying.'

'She had mud on her shoes?'

'That's it. She was wearing outdoor shoes and changed when she got to work. But I saw them in the cloakroom, caked with mud and little bits of grass, you know, like when you've walked across a muddy lawn that's just been mown. And her coat had a stain on it too, like a brown smear. I knew she'd done something she was ashamed of because of the way she behaved the rest of the day. It was always the same when she'd been unkind or gone too far mimicking a customer or some such: she went quiet and tearful and she'd keep hugging me again and again as if she wanted to be sure and make someone love her. She was like that all morning, couldn't do enough for the customers but kept looking at the door, as if she was expecting someone, or coming up to me in the kitchen and kissing me.'

'So where do you think she had been?'

'I've no idea, that's the thing. Somewhere not that nice. The coat smelled bad, you know, like it had been left in a damp bathroom. It made me think of hospital wards or an old bloke we have in sometimes who doesn't wash himself.' She glanced at me anxiously. 'And to be fair, I'd forgotten all about it. If it hadn't been for the fact she's dead and you keep asking questions, I wouldn't have brought it to mind again.'

We got off the bus on Holland Park Avenue. The rain had almost stopped and I sensed that Carole wanted to be rid of me; there was something shameful about discussing the dead girl's secrets only minutes after she was buried. I said I would take the train back to Euston Square but I was sorry that we had to part; her honesty, her desire to do the right thing were endearing and

I thought she would be a good friend, if only I could win her trust.

At the last moment I asked her to have another look at the dancer. She seemed afraid to touch it but in the end held it in her bony fingers. 'Isn't it heavy? Did it cost a lot? I shouldn't fancy it in my home. My mum would have a fit.'

'I don't know what it's worth. I'm going to try and find out.'

'Stella loved to dance. But not like this, obviously ...' Her pale eyes, as they met mine, were a little fearful. Then she thrust the statue back in my hand, got on her bus and rode away.

Later I looked at Carole's list.

Gentlemen Admirers. Stella Wheeler

1. Married man. Wore a ring. Bowler. Dark overcoat. Big nose, moustache, specktacles for reading. Seemed tired. Lunchtimes only. Never ate. Just coffee. Read The Times. *Watched her ankles.*

2. Boy. Eighteen-ish. Clerk of some sort. Sore neck from his collar. Pimples. Sunken cheeks. Worshipped Stella. Would spend his last penny on a bit of toast, just so he could hang around at a table.

3. Gentleman. Old. White hair, moustache. Specktacles. Briefcase. Always polite. Never seemed to mind who served him but we thought he looked out for Stella or Jeannie. Took the same table each time. Back to the wall. Under the clock. Watched, and sometimes got out papers and worked. Would visit odd times. Always in the week, never on Saturdays. Sometimes away for weeks at a time, we'd almost forget him, then he'd be back.

4. Another gentleman. Mr Griffiths. A bit younger than the one above. Bald on top, longish straight hair round ears. Fifty? Pinstripes. Big tips. Liked all the girls and we liked him. Asked about our love lives. Wanted to know what we did weekends. Sometimes came a few days together, then a long break. Still comes in from time to time.

5. Young man in wheelchair. Late twenties. No legs. Mother used to bring him. Proposed to Stell every month or so. Loved it when she flirted with him.

6. Fat man. Banker, he told us. Bowler hat. Smelled of cologne.

Ate cakes, loved cakes, sweet tooth. Natty shoes. Used to grab Stell's hand sometimes when she passed and ask if she'd go on a date. She used to say the touch of him made her shudder. When she told him about Stephen he said he'd got far more to offer than an insurance clerk.

7. Another cripple. Harry. Missing one arm, one foot. No job. Loved Stell. Must have drunk gallons of tea for her sake. Heartbroken on afternoon she left. Said he'd never come back and never did.

8. Prince Charming, as we called him. Too good to be true. Very tall, very well turned out. Posh voice. Not more than thirty. Always had an umbrella. Made no secret of his feelings, though overdid it we sometimes thought. Used to tease her. Brought her a posy once. Enough to make her quite hopeful – we girls used to build it up into a romance and plan a silk wedding gown for her, and a trousseau. But then, a month or so before her wedding, he stopped coming.

Chapter Twenty-Two

I arrived at the office of Breen & Balcombe very wet and hungry, my fingers itching to take up a pen and do routine work, to keep myself steady after the turmoil of the art party and its consequences. But the minute I let myself into the hall, Breen's voice rang out: 'Gifford?'

'Mr Breen.'

His office, that strangely metamorphic place, had transformed itself into a no-nonsense hub of business and he was in the kind of mood when an interview with him could go either way: he would spark fire one minute, be reasonable the next. A vast document on heavy parchment was spread before him and a pencil was tucked behind his ear as he played to the hilt the part of the overworked lawyer. There was no sign of tea, whisky or any of the other Friday treats.

'Door,' he yelled. I shut the door. 'Now where have you been?' he said on a long sigh, as if I could have been to the Antipodes for all he knew.

'To Stella Wheeler's funeral, as I—'

'And what was the value of that? Remind me.'

'Her mother asked me to be there. I didn't think—'

'It seems to me you've done a lot of not thinking recently, Miss Gifford. I have a letter here from Miss Buckley, matron of the Good Samaritan Home, copied to the chairman of their board of trustees, Bishop Ogilvie. Here it is, two close-written pages on the subject of your unprofessional and provocative conduct.'

'I had no choice, sir.'

'Hah.'

'I think if you'd been there, if you'd seen the children with their mother . . .'

'You see, this is it. When I told them I might take you on my colleagues said to me, "Steer clear of the woman, any woman. You're mad, Breen, to consider it even. Women cannot see the wood for the trees," they said. Or to put it in the words of a particularly eloquent journalist, "Women see through a stone wall what is not on the other side." *Personally* you might well have felt pity for the children, Miss Gifford, but *professionally* you had no right to do anything other than your duty as a legal representative. As it is you've probably set Leah Marchant's cause back irretrievably. Miss Buckley writes that you used threats against her.'

'I merely pointed out—'

'The entire affair shows a lamentable lack of judgement.'

'Mr Breen, I could not bear to see those children suffer. We must rescue them – they are in danger of being sent to Canada or Australia if we don't. I saw a notice of sailing on the board. My friend Miss Morrison says it's common practice to ship foundlings abroad.'

'What are you talking about? Canada! Don't be so ridiculous. How old did you say the Marchant girls were?'

'Seven and five, which I admit seems young to be migrated, but apparently it happens. They'll be sent there one day possibly, if we don't get them back.'

'Well you've just raised the stakes on that. Miss Buckley also states that you removed something from her office. I'm assuming that is simply not true.'

I didn't know whether to laugh or cry as I took the document bearing the names of board members and the list headed *Canadian Outfits for Girls* from my briefcase. As I unfolded them Breen's head sank into his hands, but then he recovered, picked up the papers and studied them. 'You are in serious trouble, Miss Gifford. You could be struck off for this. It constitutes a complete breach of trust, professional conduct, the lot. What were you thinking of? You could have copied them out.'

'There wasn't time.'

'I suspect our only option will be to grovel. I hate that. Tell me again what you meant about Canada.'

'Miss Morrison says that some children are sent overseas to be adopted. But it may be worse. I've heard that some children are forced to work as domestic servants or farmhands. Others are mistreated.'

'I'll get Wolfe to look into it. You stay clear. Don't even breathe until I give you permission. Off you go now, for God's sake. It's likely the police will be here any moment to arrest you for theft so before they arrive you might as well draw up a couple of affidavits for me.'

I could tell that I was in fact forgiven so instead of leaving I sat in the chair by his desk and lifted my sodden briefcase onto my lap. 'There's something I've been meaning to show you, sir. I brought it from Stella Wheeler's bedroom.'

He gaped. 'You didn't steal it?'

'No, no, I gave Mrs Hobhouse a receipt.'

I took the statue from the briefcase and stood it on his desk. Then, for good measure, I unfolded the ticket I'd found in Stella's sponge bag. Breen threw himself back in his chair, twiddled his thumbs and looked at the dancer. In the meantime the room had changed, as if the statue had drawn all the feeble light from a drizzly afternoon to itself and Breen's office was merely a backdrop. He leaned forward and advanced his face close. 'Now that, I'll admit, is fascinating.'

I breathed more freely as I watched him adopt a new pose, that of a connoisseur of fine art. He didn't touch the statue at first but got up and walked slowly round the desk so that he could view her from every angle. Then he sat down again and picked her up delicately by the plinth. 'You are right, she is beautiful. Utterly. Modern. It shouldn't be too difficult to find out where she was bought. A limited edition, I shouldn't wonder. French – you have to admire the French – not a Bourdelle but possibly a copy. Probably worth fifty pounds or so, quite outside our little waitress's league.'

'And then there's this. If you remember, I found it in Stella Wheeler's sponge bag when we went to the house.'

'As I said at the time, possibly significant, possibly not. When all's said and done it's only a cloakroom ticket.'

'The thing is, sir, I think it probably *is* significant because I've found out that Stella was a collector. She'd carefully tucked away a conker case and an acorn cup and other bits and pieces in a remote part of her wardrobe. Her mother thought they were remnants of her childhood but they weren't; they were freshly fallen. And now Carole, a waitress who worked with Stella, has told me that in April Stella stayed out a whole night and wouldn't say where she'd been. She came into work the next day with a stained coat and dirty shoes.'

'Well?'

'Well, don't you think, Mr Breen, that this all points to a love affair of some kind?'

'A love affair? She'd only been married a fortnight.' Despite his bluster – the words 'love affair' were spoken incredulously as if to say no one in their right mind would embark on such a thing – he didn't appear to be shocked but nodded as if this was what he'd been thinking all along.

'I've been pondering it for some time,' I went on. 'And now Carole has given me a list of men who admired Stella, although she's fairly sure none of them met her outside work.'

Breen's face was a mask of incredulity. 'Miss Gifford, a man's life is hanging by a thread. A trial date has been fixed. And you have been *pondering* a theory that could change everything? If Wheeler had cause to be jealous, then he had a motive for murder, don't you think?'

'I do. But what if Stella had become a nuisance to a rich admirer? Blackmail . . .'

He flung himself back in his chair and yelled, 'Wolfe!'

Miss Drake appeared. 'Mr Wolfe, as you may recall, has an interview with a colleague from the War Office.'

'Curse the boy. Then we'll meet first thing Monday, eight o'clock sharp. See he gets the message.'

When Miss Drake had gone I said, 'Don't you think we should tell the police?'

Few things delighted Breen more than throwing obstructions in the way of the police, though he made a show of prevaricating by chewing his lip and looking at the ceiling. 'In time. Not now. I don't want them asking clodhopping questions of our poor Mr Wheeler. Things are not straightforward. We've had a report from Wheeler's army medical officer, and we think there's a chance we may be able to run an argument of unfit to plead after all, though it's a very high threshold to cross. The defence has to convince a judge and jury that the defendant is incapable of understanding what is going on. There are many pitfalls. If we lose the argument and Wheeler, after trial, is found guilty, our chances of mitigating on the grounds of diminished responsibility are damaged because a jury has already decided he *is* of sound mind. At this stage, until we've clarified our line of defence and had a conference with Burton Wainwright, I want to play all our cards close to our chest. And, by the way, I had a call from Thorne. Says he'd like to take a look at the crime scene for the sake of completeness or some such nonsense. Damned nuisance he couldn't have come with us the other day. I said you'd go with him on Monday afternoon – ought to keep you out of mischief.' He stared at me blandly.

'I can't,' I said.

'I beg your pardon?'

'No ... I have too much work. I am at least a week behind with—'

'Wolfe can't take him on account of his asthma, and I've far too much on, so you're all we have, I'm afraid.' He threw a sheaf of documents across the table. 'You should read this report from Wheeler's medical officer, Reardon. Despite the little matter of Miss Buckley of the Good Samaritans, I'm minded to set you up for a cosy tête-à-tête with Stephen Wheeler, woman to man, see if you can get anything else out of him, especially now you suspect there was a third party in the marriage.'

Wheeler's medical report shed quite a different light on a man I had hitherto come to regard as entirely a victim of circumstance.

When recruited in August 1914 Wheeler was deemed of 'inferior' health due to a slight weakness of the lungs – asthma, like Wolfe – and the fact that he was somewhat overweight and pigeon-toed (the examining MO noted that Wheeler had been confined to a desk ten hours a day since leaving school more than a dozen years previously). He was nonetheless considered fit enough to join up. Army life seemed to have been good for his health because there were no other entries until an account of chlorine gas poisoning in 1915, which affected his already damaged lungs and resulted in severe bouts of coughing. A healthier man would have suffered less, wrote the MO, who added that Wheeler received the news that he was to be returned to England to convalesce without comment.

This lack of responsiveness became a feature of the report. When he was examined again, prior to being sent back to France, it was noted that he showed no sign of emotion, either pleasure or distress, at the thought of being returned to the front line. Later, when treated for a slight wound to the foot sustained through a display of extreme carelessness by a private with an entrenching tool, the doctor noted that Wheeler made light of the pain, hoped the other chap wouldn't be disciplined for it, and asked if he could be patched up by nightfall, when he was due to go on patrol, a duty he seemed to relish despite its dangers. 'Wheeler is one of the type of personalities who are much depended on by his fellows,' noted Doctor Reardon. 'His behaviour is utterly consistent, never showing an excess of emotion, notably fear, and even under heavy shelling he remains calm.'

When he was finally invalided out, due to the loss of three fingers on his left hand caused by handling a malfunctioning grenade, Wheeler had displayed some irritation that he would not see the war through to the end.

In a handwritten postscript to the report, Dr Reardon had scrawled,

Wheeler was in many ways the ideal soldier – unflagging, always ready to volunteer for difficult tasks, utterly dependable, able to sleep and maintain normal functions in the most challenging conditions. When I was asked, along with other officers, to select men to perform the most taxing of duties his was often the first name that came to mind. One of our regiment was convicted of desertion and firing on a military policeman whilst already on suspended sentence for a like offence. When Wheeler's name was drawn for the firing party I was relieved. I knew he could be relied on and that he would not flinch.

I have noted that there are types of personality that survive better in war than in peacetime – a man like Wheeler thrives on the routine of war and the absolute necessity to obey orders. The shocks of trench life register less with this type than with

others. At times of greatest trial to the emotions, such as after a battle, in burying the dead, he worked tirelessly. I have never known him to break down. You will note the commendations, in my view much deserved.

And yet despite, or perhaps because of, the above, I would strongly recommend that Wheeler be examined for his psychological fitness to plead. What is acceptable, even convenient, in time of war, does not allow a man to survive in more normal circumstances. His fellows thought Wheeler 'odd' despite his trustworthiness and bravery under fire, and I wonder now, on reflection, whether he wasn't of a particular type that experiences difficulty in engaging in normal human relationships, and whereas in the face of constant danger most men do at some stage show signs of fear and shock, such a man as Wheeler cannot make a genuine display of such emotions at any time. In the circumstances, I wonder if Wheeler is capable of comprehending the complexities of the British legal system or, more to the point, if the British legal system can possibly comprehend Wheeler.

I spent the afternoon in my musty basement ploughing through a heap of paperwork, much of which would have to be taken home to do at the weekend. Each envelope had been slit open by Miss Drake, the contents examined, refolded and put back. She did not prioritise my papers in order of urgency, as she did for Wolfe and Breen, or take it upon herself to respond to more obvious, non-legal queries, so I had to wade through an indiscriminate heap of licensing applications, maintenance orders, letters from an affronted husband and a self-righteous wife, a search, a couple of requests for appointments for the signing of wills, and a query over an eviction order.

Then there was the letter from Miss Buckley of the Good Samaritan, which made very unpleasant reading indeed since it was full of exclamation marks and rhetorical questions about my qualifications and fitness for the job, and stated that she felt duty bound to write a full report to the board given that her authority had been so severely undermined. My poor father, I reflected, would be spinning in his grave. Had he not, against his better judgement, paid more than five hundred pounds for my university education, articles and professional fees, yet here I was once more in peril of losing my position and hopelessly out of my depth?

Back at Clivedon Hall Gardens disaster had struck. My fault, again. The smell of smoked haddock, it being Friday, was pungent as I unlocked the front door. At dinner there was no sign of Meredith or Edmund and the atmosphere was funereal. Nobody replied when I commented on the rain and asked how they had all passed the day. Finally I said, 'Where are our visitors?'

'They are flat-hunting,' said Prudence, making the sensational gesture of pushing aside a near-untouched plate. 'Meredith says that you have told them to leave.'

I picked a bone from between my front teeth and took a sip of water. How typical of Meredith to avenge herself with this precipitate gesture.

'Your mother and I think it unforgivable that you should have acted without consulting the rest of us,' added Prudence.

'You surprise me, Aunt Prudence. I thought that you and mother disliked Meredith being in the house. I thought you would have thanked me.'

'There is such a thing as Christian charity. We would have given the girl a chance, time to find somewhere suitable. We would have made her welcome until then. Why were you so cruel to her?'

How could I announce over fish pie that Meredith had accused James of rape? 'I'll discuss it with mother later,' I said.

Mother, with the dazed expression of one who has been given her heart's desire only to find it was not at all what she wanted, had finished eating and was dabbing her mouth with her napkin. At eight o'clock, whilst we were eating tapioca, the front door opened and then we heard feet on the basement stairs. Meredith had doubtless arranged to have supper put back to be eaten later in the kitchen with Min and Rose, who adored her.

Meanwhile I planned the forthcoming conversation with mother. How would she respond if I told her about the alleged rape, given that her entire world was built around the spotless shades of her dead son and husband? In the end I took the coward's way out. When she and I were alone I said that she had been right all along: we simply couldn't afford to accommodate Meredith and so I'd told her to go. I had, however, offered to take care of Edmund.

'It seems so sudden,' said mother, glancing nervously at the door. 'I wish you'd consulted me.'

'I'm sorry. We'd had an argument, she and I, to do with the art party, her drinking. I believe that she is a very difficult woman, full of bitterness. I should like to help her but I don't think our way of life is compatible with the one she longs for. Above all we must continue to support and protect Edmund.'

Mother's mood was odd, as if her mind was on something else. She stood up, drummed her fingers on the dressing table, then swept across the room to the writing box containing James's letters, glanced at me, began to speak, but then changed her mind and started again. 'Oh, of course. I've wondered if what she really wants is for us to adopt him. Then she'd be free. Certainly we must do the right thing by Edmund. Well, perhaps it will be a blessing that you have spoken out ... But I can't help thinking, Evelyn, that with all your expensive education, you might have handled it better.'

It was a miserable weekend. Edmund was to be found in odd corners, pretending to read a book and full of questions none of us chose to answer about what was happening, and where was mommy, until at last grandmother invited him into her room to play board games and look through an album of opening-night good wishes cards. Prudence put on her hat and a martyred expression and went out on mysterious expeditions while mother paid calls and held a bridge afternoon. I was ostracised by all but tried not to mind, telling myself that I was glad Meredith was leaving and that I had far too much work preparing for a morning in the magistrates' court on Monday – routine for an experienced lawyer, an ordeal for me – to be bothered with domestic matters. All the while, the proposed excursion with Thorne haunted me.

Meanwhile, it went on raining. Meredith spent long hours walking the streets looking for somewhere decent and affordable (as I heard her tell Min on the stairs), and returned wan and soaked to the skin. The girls fussed over her, ran her a hot bath and made a dainty supper because she'd missed tea. On Saturday evening I decided I ought at the very least to apologise for striking her and say there was really no hurry, she could stay until she'd found alternative accommodation, but when I knocked on her door she appeared briefly, fragile as a flower in her delicate robe, and actually flinched as if terrified I would slap her again. Later I heard Prudence knock and gain admittance. Their conversation went on and on.

On Sunday Meredith took Edmund to church, having first established that I had decided not to go that day. How could I pray for strength in exercising the Christian virtues of restraint, continence and humility when in truth I wanted none of them? By the time the five of them came back to lunch it was perfectly clear to me that I was now the outsider, and that the others, even my mother, had united to protect the wronged little Meredith and her fatherless son.

Chapter Twenty-Three

On Monday morning even Wolfe managed to turn up for the eight o'clock meeting, somewhat rumpled and with one cufflink in his pocket because he'd not had time to fix it before leaving. The bronze dancer stood in pride of place on Breen's desk, concealed under a duster.

'Wheeler's trial date has been fixed for the fourteenth of July at Aylesbury Assizes,' said Breen. 'We have a plea of not guilty and nothing whatever to support it except for a couple of character witnesses.'

'And no plausible motive,' said Wolfe.

'Miss Gifford has come up with a motive.' Breen paused for dramatic effect, then swept the cloth from the dancer. Miss Drake, note-taker, took one look and gave me a reproachful stare, as if to say she might have known I would sully the place with such obscene statues. Wolfe sat up a little as Breen continued: 'Jealousy. This statue is evidence that there may have been another man in Stella's life. The dancer, which she could never have afforded to buy for herself, is presumably a gift, but we don't know from whom. Not her husband, I would suggest, given that it would have cost half a year's income. And I don't see Wheeler purchasing such an item. There is also the night, a fortnight or so before her wedding, when Stella went missing with no consistent explanation to her friend or sister. All we know is that she appeared at work with stained and foul-smelling clothes, and with mud on her shoes. And then there's this cloakroom ticket, which Stella hid away in her sponge bag, and a list of customers at Lyons who took a fancy to Stella when she was a waitress.' He laid out on the desk the scrap of paper, Carole's list and Stella's wedding photograph.

Wolfe picked up the dancer and turned her in his meaty fingers, a glint of appreciation in his eye. 'It should be possible to find out who sold her, even who bought her. But the kinds of establishment I have in mind are very exclusive. They will want to protect the identity of their customers. What about the police, what do they think?'

'The police searched Stella's room but overlooked the dancer or thought it unimportant. It's up to you to do their work for them, Wolfe. I'm sure you have ways of encouraging even the most discreet tradesman to divulge a little information, in the interests of justice. Miss Drake, unlock the cash box if you will, and provide Mr Wolfe with five pounds' worth of half-crowns. And now the ticket in Stella's sponge bag. Does it mean anything to you, Wolfe?'

'It could be anything. A raffle ticket? A cloakroom ticket? Number 437. No, it's slightly larger than a raffle ticket, wouldn't you say? I've seen this type a good deal, Breen, haven't you, among our clients, issued by the police when they confiscate clothing or such. But Stella didn't have a criminal record. And what about the stains on her clothes? What were they? Mud, blood? Do you suppose she had an accident or was lost, or was perhaps induced or forced to lie down in her clothes – is that what you were thinking, Miss Gifford?'

For a moment we were silent as we pondered those murky hours between Stella leaving work and turning up late the next day. Then Miss Drake spoke for the first time. 'Of course,' she said, putting the tip of her pencil daintily to the middle of her bottom lip and pausing to emphasise that she was doing us a favour by uttering a word, 'she might have had a medical emergency, but of a very *specific* nature.'

'You mean she sought an abortion,' said Wolfe.

'Child murder,' said Miss Drake firmly.

Breen sighed. 'It had crossed my mind, though one might have expected something to show up in the post-mortem. And if it was the case that Stella was in some kind of desperate situation would she not have told her friend at work? I thought you women talked about anything and everything.' Having looked from Miss Drake to me he didn't press the point – apparently he didn't find that we were representative of our sex.

'Stella's friend at Lyons did mention that the clothes smelled of hospitals,' I said.

'I could find out . . .' said Wolfe.

'I daresay you could,' said Breen, 'but in the meantime, on the basis that it's possible our poor victim had a medical emergency, I think Miss Gifford should visit the local hospitals to see if she spent a night there. Miss Drake will find out the name of her family doctor and speak to him. I may make a few enquiries among our female clients, who might have a better idea than us where a girl could go for a particular type of help. And Wolfe, get someone to check police records for the night Stella went missing, in case she ended up in custody. And now,' he added, nodding dismissively at Miss Drake and me, 'I'd like to speak to Mr Wolfe.'

An hour later I was in Shoreditch Magistrates' Court making licensing applications, this time before a bench of four lay magistrates, one of them a lady in a startling white hat. For once I found myself greeted smilingly by the bench, I suspect because the novelty of a female advocate broke the tedium of granting the Railway Arms an extension until eleven o'clock for a coming-of-age party, and another, a week on Saturday, for an engagement. The magistrates pushed back their chairs and discussed each case sotto voce as if they were deciding guilt in a capital offence and when granting the application they did so with an air of sighing magnanimity.

Later, this time with Wolfe yawning on my left hand, supposedly to lend his support, I defended a landlord prosecuted under the Intoxicating Liquors Act. 'A woman was responsible for the legislation in the first place; it's surely fitting that you should take on the extra work it brings,' Breen had said, though he'd once told me he approved of the act, describing it as one of the very few recently introduced onto the statute books that might enhance the quality of our lives.

The landlord's defence, disclosed to me when he turned up five minutes before the hearing, was that it was ridiculous to expect him to ask every young customer his age before serving a pint, and that bloody ('Excuse me, miss') woman MP hadn't thought through the consequences of her bill. 'Other landlords manage it,'

I told him. 'I shall simply suggest to the court that it was an uncharacteristic lapse and that you have a clean record on this type of offence.' I did not add that with Lady Astor's act only months old it was to be hoped that no landlord had accrued a record.

'By the way,' murmured Wolfe as we sat together under the dock while the magistrates retired to consider their verdict, 'the Marchant case. Breen told me to look into it. Devilish hard to get the children out by legal means, I'd say. The Good Samaritan Home is notoriously evangelical. Takes a hard line on the sort of background those children come from. The chair of the board, Bishop Ogilvie, is teetotal. Can't stand drink; can't stand the fact that some children don't have a father or attend church.'

'So what must we do?'

'We'll need to pull strings, Miss Gifford. I doubt your Mrs Marchant, from what I've heard, will be able to prove to the courts that she's a fit mother. Homes like the Good Samaritan will argue that children should be severed from the vicious influence of such a background.'

'We have money. She will work.'

'Money isn't enough. If the home's taken against her they will spy on her and inspect her to see if she has the moral rectitude to bring up children.'

'And if she hasn't, according to them?'

He shrugged. 'Then the home will dispose of them as it sees fit.'

We sprang to our feet as the magistrates came back and fined my landlord ten shillings.

Afterwards, still brooding on my conversation with Wolfe, I waited an hour and a half for the case of a young boy (one of Breen's habitual clients) in the children's court who was pleading guilty to stealing a pineapple. I dearly wanted to see Miss Buckley and the Good Samaritan Home subjected to the due process of law. It wasn't just that she and I had been locked in violent antipathy for those few minutes in her office; it was that Leah had all the cards stacked against her: the home had money, influence, tradition, righteousness, religion on its side. Poor Leah had only love (and the home would even regard her type of love as dubious), Mrs Sanders and me.

Meanwhile Wolfe, with characteristic ennui, represented a wife-beater who was pleading innocence on the grounds of severe provocation (adjourned for trial), and defended successfully in the brief trial of the son of a fellow solicitor accused of dangerous conduct on a bicycle.

After the pineapple case, which was adjourned so that the child's mother could attend, I was at last free to go.

Chapter Twenty-Four

By the afternoon the weather had cleared, and I took the Metropolitan Line to Chesham under a blue sky studded with small white clouds. Though I would not have admitted it to myself, I had made a concession to the fact that I was meeting Thorne by wearing a much lighter blouse than usual with mother-of-pearl buttons and a slightly scooped neck, though, in view of the recent unsettled weather, my shoes were suitable for all seasons.

As the train rattled out of Wembley Park I was conscious of a clearing of the mind that had nothing whatever to do with the sunshine. It was as if the tangle of home and work fell away and instead I was as untrammelled as an arrow shot cleanly from its bow.

I had not experienced the world in such vivid colours since the July before James was killed, when he was on leave and we picnicked on Primrose Hill, lying on our backs afterwards elbow to elbow, hip to hip. When I turned my head, about to say, 'We'll buy an ice cream, shall we?' I saw that a tear had trickled from the corner of his closed eye, down his cheek and into his ear. I didn't say a word. We got up a few minutes later and walked home. I never mentioned the ice cream.

It was as if in the years since then I had been semi-conscious but was now abruptly awake, with everything so present to me that I blinked in the sudden burst of colour, sound, touch. Beyond the train window tranquil farmland gushed past, greens and creams and browns, and within the compartment the smallest detail came into sharp focus so that instead of filtering out the inconsequential I saw it all: a crumpled ticket, the ridges in the floor where cigarette butts, mud and fluff were caught, a mole the size of a farthing on the cheek of the child opposite, the way his mother's wedding ring cut into her swollen finger. A sane voice in my head repeated, You are a legal clerk accompanying a barrister on a tour of a murder scene. That is all. It is absurd to attach any other significance to the meeting. But that voice was drowned out by a roar of expectation.

In a terse telephone conversation with Thorne's clerk I had arranged to meet him behind the church. I had a map and a pencilled plan of the terrain, together with a list of instructions from Wolfe: *Check timing. Consider hat. How did Wheeler conceal weapon?* It was barely a ten-minute walk from the station, across the High Street, through a cluster of little cottages and up the lane leading out of the town to where Thorne was waiting for me beside a natty Ford. He leaned on the churchyard wall and wore a summer-weight suit and beautiful shoes, highly polished with stitching across the toe and narrow, neat laces. His trilby was perched on the wall beside him and his hair had flopped over his brow. When he saw me he gave a start, as if of surprise, and raised an eyebrow. I walked up briskly and put out my gloved hand, registering that both his pose and his reaction to my arrival had been staged and that he was possibly nearly as nervous as I.

'Very good of you, Miss Gifford, to give up so much of your valuable time.'

It was on the tip of my tongue to remind him that I had no choice in the matter but I was determined not to quarrel. In fact my plan, upon which I had dwelt at length during the small hours of three successive nights, was that he should find my company so dull that he would want nothing more to do with me. If I didn't see him again, I reasoned, my wounded heart would begin to heal. So we set off in silence along the path running under the churchyard wall and through the gate into the field.

At first my strategy worked. I told myself that he was just a man, after all, product of a good public school, the type I had known at Cambridge, only perhaps more able and ambitious than most. Well, I had nothing to fear. What was all the fuss about? In fact, when I glanced at him I decided, He's too tall to be truly desirable and you know him to be as ambitious and guilty of chauvinism as the rest – I wonder you ever found him attractive. Sylvia, the socialite, is welcome to him.

'No ill effects from the party, Miss Gifford?' he said at last.

'None. You?'

'Oh good Lord, no. But then I didn't take a dousing in the river. And Sylvia keeps a weather eye on my drinking, if that's what you mean. I'm never allowed to knock back so much that I can't drive her home.'

'I thought your fiancée very beautiful.'

'She is. Sometimes I forget how beautiful, so that when I see her after an absence I'm quite taken aback.'

I nearly laughed aloud. Until that moment my treacherous heart had allowed the hope to flicker that Thorne had engineered this trip because, despite his betrothed, he was as interested in me as I in him. The flame was extinguished by his devotion to Sylvia – expressed abstractedly, as if he were actually immersed, for that moment, in her loveliness – and it served me right. Well, I knew how to encourage men to talk about their heart's desire; I had learned the trick at my mother's knee. 'Have you been engaged long?'

'Rather too long. I've known her for years, since she was a bouncy little girl. I was at school with her brother, Donald. He and I were best friends. I used to spend weeks of my holidays in and out of the Hardynge house in Belsize Park.' I pictured those favoured children, several rungs above my own family on the social ladder, flitting from one pleasure to the next – tennis, cricket, cycling, theatre, dancing. 'My own home was much humbler,' he added. 'My father is a solicitor in Reading but the Hardynges welcomed me nonetheless. And when I got back from the war I found that Sylvia had become this astonishing young woman. How could I not ask her to marry me?'

I congratulated myself on dealing with the subject of his fiancée with generosity and detachment, although I could not help dwelling on the strangeness of his last remark. Nonetheless the exchange, in which Thorne had disclosed so much and I so little, had given me the upper hand. 'According to the police,' I said, consulting my notes, 'this is the path taken by the Wheelers. A witness has come forward, a farmer's daughter who passed them here, on the brow of the hill, about midday. She gave a very detailed description of Stella's pink dress and hat.'

Thorne paused and looked about. Near his left hand a pair of blue butterflies touched midair then flitted away, and from trees to the left I heard the faint knocking of a woodpecker. 'The reason I wanted to come here,' he said, 'was that I thought it essential to understand the lie of the land. You will gather that I'm frustrated at not being involved in the case myself but Hardynge is taking a great interest and so am I. Maybe I'll notice something that I can pass on to Wainwright.'

'In the end details of the crime may prove irrelevant. Mr Breen is still considering a fitness-to-plead argument.'

'Is he indeed? Fiendishly difficult. Especially given Wheeler's coherence both at the police station on the day after the murder, and subsequently in jail. I'm surprised at Breen. He hasn't a chance. Wainwright won't entertain the idea.'

'Perhaps Mr Wainwright should have met us here today,' I said curtly, stung by the criticism of Breen.

'I confess it never occurred to me to ask him, Miss Gifford. I was probably being selfish . . .'

He was altogether far less at ease than on other occasions – his irritation with Breen seemed uncharacteristic and even his movements lacked the wonderful fluidity that had drawn my attention before. He opened a gate, held it for me and closed it after us. I didn't look up at his face as I passed but mumbled my thanks. Afterwards I remembered how the hinges had groaned, the snick of the latch, and under my hand the warmth of weathered wood polished by decades of passing cattle.

'Did you have a good weekend, Miss Gifford?'

I quickened my pace. The breeze was light and fragrant but my heart ached. At that moment, as my shoulder had so nearly brushed his arm at the gate, as I turned away my head though I knew he was smiling down at me, I had so yearned for him to touch me that to keep up this facade of indifference seemed unendurable. 'Much as usual, thank you.'

'We played tennis, would you believe. Whenever it stopped raining we dashed onto the court, never mind the risk of slipping. I spend more time than I can afford playing tennis, always on a Saturday, sometimes Sundays too. The Hardynges have a grass court and Sylvia and I are quite addicted, though neither of us is half as good as Donald, who is an ace. Do you play, Miss Gifford?'

'Not any more. I used to.'

'So how *did* you spend your weekend?'

'Mostly working.'

'I might have guessed. I'll bet you drive yourself atrociously hard. Do you ever let yourself have a holiday, I wonder?'

'I try to. Last week was exceptionally busy so there was some catching up to do. Unusually for me, I had been out of the office a good deal.'

'Why was that?'

'This Wheeler case, among other things. And then the Leah Marchant affair is dragging on. If you remember, her children are being looked after in a home from which we're now trying to extract them.'

'Of course. Any progress?'

'We are afraid it will be difficult to have the children released. Leah Marchant's home life is far from ideal. Mr Wolfe suggests we may need to pull strings.'

'You have only to say the word and I'll see what I can do to assist.'

I was silent, caught by the twist of anger that habitually followed one of his assumptions of superiority, imagined or otherwise. Then I said, 'Thank you. I'll consult first with Mr Breen.'

After a few moments Thorne returned to the matter in hand. 'So, when the Wheelers came up here, he was carrying a picnic basket and she presumably a little handbag of some kind. Has anyone mentioned a handbag?'

'It was scarcely more than a purse, I believe, the same colour as her dress, containing comb and compact – it was buried with her.'

'Has anyone made a suggestion yet about where Wheeler hid the revolver on the way to the picnic?'

'We presume it would have been in his jacket or the picnic basket.'

'A revolver is quite bulky. It's odd that Wheeler should have been in possession of such a weapon during the war, let alone after it. They tended to be the preserve of officers.'

'I believe Wheeler was promoted to corporal during the war.'

'Nonetheless. Non-commissioned officers didn't usually carry revolvers, as I mentioned to Breen the other day.' We were walking briskly, despite the heat. Though I didn't look directly at Thorne I couldn't avoid his shadow, which sometimes tangled with my feet. 'If you like, I could carry your jacket, Miss Gifford.'

'Thank you. No. I prefer to keep it on.' This last remark was so churlish (and untrue) that I had to make up for it by saying the first thing that came into my head. 'Actually, it's possible that you could help me with the Leah Marchant case. I'm afraid to say that when she and I visited the children's home things went very badly. My fault as much as hers. I had an argument with the matron.'

Thorne laughed, youthful, delighted, and for a fatal moment I caught his blue, brilliant eye. 'Now why doesn't that surprise me?'

'I was most unprofessional, I admit, but the sight of two little girls clinging to their mother's skirts unhinged me. So now I have to find a way of getting the children out despite having lost all hope of the matron's co-operation. And I have found that they are vulnerable in another way. Did you know that this country apparently ships hundreds of foundling children to our colonies overseas?'

'I had heard, at Toynbee. And I believe there is to be a government commission to look into the practice this autumn. Surely the Marchant children are too young.'

'I'm not so sure. And even if they're too young now, they won't be in years to come.'

'What you need is contacts, Miss Gifford. If you could find out who is on the board . . . Why are you laughing at me?'

'I was ahead of you, Mr Thorne. I took a list of board members from the matron's office. I intend to write to each in turn but maybe I should save myself the trouble and hand the list over to you. You're bound to know someone, there are a few titles. I'm sure a word in the right ear from you would save me six weeks' work.'

'Do I detect a note of bitterness there, Miss Gifford?'

'Really, you can't blame me for having a chip on my shoulder.' It was happening again, the fatal allure of pitting my wits against his. 'I've heard all kinds of arguments against women entering the legal profession, the nonsense about special spheres and women

225

having no understanding of relevance or analogy or evidence, but there is one thing that nobody can quite bring themself to mention: that unless their fathers happen to be high up, women will lack the connections that make all the difference between success and failure in the law.'

'It's the same for men. Connections help men to advance as well.'

'Connections they have formed over generations, at ancient schools and universities, through family and friends.'

'Miss Gifford, I do sympathise with you, I really do. In fact you'd be astonished to hear how much my views have changed since I met you. But in one thing I cannot sympathise: this constant wailing that life is tough for women in the professions. Instead of griping about your disadvantages, why don't you make use of them, turn them on their heads? After all, it's a device we use all the time in demolishing an opponent's argument. You, as a woman, have the advantage of surprise and novelty. You are a pioneer, which in your place I would find extraordinarily exciting rather than a bind. I do believe that women have different qualities to men – you can't persuade me otherwise – but you should play on them. Even your enemies can't deny that women are often intuitive, eloquent speakers. Since you and I last met I've listened to another of your female colleagues performing in court – a Miss Cobb. Very impressive.'

'Yes, but the reverse is used against us too. Our critics translate intuition and eloquence into an over-reliance on instinct, too much talk. Now here, I believe, is where the infamous picnic took place.'

Since my last visit with Breen and Wolfe, summer had deepened in that unremarkable field. Rain had fallen so that the meadow grass was taller and the hedgerow busier still with insects. A cloud swept across the sun and in the distance a tractor engine wheezed into life. 'Are you looking for anything in particular?' I asked. 'Mr Wolfe, for instance, is intrigued by the fact that poor Stella became separated from her hat, which suggests that Wheeler – the murderer, I should say, whoever he was – perhaps took the trouble to carry the hat back to this picnic spot although he buried her handbag and shoes. Wolfe thinks that a girl as fashionable as

Stella would not have left it here herself unless she was in a great hurry.'

'I gather she was shot more than half a mile away, is that right?'

'It is, and although I never met Stella, I just can't understand why she agreed to walk so far. I've seen the type of shoes she wore. It's one of the things that troubles me: why she should stray such a distance from the picnic spot. There must have been very powerful persuasion.'

'You don't think she was forced at gunpoint?' Thorne stood with his hands in his pockets, hat crushed under his arm, absorbed apparently in studying the ground. I slid my jacket off at last, very conscious of my bare wrists and the thin layer of cotton voile on my upper arms. He glanced at my throat, and away.

'My own belief,' I said, 'is that Stella may have been having a love affair.'

In the silence that followed there came again a thickening of the air, muffling the other sounds.

'I see,' he said. 'Based on what evidence?'

'Various clues, little things she kept tucked away out of Stephen's sight. The trouble is, if I'm right and he was consumed by jealousy, it would make him *more* likely to have killed his wife than less.'

Thorne nodded and walked on so that I wondered if he too had found the words 'love affair' almost too resonant. Our pace, under the hot afternoon sun, was much slower. The joy of being with Thorne, of finding him companionable and sympathetic, overcame my determination to keep him at arm's length, and I talked freely about how I came to study law and my experience of post-war Cambridge. He had a most engaging way (probably honed through years of escorting Sylvia) of adapting his stride to mine and inclining his head when listening. For the first time in my life I gave voice to the guilt I felt at having benefited from James's death. 'I doubt if father would have had the money or desire to let me study and apply for articles if James hadn't died.'

'Yes, but you know we are all victims of chance. I'm not so very different to you. Hardynge has proved an extraordinarily kind and influential patron but it's partly because his own boy, Donald, will never be a barrister now. In that sense I too am a replacement son.

I didn't have too bad a war. Fortunate postings – my luck was in, I suppose you could say. Like so many others, I feel a great surge of guilt sometimes that I am still in one piece, that I even have one or two fine memories, of *fun*, would you believe? But Don didn't survive. He did, physically – I mean he's alive – but his nerve broke and he's confined to a hospital. I don't think he'll ever be right.'

'What happened to him?'

He swiped the hedgerow with his jacket. 'He was in Wheeler's regiment – 2nd London Rifles – most of the men from Imperial Insurance joined at the same time. Donald fought bravely but then there was an incident – forgive me, the details are private to the family – and he collapsed, mentally I mean. Since then he has been moved from one institution to another, in search of a cure. At present he's in a place not that far from here, beyond Princes Risborough.' There was a long silence. 'Suffice to say the Hardynges are utterly stricken still. I think, in fact, they'd be better off if he had been killed outright. I'm sure they know that, which makes things all the worse for them. Sir David visits weekly, the mother seldom, Sylvia when she can. She's a trooper. I used to go quite often, but my visits distressed him – they think I'm too much a reminder of the war.'

'Is it just a matter of luck, do you suppose, that enables one man to pull through the war in relatively sound mind, another not?'

'You're thinking of Wheeler and the fitness-to-plead argument. All I can say is that if you and I, Miss Gifford, were to see a bull charging towards us from the other side of this field, we would each react differently. Of course, if we were trained to run, we might run, or if we were trained to face it with a bayonet, we might do that, but if terror got the better of us, who knows what we might do? Why, you, I suspect, would argue with it and I would attempt to pull rank, and then if we both had any sense, we'd run like the clappers. And afterwards you might recover in a minute while I would shake for hours.' I loved to hear his laughter, throaty and soft.

'But Wheeler had a good war – I've seen the medical report.'

'A good war? War is so extreme. At times it was such lunacy

228

I could have thrown up my hands and walked off, never mind the consequences. We were hungry, tired, bereaved, often shaking with fright. Death was a second away. On the morning of an offensive we woke up knowing that half of us would be dead by evening. When I ordered my men to attack, I was ordering them to be shot. And even when we thought we were safely at rest behind the lines, mishaps occurred. I saw a man who was tapping out his pipe against a tree one minute lose his head to a bit of flying shrapnel the next. Nothing surprises me about what a person would do, or become, under those conditions. He might stand up in full view of the enemy and stroll out into no-man's-land to pick up a dead friend.' Here he glanced at me and I thought, he *knows*, can it be possible that he knows about my brother? 'On the other hand, I've seen a brave man cry because a tin of cocoa dropped from a shelf onto a duckboard. But we're lawyers, Miss Gifford, we know all this. We often represent people who have behaved impeccably all their lives and then go and commit some terrible crime.'

'But have you ever known a good man to do something really wicked, not just weak or cowardly but downright wrong? Could war make a man do that?'

'Wicked? I don't think so. I've seen a man lie his way out of the front line. I've seen petty thieving. I've seen men blow a week's pay on a game of cards or ten minutes in a brothel. These things aren't wicked, are they? Ill-judged, desperate, reckless. But wicked?'

We crossed Drydell Lane and entered the bridle path, a green tunnel leading up the side of the little valley, today more sun-baked and somnolent than ever. As the quiet countryside rolled away from us, and Thorne and I were well beyond sight or sound of any other human being, it dawned on me, in the hush of mid-afternoon, why Stella had been brought so far from the picnic spot. And I also knew that I no longer had any intention of holding back from Thorne; that instead, given that this was probably the only hour of my entire existence that I would spend alone with him – or indeed any man I found so desirable – I would take from it what I could.

Nevertheless, what I chose to say next frightened me so much

229

that I shivered, even in that airless track. 'A woman called Meredith turned up on our doorstep – it was through her that I came to be at the party because she shares a teacher with Sylvia. She claims to be – she *is*, I mean, there's no doubt about it – the mother of my brother's son, conceived while she was a nurse in the war. My father met her once but I didn't know of her existence even. Or the child's. And then last week at the party she told me that my brother had forced himself on her. You see, I cannot even bring myself to say ... raped her. I adored my brother; I know he wasn't capable of such a thing. Later she and I had such a dreadful argument that I struck her.'

The sun was very hot despite dense leaf-cover, yet in places the mud underfoot was not baked dry and I had to step aside or follow a higher bit of ground. A bee, languorous with the weight of pollen, thudded against my hand. In the long silence that followed I wondered if Thorne knew that he had just been presented with my heart.

'There, up to the left,' I said, thinking, I'll change the subject and give him the chance to escape my confidences, 'is the copse where Stella was killed.'

But Thorne said, 'Are you afraid that this woman, Meredith, may be telling the truth about your brother?'

'I don't trust her. I think her capable of manipulating anything. But one thing, I believe, is authentic. She showed me a note in my brother's handwriting. Just her name. Nothing else. She claimed that he wrote it while he was dying. I do believe in that note and I puzzle over it, why he would have written her name, just hers. Love or guilt, or perhaps as the beginning of a message? And I suppose I am jealous that it was her name, not mine. He didn't write to me before he died.'

'You haven't answered my question.'

'I don't think I believe her, no. But she's sown the seeds of doubt. I thought I knew my brother inside out. It was bad enough to realise he'd had an affair. I was a fool, naive. I didn't believe he'd ever loved any young woman except me.'

'Does it make a difference whether she's telling the truth?'

'Surely it makes all the difference in the world? Above all to the memory of my brother. I loved him. I thought I knew him.'

He sighed, took my jacket, combined it with his own, slung both on his shoulder and looked down into my face. 'Miss Gifford, your brother is dead. What you have left is a mother and her son. And the memory of a boy who before the war was, I suspect, as gloriously clear-headed and ardent as you. Ever since I met you I've been meaning to say that I'd heard of a Gifford, a Captain James Gifford who died after nearly twenty-four hours in a shell hole. His bravery was something of a legend. I heard it was a heroic death and that he'd crawled out of the trench to rescue one of his men. How old was he – nineteen, twenty? Poor boy, he had little enough time to learn how to love a woman other than you. He's dead, and surely in anybody's book that's punishment enough. Please, don't cry. This bloody war. It goes on and on, doesn't it?'

As we faced each other across the lane I realised that this was the most intimate conversation I'd ever had with another soul. And I also half-understood that we were laying our cards on the table one by one, and that we were edging closer whilst maintaining a show of keeping ourselves apart.

'To look at it from another angle,' Thorne said, 'why would this woman lie to you?'

'Because she can. To increase our sense of obligation?'

I walked ahead, wiping my eyes first on my sleeve then, belatedly, on a handkerchief. Oh, I should not allow myself to cry; he would think me weak and girlish. So I gathered pace and was almost running by the time I reached the little thicket where the pheasants were confined behind their wire fence and Stella had been buried. At the gate I fumbled with the chain looped round and round the post. Thorne didn't help but stood with folded arms, peering into the trees.

'I remember a wood in the war,' he said, 'blasted clear of most of its branches; the few remaining hung with bits of bodies, gas caught in the fallen leaves so that men were stumbling about groping for their masks, blind and screaming. If, that day, you had told me I would survive, and that I might stand once again at the top of an English valley, with a woman such as you beside me and a quiet sky above, I would not have believed you.'

'And yet there's Stella Wheeler,' I said harshly. 'We're here because she was murdered. English woods are not as peaceful as you had hoped.'

I got the gate open at last. The woods were hushed and the bracken had grown since last time. Now the leaf cover was so thick that hardly any sunlight came through and the shades of green were deeper, dustier. It was as though we entered an emerald cave with needles of light flickering here and there. I floated across the soft floor of the wood in a nugget of time other than my own. I had stopped crying now, my heartbeat had slowed, my mind was quiet and it seemed to me that I was half Stella – the girl whose cotton robe still wafted perfume from a hook on the bedroom door – half Evelyn, and I knew, as I had known the first time, exactly what must have drawn Stella here.

'Nobody would hear the shot, that's why he brought her so far. And I think she came willingly, believing that they would make love.'

If I reached out, I could take him. He stood so close that I felt his heat and sensed the tremor of his nerve-endings. My hand was still, lying against the side of my thigh, a mirror of his a few inches away. I knew beyond doubt that he had engineered this trip because he couldn't help himself. He was as absorbed by me as Peter Shaw had been, and the officer with the crimson glass bowl.

I pointed out trampled bracken and a bit of rope tied from tree to tree marking the place where Stella had fallen. But even the shallow pit in which she'd been buried was already half covered with new growth. There were signs, a beer bottle, a chocolate wrapper, that others had been here, locals and sightseers probably, taking a look at the crime scene. Thorne studied it all carefully and we consulted the map. 'If he left the coppice this way he'd have had to pass the manor house but eventually would have come to the Missenden Road, which would have brought him quite quickly into Chesham. Or he might have run back to Drydell Lane and gone into town that way. If, on the other hand, we pursue the theory that it wasn't Wheeler who shot her but someone else, he might have left a car in a lane nearby and escaped in any number of directions, towards Great Missenden or Wendover or across to Hertfordshire.'

'What do you think? Could it have been anyone but Wheeler?'

'I don't know. It was well planned. Quite neat. Wheeler lacks a plausible motive unless, as you say, he was jealous, so let's suppose someone else wanted Stella dead. Is it really possible that he could have known about the picnic, ensured that Wheeler went down for a couple of beers and in the meantime lured Stella to her death, shooting her with a revolver known to be Wheeler's? And why would anyone do that? She was just a waitress, hardly a threat. Though Wolfe's right that the question of the hat is intriguing. Wheeler said he found it with the picnic things but a lady would never normally be separated from her hat. Look at you; I've never seen you without one. But if the only thing we've got is a slight problem with a hat it looks very bad for Wheeler; a premeditated crime like this, a shooting in cold blood for what the prosecution will say was purely financial gain, and a refusal to admit guilt.'

We decided to leave the coppice by the western gate, a route that someone other than Wheeler, intent on escaping, might have taken. 'You've seen Wheeler,' I said. 'Do you honestly think that Stella would have been persuaded to march all this way to these woods on the promise of a little lovemaking with him? If I were her, I would have protested that there were plenty of other private places much nearer to the picnic spot. And I would have complained about the damage that a frolic in woodland might do my pink dress. I would have been totally bemused, in fact. No, I don't think Wheeler could have lured her all this way.'

It would have to be you, Nicholas, I thought. If it had been you who found me lying on a picnic blanket, if you had stood over me, held out your hand and said, 'Come, I know a place . . .'

We left the woods and followed the farm track up the valley to the lane. And yes, there was a fringe of trees where an automobile might have been concealed, even a tyre track in the dried mud at the edge of the road. A quarter of an hour after shooting Stella a man could be in Great Missenden or Amersham, less than half an hour would bring him to Princes Risborough. 'It is possible,' was Thorne's verdict, 'but not probable. There's no evidence. In my experience the simplest explanation is usually the truth.'

I had stopped thinking about Stella. Nicholas walked a little ahead and I noted the immaculate crease in his trousers, the dust on his shoes. We were between trees again, in sudden shade. After a few minutes I took my jacket from him. Soon we reached the farm and beyond it the long sloping track leading down to the town. 'It's so hot,' he said. 'I should have thought to bring a flask or such. Could we not sit for a moment?'

'Of course, if you want to.' There was nowhere obvious except a dusty verge so I stood with my arms folded while he made a show of looking around. Then he sighed, as if exasperated, and the next moment had taken hold of my upper arm and was looking into my eyes. 'Miss Gifford. You must forgive me. What I'm about to say is something I've been rehearsing for days. And I still think I'm mad to say it. But I find I must. I cannot live the rest of my life knowing I missed the chance. You must know, Miss Gifford, that I find you devastatingly attractive.'

I stood with my arm at a somewhat awkward angle, the sleeve of my blouse rucked up under his long fingers. The fabric of his shirt was of an open weave and the collar was soft, attached, the kind Edmund might have worn. After one startled glance at his face, the look of desperate appeal, I stared down at my scuffed shoes.

Remember this, I told myself. Never forget a single detail. There was a freckle above the knuckle of his thumb and I was amazed that I should have been given the chance to study so intricate a part of him.

At last he let go of my arm and said, very clipped, 'Forgive me. Forgive me. I have behaved unpardonably,' and started to walk away. I watched the distance grow between us.

Well, Evelyn?

'I have thought until now,' my voice was tentative, a slender thread, 'that the strongest feeling I would ever have for a man was grief.' He stopped. 'But now there's you.'

He was a few paces away, shaking his head, and when he looked at me at last his eyes were soft with doubt. 'What are you telling me?'

'I think of you constantly, until I infuriate myself. I try to brush you from my mind, because of Sylvia.'

He bowed his head, nodded. His hat was off and the angle of the back of his head, nape to crown, reminded me of Edmund.

'Very well, Miss Gifford. Evelyn Gifford. I understand you. I have behaved very badly. Let us forget I spoke.'

Voices clamoured in my head: the voices of Prudence, mother, myself. You can't have him. You mustn't. Be strong. Bear the hurt of parting now to avoid worse pain later. I cried, 'Do you think I will ever forget what you said? How could you be so cruel? Could you not have exercised a little more self-control?'

'It appears not.'

'Haven't you thought about Sylvia?'

'I have tried to consider Sylvia but I can't. I can only think of you.'

'This is just because I dare to argue. You think it's exciting to meet someone who answers back, especially a woman. Can't you see that? You should put me out of your—'

'Yes, that's so true.' He laughed suddenly. 'All true. Each time I can't wait to see you because I don't know what you'll say next, what fresh remark of mine will be demolished. You must have noticed how I've cropped up time and again these past few weeks. Why do you think that is? Except for the party. To see you there was the most extraordinary shock to me, when we ran down to the jetty and you of all people stepped out of the boat in that mad dress with your hair so wild. I think you are astonishing.'

'I'm not astonishing. It's just that I'm educated and ambitious and you're not used to women like me.'

He laughed again. 'Miss Gifford, what gave you this abominably low opinion of yourself? Look at you. I admit, I dreamed of women during the war and they certainly weren't like you. I wanted softness, I wanted to slide away into someone quiet and gentle and accepting. But then I met you and felt a spark in me, and I did, yes, find you exciting but beautiful too.'

The empty track rolled away on either side. His skin was damp and his smell was of soap and male sweat, so like my brother's. I had time to imagine the heat of his mouth before he kissed me but not its softness.

'I thought you wanted to put me in my place. I thought—'

His second kiss was the merest brush of the lips, feather light. He whispered, 'I am falling in love with you. Will you believe that? Would you please not argue this one point?'

'How can we—'

I felt the unknown bulk of his body against mine, the texture, the shape, of his tie and shirt buttons as he kissed me again. He seemed to me an expert but who had I to compare him with, apart from the boy under the canal bridge and my would-be lover at the War Office? Their ghosts were present in the shade, and Stella's and even that of my brother James, but then the astonishing intimacy of his kiss blotted them all out and I was just Evelyn Gifford kissing Nicholas Thorne among trees in a lane between wheat fields, with his arms drawing me closer and my hand on his upper back, and my hat pushed off as he caressed my hair and neck.

After a few minutes he pulled me deeper into the hedge so that we were hidden from the lane. This time our hats and jackets were flung down and I was drawn up under him, my back arching over his arm, his hand on my chin and his kisses dark and beautiful. I felt them as a tearing inside me, and I clung to his warm strong neck for fear of dissolving altogether.

I drew back at last. He whispered, 'Don't say anything. We won't say a thing. I don't know what this means. I can't think. This has happened and can't be undone.'

He kissed me again and smiled into my stunned eyes, and solemnly, in between kisses, tucked strands of hair behind my ears. Then I put on my hat and we walked sedately away, although my hand was tightly clasped in his. As we neared the town we separated, and by the time a hay cart lumbered past followed by an impatient motorist I was wearing my jacket and he was decorously ahead of me. Gradually we entered the bustle of the town and found that the rest of the world was still as we'd left it, that cabbages and plums were displayed outside a greengrocer's and that the baker's window, this late in the day, was almost empty, except for a cottage loaf and three tea cakes.

At the Queen's Head, where Stephen had his two or three pints after leaving Stella on the hillside, dead or alive, we stared, standing so close that Nicholas's elbow touched my upper arm, at the red-brick, large-windowed pub, shuttered against the heat of the afternoon. And then we turned up the lane leading to the church, where he had left his car, passing the open doors of ancient cottages and the shrouded windows of much grander houses.

I wouldn't let him take me home. Instead he agreed to leave me at Ruislip station, where I would catch a Metropolitan Line train. The engine started easily and he drove, as he performed everything else, with casual competence.

'Tell me what you are thinking,' he said as we left the enclosed lanes of the town.

'I'm trying not to think of anything.'

He kissed my palm. The car was very hot but he didn't unfasten the roof. I sat, butter soft, helpless, my hands folded on my lap, turning from time to time to convince myself he was still there. The smell of the Ford – leather and oil and polished wood – seeped indelibly into my memory of that afternoon.

At the station he sat beside me on a bench at the far end of the platform while we waited for the train. 'You're so quiet,' he said.

'Be grateful.'

'But I'm not grateful. I like your words. All of them.'

I laughed. Our hands lay on the bench. He drew the tip of his index finger along the inner side of my wrist as the boy Peter had once done.

The lines sang; the train was coming. 'I'll speak to Sylvia.' He squeezed my hand then kissed my cheek. 'I'll write to you.'

I stepped into the train and took a window seat. There he stood on the platform. Nicholas. I put my hand on the window, one last gesture before he disappeared. His eyes were full of shock and tenderness and longing, as mine must have been. The train drew out of the station. I fell back against the hard seat and closed my eyes. I had no substance, was simply a parcel of light.

Chapter Twenty-Five

On Wednesday evening mother invited me to help her dead-head in the garden, where she took the unprecedented step of asking me to meet her for lunch the next day. I was so taken aback that I thought she must have got wind of the fact that I'd been kissing someone else's fiancé and wanted to put a stop to it. Then she added, 'Let's meet in the Lyons you keep talking about, where your murder victim worked. I'd like to see it for myself.'

'I thought you hated that sort of thing.'

She wouldn't meet my eye but made savage snips at a dogwood. 'Life would be so much easier if you didn't argue all the time, Evelyn.' Then she hissed, 'I want to talk to you about Meredith, somewhere away from the house.'

The next morning Breen and I drove to Wormwood Scrubs to interview Wheeler. Breen's shoulders were hunched as if he carried a great burden. 'The man is as good as hanged unless we can save him from having to plead in the first place. Or unless you can work a feminine magic, Miss Gifford, and get something more out of him today. Wolfe has left no stone unturned to find the origin of that wretched statue but it's proving to be trickier than we'd hoped. She is one of a limited edition of fifty, French, imported last November and bought by a number of so-called exclusive dealers and stores. You're perhaps not aware, in Maida Vale, that these pseudo-classical figures are terribly in vogue at the moment. The damnable thing is that Harrods, for instance, had three, and a few were sent out of London to Edinburgh, York and Birmingham. So it will be impossible to track down her purchaser with any degree of certainty unless we have some idea of his age or what he looks like. I've set Wolfe to making matches with Carole Mangan's list but it's a thankless task to expect a shop assistant to remember a purchaser who might at some date have bought a bronze, and to pick him out of the motley crew she described. Always assuming, and it's quite a leap, that it was someone on the list who gave Stella the dancer.'

'And the missing night, the cloakroom ticket?'

'We have no proof that any of these things are connected, or indeed significant. I'm afraid I lean towards Miss Drake's view of the type of thing Stella might have been up to. But in any case all this is pointing towards a motive for Wheeler, not an alternative culprit.'

We were silent as the cab stuttered along the Harrow Road, but then, having encouraged me to think the worst, Breen, exactly as if manipulating a bench of magistrates, turned the tables. 'Don't look quite so despondent, Miss Gifford. I happen to think it's worth persevering, if only we have enough time. In my experience, the truth has a habit of bubbling to the surface like gas in a swamp. Truth has its own imperative, I find. Thanks to you we know something significant: that Stella did indeed have a benefactor who could afford to spend more than fifty pounds on her.'

'And whoever it was, it was a thoughtless present,' I said. 'Of all the things he might have bought, like clothes or jewellery – Stella would have loved jewellery – he chose something useless, the kind of present suitable for someone who already has everything, unlike Stella who had virtually nothing. And a naked dancer? How was she supposed to explain that to her husband?'

'Miss Gifford,' he leaned forward, 'it was a clever present, don't you think? Exclusive enough to turn a poor girl's head but not so rare that the purchaser could easily be traced. And suggestive . . . Do you know what I think? It's the sort of gift a man might buy if he wanted to put ideas into a girl's head.'

'Ideas?'

'If Miss Drake is right – or at least is thinking along the right lines – ideas were indeed put into the girl's head. With disastrous consequences.'

The cab was warm though the windows were pulled down. We were static behind a tram and the air was fumy. All in all the conversation was far too personal for my liking. Surely Breen must see my bubble of joy; surely he must know that I had been reconstituted by love. That morning a letter had been delivered to Clivedon Hall Gardens addressed in a hand that made me tremble. I had snatched it from the breakfast table and put it in my pocket to open on the way to work, leaving the crowded bus five stops early so that I might read it without someone looking over my shoulder.

Dear Evelyn,

I write this because I think you might be as disbelieving as I am of what happened. I have lost count of the times I have relived our walk. My fear is that I shall simply wear the memory out . . .

The letter was in my pocket; I felt the corner of the envelope against my thigh. So yes, I knew all about the ideas that a beloved man might put in a girl's head. I knew that in some circumstances body and soul were pitched towards one goal. Couldn't Breen tell that I was molten with expectation?

'To give a girl a present like that suggests a relationship that has already become intimate,' Breen said, 'or perhaps one in which intimacy is being denied. We know that Stella liked dancing. In that light, the bronze is both flattering and quite shocking.'

I suspect, as I said, I may be falling in love with you. Trained as I am to analyse and dissect, I try to work out why this very inconvenient thing has happened. Inconvenient. I suspect you'll smile at that word (I should like to watch that dawning smile). But I was so solidly fixed on a particular course, and now this.

I can't write more until I have spoken to Sylvia. You will understand that I am trying to remain as true to her as possible. There is a crisis with Donald – I cannot speak to her at present.

'Don't you think, Mr Breen,' I said, 'that such a man, knowing Stella has been murdered, must be wondering whether there is some danger of the police finding the bronze dancer and asking awkward questions? He must be very worried.'

'My thoughts exactly. But I have concluded, on the contrary, that he probably feels quite easy. He couldn't have known that Wheeler would have the good fortune of being represented by the excellent firm of Breen & Balcombe. The police missed the dancer after all, and we're only pursuing that particular trail because you were observant enough to notice her.'

But might you and I meet again in the meantime? Tea? Some noisy, public place where I won't be tempted. Fortnum's. Thursday next, five o'clock. I'm bound to be finished at court by then. You can reply to me at my chambers. Mark the letter 'Personal'.
Nicholas

Mr Breen, meanwhile, had changed tack completely and was addressing the Marchant case. 'We have received a letter, Miss Gifford, from your friends Mrs Sanders and Mrs Marchant, requesting an interview. They have drawn up a petition to have the children returned.'

'Should we meet with them?'

'*You* should, of course. They need to know it's going to be a long and tortuous process. And you should draft a letter of apology to Miss Buckley, at the same time requesting a meeting with appropriate members of the board to discuss the future of the children. Meanwhile, I'll get Wolfe to follow up a few leads, make some connections, see if he can find someone who has a lever on a board member. If he's right and the home is intransigent, we will need to apply pressure on many fronts.'

By now I had some experience of prison routine, the unlocking of numerous doors and gradual immersion in a stifling interior ever more remote from the street outside. Wheeler was waiting for us in an interview room which had the sole luxury of a high, barred window, open a fraction. In the moment before he rose to greet us he was even more depressed looking than before. He might have been boneless, slumped into his soft, heavy body. I could not see him as a fighter, sinuous and brave; I could not imagine him rushing forward into battle. A prison officer stood in one corner, arms folded indifferently. But when Wheeler saw us he got to his feet, and was more animated than I'd ever known him before. 'Well?'

Breen shook his hand. 'Nothing much to report as yet. But I've brought my colleague Miss Gifford to see you. She's done a great deal of work on your behalf and has many questions.' Wheeler showed no sign that he remembered me but sank down in his chair, as if he'd used his last ounce of energy. 'I'm just Miss Gifford's escort,' added Breen. 'It didn't seem right to send a lady to a prison on her own so I'll get on with some work while she's talking to you. Forget I'm here.' And he settled himself as if he were snugly in his office, extracted a heap of papers from his briefcase, and unscrewed the lid of his fountain pen.

I was wearing the same blouse as on my trip to Chesham with Thorne – I could scarcely bear to dress in anything else – and these days I understood the effect of a woman's naked wrists and throat. When I took off my jacket and hat I was aware that the gaze of all three men, even Wheeler, flickered over my exposed flesh.

'Mr Wheeler, I'm here because I believe you didn't kill Stella. However, at the moment we can't find another suspect so we have to prove to the jury that it was impossible for you to have done it because you had no motive. In fact, quite the opposite. Do you understand? So I'd like to talk to you, if I may, about you and Stella. I thought I'd start by asking about the time before the war. When you left, Stella was just a little girl really. Twelve.'

He said nothing.

'You fought bravely. We've read the reports. You joined a regiment recommended by your employer. So you were among friends.'

Not a word.

'And Stella wrote to you all that time. It must have been a comfort to receive her letters. But she was still very young and you didn't expect her to marry you when you got back. In all the years since the war, you never seem to have put pressure on her. Her sister Julie says Stella might have married any number of men but she chose you.'

Wheeler sat with one arm flat on the table, head low, mouth so slack that a line of saliva trickled onto his sleeve. Meanwhile the prison beyond the interview room muttered and boomed and clanged and I was reminded of the Good Samaritan Home and those other pent-up lives.

'Mr Wheeler, I went to visit your mother-in-law in Acton, where I saw your wedding photographs and talked at length to Mrs Hobhouse. Meanwhile Mr Breen has spent time with your own family, who told him you'd kept all the letters Stella wrote to you during the war. We'd like to use them as evidence during the trial, if we may, to show how devoted you were to each other.' Still he said nothing and my voice rose and quickened. 'You see, the prosecution is going to find it very hard to prove that you shot your wife in cold blood simply for the insurance money, especially given the length of your courtship and your faithfulness to each other. We think that's a wholly implausible argument.' Wheeler suddenly looked up, and the glance from his grey, moist eyes was startling, as if he knew and felt more than he could ever say. 'So the prosecution will try to find other reasons why you might have killed her. And one of them might be that you were jealous. Your mother-in-law says you were jealous sometimes, is that true?'

A further sinking of the shoulders.

'Stella loved dancing, didn't she?'

Suddenly he smiled, a sad smile but full of fond memories. For the first time I noticed that he had unusually good teeth.

'I'm told that you, on the other hand, never danced.'

He shook his head.

'That must have been hard for you.'

Another piercing glance. 'I loved to watch her dance,' he said in his low, sorrowful voice, and I felt a thrill of triumph that he'd spoken to me at all. 'I loved to see her happy.'

Breen, who had been scribbling notes in the margin of a letter, paused to take his pen apart and inspect the ink reservoir.

'I'm sure you wanted her to be happy, Mr Wheeler,' I said softly. 'Tell me about Stella's dancing.'

He leaned forward and studied his damaged hand. 'I would go down to the Palais with her and watch. I'd buy her a drink or two – she preferred lemonade when she was dancing. She used to wear little frocks, showed a lot of leg, and soft shoes. After she'd had her hair cut she wore a slide to stop it falling over her eyes but it always did in the end. She used to go wild. Her arms and legs would fly up so fast I could scarcely see them. She was such a wonderful dancer others used to stand still and watch. She knew all the latest, Charleston, the lot. She used the word syncopation all the time. She'd practise on the pavement and at home, singing to herself "At the Jazzband Ball" and "It Had to Be You".'

'Did she have any special partners?'

'She'd dance with anyone, the girls from work, her sister Julie. Sometimes a young man would ask her but after one or two dances she'd point me out and swap partners so they didn't get ideas.'

'Was there ever a man she danced with more often? One she seemed fond of?' He gave me such a baleful, dismayed look that I quickly added, 'I believe sometimes she went dancing when you weren't with her.'

'I didn't mind her going dancing with the girls, as long as it wasn't down the Trocadero. I didn't like that place.'

'I was talking to one of Stella's workmates, Carole. She said one morning in April Stella came to work having been out all night. Do you know anything about that?'

'What do you mean, all night?'

'Carole said she was late to work and that she hadn't changed her clothes from the day before, and her sister Julie says the same: there was one night that Stella didn't go home.'

'Well maybe she did stay out. It's not a crime. It doesn't have to mean anything.'

But he was so rattled that I suspected he had known nothing about that missing night and was in danger of clamming up while he pondered its implications. 'And after you were married?' I asked gently.

'After we was married it was a bit different. Mainly because of money. She didn't have her own money any more, except the housekeeping. The rent, the wedding and the honeymoon and all took most of what I had and we was saving to buy our own house.'

'So how did the two of you spend your evenings, after you were married?'

'Talk. She would sew bits and pieces to her dresses. I was always very tired after work with all those figures and the travelling. She wanted a gramophone or radio, we was hoping for one as a wedding present but it didn't happen. Too pricey, I suspect. And anyway we needed practical things, saucepans, cutlery. We was intending to go out more, once we'd saved a bit more money. Stell loved the pictures. Anything. Charlie Chaplin.'

'Did she seem happy?' That word again, but now I felt I could use it with authority.

There was a ponderous silence. 'Stella was never happy,' he said at last. 'I knew her most of her life, since she was a very young girl, and I never knew her happy. I tried to make her happy. She said I made her happy but I didn't. In the end I thought, Well maybe if I marry her, she'll be happy.'

The prison officer shifted his weight. Breen's pen hovered over a document.

'Why wasn't she happy?' I asked.

'Who knows? Sometimes she said she was bored. She wanted more than she could ever have. She was always saying "if only this", "if only that", and she would set her heart on a new pair of shoes or a hat, as if they would make her happy. Sometimes I was doubtful about marrying her because she was so restless, but then I thought, she says she wants to be wed, maybe if we have children, they'll make her happy.'

He leaned towards me as if desperate to confide. I remembered Nicholas, the kiss in the hedgerow, thistles, briar roses, and I touched Wheeler's hand near where there were scars instead of fingers. 'Stephen. When you were married, was it all you hoped for, at night? You had waited for her such a long time.'

He gave me a burning, wounded look. 'It was all I'd hoped for.'

I now dipped into my briefcase and took out the scrap of paper I'd found in Stella's sponge bag. 'We found this. Do you recognise it?'

He knitted his brow and drew the paper towards him. 'Where d'you find it? I don't know what it's about.' He touched it again, puzzled over it and shook his head. Next, I took out the bronze dancer and placed her on the table, where she was utterly incongruous, the only perfect, lovely thing in the room. Wheeler stared dully. 'What d'you bring that old thing here for?'

'You've seen it before?'

245

'Course I seen it. Couldn't stand the thing. Wouldn't have it in the house. I didn't know she'd kept it.'

'Where did she get it from?'

'Heck knows. She got hold of it shortly before the wedding. Said she'd bought it as a little present to herself. Waste of money, I told her.'

'We've had it valued. We think it's worth more than fifty pounds.'

He was all grey at that moment, and it was clear that he had known the dancer was valuable and that there was no innocent explanation.

'Mr Wheeler, I must ask you this. Do you think the dancer might have been a present from a man who—'

He got up, sallow, furious. 'She would never. My Stell. Never. Never. She wouldn't dare. She wouldn't hurt me. She told me, she swore to me.'

I let his words settle before I persisted: 'So you did discuss the possibility that she might have been—'

'You seen a picture of my Stell. She was lovely. The loveliest-looking girl I ever seen in my life. Don't you think I didn't worry that she might fall for someone else? Look at me. Look at the state of me. A cripple. Old. Can't dance, can't earn enough to buy her treats. She was all I ever wanted. I dreamed of her all my life, the thought of her kept me going through the war. She knew that. She knew. She would never be so cruel. She didn't have to marry me, but when she did, I thought that would be the end of her wanting all kinds of other things.'

'And wasn't it?'

Silence.

'When you say other things, do you mean other men?'

Another agonised look. 'I don't know. I didn't believe it possible there wouldn't be, you see. I called at the café often. I knew there was men watching her. I thought it would end, once we was married and she was out of that place.'

'And yet you still suspected her.'

'I thought a baby would stop that sort of trouble.'

'But of course it was very early in your marriage for Stella to have conceived.'

Breen's voice cut in, matter-of-fact. 'Stephen, whose idea was the picnic, yours or Stella's?'

'Idea? Well hers, I think. I can't remember.'

'And, tell me again, what happened while you were up on the hill? Did you suggest you went down to the pub or did she?'

'I don't know. Me, I suppose. I can't remember. She wasn't bothered.'

'What happened then?'

'I've told you a million times, nothing happened. I left her. I went to have a beer. I come back and she was gone.' He buried his face in his arms and wept.

Then, out of the blue, Breen said, 'In the war there was an incident when you were picked to form part of a firing squad, do you remember?'

Silence.

'Describe to me what took place that morning.'

Wheeler was weeping too hard to reply.

On the way back Breen asked, 'How is it looking to you, Miss Gifford?'

'It looks to me as if he was eaten up with jealousy, sir.'

'In which case we're done for. The man is so coherent there's no way we can attempt to prove he is mentally unfit. Thorne was right.' His keen eye fixed on me. 'Thorne telephoned by the way. Said he'd talked over the fitness-to-plead question with Hardynge and Wainwright. Wheeler was far too competent an employee, they suggest, right up to the Monday after the murder. And his behaviour in prison has been impeccable. If he'd maintained his silence it would have been another matter but you've heard how lucid he is. There's no chance of us winning that argument. So it's back to motive. We won't tell the police about the dancer until we've found out its provenance and what happened on that missing night. When we're in possession of all the facts, we will decide what to do with them. But I tell you one thing: Wheeler is making very deliberate choices about what he discloses. He's a dark horse, in my opinion, and brighter than I used to give him credit for.'

'And you still think he's innocent?'

'I still have no opinion, Miss Gifford. As I've said, I believe, for the time being, what my client wants me to believe.'

'Why did you ask him about the incident in the war?'

'Because there's a danger the prosecution will pick up on the fact he was part of a firing squad and therefore, they'll say, practised at killing in cold blood.'

Chapter Twenty-Six

I arrived at Lyons well before mother because I wanted to speak to Carole Mangan privately. I spotted her at once, near the kitchen, indistinct in the smoky restaurant, one foot resting against the wall. Though white with fatigue she ushered another waitress out of the way. 'Is there news?'

'We are making progress. You have been an immense help, more than I can say. But it's possible we may call on you again if we need to have any of the men on your list identified.'

She nodded.

'And I was wondering, could you tell me any more about the day Stella came in late, when she hadn't been home?'

'Not really. She was tired and grubby. Secretive. That's all.'

'Do you have any idea where she'd been? You must have wondered.'

She rubbed fruitlessly at a tea stain on her apron. 'I suppose I did. She was so tired. And frightened, upset. I thought she must have had a bad time with someone – not with Wheeler, he'd never treat her bad – but then, why wouldn't she say?'

'And yet you didn't suspect her of having an affair?'

'There were no signs, no. And why would she, if she was engaged to Stephen? Why not just break it off with him?'

At that moment mother arrived, a somewhat incongruous apparition from Clivedon Hall Gardens, dressed in her usual hat with the spotted veil and a black double-breasted coat, both far too heavy for so warm a day. She removed one glove and looked about nervously as if she'd never been anywhere so lowly before, though I suspected that before her marriage, in the days when she was merely the daughter of a former actress and struggling school teacher, she would have been grateful for meals in establishments far humbler.

'This is my mother, Miss Mangan.'

Mother smiled at Carole in the queenly fashion she reserved for members of the lower classes not directly in her employment. Because we so rarely had lunch together and this, I insisted, was my treat, we ordered expansively: croquettes with potato salad, and tea. Mother agreed that the meal sounded tasty but took little interest and instead scanned the room as if seeking out spies at other tables. She seemed determined to make an effort to establish good relations, however. 'So tell me what you've been doing this morning.'

'Mr Breen and I visited Stephen Wheeler in Wormwood Scrubs.'

She adjusted the front of her veil. 'And how is that case progressing?'

I could not think of the Wheeler case, even in her presence, without being flooded by memories of Thorne's kisses in the hot lane. 'Badly. But I'm sure this café is significant. My theory is that Stella, the victim, had a rich admirer. And the obvious place for her to have met such a person is while she was on duty.'

'Rich, you say. How rich?'

'Rich enough to have spent fifty pounds on a present.'

'Surely nobody that rich would come here. Why on earth would they, when there are so many restaurants and clubs around Piccadilly, just down the road? Your father was scarcely what I'd describe as rich but I never knew him set foot in somewhere like this. Can you imagine?'

She had a point. Father's haunts had been his club, the hushed dining rooms of expensive hotels if a client were treating him, or the smoky restaurants around Chancery Lane. He and his colleagues feasted on roast beef, not poached eggs. 'Perhaps Stella's gentleman came in on the spur of the moment,' I said, 'in need of a cup of tea, and Stella happened to catch his eye. She was very pretty, by all accounts.'

We watched Carole clear a table and give the surface a perfunctory wipe. 'Depend upon it, there is another explanation.' Mother had assumed her role of glamorous hostess, expert at making connections. 'He will have met her elsewhere then found out where she worked. And she, the little minx, will have ensnared

250

him and given him just enough promise of future favours that afterwards he came back time after time.'

'Mother, it almost sounds as if you are talking from experience!' I caught my breath. There she was, my veiled, inadequate mother, who had spent her adult life lavishing her love on husband and son, caressing, praising, nurturing. But really, was that the only side of the story? What had father been up to on the nights he was late home? She seemed oblivious now as she dipped into her handbag, removed a handkerchief and dabbed at her nose, or was there just a hint of self-consciousness, a tremor in her hand?

'What about that other nasty case,' she asked, 'the woman who injured your face?'

'We are still trying to get her children back.'

'I can't understand why the home wouldn't be glad to get rid of them and return them to the mother.'

'It's not that simple; we have to prove that she is able to care for them.'

'And is she? She didn't treat you very well.'

'Not by herself perhaps, no, but I believe she has a good friend who will help, and in the long run the children will be better off among people they know than shipped abroad to heaven knows where.'

'Goodness me, Evelyn, it seems to me that you are taking a great deal on yourself – all this responsibility for other people's children.'

Our conversation was suspended as Carole set out our lunch. Then we talked of grandmother's deteriorating sight and of Prudence's cottage, which she planned to visit to ensure that mice or burglars had not got in while the *wretched* tenants were in Scotland.

'Actually,' said mother, shifting forward and speaking in a low voice as if about to divulge a state secret, 'did you know that Prudence has offered the cottage to Meredith, once the lease has expired at Christmas?'

'That's very generous of her.'

'I shall never understand Prudence. One minute she is calling the girl an impostor, the next she is taking her side.'

'What does Meredith say to the offer?'

'I'm afraid she laughed. She said she and Edmund would die of boredom if they had to live in the country.'

'Nonetheless, it's generous of Prudence.'

'Oh, it is, I don't deny it. And so unlike her.' Mother leaned even closer, so that her veil brushed my cheek. 'You know that Prudence has also offered Meredith money. All she has. Her next suggestion was that she, Meredith and Edmund set up house together in town on the proceeds from the sale of the cottage.'

'But that is extraordinary,' I exclaimed obediently, though in truth I had seen it coming.

'She says Edmund is heir to the Gifford name and that someone must ensure he is supported. She has changed sides *completely*.'

'And how did Meredith react?'

'She too seems to have changed her tune. Evelyn, I'm not sure that Meredith knows what she wants. I think all this talk of expensive apartments is bravado, but I'm equally sure the last thing on her mind is a ménage à trois with Prudence and Edmund.' She poured the tea, her fingers delicately crooked over the clumsy pot. 'The fact is, Evelyn, your precipitate action, telling Meredith to leave, has made me think. It is my belief that we have a duty to her and the boy and we cannot simply send them away. Oh, I don't blame you entirely. It is partly my fault, I admit, that we pitched ourselves against her in the first place. I was so shocked when she arrived that perhaps I was not as welcoming as I might have been and my response affected you. It was up to me, after all, to set the tone. Well, I've considered all the possibilities and we simply can't afford to rent her a flat in London. So what I've thought is this: perhaps we could create a little apartment within our house. It wouldn't cost us much to make her a sitting room, even a little kitchen, but we would at least be offering her a home. I was thinking of the second floor, where she could have the spare room – and James's room.'

I was stunned. That she should offer James's room, his shrine, confounded me. 'It would mean sacrifice on your part, I'm afraid,' she added, taking up a fork and pushing her croquette aside. 'If we were to give them a sitting room, and Edmund his own room, which of course he must have, you might have to move to the top floor.'

'I don't understand you,' I cried. 'This is the exact opposite of what you—'

'Hush, Evelyn.' Again she looked nervously about. 'Don't make this more difficult than it already is. Can't you see we owe Meredith a home?'

The food was too peppery for my liking but I ate several mouthfuls while I decided whether now was the time to disclose the terrible allegation Meredith had made about James. The trouble was that since my conversation with Nicholas I was less sure; the edges of my outrage had blurred. Meanwhile mother snapped open and shut the clasp of her handbag.

'The truth is, Evelyn . . . I have not been quite honest with you. Your father did tell me about Meredith and the child, though I must admit that over the years, because I heard no more about them, I pushed the fact of their existence to the back of my mind. I knew of course that your father had met her in London, and that she was expecting . . . I was too upset at the time, so soon after James's . . . And we decided we must keep it all quiet. What good would it do for everyone to know that he'd . . .? The woman was going back to Canada after all. We thought we'd never see her again.'

Mother's eyes and mouth were wet as she gave me a nervous look then again opened her bag.

'We did something else which you may find hard to forgive. I think you will be very angry but I'm prepared to risk that. James wrote to us after he'd left the hospital, a day before he was killed. The letters arrived a fortnight or so after the news of his death, while you were at work. He told us about Meredith – that he had treated a woman badly is how he put it – and that he wanted us to care for her, should she come to us for help. He said he loved her and would have married her if she'd returned his love but that unfortunately she did not. I made your father burn that letter. I was very angry, actually, beside myself, given the news came so soon after his death, to think of this woman toying with my son. And it was so unexpected to receive that sort of letter instead of his usual affectionate . . . It was so unlike all his other lovely brave letters.'

Her hand was still in the bag.

'Until Meredith turned up again, I never regretted not telling you. I was jealous of you, as a matter of fact, because you had such a fine, unsullied image of your brother, whereas I had to imagine ... But one thing I have always regretted, and that is the need to hide from you the fact that he also wrote to you. We didn't give you the letter because we thought it would contain a confession about what had happened with this woman. I never opened it – my conscience is clear on that front – but nonetheless. I could not bring myself to destroy it – it was yours – and now I have decided to give it to you because I know you are very angry with Meredith, and I'm hoping that whatever James wrote will convince you to be kinder to her.'

She brushed the surface of the table with the side of her hand then placed on it a small, poor-quality envelope. When I didn't move or speak she gripped my arm and I saw that a tear was caught in the webbing of her veil. 'Evelyn, don't be too hard on me. We wanted you to think well of your brother and we thought this would upset you too much.'

Carole was hovering to clear the table. Mother's meal was uneaten. I picked up the letter and put it in my lap. 'I'll pay for the lunch,' I said. 'You go.'

'You're not too angry with me?'

I forced myself to speak calmly; anything to be rid of her. 'Please go now, mother. Why don't you do some shopping while you're in town? Buy a new hat. Something summery and small with a turned-up brim. No veil.'

My voice was like a stranger's, low and toneless. Nevertheless she was so relieved I had not made a scene that she responded laughingly, 'I have never known you care about what I or anybody else wears! What has come over you?'

She kissed me through the veil then hung her bag over her arm and walked uncertainly away. At the door she turned and waved. As she went past the window her back straightened and I knew she would go to Selfridges and look for a hat both to please me and as a reward to herself for being so brave.

The restaurant had quietened a little. Carole approached, glanced at James's envelope and offered to bring me a fresh pot of tea. Nothing changed in that constantly changing place: the ebb and flow of diners, the straggling queue at the cake counter, the waitresses in their black dresses. I imagined Stella arriving late one morning, her eye sockets bruised from a sleepless night. She must have glanced at the clock to see how late she was and then, as she hurried to the cloakroom, felt calmer because here she was again, safe. Carole said Stella had often looked towards the door that day, as if expecting repercussions. A fortnight later she was married and in another few weeks murdered. I had no truck at all with the idea that these things in Stella's life were unconnected. One thing led to another.

19 November, 1917

> *Dearest Evie,*
>
> *It has become my habit to write you a last letter, and when I come back safely to tear it up. So here's another. I usually write the same noble words. How much I love you and hope you won't grieve for long, and that I've had a good innings and no regrets. I ask you to care for Ma and Pa but be sure not to let them talk you out of a brilliant career.*
>
> *If you get this it will be because I've taken another hit, and this time James Gifford is no more, poor lad. Well, my dear sister, my dear touchstone, here's a thing I have newly learned – that death is by no means what I fear most. Or to put it more eloquently, I would rather die than continue living in the shadow of my own lost innocence.*
>
> *When I was hit that time a month or so ago I tried out death. I lost so much blood I had to be carried on a stretcher. My head rolled from side to side and I thought any minute some sparking thing would fall from the sky and do for me. Further from the front it was quieter, I was shunted into an ambulance and in the dark I felt life wash away. I grew colder until the pain went and I slept sometimes. And then I lay in the hospital, in and out of dark hazes, aware of upright figures among the prone ones. I would snap suddenly into consciousness and realise that there'd been a change, an end of activity because another boy had died. Once, I followed.*
>
> *Do you know, it really wasn't so bad? We trod a soft floor and our hands groped forward in the dark until we found ourselves*

in a crimson room, velvety, hushed. You would have loved the colour of that room, Evie, the colour of apples and roses and the rubies in that shop where you bought my ring. A colour to keep you warm. Any minute, I knew, another door would open to another dark corridor and endless silence would begin. But then there was a tug on my wounded arm and I came back and was looking into the eyes of a woman who wouldn't hear of me dying. I was patched up and tucked up and made to drink vile stuff and when I woke again my head was firm on the pillow.

You were always better at everything than me, Evie. I don't blame anyone for the way I turned out but I came here and found I wasn't equipped to kill or be killed. I hadn't been tested. I was rightly afraid of what James Gifford might do in those circumstances. The one bit of advice I dare to give you, if you do practise the law, is don't look at just the act, look at the cause; don't depend solely on the law, depend on justice. Even if I live I could never now come home. I could not enter that house, climb those stairs, lie peacefully on my bed. I have fallen in love with a woman here, the one who wrenched me back to life – she even used the words 'I don't want you to die, Captain Gifford,' and so I lived. Evie, if she should visit you by any chance, for God's sake be kind to her, and love her, and try to convince her I was a good man but not the best. And that when I was lost I found her, and held on too tight.

There's a hellish racket overhead. Imagine Rose in a temper, clashing her pans. Doesn't come anywhere near.

Goodbye, my very legal sister.

James

Chapter Twenty-Seven

When I arrived home, after ten o'clock that night, mother was still waiting up for me. 'Where have you been, Evelyn?'

'Working late.'

She hovered about me, took my hat and hung it up next to James's. 'I told Rose to keep back a plate of cottage pie because I didn't know when you'd be in. I was afraid ... Oh Evelyn, I've been so worried you wouldn't come home at all. What must you think of me?'

'Really, does it matter what I think?'

'Of course it does. Evelyn, please, don't be cold.'

'I must speak to Meredith. Is she in?'

'She's with her art group. She didn't say when she'd be back. When I told her my idea that she might have an apartment in this house she laughed at me. She said she had to be free and she couldn't think of anything lonelier than being within the household but not of it.'

'She has a point.' There was a hatbox on the hallstand. I took off the lid and inside was a purple velvet hat with a padded brim and matching rosettes. Not summery, not dainty, but at least not black.

'It was in the sale,' said mother.

I nodded, took the hat and put it on her head, adjusting it low on her brow. She peeked out at me, fearful, and I saw how her prettiness had disintegrated through the strain of these fruitless little stabs she made at controlling her life.

'Please talk to me, Evelyn. Say you've forgiven me.'

'I can't yet.'

'I knew this would happen. I knew you would be angry.'

'Give me time, mother. Goodnight now.' I walked relentlessly upstairs, away from the thin figure in her lilac cardigan who must always be appeased.

Edmund's door was open. He was fast asleep, and the landing light fell on his bed, where he lay on his back, one arm flung out so that his half-clenched fist hung over space.

Next morning I waylaid Meredith as she and Edmund were running down the stairs on their way to his junior school in Lisson Grove, and asked if I might keep them company.

Even Meredith would not give me the cold shoulder in front of her son so the three of us set off, she very chic in her Eastbourne yellow summer frock and hat, Edmund sturdy in shorts and long socks, myself giraffe-like in a dark skirt. Edmund, never slow to seize an opportunity, insisted on walking between us so that we might swing him over the cracks in the pavement, but as soon as he'd left us, crossing the school yard with heart-rending confidence, a pall of silence fell and Meredith started to walk away, even when I called after her: 'Would you mind, could you spare a few minutes? I want to talk to you. We could perhaps go to the park, if you have time.'

'Oh, I have all the time in the world. But you, surely, have not.'

'I want to apologise for what happened, if you'll let me.' The last thing I expected was to see tears start to her eloquent eyes. 'Meredith, however shocked I was I should not have struck you. It probably doesn't help at all that I've never done such a thing in my life before. I offer you my unreserved apology and beg you to forgive me, if you can.'

She stood with bowed head until a nursemaid asked her to step aside so she could get by with her pushchair. This prosaic street of villas and box hedges hardly seemed the right setting for such a highly charged scene, whether of reconciliation or rejection. James's letter was lying in the briefcase with my love letter from Nicholas. How could father's bag, the street or the city contain such words?

'I would like us to start again, right from the beginning,' I pleaded. 'Meredith, you have received very poor treatment from my family for so long. I want to make amends.'

I began walking towards Regent's Park, and to my relief she

258

did follow, though lagging slightly behind. We crossed the Outer Circle and entered the park proper near the boating lake, made unattractive by a frisky breeze and an overcast sky. Meredith, in her light frock, clutched her goose-pimpled arms. She wouldn't meet my eye and I felt a pang of nostalgia for the much chirpier Meredith who had taken me on a trip to Eastbourne: unpredictable, infuriating, even dangerous, yes, but vivacious, intriguing, tricky.

Once we were in the park, out of sight of others, she began to cry in earnest. She did this tidily and well so that tears ran neatly down her cheeks to be caught in a diminutive handkerchief. 'I have been so afraid that Edmund and I would be destitute. I was cursing myself for the way I told you what happened, when I was drunk and not able to consider properly what I was saying.'

I glanced down at her, struggling to see her through James's eyes, to understand what he had loved. Was it just that hers was the first face he saw when he regained consciousness? Or was it her difference to us, the Gifford women, that drew him: the fact that she was small and ardent and driven by an inner light very different to our own?

'You have to understand that what you told me about James seemed entirely out of character at the time. What I have come to realise is that I probably didn't know him well enough to judge how he would be when he was away from me. I was just his sister. I didn't know what war was like.'

'That's it,' she cried. 'We all behaved out of character. But you see, if we hadn't been changed by what we saw and did, why then we'd have been made of stone. Evelyn, I want you to know this. I didn't tell you what happened between me and James to shock or blackmail you, or to kill your love for your brother. I simply told you because that's what happened.'

The bizarre thing was that I wished I had believed her before I read James's letter. It seemed so clear to me now that she was telling a version of the truth.

'But I should have said more. I shouldn't have left you to imagine the very worst. He wasn't actually violent towards me. I scarcely realised what was happening because I wanted so much to cling to him – by then I was lost too, Evelyn, the war had done

259

for me finally and to hold a young man in my arms when he needed me seemed the only reasonable thing left to do – and then, too late I realised that he was expecting far more, and he was blind and deaf to my protests.'

After a long pause I said, 'I understand mother put a plan to you and you turned it down.'

'Certainly I did.' Now Meredith was actually grinning. 'Can you imagine if I were to live in the midst of you but conveniently tucked away; Prudence and your mother on the first floor with me and my friends crashing up and down the stairs in the small hours? It would never work. And besides, I've changed my mind about what I want. I was at Sylvia Hardynge's house last night. She has a studio in the attic.'

Despite the chill air, I stood still. 'Sylvia?'

'Surely you remember her from the art party – fiancée of that barrister acquaintance of yours. She invited us back for cocktails after class to see her work. Hadley is very taken with her. We all are, except Margot, who's jealous. Sylvia's family lives in this mansion with a semicircular drive, columns at the porch, servants skimming about, mother and father at the opera. Sylvia says they're all running around looking for distraction because her brother, who's in some kind of asylum, is very sick and they're at their wits' end. For some reason he could be thrown out of the place he's in at present. But apart from the mad brother, Sylvia, it seems to me, has everything, including a studio, so I can't be too sorry for her. It's a wonderful room; part of the roof has been glassed in so that it's full of light in the day and stars at night. I should like something similar.'

She was teasing me with this extravagant request and I tried to laugh. Nicholas would undoubtedly have been up to that studio in starlight. I imagined how he and Sylvia must have stood together, like at the party, his arms round her, their kiss, and all about them Sylvia's blank canvases.

Meredith's face was peaky with cold and her fingertips purple. We took a path that led to the north of the boating lake. The wind had blown debris from beneath the trees, and scraps of dried leaves, the very last of last year's, whisked across my foot. The ghost of a memory stirred.

'We'll talk another time,' I said. 'You are too cold here and I have to go to work. But do we understand each other a little better? I do so want to find a solution.'

At the junction with Grove End Road, where I was to catch the omnibus, we parted. I should have liked to embrace her, to set a seal on my apology, but could not just yet. 'I was wondering,' I said, 'if you can spare the time, would you come with me on a trek round London's hospitals? I'm not acquainted with how hospitals work and you are. Could you ... would you help? It's to do with Stella Wheeler, the girl who was shot.'

I half-expected a rebuff but instead the old light came to her eye. 'Why I'd love to. This is your murder case, you mean ... Oh yes, please.' Then, as the bus came she asked wistfully, 'Where are you going now?'

'First to the office.'

As I stepped aboard I felt a pang for her, dressed to the nines in her yellow frock, and for the first time I fully comprehended what it was my brother had taken.

Chapter Twenty-Eight

Though I would not have admitted it even to myself, I arranged the meeting with Leah Marchant and Mrs Sanders quite deliberately to take place on the afternoon of my tea with Nicholas. I was planting an obstacle in the way – assuring myself that it was not too late to change my mind about embarking on a love affair.

So, punctually at three, Mrs Marchant and Sanders arrived in Arbery Street, both smartly turned out in clean frocks and best hats, and duly impressed by the awful significance of being in a lawyer's office. Miss Drake, who always behaved impeccably with clients, greeted them with quelling courtesy and ushered them upstairs to our bare little meeting room with its empty bookcase and round table covered by a felt cloth. Having offered to bring us tea, she left the door ajar. Wolfe was present in the building in case of trouble, but otherwise had been told not to show his face.

The meeting began quite well. Leah Marchant, who'd recently had a severe haircut, her straight fringe now drawing a sharp line under her hat, was quiet – ominously so. She sat much too still and stared at me fixedly while Mrs Sanders produced from her bag several sheets of paper on which were written names, addresses and signatures (or crosses) of friends and neighbours who had signed a petition stating that Mrs Marchant was a responsible parent and ought to have her children returned. 'Leah says she was treated shameful by that woman in the 'ome. Quarter of an hour is all the time she 'ad with them kids,' said Mrs Sanders. 'We've 'eard nothin' since. She's sick of messin' about. She wants the kids back. So we've tooken matters into our own 'ands and this is what we come up with.'

'That's very helpful, thank you. I shall ensure that this is sent to the chairman of the board.'

'And in the meantime we was wantin' to know what you been doin' to get the children back.'

'Well, in the first place we have been taking advice. I was as dismayed as Leah by the matron's attitude. However, we don't want to upset the home any further. We must tread carefully since it's a delicate area.'

'*Delicate* for who?'

'The difficulty is that the home has the right to keep the children unless we can prove that they will be materially better off with their mother. I'm afraid that the next step will be an inspection of the children's living conditions, should they be returned. We would recommend that if you are not a regular churchgoer, Mrs Marchant, you become one, so that we can get a priest to vouch for you. And it would be very helpful if there were relatives – your own or your husband's – who could show an interest in the children.'

Leah's face had reddened. Mrs Sanders said, 'Maud Grant over the way 'as a different man in every night and four kids under five crawlin' in the gutter and nobody inspects 'er.'

'We will write to the board, perhaps at the same time we send your petition,' I continued, 'requesting an interview with the chairman, Bishop Ogilvie, and asking for a timetable to be set when these investigations can begin. In the meantime we may instruct an independent person, a health visitor or similar, to support you over the coming weeks.'

Mrs Sanders put a restraining hand on Leah's. 'It's all takin' so long,' she said. 'We can't understand it.'

When Leah wept her whole face was awash. 'I want them back. I don't understand. I want them back. They never will come. I know now. I might as well give up.'

'Now, now,' said Mrs Sanders.

'It's you,' wailed Leah, shaking a wet finger at me. 'If it wasn't for you I'd 'ave 'em. That's what's keepin' them away. I seen the way they treats you. You don't 'ave any power.'

'It's not a matter of power, Mrs Marchant, it's a matter of—'

'You set yourself up as somethin' you're not. I need a man to do this for me. They'll listen to men. I don't understan' why Mr Breen's not 'elpin' me.'

The situation seemed hopeless, given that there was no trust on either side. How would this volatile woman ever clear the obstacles the system had set her? And was she a fit parent?

'We'll go now,' said Mrs Sanders hastily, then murmured to me, 'I told her not to say these things. The fact is, Miss Gifford, I believe you will succeed because you want it as much as we does. That's what I tell 'er. It's not just another case to you.'

I smiled gratefully at Mrs Sanders, shook their hands and watched them go down the narrow stairs. Leah, I noticed, left a faint, sweaty after-smell.

It was only a quarter to four. Even if I made a laborious note of the discussion there was still plenty of time to reach Piccadilly by five. I had not managed to escape after all.

My parents had escorted me to tea at Fortnum & Mason more than a dozen years before, as part of my eighteenth-birthday celebrations. They still cherished the hope that I might become a young lady – not a debutante, we weren't in that league, but mother dreamed that her bookish, wild-haired girl could yet be transformed, butterfly style, into a vision of lacy garments and soft white skin capable of breaking a string of hearts. Excursions such as tea at Fortnum's were designed to tantalise and refine. Instead I was bored. It was the summer holidays and James was staying with a school friend in Devon. For me, education was over for ever. I had nothing to talk about and nothing to look forward to as I slouched over a plate of cakes for which I had no appetite. Father glanced at his watch and consumed a coconut tart in one mouthful. Mother said that the pale blue spotted taffeta gown she'd bought me was very becoming, 'If only you'd sit up, Evelyn.' In truth, it was more of an effort to slouch in the tight corsets I had to wear.

Today, the anticipation of seeing Nicholas again was such that my legs hardly seemed attached to my body as I trod the deep-piled carpet in the wake of the very superior head waiter. All the tables appeared to be occupied by aloof ladies in exquisite hats but there was no sign of Nicholas. I was shown to a table facing the door, where I tried not to mind that my clothes were shabby or that I felt displaced among the starched cloths and waiters whose feet made not a sound as they whisked about with trays held high or pushing trolleys of cakes, their waistcoats and intensely white aprons so unlike those of their poor relations at Lyons.

My sense of dissonance grew until my head was spinning with other settings to recent unease – the boating lake at Regent's Park, the prison interview room, Lyons and James's letter dropped in my lap – and I wondered what on earth I was doing amidst these splashes of gilt and scarlet and cream, the muffled clinks, the murmur of conversation that signified wealthy people at leisure. In any case Nicholas would surely not turn up; if for no other reason than that my note in response to his had been so cold – *I shall be pleased to meet you at five on Thursday ... Sincerely yours* – because I had dreaded it falling into the hands of Miss Drake's equivalent at his chambers.

At the next table was a grandmother wearing floor-length bombazine. Her granddaughter swung a stockinged calf under a frill of apricot muslin.

My head knew that the most likely reason for Nicholas's lateness was business in court but my heart argued, If he felt for me as deeply as I for him, nothing would keep him away. Then I thought of another, far more invidious cause of absence: He's realised his mistake; he's told Sylvia of our little fling and she's brought him back into line. How could she fail with those long lashes, the brilliance of her eyes, the undulation of her hips in the white satin gown? And as the minutes passed and a waiter paused by the table to ask me pityingly would I care to order tea while I was waiting (of course not; I had less than one and sixpence in my purse), I thought frantically that the whole affair had been a terrible joke; that Nicholas had suggested Fortnum's to humiliate me, to impress upon me that this was his world and I could never be a part of it.

I had only to look at the other ladies, cut in the Sylvia mould but not as lovely, silk stockings, hats adorned with pleats and feathers, hair artfully arranged so that one little curl fell crisply on the forehead or in front of the ear, gowns draped at the neck and hips, embroidered sashes in sapphire, ruby, emerald, and hand-painted scarves in fabrics Stella Wheeler would have sold her soul for, to know that I could never compete.

Still Nicholas did not come. I'll give him just a few more

minutes, I thought. It was gone twenty past five; surely they would not be serving tea much longer? Because I'd handed in my briefcase at the cloakroom I had nothing to read but the menu: 'Anchovy toast ... Smoked salmon ... Cucumber ... Selection of freshly baked ...' My bones went liquid with misery as I anticipated leaving the store and plodding back to Clivedon Hall Gardens – the fumy pavements, the overcrowded omnibus, the unlocking of the front door, dinner at seven, as usual. My world was splintering into shards of grey and black; it was the death of James all over again. I must leave before I broke down in a shameful flood of tears.

'Evelyn.'

He was standing over the table, shockingly formal in black jacket and waistcoat, pinstriped trousers, hard collar – Nicholas, his eyes full of loving concern, his hand when he took mine warm. One glance at his face, that unique and perfect ensemble of features, made my blood sing.

'I have been in agonies,' he said, hooking his foot round the leg of a chair and drawing it to the corner of the table so that he could be a little closer to me. Immediately that alien place, the indifferent waiters, the lavish red drapes, the chattering ladies, became insig-nificant. 'The slowest judge in the world – a fraud case. And then to top it all he was taken ill at three, something he'd eaten at luncheon. We waited half an hour and I was sure we'd get away early, adjourn 'til tomorrow, but just as were packing our papers, back he comes, says we'll plough on to the bitter end. I should never have risked making this arrangement with you – I might have known we'd run late – but I had to see you. Oh God, you look done in, you're so pale and you've had no tea.'

The relief was a painful rush of heat to my numbed senses. I couldn't let go of the nightmare all at once. 'I wondered if it was wise coming here,' I said stiffly. 'I feel sure somebody will recognise you.'

'Wise? I'm not capable of being wise at the moment. I'm afraid this was the first place that came to mind. Anyway, if someone does spot us, I'll pretend we're in a meeting. But God, you're right. This is the very last place we should be. I want to be alone with you.'

266

Undone by the look in his eyes I wanted to laugh or cry or seize his hand and cover it with kisses. As it was, the superior waiter brought tea on a trolley and there was endless fuss with a silver teapot, slop bowl, strainer, jug, and wafer-thin cups with wide-brimmed fluted edges of which Prudence would not have approved – the tea could not retain its heat in such cups. Nicholas was not as deft as he had been in the café near Toynbee, and I noticed that his hand was shaking as he passed me my cup. In that highly charged moment, as our fingertips met on the edge of the saucer, I could almost have wished for the old Evelyn who, sensing the danger, would have stood up abruptly and walked away.

But it was too late. I sat so helpless before him that he laughed, buttered a scone, spread it lavishly with raspberry jam and put it on my plate. 'Eat. You must. I insist.' Then he added in a low voice, with more tenderness than I had ever known, 'How are you?'

I could only shake my head.

'I have thought of you every single waking moment,' he said.

'And I of you.'

We were pinned to our seats by the clink of china and the sudden cadences of a piano improvising a sleepy bit of jazz. A couple of ladies drifted past, jasmine perfume, the flutter of lace. And beyond this cocoon, beyond the swathed windows, was the clamorous city which would soon draw us apart.

'Tell me you have been all right.'

'I have not been all right, Nicholas, I have been very shaken.'

'Good. I want you to be shaken, at least a little. You deserve to be, since you have utterly shattered my peace of mind.'

'I have tried to concentrate on work. The trial is so soon. We think Stella really did have a lover. But on the other hand, if Stephen knew, and I think he did, then he had cause to be jealous – he has a motive ... It's looking even bleaker for him. There is a statue, a bronze dancer, someone must have bought it ...'

I, who had been praised at Cambridge for my ability to carve an argument from a ragged collection of ideas and facts, was now incoherent. My mouth formed words but the rest of my being yearned to be closer to him. I was mesmerised by the slightest movement of his hand or eyebrow or lip. A crease the size of a thumbnail came and went in his left cheek near his mouth when he smiled. Fleetingly I caught his eye. After that I couldn't speak at all.

He said, 'I was praying that you would not think, when you read my letter, that I was making an excuse for not talking to Sylvia. My mind is made up, I've not wavered for a moment.'

'Yes, you must tell her. I cannot stand secrets.'

'But it's a matter of timing, do you see? If you'll let me, I'll tell you a little more about Donald. I have hesitated because of loyalty to his family, but it seems to me that the decision not to betray is far from clear cut! You are what counts. For you to be unhappy, to be filled with doubt, seems a higher form of betrayal.'

I dared to touch his hand with my fingertips. 'Don't tell me anything that feels wrong. I trust you.'

And I did trust him. Even I could not disbelieve the evidence of my eyes. He was muzzy with desire, as was I, and a tremor ran through his hand at the brush of my fingers.

He shook his head, leaned his chin on his palm. 'Evelyn Gifford. What have you done to me? I want to kiss you and show you how very, very beautiful you are, but we have to be civilised, so I will tell you a little about Don, if I may. He's not at all well. Physically, he is in good health, if I took you to visit him you would see an immaculately dressed young man, with hair and moustache perfectly trimmed. On a summer's afternoon like this he'd be on a veranda drinking tea. But as we came closer, the illusion would become a little frayed though he would stand up very formally and shake us each by the hand. After that he'd say nothing at all. He can't, because his thoughts are shot to pieces. The war. Drugs. Recently they changed his medication and he became violent and nearly throttled a nurse. It is pure luck that he was discovered before he murdered her.'

'What happened to make him like this?'

'The war. He was always over-sensitive, perhaps over-mothered, constitutionally unfit for the shocks we had to endure. His father, Sir David Hardynge, as head of Imperial Insurance was proud of the firm's contribution – money and men, including his own son. He regarded the war as an opportunity to extend his influence and made sure that Don was one of the first to sign up. Don hated every moment. He went into that war a brave, brilliant boy and came out like this.'

The tea room was emptying while the piano played languidly on. At five, time had stretched endlessly away, second by second. Now nearly an hour had gone by and it would soon be time to leave.

'Can the family bear any more unhappiness?' I said. 'How can you hurt Sylvia at a time like this?'

'Sylvia deserves better than a man who is thinking about someone else all the time. And she is tough, I think, not to mention proud. She would never be satisfied with less than everything. She is ardent and whole-hearted about all she does. However, I will wait, if you'll allow me, until the family has got over this current crisis.'

'You know, Meredith was invited home by Sylvia after their art class. I was shocked when she told me she'd been to Sylvia's house. It all felt so terribly close, as if Sylvia and I were brushing up against each other in the dark. Or rather she is in the dark ...'

'I know. It must end soon. But there's another thing that makes a difference. I'm away next week in Manchester. Another fraud case. It would seem callous to tell her and then bolt. We need time.'

'You'll miss the excitement of Wheeler's trial,' I said, trying not to show disappointment that he was going to be away.

He paid the bill while I was brought my jacket and case. I had intended to tell him about James's letter and my attempt at reconciliation with Meredith but there had been no time. And again I felt regret for the time before Nicholas and I had kissed, when our talk had been edgy with expectation. Now we were so sad, so strained, and I knew I would spend the next week missing him.

As we walked from the restaurant he held my elbow. 'Next Friday evening when I come back. We'll meet then. That will be our beginning. I'll fetch you in the car. But for God's sake let's be alone somewhere. I can't go through a charade like this again.' He urged me past the lift to an the empty stairwell. The stairs marched down, down in gracious symmetry. I walked ahead of him, slowly, my hand on the banister, conscious that with every step the ground floor was approaching, the street door, and parting. I felt the life flow out of me. He was leaving. It was so cold, so clinical, with another meeting arranged in a week's time. The prospect of this tea had sustained me through the past days, and the world beyond Nicholas seemed a chill and very complicated place.

As we came to the last landing he got ahead of me, spoke my name, and kissed me with such violence that I lost all sense of anything but the taste of him and the cool wall at my back. The sudden contact with another body, the sense of being taken over and broken down into little fragments of Evelyn, opened me up to him so freely that I stood with my back and palms and calves pressed to that wall, unresisting as his hand covered my breast and his knee nudged my thigh. The inside of my head was dark with sensation and my body hot and yearning. I broke away at last, half blind, gasping with desire, then fumbled to take hold of his hand. We ran on down, emerged onto the pavement, and headed towards the bus stop.

There, at last, within earshot of a couple of elderly ladies each with a formidable handbag, one with darting eyes under an antiquated centre parting, I recovered a little, straightened my hat and managed something of my usual crispness. 'By the way, Mr Thorne, I have relented, since seeing you last. I need your help, if you can give it. This is a copy of the names on the board of trustees responsible for Leah's children.'

'Good God,' he said, scanning the document, still with a sheen on his lips from our kiss, 'I know both these ladies, Manningtree and Curren. Cannon Mullins. No, not heard of him. And I don't know the chairman. But there's certainly plenty here for me to go on.'

'I might have known you'd be friendly with the ladies.'

'Miss Gifford, we have already established that I am an impossible snob and move only in the most select circles.'

'How will you approach them? What will you say?'

'I'll do as I'm instructed by the solicitor. How would she like me to proceed?'

'Two things. I want the children to be released. And I want to know the policy of the trustees in relation to sending children to the colonies.'

'The latter should be easy, the former more difficult. Perhaps we should talk again, Miss Gifford. Next Friday evening then? In the meantime, I'll write.'

For the benefit of spectators we shook hands. The omnibus arrived and we were caught up in a throng of passengers waiting to board. His hand slid away from mine and I was swept forward. When I looked back, he was standing in the shade of a green and white awning, hatless and smiling.

Chapter Twenty-Nine

Meredith proved a stalwart and indefatigable companion, if anything a little too ready to enter into the spirit of our search. She was happy to discuss the possible reasons for Stella's disappearance that April night with embarrassing frankness.

'On the one hand, Evelyn, you are saying that it's possible she may have sought to end a pregnancy. On the other, you think her unknown admirer made a present of the bronze dancer to encourage intimacy. Does that add up?'

'Nothing adds up.'

'So we are looking for signs of a girl who may have met with a medical mishap or been forced to visit a hospital when an amateurish attempt to intervene in a pregnancy went wrong ...'

'Do you think it's hopeless? Would you remember such a case, three months on?'

'You have the wedding photograph. Your Stella has quite a distinctive face. So no, I don't think it's quite hopeless.'

We began with St Mary's in Paddington, the hospital closest to Stella's home, Meredith sporting a new hat in powder blue with an outsized brim that winsomely framed her little face. At first I thought her dress inappropriate – she looked more like a lady member of the board of visitors than an ex-nurse on a somewhat sordid hunt for traces of a murdered girl – but by the end of the morning a combination of the hat, her engaging smile and a glance from Meredith's enormous eyes had gained us access to at least some of the record books.

From the moment she stepped onto the polished boards of a hospital corridor and heard the distant sound of trolley wheels and the sluicing of water, or smelled disinfectant and sick bodies, Meredith acquired a briskness at odds with her usual, nervier demeanour. I remembered James's description of her expert hands, this neat little woman with unquenchable energy, and again I saw how she differed from us. It wasn't just that we were six inches taller and our limbs long and ungainly, but that our natures were so fixed, our ideas so earnestly focused on our own small horizons. The Meredith I now glimpsed was wide open, accepting of all she saw. Nothing disturbed her: not the noise, the endless waiting, encounters with authorities determined to give nothing away or nurses too busy to speak to us. Again and again she stood her ground until the right questions had been asked, the right member of staff summoned, Stella's photograph scrutinised, records checked.

At St Mary's, where we presented our letter of introduction typed by Miss Drake on Breen & Balcombe headed notepaper, we drew our first blank. 'Even if she was here that night we wouldn't necessarily have a record. We simply don't have time to write down all the ones who aren't treated or admitted. All sorts drop in late at night and most we turf out, you know, the sweepings from the park, vagrants, girls too tired to keep going. Sometimes the police bring them here for a quick check-up. They don't all get recorded.'

I produced the cloakroom ticket. 'Do you ever issue patients with tickets like this, you know, if they have to wait, or undress and hand in their clothes?'

'If only we were that well organised.'

We began the day travelling from one hospital to another by omnibus, ended it in cabs, too exhausted to consider the dwindling contents of Breen & Balcombe's petty cash box. I think we knew, by the time we'd visited Westminster, St Thomas' and Guy's, that our quest was hopeless. There was no record of Stella. And yet, despite the apparent futility of our pilgrimage, I had a sense that we were creeping ever closer to the truth. Perhaps it was simply that we were taking action, any action, or perhaps it was because we had covered so much ground that we must surely be crossing and re-crossing the dead girl's tracks. Or perhaps it was that by eliminating this one possible explanation for her disappearance that night we were leaving the way open for another to emerge.

Most of the time, during those tiresome journeys from hospital to hospital, Meredith and I were silent. It was as if we were circling each other like fencers afraid of a sudden jab, the opening of an old wound. She relented towards me a little as she teased me for loitering at the entrance to emergency departments wearing my 'Prudence mouth', as she called it, the one I put on when there was a bad smell or unpleasant sight.

Once I saw another side to Meredith altogether. At Guy's we were kept waiting for nearly half an hour on a wooden bench. Around us was the usual motley collection of the sick and walking wounded. A mother in a stained skirt and shapeless hat was holding a young baby who screamed relentlessly on and on, back arched, gummy mouth open wide, limbs thrashing. Twice the mother approached a nurse; twice the baby was briefly examined and the mother told to wait: 'Just a moment longer, we'll be with you soon.'

Meredith, I noticed, had started to tap her little foot as if irritated by the wailing like the rest of us. But when the baby stopped crying at last and seemed to relax in its mother's exhausted arms, she sprang up and asked in a commanding voice for permission to hold the infant. She put her finger to the side of its throat, her cheek to its lips and said in a low but insistent voice, 'Follow me. We will find a doctor.' The next moment, both women had disappeared.

Meredith came back alone quarter of an hour later and sat beside me, feet neatly pressed together, hands folded on her bag. 'I should have intervened sooner,' she said. 'I could tell the baby was very sick. The staff say there is an epidemic of measles at the moment. There aren't enough nurses.'

'Will the child live?'

'I hope so.'

Eventually an administrator arrived, and perhaps because of the recent drama Meredith was given the attention due from one professional to another. For once the Breen & Balcombe letter was not needed. There was no record of a Stella Hobhouse or indeed any other girl roughly her age attending the hospital on a Tuesday or Wednesday night in mid-April.

As we left I noticed that the bounce had gone from Meredith's step and she murmured, perhaps to herself, 'Yes, yes, I know. I hear it so plainly.'

'What is it?' I asked.

She laughed. 'Nothing. Hospitals. It feels as if I am being drawn back. And I don't want to be.'

'But if it's your vocation ...' In the circumstances I wondered if my choice of word was a little tactless. 'Meredith?'

'It wasn't just your brother. I was sick to my stomach. It was obscene, what we did – patch men up so they could go back and be killed. It was the opposite of what medicine is supposed to achieve. I was sick of it.'

Theo Wolfe had little more luck than us, though what with his pocketful of half-crowns, well-bred drawl, and the suggestion in his bearing that he had all the time in the world and saw no reason for going away unless he was given the answers he required, he had found that most of the very exclusive art dealers on his list were prepared to cooperate: the trouble was, they hadn't come up with any answers. By showing copies of Carole Mangan's descriptions (immaculately typed by Miss Drake) and the bronze dancer, he discovered half a dozen or so *possible* candidates for the purchaser – in fact one, the white-haired gentleman with the moustache, had apparently bought the dancer no less than three times from three different places, if the salesmen were to be believed. Wolfe even acquired names and addresses for four of the buyers who fitted Carole's descriptions of Stella's admirers.

He then took a taxi to Lyons, lay in wait for Carole Mangan to leave work, gave her, by way of a reference, my name and a card from Breen & Balcombe, and swept her away to stake out the gentleman purchasers one by one, to see if any of them was a regular visitor to the café. None of them was.

The next day, Friday, Wolfe returned to Smedley's of Piccadilly, where the salesman had assured him he'd consult his records after the close of business and come up with the identity of the gentleman who'd bought a bronze dancer and who seemed to match the third description on Carole's list. As Wolfe told us later, he had entered the emporium with a spring in his step, convinced this was the one, skirted a somewhat obscene picture of a laughing Egyptian girl and, by way of shocking contrast, a vast oil painting of the Vorticist school, and approached the desk. Today a woman was seated there, browsing a catalogue. Dressed in a cream linen frock with a brown collar she treated Wolfe with indifference once she realised he had no intention of buying. When he asked for the salesman of the previous day, she said the man in question had not turned up for work. Wolfe then confided that he needed to speak to the salesman on urgent business and may he have a forwarding address, but the cream linen woman said she had no knowledge of the man's whereabouts and could not be expected to dig out bits of information for all and sundry but would leave a note for the manager, currently on a buying expedition in Paris, if required.

At last, by means of flattery coupled with a ten-shilling note and the hint of a threat regarding the obstruction of police business, she was persuaded to rifle through a filing cabinet, produce a log book and come up with the address of the absent employee, in Isleworth.

Here Wolfe found a tall run-down house owned by a desperately thin landlady who said that the man in question, a Mr Rintoul, had gone.

'Gone where?' asked Wolfe.

She presumed on his holidays. He'd not said much but then he never did. Left with his suitcase that morning.

'Surely you must have some idea where he went.'

No idea. But he liked the sea, as she recalled. There was a cousin somewhere in the West Country.

Would anyone else know his whereabouts? Did he have any relatives locally? Might Wolfe have a quick look in his room to see if he'd left a forwarding address?

Certainly not. Who did Wolfe think he was?

'So Rintoul's disappeared,' said Breen during a gloomy late-afternoon conference, 'and coincidence always makes me uneasy. On the other hand, it's hard to see that he would take us much further, even if we found him. The police don't know we are looking for the purchaser of a bronze dancer, let alone a mythical lover, so it's a very long leap to suggest that this shady figure might in some way be connected with the murder other than to provide Wheeler with his motive.'

In other areas too, the collective endeavours of Breen & Balcombe had drawn a blank. Miss Drake had persuaded the wife of Stella's doctor to disclose that Miss Hobhouse's health had been good and that there were no gynaecological issues, and Wolfe had got a crony in the police to trawl through the records of stations in central London, looking at Tuesdays or Wednesdays in mid-April, but had found no trace of Stella.

'I'm now convinced that Wheeler will be found guilty next week,' said Breen, 'so much so that I'm beginning to regret my decision to let you sit in on the trial, Miss Gifford. You won't learn as much about advocacy as I'd hoped. How, in the circumstances, could a jury come to a verdict of innocence?'

Chapter Thirty

When the firm of Breen & Balcombe arrived at Aylesbury Assizes we had to force our way through a swarm of excited ladies in second-best hats, waiting to be admitted to the public gallery of the court house in the old town hall. I glimpsed Mrs Hobhouse in her funeral garments, and daughter Julie gripping the handles of the wheelchair to which her husband now seemed to be permanently confined. There was no sign yet of the Wheelers.

Burton Wainwright, who I met for the first time in a lawyers' conference room, deigned to take my hand and say what a novelty, no, a positive honour, it was to come face to face with one of these legal women he'd heard so much about. I thought him an unpromising figure, massively built and so fat in the face that his jowls and chins hung well below the wings of his high collar. The bottom three buttons on his waistcoat failed to meet and his trousers were old and rumpled. Yet he exuded an air of confident bonhomie, as if he had just enjoyed a very large, alcohol-fuelled lunch, and he shuffled his way so casually through a bundle of notes that I could only hope that his confidence was not based on a fatalistic belief that the outcome of this trial was inevitable.

Because I was to be merely a spectator to proceedings I did not accompany Wainwright and Breen to the cells; instead Wolfe and I sat in the lawyers' benches and waited. He bit at a fingernail then opened a copy of *The Times* while I thought about Nicholas. The week stretched unendurably far ahead. Surely there was no possibility of a letter tonight. Was he thinking of me or was he so absorbed by his fraud case that I had been pushed to the back of his mind? And at such a distance, would he remember only the worst of me: the arguments, my worn-down heels, the unruliness of my hair?

The prosecutor, Michael Warren, was a short, genial-faced man with a slow delivery and an apparently playful twinkle in his eye. The judge, on the other hand, Mr Justice Weir ('Not good news,' said Breen, 'Weir enjoys a reputation for hard-headedness'), had cold eyes and unnaturally pale skin, drained of all colour by the vibrant red of his robes. Wheeler was brought up to the dock, where he stood in what I guessed to be his wedding suit, utterly dejected as his mother wept in the public gallery, the quill in her hat jolting with each sniff. Her husband was motionless, hat on knee, gazing into the middle distance.

The jury was sworn in (there was one woman, dressed top to toe in brown including a hideous hat like a pith helmet), and proceedings opened with exactly the same lack of drama that marked the start of any trial, from the theft of an apple to treason.

'Stephen Wheeler,' said Warren, 'is more than sixteen years older than his wife. Their families were friends through the local church and the young boy, Wheeler, lacking siblings of his own, had always shown affection for the two Hobhouse girls, Julie, the older sister, and Stella. This affection was demonstrated in delightfully innocent ways – his mother tells how he built the little girls a go-cart and bought treats at Christmas. Stella was twelve in 1914 when Wheeler went away to fight, but she maintained a regular correspondence with him – letters which will form part of the defence case – no doubt motivated by the patriotic desire of a young girl to lift a soldier's spirits. At the end of the war she was sixteen years old, but Wheeler, by all accounts, made no attempt to court her, doubtless all too aware of the significant difference in their age and experience. He had sustained an injury to his left hand and might have considered that this disfiguration, albeit comparatively minor, had damaged still further his chances of winning a lovely young bride. But over the years affection apparently turned to romantic love and the couple were married this year, on the twenty-sixth of April, when Wheeler was thirty-eight, Stella twenty-two.

'Less than a month later, on Saturday, the seventeenth of May 1924, Stephen Wheeler, the defendant, and his new wife, Stella Anne Wheeler, travelled by a Metropolitan Line train from Harrow and Wealdstone in Middlesex to the town of Chesham in Buckinghamshire, in order to enjoy a picnic. After an early lunch, Wheeler left his wife alone while he went for a drink at a local hostelry. When he returned to the picnic spot some two or three hours later – we have only Wheeler's recollection as to how much time had actually elapsed – she was gone. The following day, when she still had not returned home, Mr Wheeler raised the alarm. On the Monday morning her body was found in woods, and nearby, in a separate shallow pit, were discovered Wheeler's military gloves and his Webley service revolver.

'Wheeler had a distinguished war record, and the prosecution does not seek to diminish that in any way. I cannot be alone in acknowledging the sadness of an event that has brought a man who served his country with such distinction to a court of law, charged with murder. However, Mr Wheeler, or Corporal Wheeler as he then was, was responsible for one important lapse in discipline during his years of service, and it is one that he has freely admitted both to the police and to the senior army officer brought down to interview him. Unusually for a non-commissioned officer Wheeler had been issued with a revolver because he often volunteered for night patrols and raiding parties. At the end of the war, however, he omitted to surrender this weapon. The jury would be right in thinking that such an irregularity was not unusual in the huge demobilisation that took place between 1918 and 1922, involving nearly two million young men, but the question they might well ask themselves is what kind of person would wish to keep a revolver as a souvenir of the war? Papers, mess tins, medals, gloves, yes. A revolver?

'At any rate, the revolver found a home behind a rafter in the roof of Wheeler's shed, tucked away, he says, in a tin box containing odds and ends. By Mr Wheeler's own admission, only he and his wife knew that the box was there. The box, when seized by police, was found to contain medals and documents but was empty of more significant contents – namely the revolver and the gloves that were found buried close to Wheeler's murdered wife.

'Another key element of the prosecution case is an insurance document which will later be produced for your perusal. Wheeler purchased life insurance a month prior to his wedding, at a favourable rate, since he was a long-term employee at Imperial Insurance.

On the death of a spouse, the survivor, under the terms of the policy, is entitled to the princely sum of ten thousand pounds.

'The jury will also hear evidence from the family, particularly the dead girl's sister, that Wheeler was a jealous man who kept a close guard on his fiancée. Young Mrs Wheeler was an attractive girl who worked in a Lyons restaurant. It is the prosecution case that Wheeler was driven by the twin urges of jealousy and greed to end his young wife's life. Of course the defence will say that nobody in their right mind would hope to get away with such a crime. The prosecution will argue that Wheeler was not an educated man, but performed every act of his life ponderously and systematically. Perhaps the rashest thing he ever did was marry a girl so much younger than himself, and it took him six years to make up his mind even to that. The prosecution will reason that it is quite in keeping with such a character to plan a crime meticulously, but possibly not to have a fully developed sense of its consequences.'

Warren's first witnesses, fellow passengers on the Metropolitan Line to Chesham and a couple who had been in the town at about eleven thirty on the Saturday morning, gave brief evidence that Stella and Stephen Wheeler had indeed set forth on a picnic. Only one girl, a farmer's daughter, Elizabeth Shearman, who walked into Chesham regularly on a Saturday morning and had met them on the hill above the church, was subjected to cross-questioning by both Warren and Wainwright, who seemed fascinated by the details of what Stella was wearing.

Miss Shearman was a self-important girl with thick ankles and a heavy chest crushed under an elaborate blouse. A blue cloche covered her shingled hair and she leaned on the witness box as if settling in for a cosy chat. 'Pink. She was wearing pink. A pink frock. White gloves. Can't remember what colour shoes. Something light.'

'And was she carrying anything?' asked Wainwright.

'*He* was. He had a picnic basket that knocked against his legs, I noticed. He looked awkward, a bit self-conscious. She might have had a little handbag. I can't be sure.'

'And what was she wearing on her head?'

'Why, a hat of course. A little straw hat. Very pretty but

I remember thinking it wouldn't be of much use on such a hot day because it hardly had any brim.'

'Here are three hats, Miss Shearman. One of them is Stella Wheeler's. Can you pick it out?'

'Yes, it's the one with the little straw rosette on the side. I thought it was a pretty hat. I might even have asked her where she bought it, if I'd had time to chat, except . . .'

'Except . . .'

'They seemed to be in a bit of a hurry. She was walking behind. They weren't talking. They didn't look happy. She'd picked a few flowers, I think.'

The prosecutor asked permission to re-examine. 'She wasn't happy, you say.'

'I'd say—'

Wainwright, surprisingly nimble, rose to his feet and said incredulously, 'My learned friend is expecting the witness to indulge in speculation about the state of mind of someone she passed on a hillside?'

'The point came out under defence questioning,' said Warren. 'Surely I'm at liberty to pursue it? Miss Shearman, could I confirm that you stated in open court that the couple didn't look happy, that Wheeler was leading the way, and that he seemed in a hurry?'

'That's right.'

'Hardly what you'd expect from a couple embarking on a romantic picnic.'

'With respect, Your Worship, we can't ask our poor witness to play guessing games . . .'

The next group of witnesses included the publican of the Queen's Head and two of his customers, all of whom gave evidence that Wheeler had entered the pub by the street door about half an hour before closing time and had drunk three pints without speaking to anyone but the landlord. He had seemed low-spirited and couldn't be drawn into conversation. When closing time was called, he'd departed.

'In which direction?'

'Couldn't say for sure.'

Wainwright was eager to cross-question the publican about

Wheeler's so-called depressed bearing. 'You must see many drinkers in your pub, Mr Pool.'

'I do. That's what we're there for.' (Broad grin at the jury, a few of whom responded.)

'Some must come to drink, others to pass the time of day in congenial surroundings, some but not all for both.'

'That's right.'

'So Mr Wheeler was not unusual in preferring to keep to himself.'

'Not unusual, no. He did seem low, though.'

'Your Honour,' said Warren, 'I would like you to rule on vague terms such as "seem low".'

'By all means,' said the judge. 'Perhaps Mr Pool would be so kind as to describe Mr Wheeler's demeanour that afternoon so that the jury can make up its own mind as to whether or not he was low.'

The publican, whose mouth was over-crammed with yellow teeth, was delighted to oblige. 'He was dressed in a checked shirt, dark trousers, heavy boots. He looked hot and he threw down his hat on the bench beside him. He sat over his beers like this, with his arms resting on the table. And he didn't look round or up, just stared down at his pint.'

'One further question,' said Wainwright. 'Was Mr Wheeler carrying a lady's hat?'

The publican gaped.

'Please answer the question, Mr Pool.'

'No. Just his own hat.'

During the lunch recess I asked Wolfe to elaborate on the significance of the hat and he flashed me the kind of grin he usually reserved for asking a favour of Miss Drake. 'Ladies and hats, Miss Gifford, in my not inconsiderable experience, are inseparable. So either Stella was in such a hurry or so frightened that she left it behind when she went off with whoever it was that killed her, or her murderer removed it from her head after she'd shot her and took it back to the picnic site. Wheeler certainly didn't have it in the Queen's Head, so the former explanation seems more plausible. But was she really so afraid of him that she would allow herself to be escorted, hatless, to a copse, so that he could kill her?'

'If she was at gunpoint?'

'It was a long walk. Nothing I've heard about Stella suggests an easy or compliant character. It's the one thing about the day that doesn't fit.'

'Then I should like to suggest an alternative sequence of events.'

Wolfe shot me a sideways look, folded his arms, stretched his legs and bowed his head as if to say, You have my ear. He made me nervous because I had no idea what he thought of me or indeed anyone else. In court his good humour was unwavering whether he was dealing with a wife-beating or petty larceny but it was impossible to judge his true opinion of either the crimes or their perpetrators.

'Wheeler couldn't remember clearly, but he thought that it was Stella who first suggested the picnic,' I said. 'What if she was the one driving events, and somehow persuaded him to leave her and go to the pub because she had agreed to an assignation that went horribly wrong?'

Wolfe examined his thumbnail and adjusted a cuticle with his front tooth. 'It seems an elaborate ploy. Wheeler was out every weekday. She had acres of time to conduct an affair. And how does that explain the hat?'

'She left in such a hurry – to meet someone – that she forgot her hat. The thing is we know she'd already behaved rashly at least once, when she was out all night that time in April. And if someone acts out of character once, don't you think it's likely they will do so again?'

The first witness of the afternoon was the Amersham police officer who had been woken by Wheeler early on Sunday morning. The prosecution asked for his account of Wheeler's visit to be read to the court, then said, 'Was there anything about Mr Wheeler's story or indeed his demeanour that struck you as troubling at the time?'

'I was surprised by the fact that he'd gone home at all the previous night. If my wife disappeared all of a sudden, I wouldn't go home. Why didn't he raise the alarm on the actual night she disappeared? That's what I'd have done.'

Wainwright got up. 'This court is surely not concerned with what the respected police officer might have done in the event of his wife's disappearance.'

The objection was upheld.

Then came the dog walker who had discovered Stella's shallow grave, a mousy, soft-featured woman who described her outing early on Monday morning in minute detail and wept as she said, 'I was never more shocked ... I couldn't believe my eyes when he (a mongrel answering to the name of Caspar) came out with that shoe, that dainty little shoe, with stains on it. So I thought I must just take a peek, though I was already terrified. The bracken was a little crushed, so I pushed it aside and there it was, a woman's foot, stockinged ...'

A clerk from Imperial Insurance, very self-important in a tight celluloid collar, gave interminable evidence about the terms and conditions of the life insurance policy, and the special arrangements which pertained to employees. He confirmed that the policy became invalid in instances of foul play or, as a matter of fact (apologetic glance at the dock), in the event of death by hanging.

By now the jury was showing signs of having been cooped up too long in a crowded room, so the judge allowed one final piece of evidence, a letter from Wheeler's regimental CO confirming that it was regrettable but unfortunately not extraordinary that a revolver had not been returned at the end of the war, and that the number on the revolver at the crime scene matched that issued to Corporal Stephen Anthony Wheeler in January 1918.

Chapter Thirty-One

That night I woke in the small hours and replayed the trial witness by witness. The sight of Wheeler's defeated bulk in the dock haunted me. Breen had said on our journey home that the jury would not warm to such a passive figure, but I saw him as pitiable. It was as if to retreat like that within his own soft flesh was the only way Wheeler had of defending himself. I imagined him passing nights during the war, similarly motionless, whatever horrors exploded around him.

The next morning saw an even longer queue for the public benches, and Breen reported that poor reproductions of Stella and Stephen's wedding photograph were being circulated at tuppence each. The case was a sensation in the press, which had dubbed it the 'Shot in the Heart Murder'. Breen also said, with a pragmatism that made my blood run cold, that the crowd had caught the whiff of a hanging and would soon be baying for blood. I was dismayed by the fatalism that seemed to have overcome my usually ebullient senior. It felt to me as if Breen & Balcombe was already distancing itself from Wheeler. There was no sign of Wolfe. Breen remarked that the entire firm couldn't suspend its operations for the sake of this trial and Wolfe had other fish to fry. On the other hand, my services to the law were obviously expendable. Breen told me he preferred to have me in Aylesbury under his eye and there was always the hope I might learn something.

The first witness of the day was Julie Leamington (née Hobhouse), who was to give evidence about her sister's relations with Stephen. Julie was exquisitely dressed in a navy round-necked dress with a touch of white piping at collar and hip, and more than a hint of a swollen belly. Framed by the dock she looked fragile and her little hand rested like a flower on the Bible.

From the defence point of view Julie's evidence was damning because it was clear that she'd made up her mind as to Stephen's guilt and his motive. 'He loved her to pieces, anyone could see that. But he watched her all the time. He never believed himself good enough for her. I said to her, "Stell, don't marry him. He'll want you there always, right where he can see you."'

'She must have loved him very much to go against such advice,' Warren commented.

'The fact is, Your Lordship, Stell was terrified of being left on the shelf. We all were. She thought he was the best she could get. I don't mean to be cruel to Stephen but I know I'm right. He was a good man, had a good job and she was very fond of him.'

'Your Honour, I must object. This is all speculation . . .'

'Mr Wainwright,' said the judge. 'The dead girl is not here to give her own reasons for marriage so we must pay attention to her sister. The jury should understand that in the case of murder, when the victim cannot speak for herself, hearsay evidence from those close to her is admissible. Perhaps Mrs Leamington, however, might be persuaded to give us more detail of the evidence upon which she based her conclusions as to her sister's state of mind.'

'Mrs Leamington,' Warren continued, 'you do not describe the late Mrs Wheeler, your sister, as being a contented person. What about in more intimate areas of her marriage? Did she ever give you cause to think things were not well there?'

Julie shrugged and pouted. 'I never had the chance to speak to her after she was wed.'

'You say Wheeler was a jealous man.'

'I don't want to give you the wrong impression. In some ways I thought he was too good to Stella, indulged her. He knew she loved dancing. He tormented himself sometimes, watching her dance, but apart from not letting her go to the Trocadero he never stopped her. When she was a girl she dreamed of becoming a dancer, you know, in shows. Dad paid a fortune for lessons but it came to nothing. She wanted money for her dancing frocks and such so she started at Lyons. She never saved her money, just spent it on clothes.'

'You say Mr Wheeler didn't like her going to the Trocadero. Did she conform to his wishes?'

'Mostly. Sometimes she went but didn't tell him.' She glanced at Wheeler, who sat as usual, eyes downcast, hands clasped.

'So on the one hand you have a husband who loves to watch his wife dance, on the other a man who was perhaps conscious of his own physical deficiencies.'

'Mr Warren, you are putting words into the witness's mouth,' said the judge.

'This must be a difficult question for you, Mrs Leamington, but did your sister ever give her husband real cause to be jealous?'

'Do you mean did Stella have an affair? Course not. She was a good girl. She didn't have to marry him. But did she flirt? Yes, she flirted.'

'And what form did that flirting take?'

Julie started to weep, rather daintily, and produced a lace handkerchief from her cuff. 'If she was noticed by someone she liked the look of, she would become different – more of everything, more smiles, more movement, more sparkle, you know. She would perform for them, not obviously but so only they and she would know. I've seen her do it a hundred times.'

Wainwright, in cross-examination, asked gently, 'You say Stella flirted but she never seems to have been drawn to one man in particular or allowed herself to get carried away. Yet you claim Mr Wheeler was jealous.'

'He would go very quiet sometimes after a night out. Not speak to her for days. He never shouted. Just silence. She hated his silence.'

'To your knowledge, was he ever violent towards her?'

'Never. She would have told me.'

'So the idea that he might actually have taken her life out of jealousy is, in your mind, absurd.'

'Objection,' shouted Warren.

He needn't have bothered. Julie was determined to reply to Wainwright's question. 'She's dead, isn't she?'

The next prosecution witness was Dr Reardon, the medical officer who had served with Wheeler in 1917. He was a plump, smart man, more like a naval captain than an army doctor, with a scar on his cheek and another, quite vicious, one on the back of his hand.

Once the doctor's report had been read in open court the prosecutor Warren said, 'Dr Reardon, you wrote, *I would strongly recommend that Wheeler be examined for his psychological fitness to plead. What is acceptable, even convenient, in time of war, does not allow a man to survive in more normal circumstances.* You'll be aware that the defence chose not to follow that recommendation. Perhaps you could clarify to the court why you wrote as you did.'

'It's exactly as I said in the report. I am not sure that a man's apparent sanity in times of great stress will necessarily hold in later life.'

'You think that Wheeler may be suffering from delayed shell shock or some such.'

'Possibly.'

'But you have not examined him recently so could not possibly comment on his current state of mind.'

'I could not.'

'And since the defence is not choosing to call any other experts to give evidence concerning Stephen Wheeler's state of mind at present, or indeed at the time when his wife Stella was killed, the court must draw its own conclusions. Now Dr Reardon, I have a couple of very simple questions to put to you concerning army protocol. In your report you said that Wheeler had formed part of a firing squad. I wonder if you could tell the court the process that is gone through prior to an execution.'

'What possible relevance,' asked Wainwright, 'can this question have to a murder committed in 1924 in the Buckinghamshire countryside?'

The judge said irritably, 'I'm sure Mr Warren has his reasons.'

'The man in question is given a last meal,' said Reardon, 'and allowed to pray. Then he is led before his fellows, blindfolded if he wishes.'

'And tell us how the men who form the squad are selected.'

'Again, it varies from regiment to regiment. Sometimes by lot. Sometimes hand-picked. In our case, the former.'

'And what was your role, as the doctor?'

'To declare the man dead, obviously.'

'Any other function?'

'Sometimes to ensure members of the firing party were fit for the task.'

'Anything else?'

Silence. Then Reardon said, 'It was my job to place a marker.'

'A marker?'

'The men needed a precise target to ensure that the job was done without inflicting unnecessary suffering. We pinned a square of white flannel over the heart of the prisoner, to ensure that he would be quickly and humanely killed.'

'So that he would be shot in the heart.'

'Precisely.'

Wainwright was on his feet. 'Your Honour, it's late in the morning and we're all weary but I crave your forgiveness. I repeat, I fail to see the relevance of this line of questioning to the murder of a girl in a wood.'

Warren looked pained. 'I have finished my questions. I was merely demonstrating to the jury that the defendant, Wheeler, had formed part of a firing squad in which he was ordered to shoot a man through the heart.'

Wainwright shuffled his notes and began his cross-examination. 'Dr Reardon, much will hinge in this trial on whether Mr Wheeler was capable of killing his wife in cold blood for some spurious reason to do with money. Give us your impressions of the man.'

'Your Honour, this court is surely not interested in "impressions",' Warren cried, 'particularly impressions formed more than half a dozen years ago.'

The judge bowed his head for a moment, as if summoning strength. 'Upheld, Mr Warren.'

'Tell us more then,' said Wainwright, urbane as ever, 'about the case in which Wheeler formed part of the firing squad. You say he knew the man who died.'

'It was a regrettable incident in every respect. Wheeler was a member of the firing party that executed a man whom I later discovered had been especially dear to him, all the more tragic as Wheeler was not generally known for his ability to form close friendships. This particular boy had been a junior employee at Imperial Insurance and joined up underage, at sixteen and a half, with other members of the firm. He ran away twice and was captured. In my view he was shell-shocked but another, more senior, doctor dismissed the diagnosis. The first time the boy's sentence was suspended, the second the court martial had no option but to recommend he face the firing squad. Fox – the young boy – had not been alone in trying to escape the second time, and when he and his fellow were captured, one of them turned on the military policeman and shot him in the elbow. Though Wheeler had attempted to nurture and protect this boy Fox, when his name was drawn from the hat he did not flinch from joining the firing party, though under the circumstances he would certainly have been excused. I suspect he took on the work because he knew that he at least would not miss the mark. I would say this was evidence of a merciful intention rather than otherwise.'

I was barely listening. Fox. Yes, there'd been another soldier – a pimply lad – in the only photograph of Wheeler in uniform, kept with its face to the wall in the spare room of the marital home. I'd assumed that it was Stella who had set the photograph aside out of indifference but perhaps it was Wheeler who couldn't bear to look at it. I glanced at Wheeler but he did not show even by the flicker of an eyelash that he was moved by what he'd heard.

'One question in re-examination,' said Warren, rising to his feet again: 'As you said in your own report, and I quote, "I have noted that there are types of personality that survive better in war than in peacetime – a man like Wheeler thrives on the routine of war and the absolute necessity to obey orders. The shocks of trench life register less with this type than with others ..." Does this not suggest a lack of feeling?'

'No, sir, it suggests that here is a man who has found a mechanism for dealing with what, to others, would be unbearable.'

Over lunch Breen went into conference with Wainwright so I walked by myself up and down the little streets of Aylesbury. Nicholas was on my mind, and the copse on the Chesham hillside. 'This bloody war,' he'd said, 'it goes on and on, doesn't it?' An invidious link had been made in the jury's minds between Stephen forming part of a firing squad and his wife meeting her death through a shot to the heart.

I passed gabled cottages, grander Georgian houses, cobbled alleys that reminded me of Chesham. It was all so pat, this gradual unravelling of evidence against Wheeler. Each time another witness was called a new piece was added to the jigsaw. The jury was being led inexorably towards a verdict of guilty, but if it were true, it was almost as if Wheeler had gone out of his way to frame himself. We were all being made to look only in his direction. And if that was the case, what had we turned our backs on? To what had we made ourselves blind?

Don't look at the act, implored my brother from beyond the grave, *look at the cause*. What was the cause of Stella's death? And I realised now that what we had not been seeing was the obvious: whoever killed Stella had known everything about her husband – his jealousy, what he'd kept in a tin box in the shed, his love of a lunchtime drink, his war record, every last detail, including the fact that he'd formed part of a firing squad. So what else did this person know that had led them to the terrible conclusion that Stella had to be killed? What was the cause?

And more to the point, from whom had they learned all these things? Only two people had such intimate knowledge of Wheeler. The man himself, and his wife.

But I had no opportunity to share these insights. The afternoon was filled with technical evidence concerning the finding of the corpse, a description of Stella's body and its state of decomposition, and testimony from a police examiner to say that she had been killed at close range by a bullet fired from a Webley service revolver – the same that had been issued to Wheeler during the latter part of the war. In just two more hours the prosecution had concluded its case. Not one word had been spoken of the possible involvement of any other person, and when Warren sat down with just the hint of a modestly reflective smile there cannot have been a person in the courtroom other than Breen (and I couldn't be entirely sure what he believed) and me, and possibly his mother, who thought that Wheeler was innocent.

Chapter Thirty-Two

Meredith had left for her art class by the time I arrived home at seven. Not that I was in a condition to notice because on the hall table was a letter in a heart-stoppingly identifiable hand. The Gifford habit was to delay gratification – pleasure had to be thoroughly earned by self-denial and the thrill of anticipation – so on my way upstairs I called into the drawing room, where Edmund sat on the floor at grandmother's feet absorbed in a game of bagatelle, ensuring that conversation was accompanied by the whirr of ball bearings on oak.

'Did you see your letter?' said mother, still trying to placate me. 'There is a Manchester postmark. I didn't know you had a friend up there.'

'Evelyn no doubt has many clever friends we don't know about,' Prudence remarked.

'Unusual handwriting for a woman,' said mother.

'Oh I think everyone writes the same these days,' I said as calmly as possible.

'Such a shame,' said Prudence. 'We used to pride ourselves on our dainty lettering. You could always tell a lady's handwriting by its little flourishes.'

'I love letters,' piped up grandmother, 'reading and writing them. You never know what a letter might hold. I wonder if Edmund will be a letter writer.'

'Letters often bring bad or sad news,' said mother, glancing nervously at me.

Prudence said, 'By the way, Evelyn, perhaps you will be interested to learn that I too received a letter this morning. My cottage has been valued at three hundred and fifty pounds. I am surprised it's not worth more, given the location and the beautiful garden, but at least I have taken a definite step.'

'What is special about the location?' demanded mother.

'So convenient for the village and the big house. And the rooms are a good size and have a beautiful outlook, particularly the front bedroom. The estate agent mentioned that there was plenty of space for expansion, should someone wish to add a conservatory or extra wing. In his letter, however, he states that the house has an air of neglect about it that will not be attractive to a buyer. I shall have to go out there more often to keep it aired while the wretched tenants are away.'

I said, almost before I had formed the thought, 'I could go, if you like.'

It was so unlike me to offer a favour, let alone one of some magnitude, that Prudence was incredulous. 'Why on earth would you wish to do that?'

'The trial is in Aylesbury. It is not so far for me to go on from there. If you give me the key I could perhaps visit on Friday ...'

I was amazed at myself, the suddenness with which I had conjured a plan, the brazenness of the thought that I could be alone with Nicholas in my aunt's cottage. Prudence was rattling off instructions: 'You'd have to check and reset the mousetraps, inspect the bedroom ceilings for signs of leaking pipes in the attic, throw open the windows—'

'You look so tired, Evelyn,' mother interrupted. 'I presume it's this horrible trial. I'm sure it's bad for your health, dragging out to Buckinghamshire every day, listening to all those sordid stories. Do you really want to take on the extra burden of Prudence's cottage?'

The second love letter of my life did not disappoint.

I thought mine was a steady nature and that I was not subject to extremes of emotion. I thought the war had hardened me such that I would never lower my guard fully, or be capable of what I now feel for you. Thank God the case here is straightforward, a plum for me as I am defending the most sympathetic of three, a poor stooge of a bank clerk who has been forced to defraud his unfortunate employer of tens of thousands by a couple of con men and blackmailers. Thank God, as I said, the case is relatively straightforward because through it all I think only of you.

Here are just two of a thousand things you perhaps didn't know about Evelyn Gifford. When the sun is behind you, your hair becomes electric, every strand coiled and burnished and separate in the light. Your hair is like you, Evelyn, it won't conform. Then you have this habit of looking into your teacup or into some distant part of the room and then suddenly casting me a glance with such a light in your eye that each time I want to fall at your feet.

I think of you in your ubiquitous hat – never, ever buy a new hat – in some courtroom, gravely attentive, and I want to be with you so much it's all I can do to prevent myself from leaping aboard the first train.

By way of a PS – I rejoiced in that PS, having been brought up to believe that the use of a PS was downright common – *I hear from my secretary that a prominent member of the board of the Good Samaritan Home, Lady Laura Curren, has agreed to see you at teatime on Wednesday. Here's the address. This bodes very well for the fate of the Marchant children, I think.*

I ate my supper of steak and kidney pudding (Rose's menu did not adapt to the seasons) in a daze of love, both of his letters pushed firmly into the pocket of my skirt next to James's so that I could touch them from time to time, thankful that Meredith wasn't there to notice my distraction. Meanwhile Edmund picked the bits of kidney out of his pudding and arranged them on the edge of his plate like plum stones in Tinker, Tailor ... Though Prudence drew a deep breath from time to time as if she were about to speak she'd learned not to battle with him over food because he always won.

As soon as possible I urged him to bed, carrying him all the way upstairs though it seemed to me he grew heavier each day, and in his room we had a tickling match from which we both emerged gasping with laughter. He demanded one of the crueller fairy stories, *The Handless Maiden*, for some mysterious reason a favourite, perhaps because it was rather long or perhaps, as Meredith had suggested, because it was about a banished mother and son who are finally redeemed. There was a line that he loved in particular: '"So far as the heaven is blue," exclaimed the King, "I will go; and neither will I eat nor drink until I have found again my dear wife and child ..."'

Then I kissed my nephew's beautiful cheek and whispered in his ear, 'So far as the heaven is blue, Edmundo, your Auntie Evelyn will love you.'

These days he flung his arms round my neck to kiss me in return and ask the inevitable question: 'When's mommy coming home?'

'She'll be late because of her art class but she's bound to come and kiss you goodnight.'

'I'll be asleep by then so I'll never know for sure that she's kissed me.' And his knowing look was so like Meredith's that my heart ached. Why had I never seen it before, the echo of her face in his – the inclination of the head, the compression of the lips, those expressive eyes?

'But you can be sure she will, because she loves you, Edmund.'

Even by midnight, what with the Wheeler trial and my love letter, I was still not asleep, so I heard the soft closing of the front door, Meredith's footsteps on the stairs, a pause as she looked in on Edmund, then a soft tap at my door. 'Are you awake, Evelyn?' She perched on the edge of my bed, reeking of cigarettes and alcohol having been to the Café Royal, she said: rather expensive but worth it because they'd seen all sorts of famous people there: Augustus John at last, in a corner, and Lytton Strachey, as identified by Sylvia, and about five different poets, all of whom Sylvia recognised. Sylvia had offered to foot the bill – she was drowning her sorrows while the tall fiancé was away on business – so they'd ordered three bottles of wine and Margot had got horribly drunk and horribly jealous of Sylvia because Hadley was all over her, what with the tall one being absent.

'But listen,' Meredith said. 'I want to talk to you. I have a plan, unless you're too sleepy to listen.'

She sat on my windowsill with the sash pulled up so she could smoke, and I put on my dressing gown and perched beside her. The night air smelled of mother's garden and soot; traffic still rumbled on a thousand streets. Meredith produced from her art bag a half-empty whisky bottle, a couple of shot glasses and a packet of cigarettes, and I wondered whether this late-night visit meant that she had decided we were to be friends. I, who never smoked – Clivedon Hall Gardens deemed smoking fast and unlady-like – took tentative little puffs, wishing that Nicholas were here to see me in this un-Evelyn-like pose and that I might be kissing his mouth rather than drawing amateurishly upon a cigarette.

Meredith pushed out her bottom lip as she exhaled. Her head was thrown back and my heart beat a little faster because I had no idea what she would say next.

'The night sky makes me long for home,' she said at last. 'We have skies there that would take your breath away. Stars so thick you think you must be breathing them in. And there are miles and miles and miles of emptiness between one human being and another.'

'You never talk about home.'

'You never ask. None of you does.'

'Tell me then.'

'As a matter of fact, I've been thinking of home a lot. I've been thinking I might go back.'

Pause. 'We would miss you both,' I said at last.

'Do you know what? I almost believe you.'

'You should believe me.'

She laughed suddenly and gave my calf a nudge with her toe. 'Look at you with your knees all uncovered and that old dressing gown half undone. You have become different. I've noticed that about you. Why?'

'You and Edmund, I suppose. This trial – it's toughening me up.'

'Yes, but there's something else, isn't there? Do you know what I think? I think you have fallen in love.' She stared not at me, but across the garden to the high backs of houses in the next street. I said nothing. From below came a fragrance of roses, just a whiff. 'I've seen you go soft to your core,' she said. 'Who is it?'

For one moment I was tempted. How intoxicating it would be to speak his name. But it was of course impossible, given that half an hour ago Meredith had been in company with Sylvia Hardynge. Instead I said, 'Have you ever been in love?'

She drew on her cigarette and her painted lips formed a neat little diamond where the cigarette had been withdrawn. 'Aha, that was Miss Gifford telling me to mind my own business. Well, then I shall. But I'm not as coy. Yes, I have been in love. I was in love when I entered the convent, as a matter of fact. You may think that a cliché but it's the truth. With my whole being I was drawn to love an idea – can you imagine that? But no, it was more than an idea; it was a beautiful, breathing, compassionate silence that I loved.'

'And my brother, did he end all that for you?'

'Now there's another Gifford remark. It would have to be all down to a Gifford, wouldn't it, that a lifetime's vocation ended? No, it wasn't just your brother. There was a falling off, a decline in certainty even before James. I wanted answers. If you love us, why allow the wholesale slaughter of beloved boys? And I found I loved those boys more than I loved my silent and abstract God, who I came to see as a heavenly fat boy, too darned lazy to sort things out. I loved your brother. He was so vivid, so keen to seize every last morsel of not being in the war. I was so tempted to give him everything he wanted.'

'And now?' I asked at last.

'And now here I am a little fuzzy with whisky, and you know what I think? I think, What the hell? I think nothing matters a straw. We must just get through, somehow, anyhow. Maybe do our best. Maybe not. Maybe paint a picture, maybe empty a bedpan. What does it matter?'

She blew smoke, took another swig and examined her naked feet with their crimson toenails. 'So, in any case,' she said, 'if you're in love, my girl, does that mean that you won't be interested in my proposal? I have come up with a final plan. If this one doesn't work, I do believe I'll give up and go back to Canada, so it's down to you. I arrived here and disliked you. Then you hit me and I loathed you. Then, I think, we started to soften towards each other. And now I find I am very interested in you. I even think I like you enough to want to live with you. I thought you and I could set up somewhere. Leave the others in this house, get them to take a couple of lady lodgers to compensate for your income – whatever it may be ... Within a few months they'll scarcely notice anything has changed.'

I was so taken aback that I made the first objection that came into my head. 'Prudence will notice. Prudence worships you. Didn't you realise?'

'Ah, you've spotted that, have you? Then don't you see that for her sake, if for no other reason, I must move out, and soon?'

'How would we manage? I'd be working ... There's Edmund.'

'I've thought it all out. I will return to nursing, earn some money. Yes, I'll retrain, find my way back. And I shall paint. You will look after Edmund while I'm out in the evenings or we'll hire Min to come in from time to time. Or he can come back here for his tea. And you and I will have each other and we will be wild and free, a couple of spinster girls. But all this is a pipe dream now because you have this man, whoever he is. Or am I wrong?'

Another surge of blood to the heart. Nicholas.

The sky was ink-dark except for a sliver of moon and the city was much quieter, as if the night sky was heavy, like pudding, and pressed a hush on the traffic. I said, 'But how can you forgive me for James? Won't I remind you of him?'

Her eyes were unblinking. I saw the religious in her, the ecstatic who wanted nothing less than to give everything. I felt the spiky complexity of her character and that she was constantly striving to smooth herself out, to find a way of being that would make life bearable.

'You do remind me of James,' she said. 'You were a great part of James, did you know? I never told you, did I, that he once said how much he missed you.'

'Did he say that?'

'He did. He described this house as pretty dull, I'm afraid, and the future that had been planned for him as one he would sooner get out of. But he described you as his champion, his friend. He said you were much sharper than he. I was interested in you even then.'

Did I believe her? Did it matter?

'Anyway, I want to be reminded of James,' she said. 'I have spent years trying to forget and it doesn't work. Not just what James did to me but the whole show comes back to haunt me. I have only to see a dead tree or a man on a crutch and there I am, probing a foul wound or closing a dead boy's eyes. And each time it's a blow. It makes me shrink because I'm always cowering, waiting for the next. But when I'm with you, however vile you are, I feel better. You are a consequence, a continuum, and not all bad. Do you understand?'

After a long pause she added, 'But listen, Sylvia knows of a flat in Pimlico overlooking the river, quite cheap – she thought no more than fourteen shillings a week each. A friend of hers is renting it at the moment but she is getting married so it will be vacant from next month. She's arranging for me to visit on Thursday afternoon. If you won't share with me, I might find someone else, maybe from the art class – not Margot, I can't stand her. Sylvia. But she's engaged, isn't she? She won't be looking to share a flat with anyone.'

Did she know? She couldn't know. For a moment I wondered whether this entire conversation had been staged so that we would reach this point. Her face was turned towards me, eyes huge in the moonlight, little teeth glinting.

It was on the tip of my tongue to say, 'I couldn't help myself, Meredith, I had to have him.' But how could I, to her of all people?

Her parting shot was: 'Prudence has agreed to collect Edmund from school the next couple of days because I want to come with you to the trial. Would I get a seat, do you think? After all, I went to all those hospitals with you. I feel as if I have a stake in poor Stella's fate.'

The terrible irony was that I tried to dissuade her. I didn't want her there, for the craven reason that *he* might come back early, that his business in Manchester might soon be finished. But her mind was made up. She would attend the trial, except that on Thursday she would leave early to go to Pimlico, and she would wear her green dress and hat, which she now considered to be her courtroom attire.

Chapter Thirty-Three

The next morning I found Meredith a space high up in the public gallery then joined Breen in the lawyers' benches and told him Thorne had arranged for me to visit a Lady Curren in relation to the Marchant children. Breen tap-tapped the top of his pen on the bench in front of him. 'You spoke to Thorne about the Marchants.'

'You know he was involved in Mrs Marchant's case, sir. He defended her.'

'Well, it's good of him to take an interest.'

'Are you content for me to go alone to visit Lady Curren?'

'I don't appear to have much choice. It's short notice; Wolfe is busy; I'm needed here. Keep quiet and take notes. Even you should be capable of that.'

At that moment in came the judge swathed in his stifling robes. Wainwright stood up, glanced at a watch hanging from a chain stretching from one side of his belly to the other and said, 'I'll call Mr Wheeler.'

It was something of a shock to see Wheeler's legs and highly polished shoes as he was escorted from the dock to the witness box. His posture and heavy gait were bear-like. We had no idea whether or not he would choose to speak, and when he was asked to swear on the Bible there was a moment's absolute silence. Then he read the oath in his dismal voice, gripping the edge of the box, and fixed Wainwright with those oddly liquid eyes of his.

Not by a glimmer did Wainwright betray his relief that his chief witness was prepared to talk as he began with soothing questions about Wheeler's name, address, occupation, war service and finally the date of his marriage.

'That must have been a very happy day for you, Mr Wheeler.'

'I never trusted my luck until that moment.'

I remembered the wedding photograph – Stella's regular features, the flash of a false smile. Stella the dancing girl, waitress, fashion lover. She was there in the courtroom all right, a will-o'-the-wisp to the rest of us, but such a real, marvellous girl to dewy-eyed Wheeler.

'Mr Wheeler, you wrote to your wife constantly during the war, didn't you, and she replied? It's painful for you, I know, but might the court be read some of your letters? If my learned friend is content, I shall read just two from the war, as an example of the others. But then I shall read another, written just before you and Stella were married.

'Stella to Stephen, 1917. *I think of you often and can't bear it when I hear of all the dead men. What I hope is that you're not one of them and that you will come home, and we'll go for a walk together on the common maybe and you can tell me about it. I've been at Lyons three weeks today. I like to be in London. I like it when the servicemen come in on leave, but I'm too shy to ask if they know you. . .*

'Stephen to Stella, 1917. *Saw a bit of action. Not much, nothing to be scared of. As usual, before I went up, I took out your photograph and had just a peek. I like to think the last face I shall ever look at will be yours. You are smiling but your picture's getting battered in my pocket. Send me another some time. Don't wear a hat if you have your photograph taken. I want to see your eyes.*

'Stephen to Stella, two days before their marriage, twenty-sixth of April 1924. *I promise to love you for ever. I owe you everything. You have kept my spirits up all these years, my Stella. Without you I would not see the point. You are the point. I will never let you down, I will never make you regret what you're doing for me, not for a single minute. I can't believe we are to be wed and will live under the same roof, night and day, that I'll wake up to find you beside me in the morning and when the nightmares come, you'll be there, like you said, to hold me. I will just count my blessings and let it all come about as you want. But Stella, don't forget you can pull out still, I would understand.*

'Mr Wheeler,' said Wainwright, 'this last letter suggests that you still had your doubts, even on the eve of your wedding, about whether or not Stella wanted to marry you.'

The reading of the letters had a profound effect on Wheeler. It was as if he had been struck so that even the blood in his veins trembled. There was a long silence while he dragged his attention back to the courtroom.

'I still had my doubts about whether I was good enough for her.'

Wainwright paused while the jury absorbed this information, then embarked on a different tack. 'Mr Wheeler, the prosecution has been hinting that you retained the Webley service revolver after the war for sinister reasons. Can you explain its presence in your shed?'

'We all took stuff after the war. The CO wasn't much interested in me; he was on the lookout for the real villains who would try to smuggle anything and sell it off.'

'But why keep the revolver?'

'I thought it might come in useful some time.'

Shocked murmuring in the courthouse. 'How, Mr Wheeler? What possible purpose could a revolver have?'

'I thought it might be useful, should I ever want, you know ... for myself.'

'Suicide is a terrible thought, Mr Wheeler. Why would you consider such a thing?'

'Why would I not? It was all one to me whether I lived or died, except for Stell. I never told her this, but if she hadn't wanted me, in the end, I would probably have done it.'

'Why would you have chosen to die, Mr Wheeler, having survived the war?'

'Why would I want to live? I don't want to live among the dead. They are in my head, night and day. I dream about them. It's like I told Stell, even while I was fighting the war it didn't much matter what happened to me except for her letters. She was the one bright thing. Otherwise I knew I'd be better off dead than living with what I'd seen and done.'

Wainwright again allowed the silence to extend before he said softly, 'We've heard of one incident, related to a friend of yours to whom you showed great compassion. Would you like to tell the court about the occasion you formed part of a firing squad?'

Silence.

'Why did you not attempt to be excused, Mr Wheeler, when the lad was a friend of yours?'

Silence. Prolonged. Wheeler, with his head down and his hands gripping the dock, was inexorable.

Eventually Wainwright changed the subject: 'But once you were married, Mr Wheeler, and you had won your Stella, why keep the revolver then?'

His head came up. 'Habit. And if she ever left me.'

'You say that you never told your wife you had these suicidal thoughts. But you told the police that she knew about the revolver.'

'Yes. She wanted to see what I'd brought back from the war so I showed her. She held the revolver and said how heavy it was. She wanted to know about what it felt like to kill a man. She was always asking about the war. I wished she wouldn't. It was horrible to see the revolver in her lap.'

'Mr Wheeler, forgive these intimate questions. You've heard Stella's sister suggest that you were a jealous man. Did you ever have cause to be jealous of Stella?'

'Never. Never. Never.'

'She loved dancing. Describe her to me, as she danced.'

Wheeler put his head on one side and fixed his eyes on the clerk's desk as if it were a dance floor. 'She'd wear a little dress with silky bows on the hips. They'd play something like "Tiger Rag", she loved that, and this look would come into her eye, a faraway look like she was listening for something. And then suddenly she'd be off, grabbing one of her girlfriends, or a partner would tap her shoulder and she'd give him this smile like a yes, yes please, but dancing was serious for her, and once she started her body would free itself and her eyes would shine and her jaw would set. She didn't smile when she was dancing, and those hands and feet would go. Syncopation. You know.'

'And that didn't make you jealous?'

'It made me glad. She was so happy when she danced. And then I was sad because, however gay she was, she wasn't like that with me.'

'It must have grieved you that you couldn't dance together.'

'I never danced, a great thing like me, even before the war when dancing was different. There was other things we did together.'

'Such as?'

'Talk. Plan. Watch each other. Go out.' A sudden rueful smile transformed his sad face. 'Go for a picnic.'

A note was passed from Breen to Wainwright, who scarcely paused in his questioning. 'Ah yes. The picnic. Had you been for many picnics together?'

'No, that was the first. Thing is, her mum had just handed on the basket and Stell wanted to use it. She liked the idea of wrapping things up nice.'

'So whose idea was the picnic?'

'Well hers, at first, because of the basket. But I joined in though I didn't see the point of getting on a train. I thought we could have gone up Harrow Hill.'

'Let's get this clear. Not only was it her idea to have a picnic but she chose the location.'

'She chose Chesham, yes. She'd been there with her family. And I had as a boy, fishing.'

'When you were walking up the hill, according to one of the prosecution witnesses, Miss Shearman, you and Stella both looked out of sorts. Had you had an argument?'

'We was often arguing about little things. I wanted to stop near the town so that I could go in for a drink. She wanted to go deeper into the countryside, said there was a field she knew. She kept dithering until she'd found a spot to satisfy her.'

'So you ate your picnic. Were you on good terms then?'

'Well, we didn't say much; just watched the flowers and birds, like you do on picnics. And then she said I might as well go and have a drink since I was so keen on the idea, and she would lie in the shade and have a rest.'

'So it was her suggestion that you went for a drink.'

'That was the plan all along. Picnic. Pub. Home. I was sorry she didn't come with me but Stell was in a bad mood. Nothing I did was right. So I went down and had a pint; thought she'd be better off on her own.'

'You see, the prosecution is making the absurd allegation that, before you went down for your drink, you bullied or dragged your wife nearly three quarters of a mile and killed her in a fit of jealousy or greed or some such – they seem to have an entire armoury of

305

possible motives. What do you say to that suggestion?'

Wheeler smiled sadly, showing his white teeth. 'I loved her. She was the very last person I would kill. And I'm not killing nobody, ever again. That's the vow I made to myself on the eleventh of November 1918. Except myself, if need be. Like I said.'

'And when you were in the pub, the other customers said you looked low.'

'I was hot. And I was low, yes. I'd wanted her to come with me. It seemed to me she wanted to get rid of me.'

'Mr Wheeler, I want you to think very carefully now. Was she wearing a hat when you left her?'

'She wasn't wearing it, she was holding it. When I left her she was lying down in the shade with her eyes shut and her hat was in her hand, on her stomach, like this.' Silence in court as Wheeler closed his eyes and rested his right hand on his belly. We saw her, his daintily clad wife, lying on the picnic blanket, eyes closed against the irritation of her husband's neediness.

'I've nearly finished my questions, Mr Wheeler, and then my friend will wish to speak to you, but first I must clear up three points. The prosecution will claim that the fact you apparently did nothing to find your wife on the Sunday afternoon and even went into work on Monday is proof that you knew exactly where she was. What do you say to that?'

'I did those things because I didn't know what else to do. I thought she'd gone away and might come back.'

'Gone where, Mr Wheeler?'

Shrug.

'The prosecution will claim that one of the reasons you killed Stella was because you were set to make a great deal of money out of her death.'

'You mean the insurance? Everyone knows you can't claim insurance if there's been foul play.'

'Thank you. And one more thing. The prosecution has implied that you had become hardened by your experiences in the war, that there is more than coincidence in the fact that your wife was killed by a shot to the heart when you are something of an expert marksman and had been a member of a firing squad.'

Wheeler's head went back, so that he might hold the tears

against his lids rather than let them fall. 'I loved that girl. I would a million times rather kill myself than harm her. Yes, I shot a man at close range in the war. Many, one way or another. I had to. But that was it. End of story. Do you know what I learned about death?' More animated, he leaned forward and gazed at Wainwright with those relentlessly candid eyes of his. 'This is what I learned. It's the loneliest place to be. I seen a man clap another on the shoulder one second, dead the next. I seen that same man's body lowered into the soil. Why would I want to put my dancing girl in that lonely place?'

Chapter Thirty-Four

I missed the next part of Wheeler's evidence because I had to travel back to London and take tea with Nicholas's friend Lady Curren in her house off Eaton Square. Mother would have been gratified to see me climb those marble steps, drag on the bell pull and be shown by a butler across a black and white tiled floor into a drawing room furnished in highly conventional style in pale greens and creams, including the floral arrangements. Across the polished boards and exquisite rugs French windows were open, revealing a lawn and beds planted exclusively with white flowers. Even I, with my untutored understanding of art, could tell that the walls were hung with original paintings, including an example of the Impressionist school – water, flowers, a couple of long-haired girls whose frocks merged with the meadow upon which they lay.

The diminutive Lady Curren, Meredith's height and even slighter, was seated on the edge of what I guessed was an eighteenth-century sofa next to a tall vase of lilies, whose fragrance weighed heavy in the air. On the same table were arranged a number of framed photographs in which Lady Curren and a thin gentleman (presumably her husband) were standing in a line of smiling people or shaking hands with assorted dignitaries. I recognised the Prince of Wales, Lady Astor, Stanley Baldwin.

Lady Curren wore a flowing dress in oyster-pink crêpe that provided an unsettling contrast with her hair, cut in a razor-sharp bob that must surely need the attention of a hairdresser at least twice a week, if not daily, to maintain its incredible shine and symmetry. She was dark-skinned with a thin but prominent nose and brows that arched up to a straight little fringe. Her mouth was very small, her eyes narrow and heavily outlined with kohl.

Tea was served in what might have been a set for a large doll. Perched opposite little Lady Curren with that fragment of porcelain balanced on my palm, I felt like Alice in Wonderland after she'd grown or the world had shrunk.

'So you are a lawyer,' said Lady Curren, her voice high and as creaky as a shed door, the vowels strangulated.

'I am still in training. At present I am an articled clerk.'

'How fascinating. Oh you young things are so fortunate. In my (maay) day we gels were expected to sit around and look gorgeous. Full stop.'

I smiled dutifully. Mother would have known how to deal with Lady Curren – flattered her by commenting on her *lovely* drawing room, the tea service, the flowers, the *glorious* view to the garden – but I found her immeasurably out of reach, especially having just spent a morning immersed in the Wheeler marriage. The tea was tepid and there was not even a slice of bread and butter, although I was very hungry.

'Now, to business,' said Lady Curren, dabbing her lip with a speck of a napkin. 'As I expect you're aware, you've caused quite a stir at our home, and we can't have that. We are all full of admiration for our dear Miss Buckley, who does sterling work for those poor children—'

'It was not my intention . . .'

A brow was raised. One did not interrupt Lady C. 'You see, we spend hours and hours (ares) on the board discussing every aspect of the life of the home and this includes regulations for visitors, for children's play times, for treats, for meals. All, *all*, are regulated upon the best advice of our doctor and other experts. Be assured, we consult experts, Miss Gifford.'

The word 'expert' was intended to annihilate me, as was the infinitesimal flicker of her heavy eyelid. I, in her book, was no more an expert than the women who typed her husband's letters or polished her silver. She continued: 'Then I had a letter from dear Nicholas Thorne, who I adore, and whose judgement I trust absolutely.' Her hand made a gesture like a petal opening as she picked up one of the photographs on the side table and handed it to me.

Dear God, there he was, in army uniform, amidst a group of

people sitting on steps outside French windows, probably the ones in this very room. And beside him, gripping a plait of hair that fell across her shoulder, was Sylvia, and behind her another uniformed boy and an older couple. I recognised Sir David Hardynge, moustached and bespectacled. Next to him was his wife, presumably, with her hair coiffed in a pre-war cloud of waves and coils.

'He's such a dear friend of the family, engaged to my niece Sylvia. Sylvia's mother, Margaret, is my sister.'

'And the other boy in uniform?'

Her voice tightened. 'My nephew Donald. I'm afraid he suffered tragically in the war.'

Nicholas, in the photograph, was not smiling in the way that he smiled at me but his eyes were still warm, hands behind his back as if he were a touch diffident about being in the picture. The other boy, Donald, had his sister's exquisitely well-drawn features and dark hair but his expression was stern. 'I'm sorry about your nephew,' I said.

She flicked her hand as a sign that I had kept the picture too long. We were not, then, to embark on a cosy conversation about the Hardynge family. 'I can't deny Nicholas anything. He put it to me that perhaps everyone had become a little worked up because this is an exceptional case and one that has attracted a good deal of publicity. We try to protect the children in our care, Miss Gifford. In Nicholas's view, and ours, the mother has brought the whole thing on herself, first by committing a crime that rendered her penniless, then by surrendering the children to the home. Not to mention the kidnapping of poor baby Charles. But we can see that she might have misunderstood the papers she was signing – so many of these women cannot read; it has happened before – and that she expected to take the children back at any time. Nicholas also points out that some mothers, less devoted than Mrs Marchant, might not have admitted that their children needed care, and that it was an act of self-sacrifice on her part to give them up.

'I don't need to tell you, Miss Gifford, that in all our deliberations parental rights are subordinated to the welfare of the child. However, we think perhaps that in this case the mother has shown sufficient devotion for us to consider releasing her children, under certain conditions.'

I was still so startled at seeing Nicholas's face, and Sylvia's, and the rest of the Hardynge clan that I scarcely knew what she had said. Could it really be the case that the Marchant children were to be dropped into my lap like ripe plums?

'Thank you so much. Thank you.'

'We shall expect twenty pounds to be paid as a token towards the cost of their board and education over the past months. We shall, of course, inspect the home to which the children will be returning, and our people will pay regular visits thereafter.'

'Your people, Lady Curren?'

'We have people trained in making such visits.'

Alarm bells were ringing. I saw a terrible danger to poor, sometimes drunken Leah were she to be subjected to the stranglehold of regular inspections. Thankfully, however, I had learned a little circumspection since my disastrous visit to the Good Samaritan Home, though I rather despised my honeyed words. 'It's reassuring to know that you have such a care for these children. Mrs Marchant will welcome such visits. I'm wondering if you have any written guidance about how the inspections are conducted. Presumably a procedure is set down in writing.'

'Miss Gifford, I'm afraid I have no time now to embark on a discussion of the organisation of our home. The details can be discussed later.'

She was reaching for the bell so I said hastily, 'Of course. But there's just one more thing before I go, Lady Curren. I can't help being curious about what would have happened to the children, had we not intervened.'

'What on earth do you mean?'

'Would they have stayed in the home, for instance, or been sent elsewhere?'

'The policies of the home are a matter for the board of hand-picked individuals, all highly respected members of our society, who give freely of their time and money and who work closely with the Church of England Waifs and Strays Society, an organisation with which we have close links – my sister Lady Hardynge is one of its most distinguished members.'

'I believe some homes send children to Canada. Could that have happened to the Marchant children even though their parents are living?'

This time the bell was rung and I was so terrified that she might, in a fit of pique, withdraw her offer to release the children that I sprang to my feet and said no more. Lady Curren was too well bred not to extend her fragile little hand when the butler appeared. I crushed her fingers briefly in mine and marched away though within a hundred yards I was leaning on a wall, clutching my arms about my breast.

The children were to be released and that was surely a triumph. But what would happen when Nicholas broke his engagement with Sylvia Hardynge and Lady Curren discovered that her loyalty to him had been misplaced? Would the offer be withdrawn? I had nothing in writing and I had gained nothing for all the other children perhaps destined for the colonies.

I longed to be in the library at Girton when the due process of law had seemed such a clear and obvious route to follow.

Chapter Thirty-Five

Perhaps it was my interview with Lady Curren, perhaps it was the atmosphere in the courthouse, which was of a death ritual coming to its inevitable conclusion, but as I sat in the advocates' benches on Thursday morning I wondered why anyone would choose to be a lawyer responsible for a life in jeopardy such as Stephen Wheeler's. Did I really want to spend my days as a party to this process of harrowing through people's lives, turning up the underbelly, the sadness, the weakness, the catastrophic lapses of judgement?

Breen, by contrast, was buoyant, and amused by the account of my conversation with Lady Curren. I think had we not been in court he might even have patted my knee. 'Brilliant, Miss Gifford. You're shown a short cut but insist on viewing it with suspicion until you know the price you'll have to pay. A woman after my own heart.'

'What should I do next?'

'Once the children are released we'll continue to make a nuisance of ourselves. You were right to raise questions. There could be all kinds of complications in the future should anything befall those unfortunate children or the mother slip up in her care of him.'

He told me that Warren, the previous afternoon, had dragged Wheeler through a minute retelling of events surrounding the fateful picnic. Nothing new had emerged and Wheeler had not swerved from his story.

'Did he question Wheeler any further about who planned the picnic? Mr Breen, I was disappointed that Mr Wainwright didn't press Wheeler on a couple of points. If Stella had been planning to run away that day, if she had made an arrangement with someone, she would need to be sure that every last detail remained fixed.'

'We'll see what comes out today. Listen carefully. If you think more questions should be asked, we'll pass a note to Wainwright.'

Warren began Thursday morning on the offensive. The dimple was gone and his collar so starched that it had already worn a red line in his neck. 'We learned yesterday that a week or so before her death Mrs Wheeler suggested the picnic which you described to us in such meticulous detail yesterday. At what stage did you begin to lay your plans, Mr Wheeler?'

'Plans?'

'Plans, Mr Wheeler. Plans to journey to Chesham in order to prepare the ground? Plans to take the revolver with you.'

'What do you mean "prepare the ground"?'

'You tell me. Ah, Mr Wheeler, you seem nettled. It's for you to answer the questions, not ask them.'

'I don't know what you're talking about.'

'All right,' said Warren. 'Let's look instead at the overall picture of your marriage. I can't be alone in thinking that I've heard two conflicting accounts of your life with Mrs Wheeler. You tell me that you were devoted to her but we have all heard how you doubted your good fortune and were anxious about your ability to keep her amused. The victim's sister, Mrs Leamington, says you are a jealous man and when displeased you were prone to long silences. I think we've all learned, Mr Wheeler, that you are an expert on silence. What was going on in your head while you were so quiet?'

'I was just thinking.'

'Could you be more specific?'

'Objection,' said Wainwright. 'Can a man really be expected to list his private thoughts?'

But Wheeler cut in. 'I was usually thinking about Stella. About how to make her happier, less restless.'

'She showed signs of restlessness only a fortnight into your marriage? Did you find that distressing?'

'It was her nature. She couldn't help it. When I got in from work she always wanted to know every last detail of what I'd been doing because she said her own day had been so boring. She got angry with me when I had nothing to tell her. I said she must

314

make friends in the street. She said they was all too old. I thought if a baby came . . .'

'Was there any likelihood there might be a baby, Mr Wheeler?'

Wheeler's head sank.

'Mr Wheeler, did you and your wife enjoy normal marital relations?'

Deathly silence in court.

'Mr Wheeler,' said Warren, 'I think we can infer from your silence that your wife may have had cause to be restless. I suggest you thought that you would never be able to satisfy her in any way, including sexually, and that if you couldn't please her, she would be off. After all, the court has heard that you couldn't dance with her and now, thanks to your silence, we may conclude you were unable to satisfy her more intimate needs. You were so jealous that you watched her all the time, didn't you? You collected her from work most days during your engagement. You never let her go dancing after you were married, and only reluctantly before. In other words, you kept your eye on her constantly. This paints a portrait of a very jealous man indeed.'

Wheeler was silent.

'I put it to you, Mr Wheeler, that you were eaten up by the fear of losing your wife. I wonder who, precisely, you were jealous of?'

'What sort of question is that?' interrupted Wainwright.

But Wheeler said, more firmly than he'd spoken before, 'There was no one. I trusted Stella.'

'Then why did you watch her?'

'Because I loved her.'

'So tell me again why you waited so long to marry your wife? Six years. Is it because she was a reluctant bride, perhaps?'

'No, I was the reluctant one. I couldn't believe she really wanted me. I didn't dare ask her before.'

'All those years you never hinted at marriage?'

'Sometimes we talked about it, joked. But I was saving money until I had something to offer. And then at last I thought, Now or never.'

'Did you ask her before or after you took out an insurance policy on her life?'

'Before,' said Wheeler. 'The policy only began on the day of

315

the marriage.' Just for a moment I saw Wheeler the insurance man, who must have sat innumerable times behind an oak desk, hands folded, papers neatly arranged before him as he explained to a stream of anxious clients the minutiae of each policy. And they would have listened trustingly, and he would have achieved many sales, because a man with eyes such as his could surely never lie.

'And now, Mr Wheeler,' said Warren, 'I'd like to ask about Stella's hat. The defence has made much play of the fact that her hat somehow became separated from her body.'

Wheeler's head was now so low he was scarcely audible. 'I can't explain it. She would never have left her hat.'

'And yet, despite the strangeness of finding the hat and the picnic basket, you still left Chesham and went home without her. Why was that?'

'I've said. I thought she might have been angry and taken the train on her own.'

'Without her hat? I travel frequently in trains of all sorts, Mr Wheeler, and I must say I cannot recall an occasion when I've seen a lady or indeed any woman without her hat. I put it to you that your account of what happened that afternoon is a pack of lies. You planned the picnic meticulously using every convenient detail, including the new picnic basket, which would easily have held the Webley revolver. What actually happened is that after you'd eaten your picnic you persuaded your wife to walk with you to an isolated copse, where you killed her, in cold blood, out of some bizarre mixture of tortured jealousy and greed, and that you then went hotfoot into town, where you downed a couple of drinks in order to provide yourself with an alibi, before returning to the picnic place, which was of course deserted. I put it to you that you went home that evening because you knew exactly where your wife was – under a few inches of freshly dug soil, so you didn't need to look any further for her.'

Silence.

'I put it to you, Mr Wheeler, that there could be no other possible explanation for your wife's death. Did she go to the copse and shoot herself, and bury herself and the revolver? Did some mad, invisible person appear from nowhere, lure her, hatless, to a

316

wood, and shoot her with a revolver that happened to be yours? You've insisted in cross-examination that there was no other man in her life. She was a waitress for heaven's sake. Who would want to kill a former waitress? Who could have killed her with your gun and your gloves, which only you and she knew about, on a trip to Chesham that you and she had planned in private? Mr Wheeler, everyone's time is being wasted in this court. You killed your wife that day as surely as my name is Michael Warren.'

The afternoon began with re-examination by Wainwright. 'Pay attention, Miss Gifford,' murmured Breen. 'These are your questions.'

'Mr Wheeler, I want to discuss the arrangements for the picnic one more time. You have told the court that it was your wife who decided the date and the location, and it was in fact she who persuaded you to go for a drink.'

'That's right.'

'And you've also said you would have preferred not to travel so far on a Saturday, but she insisted. Did you make any further attempt to change your plans?'

'Not really. On the day of the picnic I said I was tired and it was too hot to go on the Metropolitan Line but she said we must go, she had gone to so much trouble.'

Trouble? Corned beef and pickle sandwiches made in that joyless little kitchen?

'And after the picnic she suggested you go for a drink on your own. Were you surprised?'

'Sad. Like I said, I thought I'd irritated her.'

'You see, the prosecution has said that you used the picnic as a chance to get your wife out of town in order to kill her. I think in fact the opposite is true. It was Stella who made all the plans, and when you tried to alter them, insisted that they went ahead. Is that true?'

Warren of course had the last word. 'Mr Wheeler, do you have any witnesses to the fact that it was your wife who insisted on picnicking in Chesham and sent you down to the town for a drink?'

Wheeler shook his head.

There followed a succession of defence witnesses, including Wheeler's mother, who spoke of her son's devotion to Stella and the absurdity of the suggestion that he would ever hurt her.

'But Mrs Wheeler,' said Warren in cross-examination, 'I believe the war altered your son's previously gentle nature.'

'I wouldn't say so, not much. It made him thoughtful, maybe moody. What did you do in the war, sir, if you don't mind my asking?'

'We are not here to discuss my record, Mrs Wheeler.'

'I think you would not be so ready to judge my son if you'd fought alongside him.'

Wheeler's father, though less eloquent, made an emotional defence of his son. 'I've heard it suggested that my boy was something of a last resort for Stella. Far from it. There was a queue of girls at our church who would have married our Stephen like a shot, given half the—'

But at that moment there was such a commotion that Wheeler's potential as a husband was disputed no further. The courtroom door was flung open and Wolfe burst in, wheezing, his jacket unbuttoned, collar loose. He held a whispered conversation with Breen, who in turn passed a note to Wainwright, who immediately asked for an adjournment so that he could consult with the judge.

The court was in uproar as Breen and Wolfe disappeared with the judge and two barristers. Meanwhile I sat in the lawyers' benches, as bemused as any other spectator, in fact more so because I couldn't for the life of me imagine what Wolfe had been up to or, even more disturbingly, why I hadn't been told about it. Meredith was signalling frantically from the gallery but I merely shrugged, thinking how foolish I must look, claiming to have made inroads into the legal profession but excluded at a moment of crisis.

Time stretched and forty minutes went by before the judge returned with his entourage and addressed the court: 'Gentlemen – and ladies – of the jury, the defence has produced three additional witnesses at very short notice. This is highly irregular, not to say lamentable because one regrets any tendency in one of the parties to spring surprises upon the other. It appears, however, that there has been a degree of confusion on both sides and some failings in the police investigation which have led me, with my good friend the prosecutor's reluctant permission, to allow this irregularity, especially in view of the fact that we are dealing with a capital offence. I might add that despite the drama with which the defence has introduced these witnesses, it may be that they lead us nowhere. It would be quite wrong of you to read anything into the suddenness with which they've been produced.'

Breen refused to meet my eye and I tried to quell my growing frustration. It was as if I were a child again, clamouring for the attention of my father while he quizzed James on what he had learned in school that day.

The next scheduled witness was Carole Mangan, pale and dignified under her dark hat, surely the one she had worn at Stella's wedding. She gave evidence about Stella's work at Lyons and how she used to be admired by many of the customers. I was a little soothed by the knowledge that Carole had come to court partly at my instigation; she was my witness, I had discovered her.

'You say Miss Hobhouse, as she then was, had plenty of admirers. Did she have any particular followers?'

'There was lots. I made a list and gave it to Miss Gifford. And the police asked me about it too.'

'Miss Gifford?'

'The lady lawyer, sitting there.' Wainwright smiled benignly at me. The spectators muttered. I met Carole's eye and we exchanged a private smile.

'Despite these several admirers, did you ever have cause to believe that Stella was seeing anyone – I mean romantically – apart from her fiancé, Stephen Wheeler?'

'No.'

'Have you seen any of those admirers since Stella Hobhouse's marriage?'

'One or two of them pop back to Lyons for a cup of tea from time to time. And I seen one just now outside the court.'

In the flurry of excitement that followed this remark, I saw Wheeler's head snap up.

'Miss Mangan. I am about to produce an object – as agreed with the learned judge and the prosecution – that was found in

Mrs Wheeler's childhood bedroom. I wonder if you could tell me whether or not you've ever seen it before?'

Wainwright opened a cardboard box, about a foot square and four inches deep, of the sort used for transporting shirt collars to and from the laundry, and from it he lifted the bronze dancer. There she stood on the bench before the pallid judge, a tiny foot extended, her hair flung back, every curve in her sinuous body exposed, poised to run clear off her plinth if only she could.

'I seen it once, when Miss Gifford showed it to me.'

'You don't know who gave it to Stella?'

'I told her. No.'

'Finally, Miss Mangan, this court has heard the prosecution suggest that the Wheelers' marriage was troubled. Forgive me for being blunt, but the suggestion was that Mr Wheeler could not satisfy his wife, if you understand what I mean. I believe you met her once after her marriage. Did she give you any indication then that all was not well.'

'No.'

When he stood up, Warren pretended to have no interest in the bronze dancer although his eyes were drawn to her from time to time, as they might have been to the bosom of a woman seated opposite him in an omnibus. In his cross-examination he concentrated on Carole's recollection of the Wheelers' betrothal. 'Do you think Stella loved her husband-to-be?'

'Yes. She was very loyal to him and talked about him often. She was always in a hurry when she knew he was going to meet her after work.'

'Did she ever show interest in any other man?'

'I've already said. No. No one special.'

'What does that mean, *no one special*?'

Carole fixed him with a cool gaze that made his colour rise. 'What do you think?'

'So you have no cause to think she had any involvement with anyone except Stephen, her husband.'

Wainwright, in response to a note from Breen, had one question in re-examination. 'Is there anything, in all your time of working with Stella, eight years in all, that gave you cause to think she was not quite faithful to Stephen?'

'Only the thing I told Miss Gifford.' Her pale eyes again met mine. 'There was one night she stayed out and come in with her uniform dirty and smelly, and there was mud and grass on her shoes. She was very tired, red-eyed. I never did find out where she'd been.'

Wainwright had no further questions but invited Miss Mangan to sit at the back of the court, if she could spare the time. He wiped his brow, folded his hands across his immense chest and fixed the usher with a benign eye. 'I call Mr Smedley.'

Mr Smedley was a diffident gentleman in a frock coat who identified himself as a dealer in fine art, owner of the eponymous Smedley's of Piccadilly.

'Mr Smedley, I wonder if you would be so kind as to look at this object. Do you recognise it?' Wainwright asked.

'I do. I bought one of an edition of fifty last year in Paris. Lamourdedieu.'

'Could you tell the court where you have been for the last ten days?'

'In Paris.'

'For how long had you been planning that trip?'

'I go every three months or so. I plan the next as soon as I've finished the last.'

'And what happened early yesterday morning, when you were at your lodgings in Paris?'

'I was told I had a visitor. A lawyer. Mr Wolfe.'

'Mr Smedley, if you'll forgive me, nothing in your demeanour suggests that you are a man of impulsive habits. What persuaded you to dash back from France to appear in court today?'

'Mr Wolfe told me that one of my most trusted employees had suddenly left the business, and that I was needed in his stead to give evidence of a particular sale. I confess that it was largely because I couldn't understand why my man had left in such a hurry that I came back so readily. I still haven't got to the bottom of my employee's desertion but I did search our books for a record of sale. At first I found nothing but fortunately we make records in triplicate – that is obviously in addition to the receipt we give the customer. I have often been reproached by my wife and sometimes by my senior staff for my insistence on this laborious procedure. The triplicates file is locked away in a safe for just such eventualities as this. We deal with very costly and rare items, you see, and it's therefore essential to keep punctilious accounts. At any rate, in the triplicates file I found that the bronze dancer had indeed been bought, on January the eighteenth, by one of our regular customers.'

'Could you tell the court who that customer was?'

Smedley showed considerable reluctance and had to be prompted. 'Sir David Hardynge.'

Hardynge. But there was no time to ponder this extraordinary development; Warren was on his feet. 'My learned friend has insinuated that your employee Mr Arthur left under suspicious and irregular circumstances. Do you have any cause to believe this was the case?'

'It is very odd. Mr Arthur had been in my service for more than fifteen years. I would expect him to have given adequate notice.'

'Odd, you say. Not suspicious.'

'Decidedly odd.'

'You say you had to look in the triplicates file, again implying, perhaps, that it was irregular not to have found a record of the sale elsewhere.'

'It was irregular. But then the files were in a very bad way. I'd been gone more than a week and I'm afraid it showed in the disorganisation of the accounts.'

I was as transfixed as the most prurient spectator in the back row of the public gallery. Why hadn't I been told about Wolfe's excursion to Paris? After all, it was I who had discovered the bronze dancer and realised her significance. But the next witness, even more astonishing than the rest, had already been called, and the courtroom doors swung open to admit Sir David Hardynge.

In he came, Nicholas's prospective father-in-law, somewhat older than in the photograph Lady Curren had handed me yesterday and dressed from head to toe in black apart from collar, cuffs and pocket handkerchief. He was precisely as I remembered from my brief glimpse of him at Wheeler's earlier court hearing: a good-looking gentleman, slim, smiling slightly as if bemused but by no means discomposed at finding himself in court.

In clipped tones he gave his date of birth, 12 March 1868; his address, 18 Belsize Square; his occupation, government adviser, parliamentary candidate, entrepreneur, company director and financier; and his marital status, married, two children, now both grown up.

'Sir David,' said Wainwright, oily with deference, 'could you tell us, were you acquainted with the dead woman, Stella Wheeler?'

'When I knew her I believe her name was Miss Hobhouse. And yes, I saw her from time to time when I went to Lyons for tea.'

'And what did you think of her?'

'I thought she was a very sweet girl.'

'Did you ever single her out in any way?'

Hardynge's smile was a touch wistful. 'She must have been some thirty years younger than me.'

Wainwright smiled too. 'Quite so. But perhaps you could answer the question, Sir David.'

'Single her out? Rather the other way round, I should say. She was very patient with me. She knew that I couldn't tolerate tea that wasn't piping hot and strong.'

'Did you ever see her outside Lyons?'

'Once or twice perhaps. She was the girlfriend of one of my employees, after all. I first met her, I think, at one of our Christmas parties.'

'And on that occasion did a relationship develop?'

Sir David seemed puzzled. 'She and I had a dance. I make a point of dancing with the wives and girlfriends of my employees; they seem to like it and it helps me get to know them better. She told me she worked at Lyons so I looked in one day when I was passing.'

'If you would specifically answer the question.'

'Our relationship was always within the boundaries I have just described: she a waitress, I a customer.'

'Did you give her a wedding present?'

There was a long pause. 'Why yes, I believe I did. I made her a present of a little statue. Yes, that one there.'

'That statue is worth some fifty pounds.'

'Good gracious, is it? I don't remember. I bought it some time ago, for my daughter, but my wife decided it was inappropriate.'

He gave a rueful smile as if remembering a painful conversation. 'So I gave it to Miss Hobhouse instead, when I heard she was to marry. As a matter of fact I'm surprised to learn she kept it. I thought she would sell it immediately.'

'When exactly did you give it to her?'

'I'd say in spring some time. I don't recall.'

'An extravagant gift for a girl you barely knew.'

'I thought it would amuse her. She had looked after me so well.'

'A rather suggestive gift, I think.'

'Suggestive? I see it as a rather fine piece of art.'

'Sir David, did you know that the wife of one of your clerks, Stephen Wheeler, had been murdered?'

'Of course I knew.'

'And that Wheeler had been arrested?'

'I not only knew about it but have taken every possible step to give him my support, financial and otherwise.'

'Then perhaps you'd tell the court why you didn't inform the police that you knew the dead girl.'

Sir David smiled. 'As I recall, I did. I told them it is one of the privileges of my position to meet most of the wives and girlfriends of my employees. I believe my company is admired for its family spirit.'

'And did it never occur to you to mention to the police your gift of the dancer?'

'Forgive me, but I had well-nigh forgotten about it. And had I remembered, I would have wondered what possible relevance the dancer might have.'

'Sir David, I'm nearly finished, if you'll bear with me. We have heard from a witness that one morning in April not long before her marriage, Stella came to work very late. Do you have any knowledge of why that might have been?'

Sir David blinked twice, as if working through a mental calendar, then shook his head.

'Was that a no, Sir David?'

'It was.'

'You were never with Stella Hobhouse, as she was then, other than in Lyons, during an evening in mid-April?'

324

'I have said. Our relationship was within the boundaries I have already described.'

'If you would answer the question, Sir David.'

'I have no idea what you are talking about.'

'Please answer yes or no, Sir David. Did you spend an evening in April with Stella Hobhouse?'

Sir David smiled patiently. 'The third time of denial. I did not spend any evening with this Stella Hobhouse.'

'Two more questions. Did you ever visit Miss Hobhouse at home – I mean Mrs Wheeler – after her marriage?'

'I have no idea where Mrs Wheeler lived.'

'Where are your staff records kept, Sir David?'

'In my secretary's office, I think.'

'So you could have had access to them if you'd asked?'

He shrugged. 'Presumably.'

'And just for the record, Sir David, where were you on the day that Stella was murdered, Saturday May the seventeenth of this year?'

There was a long pause. Hardynge seemed to be counting back across the weeks. 'I would have to check with my secretary, but I believe I was at home with my wife. Late in the afternoon I would have gone to visit my son, as I do every Saturday. He is in a type of hospital, near Princes Risborough.'

'And for the sake of the jury, where is Princes Risborough?'

'I would have thought the jury would know well enough. It is a town in this county of Buckinghamshire.'

Warren was obsequious. 'The jury will forgive me if I am somewhat ill-prepared but perhaps I could begin by having Sir David Hardynge elaborate a little, by way of background, on an extraordinary career in both business and public service.'

Hardynge was charmingly modest but after ten minutes it had been established that he served on committees concerned with the financial support of veterans and widows, that during the war his company, Imperial Insurance, had been responsible for a number of charitable endowments to aid refugees, and that having recently been selected as a candidate for a north London constituency regarded as a safe seat for the Conservative Party, he was

325

about to embark on what promised to be a distinguished life in politics.

'And now, Sir David, I have to put it to you that my learned friend, at a very late stage in this trial and for motives that I would suggest are less than commendable – notably to cloud the glaringly obvious – is suggesting that you had an improper relationship with the unfortunate young waitress Stella Wheeler, née Hobhouse. How do you answer that accusation?'

'I'm afraid I find myself so incredulous that I am at a loss how to reply.'

'Much has been made of this gift, the dancer in bronze. Yet from your point of view it was simply a rather generous wedding present. Could you tell the court what was going through your mind when you gave it to Stella?'

'Obviously not quite enough. It was, in retrospect, an ill-judged gift. But I knew that the girl liked dancing so I thought she would love the dancer. It also crossed my mind that, should she grow tired of the present, she could sell it for quite a significant sum. For instance, if she were to become a mother, she might well need extra funds. You see, her husband Wheeler had been an outstanding employee and a gallant soldier. I thought the dancer would be a way of helping them both informally – I did not want to make a precedent of such largesse to all my employees. I'm afraid I simply couldn't afford to make exceptions to the favoured few for fear of exciting jealousy.'

'Did it occur to you, Sir David, that such a gift might cause Stella embarrassment?'

'I'm afraid not. Perhaps it was thoughtless of me but after all I'm surrounded by ladies, wife, daughter, sisters-in-law, and I can never resist buying beautiful things for beautiful women.' Here his short-sighted eyes scanned the women in the galleries, the jury, Carole Mangan, even me in the lawyers' benches. Although there was no flicker of recognition, in the split second that I had his attention I suspected that I had been assessed as a possible object of desire and dismissed.

'If you came to my house you'd see it is full of artefacts. I have an eye for them and I like to share my pleasure with others. My daughter is an artist and I'm afraid we egg each other on when it comes to buying art.' His gaze flickered back to me and his brow contracted with momentary irritation, presumably as he tried to work out what I was doing amidst the defence team.

'My friend has tried to suggest that you had some sinister motive in not mentioning the gift of the bronze dancer before now. I wonder if you could again give the court your views on the matter.'

'As I said earlier, I had no idea the gift was of any relevance. Good Lord, if I had to appear in court to account for every present I've given, I'd rarely be at home.'

Wainwright got ponderously to his feet. 'A few additional questions, Sir David. When did you say you gave the bronze dancer to Stella?'

'A few days before her wedding, I believe. I can't recollect for sure.'

'Isn't it odd that none of the other waitresses noticed you giving her the present and that she didn't show it to any of them?'

'As to the latter question, I can only assume she preferred not to excite jealousy. As to the former, I really can't say.'

'And finally, you told my learned friend that you knew that Stella liked dancing. How did you know?'

Another smile. 'I expect because she told me so.'

'I have no further questions, Your Honour, but I wonder if Sir David might be required to remain in court while we call the next and final witness.'

I saw Meredith and Carole leave the court as Mrs Ball, a pop-eyed, full-chested neighbour of the Wheelers in Byron Street, came in. Presumably, despite the drama in Aylesbury, Meredith could not resist the chance to view the flat in Pimlico and I had no doubt that Lyons had demanded Carole return to work immediately her services were no longer required by the court.

Mrs Ball was first asked to give her opinion of the Wheeler marriage.

'I hardly had time to get to know them,' she said. 'The young girl was very quiet. Came in for a cup of tea once but didn't say much. To be honest, I thought twice about asking her again. Of course had I known what was about to happen to her, I'd have tooken more trouble.'

'Did she receive many visitors, Mrs Ball?'

'Well I can't say, obviously, because I spend most of my time in the back. Her mother came sometimes, I think, and *his* family. And there was one gentleman caller, I noticed.'

'Can you describe this gentleman to us?'

'Not really. I only seen him from the side and back. But he was very smart, I know that.'

'I wonder if you could look around the courthouse, Mrs Ball, and tell me if you see that gentleman here.'

She cast her eye solemnly over everyone present, even the jury, even Stephen in the dock. It seemed to me she took a very long time scanning the public benches, perhaps dwelling longest on Sir David, but in the end she shook her head. 'I seen the gentleman from the side and back, not the front. I couldn't say for sure.'

'That is very honest of you, Mrs Ball,' said Wainwright, though I sensed his disappointment. There was no cross-examination.

By now it was four thirty, too late to hear from a succession of character witnesses: fellow soldiers and workmates. The judge, looking thunderous – on account of his Friday-afternoon golf match being doomed, muttered Breen – thanked Hardynge with unnecessary effusion and announced that the court would re-convene at ten o'clock sharp tomorrow morning.

As soon as Wheeler had been taken down and the bench had risen, Hardynge, assuming the demeanour of benefactor and future MP, shook hands with both defence and prosecution, thanked them for their trouble, told Wolfe he'd been commendably thorough and that it was only right that the defence should leave no stone unturned in so tricky and painful a case. Altogether his attitude was that of a wealthy patron participating gamely in the fathers' race on sports day.

Afterwards Breen told me I should go home. He had a meeting with Wolfe and Wainwright and I was not required. So I was left to make my lonely way to the station, bewildered by this continued ostracism and thwarted in my need to discuss the sensational events of the day.

Chapter Thirty-Six

Despite my weariness and confusion I had a dogged sense that I must fulfil my commitment to Meredith so from Marylebone I took an omnibus to Pimlico, where I found a narrow street of shabby houses and had to hunt long and hard among a cluster of bells to locate 11A. After a wait of several minutes Meredith appeared at the dusty front door, eyes ablaze with excitement. 'I was hoping you'd make it but that trial was so riveting I thought you probably wouldn't. The girl who lives here has gone out for an hour and left me to get the feel of the place. It's just perfect, you wait and see.'

She led me up four flights of stairs until we came to the top landing, which was narrow and had a door on either side, the one on the left ajar. My first impression was that the flat was oppressively small and low-ceilinged though full of light, being in the roof. Meredith had certainly made herself at home – a gramophone was playing a tune called 'Margie' and a kettle was heating on the gas ring. The cubbyhole of a kitchen was more modern, with its neat little cupboards and enamel surfaces, than the vault of a basement kitchen in Clivedon Hall Gardens; there was a box room for Edmund and another room with a sloping roof and skylight which Meredith and I would have to share.

The glory of the apartment, according to Meredith, was the long living room overlooking the street, from which, if one craned one's neck slightly, one could see the Thames through a gap in the buildings opposite. In this room, said Meredith, we would live, eat and work. She would have an easel at one end and I would have a desk of my own. We might even use screens to give each other a little privacy. And we could hold parties; it would be possible for two dozen people to cram into this room with no difficulty at all.

She made a pot of tea, which we drank from unevenly shaped cups with rough edges and designs that seemed to have been created by spattering them with coloured glaze. As she talked, 'I'm Goin' South' played, and Meredith hopped from side to side, picking up the rhythm. The present tenant, Sylvia Hardynge's friend, was obviously blessed with a bold artistic nature because the flat was filled with cushions in brilliant colours, curtains in bottle-green velvet, striped rugs on the bare floors and on the wall an assortment of paintings, some very primitive indeed.

I play-acted admiration but the idea of actually living there seemed too unreal for me to take seriously. The flat occupied less space overall than the servant's floor at Clivedon Hall Gardens; there was no obvious means of heating apart from one oil stove; the bathroom, on the floor below, was shared with three other flats; and all in all it seemed absurd to reduce myself to Leah Marchant conditions. Fresh from the humiliation and, as it seemed to me, chaos of the Wheeler trial, my thoughts were all negative: I couldn't possibly work in such a cramped space; we couldn't afford it; we would be bound to fall out; and above all I could not abandon mother and the heart-broken Prudence.

'So now,' said Meredith, 'tell me what happened after I left. Weren't you just so surprised to see Sylvia's father in the witness box? I was. Whatever will poor Sylvia make of it when she finds out? Surely all that stuff with the dancing girl was a bit of a red herring.'

'Maybe. But when I found her I thought she was significant. So much didn't quite fit, notably that the dancer was worth a small fortune yet nobody seemed to know how Stella came by her.'

'And I don't understand why there was such high drama. Why drag Hardynge in at the last minute, without warning?'

'Because up until today we couldn't connect the dancer with the person who'd bought her. We tried but—'

'It's so unfair. Here we are, scrimping to find a few shillings rent; there he is, splashing out on bronze dancers. But then he is an extravagant soul, as I well know.'

'What do you mean, you know?'

'Remember I was in his house only a week or so ago. The place positively reeked of money. And do you know what? When he walked into court this afternoon I recognised him from the war. Like that man Warren said, he was a benefactor, fetched up at one of the hospitals from time to time bearing gifts, treats. But we didn't like him. Oh, he had an eye for the young nurses all right. Some men are like that with women in uniform. And there was something about his son – rumours that he'd bought him out, got him sent home. We didn't like the sound of that either.'

'You knew Hardynge's son, Donald?'

'By reputation only. Through what they said about the father. We were supposed to be grateful to Hardynge; he bought the hospital supplies of medicine when we were very short, and chocolate and cigs for the men, you know. But we couldn't like him and avoided having to speak to him. There was something calculated about the favours he did us, as if he were bound to want something in return.'

Sylvia's friend came back and I offered to wash the cups while she discussed the flat with Meredith. From the kitchen I glimpsed her, a girl from another world – plucked eyebrows, luminous skin, flitting from room to room as she gushed about the views, the convenience for Victoria station and shopping, the whole of London in fact, though she skimmed over the question of how many people actually shared the bathroom and whether the temperature was bearable in winter. Finally we all shook hands and Meredith and I ran down the steep staircase.

Outside, the skies were grey and there was an untidiness about the streets typical of London on damp and blowy summer evenings. The gutters were full of litter and smoke gusted from chimney pots. We had agreed to catch an omnibus, the number 16, which carried us along the side of Hyde Park, and we sat side by side on the top deck, second seat from the front, she with her little green bag on her lap, I with my briefcase.

Meanwhile, beneath all this activity, I was trying to work something out. Surely Meredith had said nothing of significance? Only that Sir David Hardynge had visited her hospital in France. Well, our post-war world was full of people who'd known each other in that other life. But then, as the omnibus rumbled along the

331

Edgware Road and the familiar nausea of travel sickness set in, I became aware of a weight settling in the pit of my stomach that had nothing to do with the swaying motion of the top deck, and there was such a ringing in my ears that when Meredith gripped my wrist and spoke to me – something about preparing the ground with mother – I couldn't attend to what she said. We got off the bus and walked in silence, I stumbling occasionally and even knocking into her. At the door I pleaded a splitting headache and said I would go straight to bed.

Upstairs I turned the key in the lock, flung off my skirt and blouse and lay with my hands clasped on my breast, gazing up at the glass bowl of the light fitting as the evening grew darker.

Hardynge. Bronze dancer. Stella Wheeler. Donald Hardynge's career as a soldier. Connected. Breen said he mistrusted coincidences and here was an entire parcel of them.

A witness in a murder trial, unearthed through the dogged ferreting of the commendably persistent Theo Wolfe, had turned out to be none other than the only suspect's employer and benefactor, who also admitted to a passing fondness for Stella Wheeler, former waitress. Was that all?

No. Meredith, a chance spectator to proceedings, had recognised Hardynge from the war and knew him to have a fondness for young nurses – or at least their uniforms – and a reputation for some kind of distasteful dealing to do with his son. Was that all?

No. I had been sent to Lady Curren's house where I was offered the release of the Marchant children. And there, on a side table, was a photograph of her close relatives the Hardynges, and in their midst, Nicholas. Was that all?

Yes, surely.

No. There was something else. What was it? 'Why drag Hardynge in at the last minute, without warning?' Meredith had asked. The reason was that the salesman at an exclusive dealer of fine art in Piccadilly, who had promised to connect the bronze dancer with the name of its purchaser, had disappeared. And what day was that?

Last Friday. The day after my tea at Fortnum's with Nicholas. I had told him, as an aside to hide my anguish at his lateness,

'There is a statue, a bronze dancer. Someone must have bought it ...'

I got up, strode about the room, seized a pen and paper and wrote everything down: the date of Stella's murder, the date of Wheeler's arrest, the date that Nicholas came into my life during the Leah Marchant hearing. He had spoken my name on the steps of the court. *Miss Gifford*. He even claimed, during our afternoon on the hill above Chesham, to have heard details of my brother's heroic death.

There was a tentative knock on the door, a testing of the latch. 'Evelyn, may I come in?'

I unlocked the door. Mother was very pale and too distraught to notice that her blouse had lost a button and was gaping at the breast. 'Evelyn, what is this I've been hearing from Meredith, about you sharing a flat together?'

'Oh it's nothing, mother. Nothing will come of it.'

'That's not what she's saying. Prudence is hysterical. I've never seen her like this. Meredith made her lie down with her feet on a cushion and we had to ring for Min. Meredith says you went to see the flat this evening. Why didn't you mention it? Is this to punish me because I didn't tell you about James's letter?'

'It is nothing of the kind. You know I would not be so cruel. It was very wrong of Meredith to mention it without consulting me first.' Or perhaps she had consulted me on the bus and I hadn't been listening. 'I really have no intention of falling in with her plans.'

'I thought we were getting on so well together. That lunch we had. I told you I was sorry, what else must I do? Oh Evelyn, I really don't think I could abide it here without you.'

'You're always saying I should marry,' I said, rallying suddenly. 'What's the difference?'

'You know full well that if you were married I would have a second home. Grandchildren. Perhaps, in time, a refuge. And I sometimes thought that if you married, you might choose to live here with your new husband. To save money, you know.'

'Mother.' I couldn't help laughing.

Her mouth turned down at the corners, a familiar look of hurt disappointment. 'I brought you a letter. I always seem to be delivering letters these days, don't I? It's been sitting in the hall all day. Your friend from the north, I believe.'

I took the envelope, kissed her, closed the door and locked it again. This time I waited many minutes before I could bring myself to open the letter.

I have received your note. I'll collect you as you suggest, Friday evening at the corner. I'll be there soon after five. Touch and go whether I can exist that long without you.
Nicholas Thorne

Chapter Thirty-Seven

I lay awake most of the night and every so often made another jotting in my notebook. The nightmare went on and on. I wanted there to be a flaw, something to call a halt to this speculation. But no. The more I thought about it, the more plausible it all became.

By five o'clock I had a plan of sorts and at last turned on my side and slept for an hour. Then I dressed, bathed my stinging eyes, went down to the kitchen and begged a cup of tea from sleepy Rose, who was coaxing a flame from last night's embers. I ate a slice of bread and butter and told her I would not be back until very late and that nobody should wait up for me. Then I crept out of the house and into the early morning, which was already humming with a new day's activity. There was no sign of yesterday's cloud except for a faint pallor in the west and the streets were skimmed with mist in the early sunshine. I presumed that Wheeler, in his cell, would have no idea whether or not the sun was shining. And I thought of Nicholas, in Manchester, rising from his bed in some rather grand hotel, dressing in his wonderfully tailored garments, packing his bag, eating a substantial breakfast, thinking perhaps of me.

I had plenty of time so I took an omnibus to Hyde Park, entered by the Albion Gate and walked down its eastern side to Hyde Park Corner. As the morning advanced a breeze got up and a few early-fallen leaves rustled along the path and settled at the edge of the grass. I passed the bandstand, deserted of course, heaped deckchairs, clusters of trees and shrubs, my head full of images of the lost. The day after we'd received news of James's death I had got up early and taken this identical route to the Censorship Office, my feet performing their regular task of carrying me forward, my heart stone, my mind refusing to recognise the indelible line that had been drawn beneath my brother's name. And then there was Stella, who had met her death among trees, a fearful end for a city girl. Yet she had made a sorrowful little collection of acorn cups and conker cases. What had she been trying to cling to when she tucked them away at the back of her wardrobe? The nurse at St Mary's emergency department had said that they regularly received scrapings from the park, an assortment of vagrants, drunks and prostitutes, some of whom, as I well knew, appeared in the magistrates' courts each morning. Perhaps Stella had also spent ilicit time in London's green spaces. Alone? With whom? With him?

Next Green Park, St James's Park and the long path by the lake. Every moment London was growing louder. And then I was in Great George Street, among the significant buildings of Westminster. It was nearly a quarter to eight.

All but a handful of women had been dismissed from our office after the war but I hoped that some men, or rather one in particular, might have been retained. So I found a bench with a good view of the side entrance where we used to bundle in each morning, having wrapped ourselves deeper in coats and scarves because we knew it would be far colder inside than out, and watched as hopeful pigeons approached my feet. Men in trilby hats, clean collars and rolled newspapers; the occasional office girl in a cheap summer frock with its skirt crumpled at the back; an older woman in a light-green knitted suit. I saw a brown paper bag tumble over itself, and automobiles, with their hoods up against the morning chill, a queue of omnibuses, cabs, delivery lorries, a brewer's cart.

Just after eight thirty I saw him approach, recognising him at once even though he was not in uniform. It was his gait that marked him out, somewhat apologetic, an air of being guarded against the world. Perhaps he had retained his chic little flat behind Harrods, where he slept each weekday night; perhaps he had even kept that startling red bowl. One arm still hung awkwardly and his face had grown thinner. I had pondered for hours how I might approach him; as it was I simply stood in his path and spoke his name.

At first he was very puzzled, as well he might be when his mind had to stretch back more than six years. Perhaps, I thought with the ghost of an internal smile, I had made no real impression upon him at all. But finally a light came to his eyes, then clouded as the memories awoke.

'I need your help,' I said.

He considered me for a few moments with his thoughtful, rather beautiful eyes, the colour of sky just before dawn. Then he instructed me to follow him, and we went through the main entrance into the lobby, where the porter whipped off his cap and hurried to summon the lift. We waited in silence for the doors to open, ascended three floors without speaking (in the old days the lift had been out of bounds to girls like me and we had clattered up flights of tiled steps) and came at last to his office, which was very grand with book-lined walls, a silken rug and south-facing windows. He sat down behind a vast, empty desk topped with leather.

'I took your advice,' I said. 'I never did tell anyone I could type. So now I am training to be a lawyer.'

He put his fingertips together and smiled. I was touched that he seemed to have remembered the details of our few conversations.

'I have a great favour to ask you. But I also have to be sure that you will treat our discussion in absolute confidence.'

He raised an eyebrow. I remembered why I had found him so attractive: the stillness, the air of knowing so much more than he would ever say.

'You ask a great deal.'

'A man is on trial for murder. There is one detail missing, from a witness who I believe is concealing something, maybe to do with the war, that might shed some light ...' Could he tell that even my lips were shaking?

'Who is the man in question?'

'A businessman and would-be politician, Sir David Hardynge.'

He nodded as if to say, I've heard of him.

'I want to know about his connections. I want to know if there is anything at all untoward on his record.'

He sat for a moment considering me. I wondered if he remembered the red bowl, the unyielding silence when he had removed it from my hands, the hopelessness with which I had received his touch.

'I'll see what I can do,' he said suddenly. 'It will take a while. Perhaps you could come back next week?'

'I don't have any time. The case is being heard now. In fact it may already be too late.'

The fingertips tapped together. Then he sighed, told me that he would order someone to bring tea and that he would show me to a room where I could wait.

I was ushered to a hallway where I sat in a red plush chair with gilt arms like a throne. A young clerk went by wheeling a trolley stacked with files. After ten minutes a woman wearing a shapeless grey skirt and with untidy hair escaping from its pins (like yours, Evelyn, I thought drearily) brought me tea in a plain white cup and saucer. A clock somewhere struck nine thirty, then ten, and I wondered what Breen would say when I didn't turn up at the trial. My life was in the balance, or so it seemed to me. I didn't know what I dreaded most, a report which revealed nothing or a report which somehow gave substance to my gnawing fears.

At about twenty to eleven another woman appeared, this one very neat in a pale blue dress with a narrow belt, and with well-cut hair. She offered to escort me back to the office.

His desk now had one file upon it.

'I cannot of course let you read the file but I can summarise the documents within, if you like, and see if any is of interest to you. Hardynge's activities extended far and wide during the war. He served on various committees related to the funding of the military. And he seems to have had a benevolent streak, setting up a significantly well-endowed fund for refugees and the wives of prisoners of war. He was also trustee of an organisation that gives relief to families in which the main breadwinner remains incapacitated by the war.'

'Is that it?'

'That's it. More or less. There is one thing.' And he removed from the file a letter, typed on thin, yellowing paper. 'Hardynge seems to have some very prestigious friends. A brief cor-respondence with General Haig has found its way into the file. In his letter Hardynge pleads for clemency on behalf of a young officer who, together with his companion, a nineteen-year-old private, was court-martialled for desertion and for firing at the military policeman who attempted to arrest them – both capital offences, as you doubtless know. Hardynge's petition was successful; the officer was sent home and confined to an institution dealing with shell-shocked patients. The other boy was executed. The court martial accepted the officer's word that it was the young private who had fired the gun.'

'What was the name of that boy?' I whispered.

'Fox. Private Fox. The officer in question was Captain Donald Hardynge.'

I went back to St James's Park, where I strode about, sat on a bench, got up. It was midday. What was happening in Aylesbury? Perhaps the closing speeches had already begun. The park was full of people with time on their hands, nannies and toddlers, the wheelchair-bound, the limpers, the men in broken boots who sat with their hands hanging between their knees or scouring the columns of a discarded newspaper, ladies in flirty summer dresses, a listless girl making a halfpenny bun last a lunchtime. One of Meredith's favourite songs replayed in my mind: 'What'll I Do'.

I walked along the other side of the lake, too restless to stay anywhere long. Mostly I kept to paths; sometimes, where permitted, I crossed the newly mown lawns. Stella Wheeler. Mud and grass on her shoes. A pathetic collection of acorn cups and conker cases. Scrapings from the park. I remembered Hardynge's eyes half concealed behind his glasses when asked about Stella's missing night. Blink. Blink. He must surely have been with her, but where? Her clothes had been stained with mud and grass and smelled bad. What had she been up to? Was that the night he'd presented her with the bronze statue? Or – as seemed more likely now – was the statue a reward or recompense for something that had happened that night? He was drawn to women in uniform, said Meredith, and that little waitress, the thwarted dancer Stella Wheeler, would have been easy pickings for a rich gentleman liberal with promises.

Stella had worked in Lyons in Regent Street so where was the nearest place a man and woman, intent on a secret meeting, might lose themselves? Green Park? *Hyde Park*. Hyde Park, notorious haunt for those after a quick fumble, a clandestine rendezvous. The newly appointed women police officers were constantly making a nuisance of themselves by plucking couples up to no good from the bushes.

Breen had ordered a search of the police records for the middle of April and uncovered nothing. No matter, I would look again. I was now walking fast and purposefully up Constitution Hill. There were various police stations in or on the fringes of London parks; in Hyde Park on the slope above the Serpentine among trees. The last time I'd confronted that innocuous red-brick frontage I was tagging along after Breen to bail out one of his female habitual clients, accused of using foul language to a woman police officer whilst resisting arrest. Breen treated police stations as if they were his club; a genial wave to passing officers, a thumbs up to the administrative staff, who fell over themselves to supply him with tea and biscuits.

Wolfe had said, when fingering the cloakroom ticket found in Stella's sponge bag, that he'd seen its type before when his clients redeemed their belongings on release from a police station. We had considered the possibility of Stella spending the night in a police cell – certainly that would explain the smell on her clothes – but had found no evidence. Now, though, I knew what I was looking for. I had seen Hardynge, under oath, deny that he had been with her one night in April but he was like a boulder buried in sand – the more we cleared away, the more I discovered what had been obscured from view. And I was driven by the kind of momentum that comes in moments of extreme tension, as in the examination hall. I did not consider that I was tired and hungry or that I would face the usual opposition from the male Establishment as I pushed through the swing doors and entered the fug of the outer office.

There was, as in every police station I had ever visited, a motley collection of customers awaiting attention. A woman at the head of a languid queue was describing a lost cat to an officer filling out a form. Breen would have marched straight up to the desk but I bided my time as first the cat woman was dealt with, then a man with a crushed cap who wanted to visit his son who'd been 'banged up' for assault, then a gentleman who wished to report a stolen bicycle.

When it was my turn the interview that followed was predictable. 'I am from Breen & Balcombe, solicitors. I wish to consult your records of arrest for April.'

The officer was tall with childish round eyes. 'You are from where?'

I produced letters addressed to me at Breen & Balcombe but he wasn't satisfied. 'We don't show our custody records to the public. They're confidential.'

'I believe Mr Breen has already had the records checked. Whoever looked before might have missed something. New evidence has come to light since then.'

'Then Mr Breen should come back here hisself.'

'Mr Breen is in court in Aylesbury.' My control was wafer thin. 'If you want, you could ring our office and his secretary will vouch for me.'

The officer was torn. He knew Breen, of course, and probably feared his wrath. In the end he pulled the telephone towards him, asked the operator for the number of Breen & Balcombe – he didn't trust me to give the correct one – and dialled. I prayed to a God I no longer believed in that Miss Drake would answer the phone promptly and then cooperate. The policeman's gaze raked up and down my face as he introduced himself to the invisible presence on the end of the line. 'It is a matter of verification, madam. Could you confirm for me that a Miss Evelyn Gifford works for your firm of solicitors.'

Long pause before I heard Miss Drake's voice scrape across the wires.

'In what capacity?' the policeman asked.

A longer pause before the voice began again. I heard the words 'junior' and 'clerk'. Then the officer passed the receiver to me. 'She wants to speak to you.'

'Miss Gifford,' said Miss Drake in her heavily enunciated telephone voice. 'Mr Breen has telephoned me twice this morning to ask if I know of your whereabouts. What am I to inform him if he calls again?'

'Tell him I was delayed.'

Pause. 'Miss Gifford, do you intend to go to Aylesbury today?'
'I cannot.'

A long silence. Then she said something very surprising indeed. 'Take care, Miss Gifford.'

At last I was led through the back office, down the stairs to the cells and surrendered to the custody sergeant, a cosy man so glad of the diversion that he even offered me tea. Someone, possibly the assault case, was hammering rhythmically on a cell door.

'Could I ask about your procedures?' I said as he loaded a tin tray with cups and, rather touchingly, a china milk jug patterned with harebells. 'Should a prisoner have valuables of any kind which you wish to confiscate whilst they are under arrest, what is the process?'

'We writes them down in a book and we issues a ticket. When they leave they show the ticket and we returns their things. Unless of course we want to use something in evidence. We enter the number into the log.'

'Could I see the type of tickets you issue?' But I knew already that he would produce a book of mushroom-coloured cloakroom tickets.

So I sat in that stuffy little chamber, corridors of cells to the right and left, as the custody sergeant shuffled about with kettle and teapot, and opened the ledger at 1 April 1924. It seemed to me that I must read each entry, one at a time, skipping nothing, or the spell would be broken.

On Tuesday 15 April I found what I was looking for, inscribed in painstaking copperplate, each column across two double pages filled in. The date. 'Time: *11.04 in the evening.*' Name of the arresting officer. 'Name of the arrested party: *Julie Fox.* Date of Birth: *23 March 1902.* Address: *4 Lyons Street, Acton.* Occupation: *Servant.* Charge: *Behaviour reasonably likely to offend against public decency.* Legal representative: *None.* Outcome: *Caution.* Released: *9 a.m. morning of Wednesday 18 April.* Chit *437.*'

And beneath, another entry. '*Miss Fox arrested in association with: Name not supplied.*' Legal representative: a scrawled signature. '*Released without charge.*'

I managed to speak though my index finger would not hold still as I pointed to the entry. 'Do you remember that night?'

The sergeant smiled kindly. 'I don't, miss. The officer in question has since moved on. I only been here since the beginning of May.'

'Isn't it unusual for a name not to be entered in the book?'

He pulled it towards him. 'Very. But some hold out until they've tooken legal advice. Looks like this all came to nothing.'

I nodded, shaking so hard I couldn't hold my cup steady. The sergeant was talking about his previous posting in Stepney, which he had preferred. 'You get used to the regulars. Here you never know what'll come in next.' I nodded again, shook hands with him, and then at last escaped into the daylight.

The name Julie Fox would have meant nothing to a policeman requested by Breen to scan the records for Stella Hobhouse, and the signature of the legal representative was such a scrawl as to be almost indecipherable. But I knew it. Oh, I did. Had I not, in the past couple of weeks, read three letters over and over again, each signed Nicholas Thorne?

Chapter Thirty-Eight

By now it was gone three. I bought a newspaper and ordered tea and toast in a café as my eyes passed over the usual headlines – queues lengthening outside labour exchanges, miners rebelling, government failing. On page 3 there was an update on the 'Shot in the Heart Murder' in which Sir David Hardynge, philanthropist and parliamentary candidate, was described as a surprise witness whose generosity in private led to his unexpected embroilment in a murder trial and whose modest dignity in court was exemplary. At a quarter to five my feet carried me to Maida Vale and the corner where Nicholas was leaning against the side of his car, arms folded, head to one side, casually dressed, no tie, open waistcoat, blazer.

He flung open the door, helped me in and at once the horror faded a little as the truth of Nicholas – the clean lines of his body, the shape of his smile, that upward tilt to the left side of the mouth – soothed my aching heart. He kissed me, studied my face, told me I looked desperately tired, kissed me again and asked where shall we go?

I said I had the key to Prudence's cottage and we would certainly have privacy there. Making no comment he gave me a quick, warm look then turned on to the Harrow Road. I was incapacitated by the shock of being all day alone and now with him. Here he was, the man I was so in love with, the same as when I last saw him outside Fortnum's though perhaps even more impossibly, unreachably Nicholas, his competent hand on the wheel, the intelligent fingers, the contrast of the white cuff with his skin, the changing slope of his thigh as he worked the brake.

At first he tried to make me talk. What was the outcome of the Wheeler trial? 'Not finished yet,' I said. 'Did you not read about it in the papers?' He'd only glanced at *The Times* in the train and there'd been no mention. What about my interview with Lady Curren? 'The children are to be released though it was an uncomfortable half-hour. I wanted to know more about the home's policy on child emigration and Lady Curren thought I was being ungrateful. You obviously exert quite an influence on her, Nicholas. She spoke of you fondly.'

'Well she's Sylvia's aunt. A formidable woman for her size but her heart's in the right place. Between them she and her sister sit on practically every committee in town.'

He didn't seem to notice that I rarely spoke after that. Instead he told me about his brief in Manchester and how he'd managed to get his defendant off with two years' penal servitude, a sight better outcome than for the others, who received ten years apiece. 'The fact is, though, that the sums involved, more than a hundred thousand pounds stolen from the bank over six months, made it a high-profile case that hit the national press. Others like it may follow for me. It's all good.'

Summer had matured since we walked together in the fields above Chesham. In the luminous late afternoon there was scarcely a movement among the dense greenery of the woods. I remembered the acute sense of excitement as I travelled out, alone, on the Metropolitan Line, the child in the seat opposite with the farthing-sized birthmark, the miracle of finding Nicholas awaiting me under the churchyard wall. And now I was with the same man but with the dream, it seemed to me, in ruins.

For the first time I admitted to myself what I had wanted from this evening when I made my offer to Prudence and asked for the keys to her cottage. Him. Yes. All. And now?

Prudence's cottage was in a lane just outside Beaconsfield, a few miles from Uxbridge. It was familiar to me from reluctant childhood visits to the recently orphaned Aunt Prudence, who had sat in rustling black satin and served us meagre Sunday teas, agony for James and me until we were released into the garden and allowed to play hide-and-seek among the gooseberry bushes. The cottage, of charmless stucco, was set four-square in its gardens behind a low wall, a quarter of a mile or so from the much grander Georgian house that had once belonged to my grandfather.

Prudence had an eye for function rather than beauty. The garden was rigidly carved up into vegetable patch and fruit bushes with stepping-stone paths in between and squares of flower bed outside the front and back doors. Inside there was no electricity, the fires were rarely lit and the furnishings, hastily selected from her dead father's house, the worst of mid-Victorian. On the evening I visited with Nicholas, though the mellow July light was flattering, the angular little house seemed resigned to a future of creeping decay. Leaving me at the gate, he drove off to park in a wider part of the lane. My key gave access to the scullery with its red-tiled floor and dripping tap where, as a child, I had been condemned to spend damp half-hours with Mrs Lime, the help, peeling vegetables or washing up.

No wonder the tenants had gone elsewhere for the summer. Prudence's furniture was still there, the unforgiving chairs at the swept hearth, the heavy sideboard in the parlour. The windows were too small and deep-set to let in much light or any heat. I looked under the sink but found neither ants nor mouse droppings, only an evil-looking but mercifully empty trap, and ran up the steep little staircase to check the two bedrooms, one containing twin beds, the other Prudence's, with a three-foot iron bedstead and pious prints on the walls.

Once, when I was eight, James and I had been sent to stay with Prudence – 'to keep her company now she's lost grandfather', mother said. James was allocated the spare room while I had to undergo the torture of sleeping head to toe with my aunt, who was outraged when I suggested I share my brother's room. I lay awake with her feet on my hip, swamped by her very distinctive smell. What was it? Coal tar soap, hair washed once a week, clothes often aired but rarely cleaned and, most pungent of all, the odour of distaste. I regarded Aunt Prudence as an unknowable woman who avoided touch beyond a peck at arrival and departure, whose activities were rigidly regulated and included numerous trips to the village with a basket and a list of dull messages: call in on old Mrs P. to check her feet, visit Mrs Carstairs (the vicar's wife) to offer a seed cake for the bring-and-buy, deliver a parcel of largesse (rhubarb and a cast-off pair of lisle stockings) to the indigent Lawrence family, buy

346

stamps and postcards so that we children could write home daily.

James, at five, was not expected to participate much in Prudence's life, and a son of the vicarage was summoned so that the pair could form a reluctant bond. They were even given an old sheet to make a wigwam. I, on the other hand, was to be Prudence's little helper as she paid her calls, fussed over church matters, sewed or worked in the garden. By the end of two days I was near to screaming with boredom. The next morning I took James for a long walk in the enticing country lanes. I remember his hot, rough little hand in mine, the ache of responsibility as we ventured further and further from the cottage, his questions: 'Where are we going? How much longer? What's a baby bat called?' We ate blackberries and stopped to look at everything – a foal rubbing its ear on a gate, a scattering of feathers betokening some dreadful death, a well with a small pitched roof. We got lost, had to ask the way back and arrived at the cottage with berry-stained mouths and filthy hands. Prudence slapped our legs and refused us jam at teatime. James obligingly howled all evening and far into the night until at last I was allowed to sleep with him, his delicious fruit-scented cheek pressed against mine. The next day we were collected by Min and brought home to Maida Vale.

I stood at Prudence's bedroom window, facing the front, and watched Nicholas, who was leaning on the wall by the gate in a stance that was already wrenchingly familiar, arms folded, head down, legs crossed at the ankle. Bathed in that steady golden light, he seemed to be on the brink of something, of an entirely different world to mine.

Where had my dream of a happy ending come from? Happy endings of the fairy-tale variety had not been part of the plan since war was declared, since the toasting fork had clattered onto the hearth, since I had listened to that fateful lecture in Girton. What a fool I had been to think that a man so beautiful, so full of promise, so sweetly inclined to fall in love, should actually have been destined for me. He, after all, like most other eligible men over twenty-four in Europe, was deeply, fatally entrammelled by the past.

I stood at the window a little longer making up my mind, then I went down to him.

'What is it?' he said. 'What kept you so long?'

'I want you to do something for me.'

I led him inside, closed the scullery door behind us, passed through the kitchen with its blue gingham frills on cupboards and windows, and climbed the little staircase leading to Prudence's bedroom, where the net curtain at the window was still thrust to one side.

'What is it?' he asked again.

I lifted his hand to my breast. 'I want you to give me this, only this.'

He took a little indrawn breath but shook his head. His fingers pressed momentarily, promisingly, on my flesh, then withdrew. 'Evelyn, we'll have a lifetime.'

'So much could happen. I want to take this now.'

'My very, very dear girl.' Stunned, wrong-footed, he took a step back. 'Do you know what you are doing?'

I sat on the edge of the bed, hands in my lap, waiting.

'Evelyn.'

'You said you wanted to be with me.' I pulled the pins from my hair and placed them on the quilt, then undid the top button of my blouse. His back was to the light. I thought, If he refuses me, I shall die.

At last he pulled me up so that we stood one on either side of the window looking half through the lattice, half through net to the overgrown fruit bushes now in deep shadow. Sighing, he reached out his other hand, lifted my hair, held the back of my neck and brought my face close to his. I was weeping so hard that I had to take long, deep breaths as he kissed my mouth.

Everything broke apart – the pink and brown trellis pattern on the wallpaper, the greens of the garden, the darkness of Nicholas. I kept my eyes open because I wanted to know what happened to the world when lovemaking was involved. I heard my own stunned cries as his kisses intensified, my hands tore at his clothes, my flesh shivered under the shock of his touch as he slid his hand inside the neck of my blouse and stroked my breast.

He whispered, 'Are you sure?'

I drew him back until I felt the side of the bed against my knees. When we lay down I guided his hand onto my thigh. He watched me for a moment then tucked me under his arm so that we lay clasped together as he undid the buttons on my blouse and pushed the fabric aside.

'You're so perfect,' he whispered. 'You don't know. My head has been full, all these years, of images of men who have been most obscenely broken. I don't know how I shall bear it, the beauty of you.'

'All. Not just men. All of us broken.' Our kisses deepened and I laid his hand on the fastening of my skirt. I had time to wonder, in those kisses, about other women, Sylvia. And then I gave in.

Pay attention, Evelyn. Don't miss a thing. I followed his hand as it cupped my knee and swept my inner thigh. My flesh shuddered at the impossible intimacy of his tentative fingers. I loved the conjunction of our bodies, the beat of his stomach and thighs so that the pain in my heart was crushed to a distant echo. My fists clenched, ankles flexed, neck arched until I didn't recognise my own body. How could I, when it had been shrouded for a lifetime in constricting garments, and was now unwrapped at last, being made love to by this man and no other? I wept to see Nicholas exposed, connected, revealing a face not as it was in public but absolutely stripped of any defence, soft-mouthed, soft-skinned, blurred with love.

This was the opposite of all the rules I had grown up with – cover up, avoid touch, treat your body merely as an inconvenient, suffering vessel for the soul. What a lie to pretend the body wasn't packed with sensation and desire, capable of embracing and opening itself up to be filled with a new light, a new freedom. Evelyn Gifford, alive, alive.

But afterwards as I lay in his arms, even as I marvelled at the touch of his warm moist skin against mine, they came back, softly at first, whispering against the window, a million dead mouths, among them James, the shadowy Private Fox and Stella Wheeler with her bronze dancer and her false smile.

I shut them out again and for a while longer spun on the pivot of our brief time together while he covered my neck and breast with kisses. I couldn't believe that he didn't love me.

The shape and contents of the room emerged again: a print of a child kneeling at prayer, blond curls, eyes shut; a spider, legs thin as hairs, twirling from the picture rail. Nicholas's face, close up, was full of movement: the flutter of his eyelid, a momentary tic at the side of his mouth, the adjustment of his lips as if the muscles were relaxing in preparation for sleep. With one arm he held me, the other hand rested on my stomach. I heard a car in the lane, remembered the gooseberry bushes and how their thorns used to tear at my hair when I hid among them as a little girl.

He opened his eyes and smiled. Was that love, the softness and heat in his gaze, or was that how all men looked after sex? I stroked his face, waiting. It's not too late, Evelyn, to say nothing. He caught my finger between his lips and kissed it, leaned over me and kissed me again.

The last thing I did, before I spoke, was to trace the shape and texture of him from chin to navel, the slight roughness of his throat, the muscular breast, the soft, tender skin of his stomach. Then a voice I scarcely recognised as my own said, 'You know that Wheeler will hang.'

He tightened his arms about me. 'I fear so.'

'Despite the fact that at the last moment Wolfe found a new witness, an admirer of Stella's who bought her that bronze dancer I mentioned to you.'

'How clever of Wolfe. But it made no difference?'

'Nicholas, you'd know the answer to that because the gentleman was Sir David Hardynge.'

His muscles became rigid. 'Hardynge?'

'He met Stella at a Christmas party, so he says, dropped into Lyons on a whim, and bought her the bronze dancer as a wedding present. We could pin nothing else on him, even if it were plausible that he wanted her dead. He has an alibi for the day of the murder – at home with his wife over lunchtime, then visiting Donald.'

He said again, 'Hardynge.'

'Yes. I don't expect you're entirely surprised.'

'You're mistaken. I'm shocked to the core.'

I lay for a moment longer in his arms, inhaling his scent, then jolted upright and knelt above him, my hair tumbling onto his chest, my arms crossed to cover my naked breasts. 'Tell me the truth. Please. I need to hear it. Tell me you are not somehow bound up with Stella's murder.'

He put his hands behind his head and stared at me. I saw the shadow of a defiant boy in him, a tightening of the lips, eyes voided of expression. Already we were so far from what we had been minutes ago. 'I can only tell you what I believe to be true.'

'Tell me. Nicholas, don't you understand? Wheeler will hang. Who is protecting who? What's going on? You can't let a man die, Nicholas.'

'I didn't know that Hardynge had bought her the bronze dancer.'

'I wish I could believe you.'

'When Wheeler was arrested, Hardynge telephoned my chambers and asked me to keep an eye on the proceedings as they concerned a loyal employee – one for whom he had a particular affection and respect, especially bearing in mind Wheeler's wartime service – and if possible to protect the good name of Imperial Insurance. He said he was worried about poor Wheeler and wanted him to have the best possible defence. He wanted be kept in touch with developments. That was all.'

'No. It wasn't all. You deliberately befriended me. You approached me after the Marchant case not because you admired me but because you wanted to keep your eye on Breen & Balcombe and I was the easiest way in.'

'You knew that; I told you so in the café near Toynbee. You were utterly incensed, as I recall. But I was hooked after that. Believe me.'

'You looked up my brother's war record so that you could form a bond with me.'

The briefest of pauses before he answered: 'That was before I knew you. Once I'd met you everything changed.'

'I told you we were going for a fitness-to-plead argument. You dissuaded us after consulting with Hardynge, who I now realise would have been most unhappy if there had been excessive probing into Wheeler's war record. And then the bronze dancer. Who did you tell about the bronze dancer after I mentioned her to you during our tea at Fortnum's?'

'I might have said something to Hardynge ...'

'And he somehow got to the salesman, who disappeared, heaven knows where. We still haven't tracked him down, though apparently Wolfe has discovered he has family in Devon. There are too many connections and too many things that don't fit. And I haven't told you the most significant of all. Do you remember an incident late at night on Tuesday the fifteenth of April, when you were called to Hyde Park police station?'

All this time he had lain with his hands behind his head, watching me. Now he raised himself on one elbow. Even in the last of the twilight I saw his sudden pallor. 'Possibly.'

'Your name is on the records in the case of a Julie Fox and an unnamed other party. Julie Fox was Stella, I'm sure. Julie came to mind because it's her sister's name and Fox … I'll tell you later why she chose Fox because I think it could have been that use of a false name, on a whim, that resulted in her murder. Who was the man you bailed out, Nicholas?'

He lay on his back with his palms crushed to his eyes. 'Christ.'

'Nicholas.'

He sprang from the bed and began to dress. After a moment I did the same, though it seemed a dreadful thing to be struggling with buttons and hooks, arming myself against him. We didn't look at each other. Now that I had wrenched myself from him the process of dressing was cumbersome and shameful. Nicholas stood at the window once more, head bent in the low-ceilinged room, holding his elbows.

'Tuesday evening,' he said at last. 'Mid-April. About eleven o'clock. I was telephoned from Hyde Park police station. A gentleman wished to speak to me. Hardynge. He sounded flustered. "In a spot of bother," he said. "Come down to the station, Nicholas, I need your help." Turned out he'd been caught among the trees in Hyde Park embracing a girl, rather more than embracing. The pair had been arrested. Hardynge was agitated as he didn't want it to come to court, didn't want his wife to find out, and was obviously terrified lest it spoil his chances of being selected for his constituency. I had to use all my powers of persuasion, and summoned the inspector, who fortunately was of the opinion that women police officers were forever bringing time-wasting cases back to the station. I made a few promises, alluded to a couple of influential people and managed to get Hardynge out.'

'And the girl?'

'I knew nothing about the girl.'

'Not even her name?'

'I wasn't told her name. I never saw her. I simply got the police to agree that a caution for her was the most convenient resolution for all. The thing was, Evelyn, I wasn't surprised when I got the call from Hardynge that evening. It was an inconvenience to me rather than a shock. I knew he had a weakness for young girls – I suspect even his wife has an inkling – because I'd bailed him out before.'

'And when Stella was murdered it never occurred to you that she might have been another of his dalliances?'

'It did not. I trusted him. As I trusted you.' It was too dark now to read his eyes as he said very low, very cold, 'I never thought I would be used by a woman as you have used me this evening. You knew all this. You believe me to be implicated in whatever it is that Hardynge has done, you were determined to confront me with all kinds of accusations, and yet you asked me to make love to you first.'

'Was that using you? Perhaps. I love you, Nicholas, you have no idea how much, or how sure I am that it will be the only time for me. For once I took a risk and asked for what I wanted. But it's hopeless because you are in Hardynge's pocket. He whistles; you jump. A woman is dead and her husband will hang for a crime he almost certainly didn't commit because you couldn't resist doing him another seedy favour. Can't you see what happened after Stella was released that night? She had a hold on him, or thought she did. Perhaps he assumed he could buy her off with the bronze dancer. I'll bet she tried to pester him into providing her with some other kind of life than that little terrace with Stephen Wheeler.'

He was a stranger, face averted. And still I loved him and wanted to take the step that would bring me back to his arms, surely, soften the steely perfection of his profile, restore his kisses.

He said, 'Doesn't this give Stephen the motive we've been looking for, if he got wind of the fact that Stella was having an affair?'

'Wheeler didn't kill Stella. You know he didn't. My God, what that man could teach us all about love. At first, when I was at the police station today, I thought Stella had probably tried to blackmail Hardynge after that night by threatening to tell the press about the sordid outing to Hyde Park. But even I know that a man like Hardynge could buy off any number of newspaper editors or pushy little waitresses.' I thought, but didn't say, After all, Nicholas, he appears to have bought off you. 'Unless Stella threatened to reveal a much more significant truth, one Hardynge couldn't bear even to speak about. Nicholas, do you know what your friend Donald got up to in the war?'

At last he faced me and grasped my shoulder. 'Jesus Christ. Jesus.' Thrusting me aside he clattered down the narrow stairs and through the kitchen, where I heard him fumbling with the bolt on the scullery door. By the time I'd caught up with him he was outside at the gate, white-faced, trapped within the low walls of the garden.

'Can't you see?' he said. 'Have you any idea how much this hurts? Donald. If I'd known Hardynge had bought the bronze dancer ... I might have ...'

But the next moment he laughed, as if in rueful surrender to the fates that had so perversely brought him to Prudence's cottage. He looked about him at the darkly shadowed garden where the unruly gooseberry bushes extended vicious spikes, then sank down against the wall of the house under the parlour window, hands locked about his knees. 'Don't tell me, the other boy was called Fox. Is that where Stella got the name? I was never told it, though I knew Don liked boys, of course I did. He always had. And I knew that he'd run off with someone and that one of them had fired a shot. I knew that Hardynge had got Don home, even though he was the officer and older, and therefore more culpable.'

'Did you never probe what had happened? How Hardynge managed it?'

He sank his head into his arms. 'I owed him too much to ask questions. My life, probably. A month or two later he had me moved to a safer posting behind the lines. I wasn't given a reason at the time, just thanked my lucky stars. Later, after the war, Hardynge told me he'd had a word in someone's ear: he'd lost one son, he said, and couldn't bear to lose another.'

We sat shoulder to shoulder against Prudence's cottage, just where James and I used to crouch safely out of sight. The stucco at our backs was still warm.

'Stella knew all about it,' I said, and as I dropped words into the soft air they became nuggets of truth. 'She'd have drawn the story out of Wheeler: how he was part of a firing squad and all the details of the young boy's crime, including the name of his accomplice – or rather leader, I should say – because he couldn't deny her anything. Perhaps he even hoped she would comfort him. There was a photograph of Fox in their house. That's why she used his name at the police station, as a hint to Hardynge that she had a hold on him. Imagine if Stella had told the world not just about her little fling but that Hardynge had sacrificed the life of a frightened young boy for the sake of his own son, who was, incidentally, a coward and a liar. Do you really imagine it was the boy Fox who shot the military policeman?

'Hardynge killed Stella, or had her killed – he has an alibi for the afternoon of the murder – because she was a liability. The gift of the bronze dancer wasn't enough to satisfy her so he visited her at home and perhaps promised her a tryst, an elopement even. I think he planned every detail so that we'd all focus on Wheeler. It was only the bronze dancer that betrayed him – a matter of pure arrogance to overlook the value of something that to him was a trifle. Once Stella had told him about Wheeler's war souvenirs, it would have been simple for him to get hold of the gun and gloves, which were kept in an unlocked shed. After all, he was a dab hand at using scapegoats. Like father, like son.'

The garden was warm and mothy, and though ill-kept some flowers had struggled up through their weedy beds so that I could smell the dusty perfume of perennial sweet peas. Still, in some drowning part of me, I hoped we might soon come to a resolution that would extract us from this dreadful place. Nicholas was bound to say something that would save us.

'What will you do with all this speculation?' he said.

'I don't know. Tell Breen. As you say, it's only speculation. But perhaps there's enough to convince the judge that to convict Wheeler would be unsafe. Perhaps it will buy us time.'

There was a long silence. 'You know it will destroy me,' Nicholas said, 'if it comes out that I put pressure on the police at Hyde Park, especially if Hardynge is brought back to court and has to admit to being with her that night.'

That was the worst. Until then I had thought that he might not be culpable. After all, my lips were still swollen, my body thrumming, overturned by our lovemaking. And yet there he sat murmuring about the damage this would do to his career.

I went to the back of the cottage and locked the scullery door. Then I walked to the gate and waited. At last he too got up, brushed himself down and followed me out of the garden. When I closed the gate behind us I listened for the click of the latch, remembering the flash of joy as James and I had been led away by Min, in such disgrace that Prudence couldn't bring herself to shake our hands or wave from the window; how the gate had snapped fast behind us and how we had pranced off, one on either side of Min, who was in great spirits due to the unexpected excursion to bring us home. Leaving the cottage, I had felt triumphant. By the time I reached home, I had been overwhelmed by guilt.

It was quite dark now in the surrounding woods, and through the trees I saw a gleam of orange – low sunlight reflected on a window-pane. The inside of the automobile was quite cool and steeped in that unforgettable scent of leather and oil. Nicholas's hands gripped the wheel but he made no attempt to start the engine.

'I want to take you somewhere, Evelyn, that might make it easier for you to understand.'

I said nothing.

'Will you come and meet Donald?'

I drew a long breath. 'What difference would it make?'

'Perhaps none, I don't know. At least you'd have the full picture.'

'You want me to keep quiet. This is just an attempt to win my sympathy.'

'Think that if you must. But perhaps it will give you more evidence. After all, wouldn't it help to check the records at the nursing home and find out what time Hardynge visited on the day of Stella Wheeler's murder?'

Of course I couldn't object to that. Besides, anywhere in Nicholas's company still seemed the only bearable place to be. It was well past eight o'clock and the lanes were dusky, though the sky in open countryside was luminous. I sat neatly, not allowing my elbow to touch his, as I watched the occasional flicker of light in a cottage window, a passing car, a cluster of houses.

Chapter Thirty-Nine

The Grove, to the north of Princes Risborough, was reached by a narrow lane, and our way was eventually blocked by wrought-iron gates. Nicholas had to knock at the door of the lodge until a bent little man in an oversized cap and jacket emerged.

'It's late to come visiting,' he said, but having recognised Nicholas, he let us in. Because the shrubs and trees were in full leaf, the house, a rather beautiful white-painted mansion with a colonnaded porch, only came into view when we were a few hundred feet away. As I got out of the car at the foot of a short flight of curved steps, I stumbled, unable for a moment to remember what I was doing there.

The door was opened by a nurse, Sister Phelan, who wore a flowing apron and complicated headdress, and was as surprised as the gatekeeper had been to see us.

'We never usually allow visitors so late in the evening. It's too disruptive. Our men are nearly ready to go to bed.' She had a strong southern-Irish accent, and her staring eyes were emphasised by the fierceness with which her hair was dragged back from her forehead. However, she too remembered Nicholas, as she shook him by the hand and exclaimed: 'Don't tell me there's bad news in the family.'

'We were in the area on business,' Nicholas said. 'Miss Gifford is also a lawyer. We thought we'd call on the off-chance that Donald was still up. He won't want to see me, I'm sure, but I thought he might appreciate a young lady visitor.'

'It's true he has a softness for the girls. Are you a family friend, Miss Gifford?'

'An acquaintance, rather.'

'My goodness, but you look all in,' said Sister Phelan. 'I can't imagine what possessed you to come calling so late. Shall I be getting you a cup of tea? Shame on you, Mr Thorne, for asking so much of your young lady friend.' But she asked no further questions and bustled away to order tea. Meanwhile Nicholas and I avoided each other's eyes as he picked up the visitors' book from an occasional table, leafed through and found the entry for Saturday 17 May, with Sir David's name and signature. Hardynge had arrived at four thirty, left just after six.

In my trance-like state I thought, How easily the world moulds itself for Nicholas. Everything he wants, he gets. Even me.

'Does Donald Hardynge have many visitors?' he asked Sister Phelan when she was pouring the tea.

'Just the family. His father is a wonderful man – never misses a Saturday, though he must be in such demand elsewhere. And as you say, Sylvia is a very popular visitor here, with all our men.'

A few sips of tea revived me a little and afterwards Sister Phelan led me through room after room across one highly polished set of floorboards after another. Glass doors divided the old house, with its elaborate plasterwork and graciously proportioned rooms, from a much newer wing consisting of long, low corridors with closed doors on either side. Turkish rugs dotted the floor, semicircular tables held floral displays, and the walls were adorned with photographs of the staff arranged in blurred ranks so that I could scarcely make out their faces, and delicately tinted prints of botanical specimens. The house, said Sister Phelan, had until the war belonged to a private family and was not ideally suited to its present function; food had to be carried too far and the rooms in the old house were not secure and therefore good for little except meetings and staff accommodation. Occasionally we passed a deferential nurse, who fell back against the wall to let us pass, but we never saw a patient, and as I watched the floating wings on our guide's headdress and heard the rustle of her starched uniform, I wondered at the profundity of the silence beyond.

Donald Hardynge was seated exactly as Nicholas had once described him, on a ladder-back chair in a glassed-in veranda, overlooking a garden graced by a cedar and S-shaped flower beds. Perfect lawns were edged by shrubs and crossed by gravel paths. A couple of other men, young and crisply turned out with sleekeddown hair and spotless shirt collars, sat tranquilly reading their newspapers. Donald Hardynge, who was not doing anything, was also dressed smartly, in a buttoned-up waistcoat over shirt and tie, neatly pressed trousers and gleaming shoes as if he were about to stride off and meet a client.

All three men leapt to their feet, and I was introduced to each as a friend of Sylvia Hardynge. One had a dreadful facial wound across which skin had been grafted, but the corner of his mouth and eye were dragged down and his right ear was gone. Donald's grip was firm but cursory. He was very thin with high cheekbones, cleft chin and lightly curling hair. I saw echoes of his father and sister in the shape of his bones; I saw nothing in his eyes.

Once we were both seated we stared at the garden and Donald drummed his fingers on the arm of his chair. Sister Phelan said she would return in ten minutes. At the far end of the veranda a nurse was knitting a garment in pale blue wool.

'It's getting dark,' I said, sensing that the banal words seeped into Donald's mind as if it were a sponge, spreading out until they didn't fit together at all.

After a pause his cultured voice, like his father's, said, 'I have not been out all day.' The next moment he got up and offered me his arm.

The young nurse in the corner set aside her knitting. 'He wants you to go out with him. He always wants to go out. But he won't stay long, just a few minutes.'

She slid open the glass door and Donald Hardynge and I stepped first onto a gravel path, then a lawn. His arm was rigid under my hand. I tried to imagine him in another, pre-war life: the tennis-playing schoolboy, his future mapped out by an ambitious father; and later as a young man bolting across a desolate French landscape in the company of a frightened boy soldier. Meanwhile I was being guided in a very straight line across the lawn, under the cedar and beyond, towards the shrubbery.

At the edge of the lawn Donald stopped. From here we could see both the front of the house and the bedroom block with its glassed-in verandas, where his two companions sat exactly as we had left them. 'Have we walked far enough?' asked Donald.

'I should say so.' The last of the sun had sunk away and the shrubbery was very dark. We did not go back across the lawn but walked on round its edge in what I assumed was a well-worn ritual. I glanced up into Donald's face, but he was staring straight ahead and did not acknowledge me at all.

So this was why Stella had died, this long-dead boy. I leaned on his unyielding arm and thought how fruitless it had all been – Donald's attempt to escape the war, his father's efforts to save him. And as we circled the lawn, I could not help giving thanks that it was Donald Hardynge's and not James's arm that lay under my hand, Sylvia's brother and not mine who marched sightlessly along the gravel paths leading one to another in the garden of an old mansion.

Nicholas and I drove back to London in near silence. Occasionally his fingers drummed the wheel or he sighed deeply and shifted his weight on the seat. When we reached the corner of Clivedon Hall Gardens I moved to open the door, and for the first time in over an hour he spoke. 'Evelyn, I've been thinking. There's something else you should know. I remember the weekend of the murder very clearly because of course on the Tuesday of the following week, I met you. That Saturday I played tennis as usual with Sylvia in the garden of her house. You say Hardynge's alibi is that he was at home. I saw him at twelve when I first arrived, but I didn't see him again.'

'He could have been anywhere in the house, surely.'

'I don't think so. Lady Margaret was there with a luncheon party – they were having a committee meeting or some such and in the early afternoon they all came spilling down into the garden to watch us. There was no sign of Sir David.'

I couldn't take in either the implications of what he said or the fact that he seemed to be offering this information as a kind of plea, or pledge.

He said, 'Can you forgive me?'

But you are a stranger, I thought. What I knew of him was that if I lifted his hand to my lips his wrist would smell of soap and, very faintly, the leather of his watch strap, and that if I were to lean my head on his shoulder I would see the pulse in his throat and how the soft hair above his ear sprang a little sparsely so that

I might actually have counted the follicles, one by one. I would try again to puzzle out what it was about his face, his mouth, his eyes that quickened my pulse, why I found so beautiful the fall of a lock of hair on his brow and the sweep of his fingers thrusting it aside. But what enthused and inspired or disgusted and deadened him, what kept him awake at night, I did not know at all.

'How can I forgive you,' I said, 'when I have no idea now whose side you are on?'

I got out of the automobile and was about to close the door behind me when I thought I heard him say, 'Yours. I love you.'

A light was burning in the hall, where Edmund's little blazer was hung carelessly on the stand, his satchel tossed alongside. My brother's hat, I noticed, had been shuffled to a less prominent hook. Perhaps soon someone would take it upstairs and put it away.

I crept to the kitchen, fumbled for the light switch, and went to the scullery in search of bread. But I could not escape Meredith, who came pattering down in pale green silk pyjamas. 'Evelyn. For heaven's sake, where have you been? You missed everything that happened in court today. Your Mr Breen was so concerned he kept looking at the doors hoping you'd come in. He says you're to telephone him when you get back, no matter how late it is. But in the Lord's name, what are you doing with that knife? Give it to me.'

The knife clattered off the board and onto the floor. She pushed me into a chair and held my cold hands as a tidal wave of exhaustion overcame me. When the wrenching sobs began she held my face against her stomach, stroked my hair and would not let me go.

Later she revived the fire in the range, boiled an egg and heated milk. She talked about the trial, how the defence lawyer had done his best to persuade the jury that Wheeler should not be found guilty: there was too much doubt, evidence of another man in Stella's life, evidence that she had planned the picnic, above all overwhelming evidence that Wheeler loved her so much that the idea he might have killed her was quite absurd.

Mr Breen ('your Mr Breen', as Meredith put it) was pessimistic, however.

She watched me eat, nudging the plate closer, as she did with Edmund, to remind me to take another mouthful, then went to telephone Breen and tell him I was home safely and would speak to him in the morning. Not once did she ask what had happened, though she must have longed to know. Instead she switched off the lights and urged me upstairs, where she turned back the quilt of my bed and plumped the pillow.

And I discovered, as I lay down at last, that beneath the pain there was a spark of hope, because this time, when I'd lost my love, I'd been given a hand to hold.

Chapter Forty

Next morning Breen and I sat on either side of his desk in the Arbery Street office. He rocked back in his chair, twiddled his thumbs and gazed at the ceiling while I recounted the events of the previous day, though not of course the detail of what had happened between Thorne and me.

'There's no need to be so woeful and melodramatic about all this,' said Breen, fixing me with his blackbird eye. 'I'm not a complete fool. The moment we got back to London last night Wolfe and I visited Hyde Park police station to see what you'd been up to. I found the entry in the ledger, same as you did. And we were well aware that you had developed feelings for Thorne and, incidentally, he for you. Why do you think I excluded you from our investigations? You should not reproach yourself. As you well know, the world is oiled by people making connections with each other.'

'I let my feelings interfere with my—'

But he'd had enough of this talk of feelings. 'None of us is made of stone, Miss Gifford. And if we become stone, we should give up criminal law at once and stick to conveyancing. It's simply a matter of watching one's tongue and keeping confidences where appropriate. I'd say, on the whole, feelings aside, that you have done rather well.' He was, I realised, concealing considerable excitement by shuffling papers and adjusting the knot in his tie.

'I really do believe, Miss Gifford, that with all this new information, we shall be able to save Stephen Wheeler.'

Next we took a cab to Wormwood Scrubs, where an officer friend of Breen granted us an interview with Wheeler, who received us as if we were paying a social call and expressed amazement that we had troubled ourselves to visit on a Saturday. Altogether he was a different man to the one who had been confined each day to the dock. His beard and hair had been trimmed and he looked more comfortable in his laundered prison shirt than in the cheap suit he wore in court. We took him the gift of half a fruit cake, the remains of one of Miss Drake's offerings to Breen, for which he was touchingly grateful. Then I took out pen and paper and placed it neatly on the table. Breen and I sat facing Wheeler, my heart beating fast in anticipation of his reaction to our news.

Breen wrapped his hands round one knee, cocked his head to one side and looked Wheeler in the eye. 'Stephen, we are here because more evidence has come to light about Hardynge's involvement with Stella. I always counsel caution – I would advise you not to raise your hopes too far – but we think we have enough to suggest that there should be further investigation. Even his alibi for the afternoon of Stella's murder is now questionable. And if the judge won't allow us to suspend proceedings at this stage, we definitely have grounds for an appeal.'

Wheeler's reaction was not at all as I'd anticipated, in fact it was the opposite of hope. The genial light went from his face and he adopted the same posture as he had in the dock – body slumped, head bowed.

'You served with Hardynge's son, Donald?' Breen said.

The slightest nod. 'What has that to do with my Stella?'

'Stephen, you have asked us to defend you but I think that you have been less than helpful in telling us what you know. You have kept quiet when you might have given us information that would have saved a lot of time. So now that we have found everything out, I hope you're going to cooperate with us.'

Wheeler sat more upright but still would not look at Breen.

'Go on then. Ask me whatever you like.'

'What happened between your friend Private Fox and Donald Hardynge, Stephen?'

This time Wheeler did not seem in the least surprised by the question but nodded as if we had confirmed something in his mind. 'The Hardynge boy got off; the young lad was sentenced to be shot. I'd known Fox since he was twelve – he used to be a messenger at work. Knew him to be a soft sort of boy.' He glanced at me. 'Forgive me, Miss Gifford, but he was a bit of a honeytrap for men who took their pleasures that way. I kept my eye on him as far as I could but there was always someone else wanting to offer him a different type of protection.'

'Did you find it surprising that Hardynge was sent home while the boy was left to face a firing squad?'

'Neither of them should have died. They were too scared, not right for the war. I saw them when they were brought back to camp. Both crying.'

'Did you know which of them shot the military policeman?'

There may even have been a glimmer of humour in Wheeler's eye. 'Well it couldn't have been the boy now, could it? Everyone knows that common soldiers aren't issued with revolvers.'

'Weren't you angry, then, that Fox was shot?'

'Course I was angry. But it wasn't the Hardynge boy's fault. It was the way things were bound to turn out, given who each of them was.'

'Did Stella know this story?'

'I told Stella everything.'

Breen said, 'You've heard already how Sir David made Stella a gift of the bronze dancer. And now we discover that there was a night in April when they were caught red-handed, Stella and Hardynge—'

Wheeler leaned forward. 'What are you saying?'

'We think that Hardynge committed perjury last week in court or came damn close to it. I suspect he chose his words very carefully – I'll have to look at a transcript. He knew exactly where Stella was on the fifteenth of April because he was with her. We think that afterwards Stella tried to blackmail him by threatening to make public the story of Donald and Private Fox, and that's why he killed her.'

Breen had spoken in the soft tones he normally reserved for soothing distraught female clients but Wheeler was stricken. I saw dawning comprehension in his eyes, then a kind of horror. Next he sprang to his feet so abruptly that his chair scraped back, teetered and clattered to the floor. 'If you bring this up in court on Monday, I'll change my plea to guilty.'

'Stephen, you've said all along you're not guilty. It is quite wrong to plead otherwise if you're innocent.'

'Then don't make me. I'm not having my girl's name dragged through the mud. I don't want to know any more about it, if she was connected to him.'

'Stella will not come out of this badly. Hardynge is the seducer, the manipulator. She was just a girl. Stephen, you cannot allow a guilty man to go unpunished.'

'I'm not interested in what happens to him. I'm interested in my girl and what people will say about her.'

'You'll hang, Stephen. I cannot let an innocent man hang,' Breen said.

'It's not your choice. I want Stella to myself. I'll change my plea to guilty if you bring this up in court. For all you know, I am guilty. For all you know, I knew about Hardynge and Stella all along and killed her because I couldn't bear that she had an affair with my boss. That's what they've been saying in court. Maybe it's true. What do you think of that?'

'Then why have you pleaded not guilty all this time, if you suspected Stella of having an affair and didn't want it to come to light? Why did you put yourself through a trial?'

Wheeler's smile illuminated his face, allowing a glimpse of an utterly different man. 'I'm not such a fool as you all think me. I didn't know what had happened to my Stella. Before they found her body I thought she'd met up with someone after I left her at that picnic place. Soon as I saw her hat I knew she'd gone off in a tearing hurry. Eloped, I thought. I'd known for months, before we was married, there was someone else on the scene though I'd never have believed it was him – that was a bad shock, to see Sir David in the dock and think it might have been him. He has always been very good to me. But he was old and Stella ...' He looked away and bit his lip. 'I could tell by her eyes, the way she seemed to be listening to a voice in her head sometimes, that she was distracted. Even on our wedding day she was waiting for something else to happen. Then, when she was dead, of course I wanted to know who'd got hold of my revolver and killed her. Mr Breen, you was just the man, I thought, to find out for me. And you have. So now

I'm satisfied. I've got what I wanted, thanks to you.'

Breen said: 'Well, I suppose that's the greatest compliment I've ever been paid. But now Hardynge must be charged with murder and we can only achieve that with your cooperation.'

'As I said, I don't choose to say anything more about this. Stella is my dear girl. I won't have her name linked with his again.'

'But Mr Wheeler,' I cried, 'we are sure Sir David Hardynge is guilty. All we are trying to do is bring him to justice. You can't mean that you are prepared to hang instead of the man who seduced—'

'Now you just listen to me, Miss Gifford.' Wheeler held fast to the back of his chair and fixed me with fiery eyes. 'In my book, this has nothing to do with the kind of justice you're talking about. In my book, I have the right to be given what I want, and what I want is to save my Stella's name. Her name is the one thing, the *one* thing, Miss Gifford, that has kept me alive for the last ten years. Oh, I'm not saying I'm different to anyone else. I daresay you have your own terrible story from the war and Breen here, I know, was out driving ambulances. I might have guessed,' and he grinned at Breen, 'that my old school fellow Daniel Breen would be close to the thick of things, running about, getting people organised. But I, I took one look at that war and thought, I'm done for; Stephen Wheeler cannot survive this. When I was a young man, before the war, these hands were good hands, Miss Gifford, they did good things. They held a pen and filled out insurance forms that made people feel safer, God help me. They made things about the house and served others in small ways. In the war they was required to be killing hands. And there was nothing in me that could find justification for what we were doing. There was not a scrap of sense that I could see in living like insects, killing men we had no reason to hate, except they were the mirror image of ourselves. So I died to myself, I did what was required and I did it as best I could.

'Haven't you asked yourselves, how I could have been part of a firing squad, taken a rifle and pointed it at the heart of a boy who was very dear to me? I see him now, every hour of every day, that scrawny, snivelling lad, sniffing and sobbing, unable to stand upright so he had to be tied to a post, unable to control his bowels.

I killed him as I would a rabid dog. It had to be done and it had to be done well. But what kind of a world was I in, that made the killing of that boy the kindest thing I had done in three years?

'And do you know why I'm here still, why I never pulled back my shoulders and walked into the teeth of machine gun fire? It was the thought of a little girl who wrote to me every week and signed her letter *Love, Stella*. Those nights when there was no sleep because there was rats and lice and mud and icy rain instead of a bed, there she was, light as air, this good, soft, rushing thing, this girl who had nothing whatsoever to do with the war but who wrote me letters because she remembered the old Stephen who used to carry her on his shoulders and admire her dancing. Oh I knew I would lose her in the end, she was always just out of reach, but she gave me all the joy I have ever known and I won't barter her good name for the sake of a life that means less than nothing to me.'

For a long time after he'd finished speaking we were still. Breen's chin rested on his palm as he stared at Wheeler; I looked at the blank sheet of paper before me. 'So,' said Wheeler, as if to recover himself and stir us into action. With the hint of a conspiratorial smile he held out his good hand to Breen.

We gathered up our things. Breen clapped Wheeler on the shoulder, gripped his upper arm and said, 'At least let me be there.'

Wheeler nodded. At the door I looked back to where he sat, back straight, hands resting on the table edge like an obedient schoolboy. He was already far away from us and the look in his eye was achingly familiar. Hadn't I seen the same in a thousand nightmares as I floundered across no-man's-land, trying to reach my dying brother? And hadn't Donald Hardynge sat just so on the veranda at The Grove: nowhere to go, nothing to do but attend to unquiet ghosts?

On Monday morning we went back to the court in Aylesbury to witness the inexorable process of Stephen Anthony Wheeler being sentenced to death.

With remorseless precision Mr Justice Weir punched out advice to the jury. 'Defence case ... Wheeler devoted to his wife ... no plausible motive for killing her ... much emphasis has been put on spurious bits of evidence such as a hat left with the picnic blanket. Although there is some evidence that Mrs Wheeler had other admirers, one of whom was generous enough to buy her an expensive wedding gift, there is no evidence at all that anyone else with sinister intent was on the hill that day or had access to Wheeler's gun ...'

At the end of just two hours the jury returned a unanimous verdict. The judge pronounced that Wheeler had cold-bloodedly, and with malice aforethought, murdered his wife of less than one month by shooting her through the heart with his own service revolver, and in these circumstances the only possible punishment was death by hanging.

Wheeler's head went up. As he was led from the courtroom he smiled lovingly at his mother, who sobbed, a handkerchief pressed to her mouth in a tight ball, as if it wasn't polite to show so much feeling in so public a place.

Chapter Forty-One

In the days between the end of Wheeler's trial and the date of his execution, set for Friday 15 August (the day after my birthday), I found that everything had changed.

In the first place I could not tolerate the prospect of living indefinitely at Clivedon Hall Gardens. Perhaps the outcome of Wheeler's trial was in some way connected with this decision. The fact that he had not allowed us to save him made me all the more determined to save myself. Besides, in the brief spell – the week between tea at Fortnum's with Nicholas and discovering his signature in Hyde Park police station – when I had tried to envisage myself as the wife of a rich and successful man – one image I had particularly relished was the leaving of Clivedon Hall Gardens. In my mind's eye I saw myself close the front door, run down the white steps and walk away. So I told mother that I would move in with Meredith and Edmund for a trial period, in Pimlico, and in the meantime I would help her find a lodger or two. To my great surprise, and slight mortification, she didn't put up a fight – I suspect she was relieved that, thus punished, she had done sufficient penance for concealing James's letter from me.

We heard through Meredith, who met Sylvia at art class, that Sir David Hardynge was reconsidering his decision to stand for parliament. He was drawn, said Sylvia, to more philanthropic activities and thought that politics might be a distraction. If this was the only price he was prepared to pay for what he'd done it seemed inadequate, and I was sickened by the knowledge he might yet elude retribution, but for the time being I was distracted by Sylvia's other news, which from my point of view was even more sensational. Her engagement to 'the tall one', as Meredith insisted on describing Nicholas, was over. Sylvia said that he had disappointed her, kept her waiting too long, and she'd called it off. So heartbroken was Thorne, according to Sylvia, that he intended to leave London altogether and return to his home town of Reading, which meant the death of his career.

A fortnight later a letter duly arrived, postmarked Reading. I burnt it, unopened. Wheeler was to hang and I wanted nothing to do with Hardynge or Nicholas, who had been his creature. Then I spent fruitless minutes trying to rescue the letter from the flames, but when at last I'd salvaged a few scraps I thrust them back. Hardynge's influence was so far-reaching, so insidious, I told myself I could never trust Nicholas again. In fact, at Breen & Balcombe we thought it expedient to get the Marchant children out of the clutches of the Good Samaritan Home as soon as possible, in case Hardynge took it into his head to take some sort of devious revenge on us for bringing him to court by having the little girls sent to Canada. But after a flurry of letters, payments from the *Daily Mail* fund and a cursory visit by Miss Hands, assistant matron, to Caractacus Court, we received notification that the children would be released. A qualified lawyer was required to be present. Breen sent me.

Leah and I met outside the gates of the home at a quarter to two on a blustery Thursday afternoon, a week before Wheeler's execution. She was looking very trim in a neat grey coat – cast off, she told me, from one of the new ladies she charred for – and her best hat with cherries. When I offered to shake hands she ignored me, but I told myself it was not so much that she was choosing to slight me as that her whole being yearned towards the release of her children, and she would allow herself no distraction. As we crossed the yard I noticed that she avoided treading on the painted squares of hopscotch.

The door was answered by the ubiquitous Miss Hands, who informed us apologetically that there were yet more papers to be signed before the children could be released. Miss Buckley had not chosen to be present – she was out on charitable business, according to Miss Hands – so we were shown into a cubbyhole of an office the walls of which were bare, presumably to ensure that I was not tempted to steal information from them. There I read out a document stating that Mrs Marchant was a fit parent and would bring the children up in a moral Christian environment, and Leah put her cross on the dotted line.

Miss Hands glanced at me so often that I suspected she had been given dire warnings by her superior. Or perhaps she remembered the horror of our last visit, when she had attempted to tear the children from their mother's arms. Or perhaps she wanted to speak to me but didn't have the courage. As we left the office I gave her Breen & Balcombe's card, which she scrunched in her hand and thrust into a pocket. Then we were directed to a row of hard chairs in the hall and told to wait while Miss Hands disappeared upstairs. A clock ticked on a wall to the right and beyond was the institutional mutter of a hundred children and their female teachers.

Leah was supernaturally still, her spine tilted towards the stairs, and I realised that this was the first time I had troubled myself to regard her as a woman worthy of respect rather than as a weak and reluctant client. She, after all, in the face of overwhelming odds, had remained unswerving in her devotion to her children. To her mind, sheer force of will had prevailed in the end.

A door opened and then came the sound of feet on a corridor above. First to appear on the landing were the little girls with their tightly bound hair, dressed not in uniform this time but in skimpy summer frocks. Each wore new shoes, courtesy of the *Daily Mail*, and carried a small parcel. Next came Miss Hands, then a woman in a nurse's uniform clutching a fat baby.

For a moment the group paused. Then Miss Hands gave the youngest girl a gentle prod with her knee and she moved down a step. Leah stood up. The children came slowly, one step at a time, their eyes fixed on their mother. When they reached the bottom they waited as she crossed the space between them. Even when she held them they didn't respond but I noticed the youngest had taken a fistful of her mother's skirt and wound it round her wrist.

The baby, when passed to Leah, cried lustily and arched his back. I tucked my briefcase under my arm and held the little girls' hands. At the gates of the home mother and children were photographed and Leah made an incoherent speech of gratitude to the reporter, then we bundled into a waiting cab. The baby, plump after weeks with an indulgent foster parent and with a dazzling crop of blond curls, hurled himself about in his mother's arms while the girls sat one on either side of her and fixed me with unblinking eyes. They did not smile or respond to their mother's questions. The youngest, Cathy, had not released Leah's skirt. Meanwhile I pointed out sights along the way, the trees of Regent's Park and, 'Look, behind this road is Arbery Street, where I work, and there's St Pancras station.' The girls swivelled their eyes obediently but didn't comment. Leah struggled with the baby and from time to time squeezed the shoulder of one or other of her daughters.

At Caractacus Court Mrs Sanders had laid on a substantial tea. Her spotless overall was removed when the kettle had boiled and she wore a brooch of tiny mosaic pieces pinned to her collar which Cathy could not resist touching. I admired Mrs Sanders for her thoroughness, the absolute commitment she gave to a task, even one as mundane as filling a teapot. She gave me the impression that her life consisted of a series of unwieldy packages, each of which had to be dealt with and dispatched before another was opened. It was reassuring to believe that the Marchant family was her latest mission.

The girls' eyes were full of wonder as they took in the jam, the fairy cakes, the lemonade. Sometimes they looked at each other, sometimes at Mrs Sanders, sometimes at their mother, who dandled her baby on her lap and pressed bread and jam into his mouth.

I drank a cup of tea, ate a slice of bread and butter and became aware that my status had changed from officious intruder to honoured guest, and that a speech had been prepared. 'We 'ope you will call again, any time, Miss Gifford,' said Mrs Sanders, 'to see 'ow we are all gettin' on. It's a rare thing to find someone who don't give up on people like us.'

These words, which should have been a balm to my soul, were salt on a wound. To my mind the fact that Leah had been reunited with her children was inextricably linked to Wheeler's fate. The Hardynge machine and its instrument, Nicholas, had sprung to the assistance of Breen & Balcombe in the Marchant case because it suited them to do so. By another flick of his fingers, Hardynge might have ordained an entirely different outcome.

Afterwards they all crowded into the court to wave me goodbye. I produced chocolate for the girls and kissed Charlie, whose cheek left a sticky smudge on my lip. When I stooped to embrace her, the older child, Ellen, suddenly put her thin arms round my neck and squeezed hard.

Chapter Forty-Two

My birthday, 14 August, coincided with our next meeting of
women lawyers. As the Law Society restaurant did not run to
birthday cake my friends clubbed together and bought me a pink
concoction from the ABC tea rooms. Altogether the day promised
to be far more festive than usual. That night in Clivedon Hall
Gardens there was to be a party, arranged by Meredith, to include
the new lodger, Miss Griffiths, who had been recommended by
an acquaintance at church, who taught the piano (the prospect of
music in the house delighted grandmother) and who was over-
whelmingly grateful to be offered a room and therefore, on all
three counts, was considered to be *ideal* by mother. Prudence
made no comment but cast wounded glances at Meredith and bit
her lip to prevent unaccustomed tears falling. At the weekend
Meredith, Edmund and I were to move out, but in between these
two dates – my birthday and the new flat – was the horrifying fact
of Wheeler's execution.

During our meeting of lady lawyers I was not the only person
with news. All had been busy. Whilst I had allowed myself to
be distracted by a murder trial and love affair, the others had
forged ahead. Maud was halfway through a book entitled *Women
under English Law* and Carrie had been working on a divorce
case, which she would conduct herself under the Poor Persons
Rules and thereby be the first woman ever to handle the
breakdown of a marriage. For my own part, I told them that
we had failed to save Wheeler, that I was about to move out of
Clivedon Hall Gardens and that I had rescued Leah Marchant's
children from the threat of emigration by reaching an out-of-
court agreement.

'You did *what*?' said Carrie. 'Well that's not going to get the law changed. I was hoping your Marchants might be a test case that would raise the issue of child migration.'

'These are real children. We could not use them as legal pawns. We had a chance and we took it.'

'You should have gone through the courts. That way you could have brought to public attention the sometimes barbaric way destitute children are treated.'

'And what if we'd lost? The mother is known to be fond of the bottle, the father is absent. We risked her losing the children altogether.'

'The good news is that Canada is putting its foot down about accepting unaccompanied children under fourteen. All the British charities which ship them out there are terribly worried. After we spoke last time I got hold of these minutes of the Church of England Waifs and Strays Society. You can take them away with you if you like. And you know Mrs Bondfied is conducting an inquiry on behalf of the government. There'll be a rush to send children this year and next but then there'll be a tightening up of the rules, I hope.'

'Perhaps we can find another way to expose the policy of child migration?'

'We're not social reformers – first and foremost, we're lawyers. That's why it's a pity you missed your chance,' said Carrie.

'You're wrong. I took my chance. And there'll be other opportunities to see justice done.'

Breen & Balcombe had rustled up a birthday card, bought out of petty cash by Miss Drake, who had selected a picture of a white puppy with a blue ribbon tied to its ear. I was also instructed by Breen to go home early since 'You women like to have such a fuss made of you when it comes to birthdays.'

It was odd how, when I reached Clivedon Hall Gardens, I already felt like a visitor. For once I was back earlier than Meredith and Edmund so that only women's hats and scarves adorned the hooks on the stand, though it still held a collection of massive black umbrellas. ('If there was to be an intruder,' said Prudence, 'he would note the male umbrellas and be deterred.') On a tray under the mirror were a few cards addressed to me,